Also by Bradley Ernst

MADE MEN
By Vardo, Mostly

ADDITIONAL PRAISE FOR *INHUMANUM*

"A well-written page turner ... more than just a hunt for a killer! Highly recommended."

—*Amy's bookshelf Reviews*

"I simply could not put this one down ... The characters are complex and even though their actions might not be acceptable or the norm, it seems justifiable given their metamorphoses and the reasons for it ... intricately constructed, layered and immersive novel with a look into the makings and the mind of a killer who is convinced of his moral right to right the wrongs of the world.

—*Cover2Cover*

"The prose is thick, intense, and urgent ... runs the gamut from the grotesque via the absurd and back again, and it never strays far from the baroque ... At the beginning my analytical brain came up with comparisons to other authors. I thought James Ellroy meets John Irving, with Lewis Carroll thrown in for seasoning purposes ... soon it became obvious that all comparisons were vain..." (Ernst) "has big lungs and his out-breath takes you on a narrative ride that catches a long wind. Stretch out the wings of your imagination and cruise along."

—Magnus Stanke, author of *Falling in Death and Love*

"In a lifetime of love for literature, spanning four and a half decades, I have only ever doled out two 5 star ratings; *Inhumanum* will be the third recipient ... To engage a reader from start to finish in such a manner is the work of a master storyteller who has perfected his craft. I, for one, am envious of this skill ... flawless with meticulous attention to detail and extensive research in his subject matter. This is a great, shining, new voice in the world of literature..."

—Shervin Jamali, author of *The Devil's Lieutenant*

"This and it's sequel have made my "best reads of 2016" list."

—*Megalion*

"Breathtaking in its imagination, sly wit and killer prose, *Inhumanum* (and its companion, *Made Men*) went straight to the top of my lifetime best reads list. *The Law of Retaliation* duology belongs on your shelf beside absurdist classics like John Irving's *The World According to Garp*, and Kurt Vonnegut's *Slaughterhouse Five*."

—*Zippergirl*

INHUMANUM

By Bradley Ernst

Nick —
I hope you enjoy my
first book!.

All the best —

Bradley Ernst Oct
2016

To Sara
the love of my life
for laughing at my jokes

Inhumanum: (Latin) "Brutal."

"When you meet a swordsman, draw your sword: do not recite
poetry to one who is not a poet."
~Ch'an (Zen) Buddhist aphorism

"As surely as I live, says the Sovereign Lord, since you show no
distaste for blood, I will give you a bloodbath of your own. Your turn
has come!"

~Ezekiel 35:6

"I will fill your mountains with the dead."

~Ezekiel 35:8

Table of Contents

~Prologue

The '69 Mercury Marauder's aged suspension moaned as though a heavy corpse was in the trunk. It was not a body—just money. The driver stuck to back roads. Operating the aged car, hoary with rust except for its glistening black skin, was a joy at highway speeds. Although he had hit a flat stretch of road, the needle on the accelerator wavered between seventy-five and sixty. New York City wasn't built for speed of transit. It was built to shelve millions of people, each with their own goals and reasons to want or need to be shelved. His mismatched eyes didn't blink as the windshield took a bullet-sized rock low and to the left of his field of view.

Better still. He liked the car's imperfections.

Old. Drafty. Aged vinyl turned sweet-smelling by years of sun exposure, motor oil, lead and oxidation. The metal harmonics of the springs in the bench seat groaned as they compressed unevenly beneath his solid weight. It was nearly 2 AM. Odors from the countryside hammered through the cracked driver's side window. *Whup. Whup. Whup.* Hay. Mud. Wet stones.

A cellphone rang for the last time—a glance.

Detective Grimaldi's number.

Cool, dry hands hardened by extreme measures stayed on the thin black steering wheel, but the set of the man's jaw changed. The call went to voicemail. The fingers of his right hand flared. He palm-spun the wheel into a turn and slowed to enter a covered wooden bridge— one of many in New England. It was a flimsy avian bivouac badly in need of restoration, like the car.

A nice place to stop.

Easy pressure on the brake, new pads hissed rust free from the drums onto the patchy creosote. The white dice hanging from the rearview mirror swung. Front, back. Front, back. The well-dressed loner turned the smooth key counterclockwise and walked the tarred planks while he listened to the voicemail. Detective Grimaldi seemed hesitant—he didn't speak right away. Finally the ex-boxer cleared his throat. "You should know I've been promoted. I took Bill Turret's spot. I'm the station chief—"

Tall, broad through the chest, the man leaned against the bridge railing for a moment. He peered over the edge, into the water. Almost absent mindedly, the vigilante tossed the well-used police baton into the river. "—and although I appreciate what you were trying to accomplish ... what you *did* accomplish, I remain in steadfast disapproval of your methods—"

A sleepy bird peered down at the specter from an overstuffed nest. He glanced at the bird for a moment then leaned into the decrepit muscle car to push in the cigarette lighter on the cracked dashboard. "—in summary, we remain in pursuit. If you and your—" The lighter popped out. The man tugged the knob from the dash and rolled the device between his fingers. The hot coil cast a glow like an angry electric ring. Cracking the phone open as easily as an egg, the most wanted criminal in New York state history removed the SIM card from the device, placed it on the railing, and pressed the hot coil of the cigarette lighter down.

The woman he loved was safe—the Germans would assure it. So would the other man. That mattered.

A deep black pool had swallowed the baton. In his pocket lay his last link to New York. The Germans had made the tubular device. Titanium—anodized to a dark bronze. A green led light recessed in one end, a rounded screw cap with ornate crenulations for grip adorned the other. If the green light flashed, they needed him. If he unscrewed the cap and pushed the button beneath, the Germans would dispatch help his way. Satellites were involved, amongst other technologies. Pulling the device out was instinctual—cathartic. For a moment, he held the tube out over the water. Relaxing his grip, he let it roll to his fingertips. A car approached the tunnel. It stopped at the entrance of the one-way bridge and flashed its lights. Amiably, the fit man waved and slipped the tube back into his pocket. The springs in the seat sang their complaint. He turned the smooth key clockwise. He wasn't on the run—

This was a trip about perspective.

He would let fate steer his actions.

You can look, Detective Grimaldi, but you won't find.

2

~Conspicuous Consumption

Ithaca, New York.

Troy and Raquel Maddox received frequent compliments on their son's good manners, however it made the five-year-old feel uncomfortable. He wanted—more than anything else—simply to be left alone.

Bonn is such a well-behaved child. He seems just like a little man, Troy. Raquel, you must be so proud of him. I see a lot of your influence there.

Tonight Troy entertained his client at the Black Bow Inn. The old stone building had elegant chandeliers. The expensive wine list afforded the chef license to serve pigeon, but call it "squab." The little boy liked to watch people, but he despised being scrutinized himself. He wondered why everyone fussed over him.

Good manners came naturally. Why did everyone feel obligated to comment on his?

Bonn finished his meal. He wiped his mouth and folded his napkin, crossed his silverware on his plate to indicate he was finished. People stared rudely. Some went so far as to point in his direction. A well-dressed couple stopped at the Maddoxes' table on their way out. The man seemed to know his father and tousled Bonn's hair aggressively. His date, a well-dressed younger woman, loomed awkwardly. She seemed out of sorts, unsure where to stand or even to look. Bonn could appreciate her dilemma: seating was tight, the tables close together. It would have been rude for her to march on past when her date stopped to rub elbows, yet no matter where she pointed her shapely bottom it faced someone seated nearby.

Some of the men didn't seem to mind, but the women sure did. Perhaps for several reasons.

The boisterous man had failed to introduce the attractive woman who seemed a transient, nervous orchid in a marigold patch.

She had been set up to fail.

The glad-hander had planted them all in the social muck. He, for instance, would have preferred to shake hands with the man rather than suffer the pet-grade hair fondling.

Bonn remembered the steps his father taught him—steps to ensure the success of a handshake:

1. "Don't be the first one to squeeze."
2. "When you do squeeze, make eye contact."
3. "Never let anyone turn your hand 'palm up.'"
4. "Steer the conversation when you can."
The most important step came at the end:
5. 'When shaking hands, never be the first to let go. No matter how awkward it becomes."

Bonn didn't know why that would feel awkward but remembered the rule anyway. The woman loitering uncomfortably above him blinked apologetically and offered Bonn a small smile.

One of the other adults should have engaged her by now. If they wouldn't help her, he would. Someone had to do it.

"Did you enjoy your chicken?" Bonn asked pleasantly. "Francois frequently sends it out a bit dry."

His father's client sat just to his left. She was a wealthy woman. A very proper woman. A lady. To that point, she had managed to ignore the impromptu visitors at their table, though her crossed arms indicated the imposition on her dinner felt—offensive. The boy was correct to address the interloper, and her eyes shone with pride and perhaps a bit of embarrassment that she, herself, had not risen to the girl's need. The unseemly interaction and Bonn's salutation caused a chuckle to bubble up from her chest. She attempted to stifle her belly laugh by pressing an embroidered napkin against her lips. Her mirth spilled around the edges nonetheless. She couldn't help herself. She laughed harder still. When she came up for air, she sucked in a piece of inadequately chewed shellfish and began to choke. The scene intrigued Bonn. Each adult took a break from their struggles for power, money, or validity to watch his elbow-mate suffer. The shrimp was hopelessly lodged in the lady's airway. His father stood, grasped the woman from behind, performed an inelegant maneuver, then—

Entropy made its move.

The woman's breasts bounced with each jagged squeeze. Her dark wig shifted to a rakish angle. The clasp on her necklace broke. Gleaming gems joined the shallow pond of shrimp, butter, and wine from inside the woman. Each of them was spattered, except for the young orchid-lady. She ran.

The catalyst that kicked off the event—what was it?

Bonn reviewed events:

It was him.

4

Once it was clear Troy's client would live, the intensity in the restaurant waned. The waitstaff banded together, each person—white shirt and black slacks—smiled with insincerity, yet made no eye contact with patrons.

Nothing must be misconstrued. There was a protocol to follow.

Order was, eventually, restored. A new tablecloth was placed with a flourish. Troy Maddox checked his shiny watch too frequently and lit a cigar to occupy himself. Raquel gamely failed yet attempted to reassure the gentlewoman that no one had noticed the scene. A thought occurred to Bonn—a thought that would become truer as he aged:

People should be careful around me.

His mother stared at him with what appeared to be—disgust?

He was never sure.

Bonn and his mother exchanged unblinking gazes.

What could she be thinking?

Raquel returned the dead-eyed look her son cast her way. Life was increasingly unbearable. She wished he would give her a short, happy wave—or even stick his tongue out at her like a normal child might. It was terrifying when he spoke like a Rhodes scholar. She wouldn't be a bit surprised to see him pull a sleek tin from his toddler-sized suit coat, pluck out a cigarette, ask her for a light. Raquel felt cold. As her son studied her, she made an odd realization—one she would have shared with Troy if she loved the man:

She'd never seen her own son smile.

~The Stray

Ruka, Finland

Four-year-old Henna watched as the forest closed in on the road. The driver of the rented Mercedes was her grandmother.

Henna's grandmother, Lucrece, seemed only to care about clothes, perfume, and money. Lucrece Cloutier was elegant, but emotionally barren. She wasn't born wealthy. That was part of her problem. She was, as much as a person is something they have, "new money." Unlike people with "old money," her wealth mattered greatly to her. When a family prospers for several generations, plentitude is often taken for granted—whereas those with new wealth remember their struggles. They grip their fresh prominence with aching hands, afraid to sleep for fear of loss, afraid to wake in case they simply dreamed their good fortune.

Lucrece didn't intend to lose her stature.

Her maiden name was Mokri. She was the daughter of an unexceptional Iranian cartographer. To date, Lucrece collected three married names. She was Lucrece Takala, then Lucrece Dupont, and most recently, Lucrece Cloutier. She liked the sound of Dupont the best, however—now that she'd tucked Mr. Cloutier into the ground she considered changing her name back to Dupont. Although she grew up Persian, Lucrece's mother was from Saint-Germain-en-Laye. The woman refused to speak any language but French and frequently reminded her father that she gave up a lovely life in France for him. As a girl, Lucrece felt she, too, belonged in France—so she joined her mother's cause and spoke French exclusively. Lucrece still preferred all things French—unless she could find a superior Swiss or Italian replacement. She vehemently resented the scrutiny of her undiluted Parisian associates. To them she was "exotic."

"What *are* you?" They asked too frequently. "We *must* know." Lucrece wouldn't say her father was "Iranian." She preferred "Persian." "Persian" sounded similar to "Parisian" if said quickly, however some caught her trick. She resented the task, but became accustomed to confessing her heritage in a dismissive tone:

"Persian. Of course I said Persian. A great man."

"Yes. Persian. Persia. Near Pakistan."

"A cartographer—an excellent one. He gave up so much in the move." If her audience knew about the Middle East, she'd lie. She was born in Qom, but she was prepared to say "Tehran."

Tehran sounded less ordinary.

Lucrece was eight when her family moved to France. Her mother was tired of Iran. She gave her studious husband an ultimatum. Lucrece watched her father mull over his decision. For a while it appeared he might choose to live a quiet life, alone with his maps, in Qom.

"Of course, you will go—we will ALL go," her mother exclaimed with finality and too afraid to argue, he went. Lucrece immersed herself in French culture. She practiced being Parisian as only the non-Parisian can and increasingly resented her father. When conversations arose that involved the man, she would promptly change topics. Lucrece was confident that what her compeers genuinely meant when they announced she was "exotic" was: "Lucrece, the unfortunate mongrel."

On her nineteenth birthday Lucrece attended a talk at the university. The debutant practiced her seduction skills on the speaker, a Finnish chemist, with marked success. Lucrece enjoyed the prestige gained by fraternizing with the scholar—and wanted more of the feeling. The perfumed temptress married him and embarked on an adventure. The self-made Parisian would bring elegance with her to Scandinavia—dole it out there—and be revered!

No one in Finland would guess she wasn't French.

Unfortunately for Lucrece, no one in Helsinki gave her much thought whatsoever. Lucrece learned to speak Finnish, but the language felt coarse in her mouth, like freshly salted sprats.

Tails flicking in their reluctance to perish.

Fortunately the chemist spoke French. When her mother invited the family to convalesce in Saint-Germain-en-Laye after Alvar was blinded in the war, Lucrece returned to the country and language she loved most. Alvar faked a Swedish accent. The French seemed able to overlook Sweden's steel profiteering with the Nazis but would never tolerate a Finn. When she met Mr. Dupont, Lucrece promptly left Alvar.

He was damaged by the war after all.

She moved up! Closer to her natural station. She deserved a richer life—one without sprats and moldy bread. Who could blame her? If Mr. Dupont was able to endure children, she would surely have brought her baby daughter along, but he clearly could not. Lucrece convinced herself the girl was better off. Now she could send money her daughter wouldn't have benefited from otherwise.

"Dupont?" Lucrece whispered to herself—maybe Dupont was also inadequate. If she moved somewhere completely new, she could be anyone. Nice perhaps? Her money would certainly go further in Nice. She gave it some thought.

It must be Nice.

Paris was saturated with privileged, beautiful people, but Nice was not. She could re-invent herself in Nice. She could be "Lucrece Chalon," or perhaps "Lucrece Montebeliard."

Now those were names.

Mr. Cloutier made his fortunes selling hardware—although his estate eclipsed that of her second husband, she felt the name Cloutier unworthy.

The meaning of a name mattered.

"Cloutier" meant: "one who sells nails." He did sell them actually, yet to Lucrece nails, though no doubt necessary, seemed grimy and plebeian.

How exciting! Perhaps she'd change her first name too …

Lucrece tried to conjure one she liked, but each name that came to mind reminded her of someone she disliked. Her face became pinched with disappointment. She dismissed the new idea as overly complicated. She checked her lipstick in the mirror. It didn't matter of course. The blind dullard wouldn't appreciate the precious maquillage, and she certainly wouldn't kiss him.

A vulgar woman squatted to weed a roadside garden as the car thrust forward. Lucrece couldn't imagine dirt on her hands. Those who chose to grow their food seemed very bad off. Fortunately, it hadn't been necessary to breathe even a drop of Finnish air since the Winter War. Helsinki was bad enough—but the *north* of Finland? Alvar must intend to hide until he became a part of some garden.

Well let the old women squat over your bones. I did what I had to do.

Lucrece glanced back to the mirror to check her teeth. The sullen foundling peeped back at her. In the will, her daughter had entrusted Alvar of all people with the girl. No one in Connecticut knew how to reach him—how would they?

He had no telephone.

If his address was in her daughter's home, it burned in the fire. Lucrece was only able to find him through the university. Finland's stagnant mail system made correspondence of any sort difficult. She had written him the very moment it became clear she couldn't tolerate the child and didn't hear back from him for weeks. Henna was a pretty girl—

If her inheritance was accessible, maybe she would raise her herself …

Some work was needed to erase the intellectual damage. Most parents didn't realize that a girl who knew so much would never attract a mate.

How would she ever support herself? No bother. Her inheritance was locked in a trust.

Lucrece wasn't privy to the amount, though she'd tried valiantly to find out. Henna would get the money at age twenty-five. Twenty-one years was a hell of a time investment to help the girl with her money. If the orphan weren't so contrary, she might be worth it as the fund could be immense, but she was quite contrary indeed. Lucrece was amazed the social worker in Connecticut was able to track her down as she hadn't seen her *own* daughter since she was this girl's age.

News of her daughter's death didn't surprise her—people died all the time. Who she'd married, however, was a surprise. The man was a mogul: an absolute jet setter. Lucrece still pictured her daughter in a dirty little frock, asleep in the apartment in Helsinki. She glanced at the child in the backseat. She looked the same as her own daughter at that age—except for the clothing. For all her smarts, Henna didn't appreciate Lucrece. She didn't grasp what she could offer her. The toddler was certainly intelligent enough to learn how to live well, but what the girl knew and what she said didn't match. If Lucrece kept the child, it was just a matter of time before the overly candid youngster embarrassed her, or worse. What if she took her to Nice?

People would ask questions.

The girl wasn't capable of maintaining a story. She wouldn't keep her mouth shut. Henna fell into the boorish percentage of people for whom the truth was more important than comfort. Lucrece focused back on herself. She smoothed a bit of hair from her face. The fact was, she'd stepped up proudly to claim the girl. They simply weren't a match. For instance, the child recited the alphabet in several languages when she should be asleep. When Lucrece asked about it, she said: "Daddy and I said them every night. Sometimes he would say one wrong—so I could catch him."

What a terrible habit! It was disconcerting to hear.

She sounded like a tiny teacher in a refugee camp—it was downright creepy. "French is the only language you'll need from now on." Lucrece reassured her. "There is no reason to learn inferior languages." The girl regarded her coldly. She still spoke in tongues at night, she just did it discreetly. Henna seemed to enjoy aggravating her. She refused to sleep on the daybed Lucrece made up for her as well.

She'd even put the Frette linens on it!

Instead of thanking her, she soiled them in the night. Lucrece scolded, but it didn't help. Once the brat knew it bothered her, she wet the bed often. Her well of patience was dry.

She felt no connection with the girl.

That very morning she'd found the stray curled in a blanket near the radiator. She was like a dog and seemed to choose her quay more based on heat than dignity. Lucrece rammed the accelerator with the toe of her delicate shoe. She hoped this sodden path led to Alvar's burrow. If she couldn't leave the disagreeable stripling there, she'd take her to an orphanage.

Let Finland raise her.

Perhaps the little beast would *enjoy* these unseemly mountains—this vacuous countryside.

Henna boosted herself to look out the window. She wondered how the ground could change so quickly underneath a plane as you rode in one. It was drastic. Sunlight flickered through tree trunks as pines turned to birch. Her mother liked trees—she'd known all their names. The powerful car shot through a meadow. Lucrece cursed in French and they careened sharply around a corner. The trees seemed too close to the car. Henna felt her empty stomach flatten into her back like a crepe. They rocketed up into thinner trees. Henna tried to identify them, but they were going too fast—up and up they catapulted—into a thin spruce forest. Lucrece stomped on the brake so hard that Henna nearly slid off the seat. She craned her neck to see what she could—a small stone house stood nearby. Lucrece got out. Henna hadn't been told their destination, but she knew they were in Finland. She read the signs at the airport. Henna used to practice speaking Finnish with her mother.

Lucrece wouldn't know that.

Two nanny goats approached. Each wore a bell around her neck that clanged when they walked. A dog with a head like a lion arose from the porch. It looked from the car to the door of the house and back then shouldered open the door and gave a low *woof*, to broadcast news of the arrivals. Henna broke off handfuls of wild grass for the goats. The animals nibbled at the offering while the adults concluded a hushed exchange. Lucrece pursed her lips—she didn't stay long. She patted Henna's cheeks with both hands and roared off in the big car. As the thrum of the engine faded, the dog swept his great tail and came to inspect her. A goat nibbled her hair, but the Leonberger gave a warning cough and the goat darted off. The dog folded himself earthward for inspection. Henna threw her arms around the beast's neck and squeezed until his eyes bulged. The man grinned.

"Gertie likes your hair." He nodded in the goat's direction. They didn't seem selective about what they ate—one chewed a bit of fence wire. "If Mortimer likes you, you've passed security. How about a hug like that for your grandfather?"

"Are you my grandfather?"

"Yes."

"Do you have a cat too?"

"Do I have a cat that I feed? No—" The man looked thoughtful for a moment. "There are a few cats in my barn, but they belong to themselves. Mortimer's enough company for me. The other animals are sort of ..." The man grinned when he thought of the correct word. "Livestock." Henna looked around for the barn. "I have a few chickens also. They like to hide their eggs from me. Would you use your good eyes to hunt eggs with me? Mine don't work. I suspect Mortimer here steals most of the eggs he finds." Mortimer looked into the forest innocently, as though he couldn't recall such antics.

His eyes don't work? Was he blind?

He looked young for a grandfather. Trim through the waist. Thick grey hair. He looked strong. Henna stepped closer. "Did you miss me before you knew me?"

"I've always known you." Alvar held his hand out. "I'm so sorry about your mom and dad. I never got to meet your father, but I'm sure he was great. Your mom wanted to bring you to visit, but it would've been a really long trip from the United States." Henna wilted and looked at her feet. "I'm glad you're here," Alvar offered brightly. "My guess is you've had a rotten few weeks since the fire.

11

There isn't a great way to sort out what happened, but we can try." Henna stepped closer. His face smelled like mint, limes, and pipe smoke.

"So it *was* a fire. No one told me directly, but I figured it out. It is good to hear someone say it. Not good—more—cathartic. My problem with most adults is that they whisper just as loud as they talk. If something is so secret that whispering is considered, adults should just leave a room. It would be more effective and less patronizing. Less ageist."

"What did they tell you?"

"The social worker told me they were 'gone' and she was sorry. I asked what she meant by 'gone.' If she'd said, 'Henna, your parents have been killed in a fire,' it would've been better. 'Gone' sounds like they might come back. 'Just gone' she said—then she cried. She didn't know my parents, or how special they were. That wasn't empathy, that was laziness. It was unfair. I don't think she wanted to 'go easy' on me since I'm little. I think she assumed me incapable of conceptualizing death and she couldn't be bothered to explain it to me."

"Yes. That was unfair. Well, I won't do any whispering unless I whisper something to you."

Alvar recalled the letters his daughter had written since Henna had been born—she'd written so many things to be proud of, but Alvar knew how a parent's estimation of their child could be magnified. If anything, she'd been humble in her accounts—it was obvious. He grinned at the tiny intellectual appreciatively, as though she had a bus engine sitting between her ears.

"Why are your eyes funny?"

"I put some glass eyes on top of my real ones, so people wouldn't think I looked spooky. It doesn't usually matter—I don't get many visitors, but there is a lady who helps with my mail. I've never wanted to disturb her and now, you. I want to look handsome for you."

"Oh…" Henna ran a finger along her own eyelid "…that's sad, but thank you." Henna started to cry.

Alvar knelt down and Henna wrapped her arms around his neck. It was his first human contact in over a year—the directness of the girl's affection was overwhelming. For years he'd felt—useless. He cried with Henna for a while, then dabbed at their cheeks with the cuff of his sweater. He cleared his throat.

"Should we see about those eggs?"

12

"What are the rules? Grandma has so many. I don't agree with some of them."

"Only one. Find the eggs before Mortimer does."

Henna smiled. "Can I say my alphabets at night? She hated that, but I like to."

"Of course. Your mom told me in a letter that you've done that for a couple of years. Maybe you could teach me."

Henna reached for Alvar's hand and pulled him toward the chicken coop. "Yes, but we should hurry. Mortimer must have heard you."

"Heard me say what?"

"Grandpa, he's going for the eggs!"

~Troubled Child

Troy took the call from Bonn's scoutmaster in the library. There was trouble. From the range of pained facial twitches his father broadcast, Bonn correctly guessed he was the cause. It wasn't the first time. Trouble took root years ago. It was well established now. Bonn didn't seek trouble out—it seemed naturally fond of him. A week into the second grade Bonn asked his homeroom teacher a question. "May I please have a copy of the curriculum you intend to use the rest of the year?"

Bonn's homeroom teacher balked. She used the word "disquieting" in her report to the principal. In truth, it completely derailed Barbara Stebbins. It was the first thing Bonn said to her. Although his reading and spelling scores were perfect, she suspected the boy suffered from stunted social skills. He used a lot of eye contact. That shot her earlier autism theory, but something was certainly amiss. She'd taught for thirty years—she knew when something was wrong. Most children doodle on their schoolwork—extraneous creations, sneezed from developing minds through busy fingers. Drawings, shapes. Even little scenes were common. It was the small things that cued an apt educator to look more closely at certain children, and Barbara hoped she was that educator. She sensed trouble with the Maddox boy, but couldn't put her finger on it—that was before the request. To Barbara, the request for her curriculum was a cry for help. She reviewed Bonn's schoolwork then and found the doodles.

"Well not doodles, exactly," Barbara told the principal, "graphs." They hadn't *covered* graphs yet. To Barbara, the graphs seemed a logical way to start a conversation with Bonn's parents. She needed to know more about the unusual boy. She couldn't let him slip through the cracks if he needed something more—or something entirely different. One graph was a bell curve with initials written neatly along the probability density. She couldn't decipher it. "B.M." was written at the far right hand of the bell curve. Barbara assumed that was Bonn himself. He'd also made a bar graph—on the back of a spelling test. Initials were printed neatly below each column. The school's principal was unimpressed. To get her out of his office he encouraged her to consult the school's new counselor, which she did.

Someone needed to speak with the boy's parents! Raquel Maddox agreed to meet. Tom, the counselor, would sit in too. Barbara didn't like Tom, but since the principal wanted him in the meeting, she agreed. Bonn and Raquel Maddox were on time. The boy sat quietly. Unlike Barbara, he seemed completely at ease. Barbara pulled the graphs from a folder and handed them to Raquel.

"I hoped we'd discuss these graphs first. We haven't covered graphs in class yet, but these are quite good. It's the content I'm interested in. You should know, I'm a worrier." Barbara chuckled, hoping her icebreaker would be well received. It was not.

Barbara cleared her throat and continued. "Today, I am worried that Bonn's trying to tell me something and I don't understand it."

Raquel shrugged. "Did you ask him what they mean?" Since neither she nor Tom had, an uncomfortable silence followed. Tom forced his gaze from Raquel's cleavage. He looked at Mrs. Stebbins expectantly, as if he had asked the question. Barbara shook her head, embarrassed. Tom Talbot fancied himself a modern Casanova. So far in the new job, he had bedded one first grade teacher and two fourth grade teachers. He hadn't considered tapping into the deep pool of children's mothers yet, but Raquel Maddox was very attractive.

"Good idea." Tom grabbed the stack of papers. He held the first aloft for Bonn to see. "What's this one?"

Bonn thought the question was premature. "Could we start with introductions?"

Tom's face flushed. He forced a smile and wrote something in his notepad. "I'm your counselor. My name's Tom and I'm here to sort things out. In order to do that, I need to ask you questions."

Bonn looked incredulous. "I have a lawyer? That's curious. I must be in quite a bind. What is your last name, Tom?"

Raquel shook her head. "At our house, counselors practice *law*— Bonn's father is an attorney."

Tom suffered a feeling of inadequacy, but in the time it took to straighten himself in his chair, it passed. He wore a disconcerted look that said: "I'll have to be on my game with this kid." Tom started over. He stood and walked around the table to offer a handshake to the boy. "Thomas Talbot."

Bonn scanned the walls of Tom's office for a diploma, but found none. A print of a woman on a horse hung above Tom's desk—she was naked except for her long hair. The counselor waited, hand extended and nervous. He stared down his hooked nose at the little boy, who seemed determined not to notice his gesture. Finally Bonn extended his hand, but let Tom clasp it before he gripped back.

Steer the conversation when you can.

"Lady Godiva ..." Bonn studied Tom's face. "Do you know the story?"

Tom squeezed Bonn's hand hard.

When you do squeeze, make eye contact.

Bonn squeezed back. He raised his eyebrows to illustrate his ongoing expectation of an answer—

If Tom did know the story, it was a foolish choice in artwork.

"I'm sure we all do. Let's talk about the graphs instead." Tom released Bonn's hand.

Since Tom hadn't attempted to turn his palm up, Bonn realized the handshake was a success all around. Bonn folded his hands. It was a large table so it took Tom a while to walk back to his seat. If the man was trying to intimidate him with the gesture it had failed miserably. Tom wrote some notes and held a graph aloft for all to see.

"Thank you, Mr. Talbot. I am interested in your questions. Please do ask some."

Though the tension in the room was thick, Barbara appeared relieved. She was right to worry. There were obviously issues to illuminate. Now she shared the burden. After all, it was called a school *system*. Barbara glanced at Raquel, but the woman was busy rummaging through her purse and didn't notice.

Tom seemed increasingly irritated. "What is this Bonn?"

"It's a bar graph I drew on the back of my spelling test."

"Correct." Tom smiled like an idiot. "What is 'L.F.?'"

"Who, actually. Those are initials. That may not be immediately apparent however, so I appreciate your need for clarification. Mrs. Stebbins, should I discontinue the habit of using the margins for my thoughts, or would a key afford less worry for those, like yourself, who find it necessary to analyze my diagrams?" Barbara didn't know how to answer. "If my childish scribbles have puzzled you, I apologize. I try to occupy myself quietly. I seem to finish my work before the other kids. I'm left with ample time to scribble."

Tom wrote something down. "Who is L.F.?"

"Lou Ferrigno."

"Lou Ferrigno? Incredible Hulk, Lou Ferrigno?"

"Yes. I'm a child. I think of superheroes often. Most likely it appeals to my powerlessness. Do you like superheroes too?"

16

The counselor's eyes narrowed. He might suspect Bonn would try to bait him. Tom seemed inclined to prove this a tempest in a teapot.

"Let's stay on track, Bonn. So you feel powerless?"

"Actually, I am powerless. I'm a small boy. I'm pretty much stuck with what adults decide for me for another decade."

"Do you think the adults in your life are unfair to you?"

"That's an interesting question—since my frontal lobe is still undeveloped I'm thankful for any guidance I get. I'm not capable of rational decisions yet, so I don't worry about what is fair and what isn't. What could a small child do even if they perceive an 'unfairness?' I certainly do enjoy superheroes, though, Mr. Talbot. I'll tell you why. They exact unfair justice upon unfair people. Let me illustrate. What if it were you, Tom, that watched Lady Godiva gallop through the streets of Coventry in all her naked glory—in order to decrease your taxes? You recall, of course, the reason for her historic ride? It was an act of support for the commoners her husband had too-dearly taxed. Anyhow, if it were 'Peeping Tom Talbot' who broke the agreement to avert his eyes and Superman flew in and said: 'Shame on you, Talbot,' and fried your eyes with his laser vision, would that be fair?" Tom was dumbstruck. "In my view, it wouldn't. Superman is bigger, faster, smarter, stronger, better dressed—has a superior intellect, Tom. He's better than you in every conceivable way. You wouldn't stand a chance. The more important question is: would it be just? I'll give you my answer: it would. If you, with your grubby eleventh-century peasant tongue agreed to avert your eyes, then peeked? You lied. That's on you. That, Tom, is a society I want to live in. The problem arises when the citizens of Coventry lament the fate of the poor liar: 'But it was just a peek, Superman. The punishment doesn't fit the crime.' How naïve. Superman did the only thing that works—you won't peek again, will you? And since he allowed you to live, you fulfill a greater service to your fellow citizens than if you had politely averted your eyes. You become a beggar—a daily reminder for the people of Coventry that justice must be unfair to work."

Tom found his voice, but it didn't emanate from a stable place. "So S.M. is—"

"Superman. Yes. Are you certain you still wish to talk about the graphs? I thought we had moved on."

"Yes," Raquel announced, "we're quite done. Tom? Barbara? Please write your suggestions and thoughts down—I'll share them with my husband."

In the letter from Thomas Talbot, he urged the Maddox family to "seek the help of a psychiatrist." In Tom's estimation, "the magical thinking" Bonn used, "could lead to a downward spiral of superstition and behaviors that may harm himself or more likely others." Troy took Bonn to a psychiatrist. They left with a piece of paper. Raquel handed the paper to the principal on Monday.

"I strongly suggest B. Maddox skip to fourth grade. B. Maddox tests at AP college level equivalent math—higher still in linguistics. His behavior borders on asocial, however diagnosis is impractical due to child's advanced use of redirection (of observer.) IQ testing deferred due to a pseudo-philosophical discussion involving the math required to define the word: 'quotient.' Aforementioned discussion spurred by B. Maddox. In short—please keep this child challenged. We may all be sorry if he is not. Follow up in six months if re-evaluation is desired."

Bonn was moved to Ms. Rothknot's fourth-grade homeroom. Troy and Raquel tried to find challenges for Bonn. They tried hockey, piano, and golf—all before Bonn finished the fifth grade. Bonn, however, applied hockey rules to his golf game and took the piano apart while his teacher was in the bathroom. He remained polite throughout. Having finished the fifth grade, Bonn could enter Boy Scouts. Technically the minimum age for Boy Scouts was eleven, but exceptions were made for advanced younger boys—especially those with wealthy fathers with successful law practices.

Troy tired of the scoutmaster's diatribe. Bonn could see it—whenever Troy said "uh huh" he no longer listened. After all, Troy spoke on the telephone much more often than he spoke to his family. Bonn recognized the cues.

He had read the Scout handbook in a sitting the night he was accepted. The eight-year-old carried himself with confidence: shoulders back, head high. Older boys assumed he was cocky. They ganged up on him. Bonn didn't mind, really. He didn't even fight back for a while. He learned from the beatings—about human nature, about groupthink, and about charisma. It took a dynamic ringleader to convince others to follow him. He also learned about pain. He absorbed pain. He categorized it. He both felt, yet was indifferent to it. More importantly, he learned about those who doled it out—those willing to hurt someone simply because they seemed weak. It spoke to poor reasoning on the part of the persecutor.

If you didn't kill someone eventually they would come for you.

If you didn't destroy them, you had better disrupt their motivation to seek a fight with you in the future.

That's where his tormentors fell short.

Bonn also had trouble when he decided to use the slide—he had only gone down once—when he was six. Bonn preferred to remember the smooth acceleration in his raw and virgin run. He waited in line for the slide like he should. He didn't *want* to wait with the others but knew it was expected. He was bumped and jostled by careless classmates. The boy in front of him paused to tie his shoe when it was his turn to go, so Bonn went up the ladder instead.

It was the efficient choice. The kids behind them would wait less—everyone benefitted.

A boy twice his size kicked him in the mouth at the bottom of the slide. "You took cuts. That's what you get!"

The blow nearly knocked out his tooth. Bonn faced the laughing bully and tongued the bloody incisor. Then he wiggled the tooth with a finger and snapped the remaining shred of torn dental ligament himself. He held the tooth out to the bully, who turned green. The boy's knees locked. He reeled for a moment and went down. A circle of children formed. Bonn sat on the bully's neck and forced his mouth open. When he struggled, Bonn rammed the bully in the diaphragm with his knees and dug his fingers into his trachea. The boy coughed and gasped. Bonn shoved the tooth down his throat like a veterinarian force-feeds a pill to a cat. The boy gagged and swallowed the tooth. Bonn got up and left. The bully sat up.

A beaming girl in pigtails squatted down to look at him. "Sometime tomorrow Bonn's gonna bite you in the BUTT-hole, Gulp-tooth."

The circle of breathless children shrieked like jungle birds who have spotted a snake. "Gulp-tooth! Gulp-tooth!"

It was a big win for all girls. Girls were special targets for the bully and the one with pigtails was a hero. It took guts to do what Bonn did, sure—but a nickname like Gulp-tooth? That took away the bully's power.

The principal called Raquel to report the event.

"There was a playground altercation. Your son lost a tooth, but, ma'am, he—well, he forced the other child to *swallow* the tooth. His actions incited what can only be described as a riot." Troy locked him in the library. It struck Bonn as a poor choice of punishment, however. He chose to spend his time there anyway.

At long last, Troy finished the call. "You know what that was about?" Bonn nodded. Troy poured himself four fingers of scotch. He swallowed greedily and sat in a leather chair near a bank of windows facing the gorge. "Didn't you want to get signed off on your knots?" Bonn didn't answer. Troy glanced around the library for him. His son stood at the sideboard. He poured himself a scotch.

That was new. Was the boy looking for limits?

Troy decided not to redirect Bonn from the decanter.

The burn from the liquor would teach him.

Bonn sat in a chair next to his father and held his drink the same way. "A good knot can be untied. I accomplished that."

"Yeah, you did. Several times. I'm most interested in why you tied up eight boys."

Didn't he spend enough time with Bonn? Was it a cry for attention? Somehow it didn't seem so—he had plans to spend time with Bonn. Later. When he was older. The intense little character seemed to be more comfortable alone anyway.

Troy downed his drink.

By the time Bonn was twelve or fourteen—old enough to really throw a football, they'd laugh about this.

Bonn tracked a crow that flew from the gorge. It carried something small and dead. The wind in the trees added a blur of green monochrome. Rain tapped at the windowpane with each gust. Corvids were tough. They barely needed shelter—they just weathered the storm.

You could hide in a storm, if you were a crow. No one would come to look for you. Maybe he didn't need to be a crow. Maybe he could stand still in the gorge and not be seen. Maybe everyone would leave him alone. Animals on TV that held still blended in unless they moved.

20

Bonn envied crows. He wished he were one.

He'd sprout wings. He'd carry dead things. Large dead things.

"A couple of boys tied me into my sleeping bag. I couldn't breathe. I called for help, but even though they all heard me, no one came."

"So how did you get out?"

"Well, I followed the motto—you know, 'be prepared.' I had a knife. I cut my way out."

"Ok. That was good thinking. What happened next?"

"I decided what the right thing to do at the moment was and I did it. It's all in the handbook."

"What did you 'decide' to do?"

"I elbowed one of the kids in the nose. One of the guys who tied me in my bag—when the other kid came at me, I kicked him in the balls, then I tied them up."

"What about the other six? Why did you tie *them* up?"

"Because they didn't help me. They let the other two do what they did. So I treated them all the same."

"How were you able to overpower six of them at once?"

"Sheep don't fight, Dad. They just let me. If someone will stand by and let others be hurt, they will likely allow themselves to be hurt too."

"You didn't tell them you'd 'cut them' if they didn't let you tie them to trees?"

"Of course I said that, but they didn't fight."

"Would you have cut them if they'd fought?"

"Of course—but after I cut the first one, the rest would have let me tie them up easily."

"How would you have cut him—the first one?"

"With my knife."

"Where Bonn? Where would you have cut him? Where on his *body*?"

Bonn looked into the amber fluid in his tumbler. He smelled it next. The silence was uncomfortable for Troy—like knots, Bonn had mastered the pregnant pause. Troy used the engineered silence himself in court, but only when he needed to make someone very uncomfortable. Juries didn't like the trick, so it had to be used sparingly.

Silence was a weapon—a damned effective one.

Bonn raised his glass. "I learned what I needed to learn. Here's to the Scouts' handbook—may my victims now read it and avoid the

21

pitfalls of treachery." He took a big swig from the tumbler and set the glass down on a table. Troy watched for the boy to react to the strong alcohol, but he didn't. He just looked out the window.

"You can't go back to Scouts. You can't assault a whole group of kids, threaten them, tie innocent ones to trees for crying out loud, and expect to make friends. It isn't how things are done. It isn't how the world works." Bonn sat quietly. "If you want to make friends, you have to play. Visit with the other boys. Make allies. If you want to be normal, you must temper yourself. We all want to do things that are crazy sometimes, but, Bonn, we don't actually do those things. I don't know what in the hell you're thinking."

Normal? He didn't want to be normal. Normal seemed weak. Friends would be nice, but who shared his ideals? No one. No one he knew anyway. He had more in common with the crow than his father.

The dark bird watched Bonn through the window.

The crow had ideals. It had sets of rules that it followed and it didn't take $400.00 bottles of scotch to make the bird happy. Just a scrap of something dead.

"What makes you happy? Do you want a dog? Do you want to try baseball? What do I need to do to get you to make friends?" Bonn smelled the rain licking the gray stones of the house. He heard it tick on the roof. The angry static from his father seemed like a part of the storm, just another mineral flowing sideways. The crow finished its meal and hopped to the window ledge to avoid the pelting raindrops. The wind changed directions, and the bird leaned into the gale on scaly legs to keep from being blown from the ledge.

I want a crow.

"I don't need friends, but a dog would be nice." The crow swiveled its head to blink at him—disapprovingly. Something about the bird's gaze said "turncoat."

Troy seemed relieved. He followed his son's gaze outside. Bonn's answer had the countenance of today's harsh weather. Troy boomed with sarcastic levity. "Will you tie the damned thing to a tree?"

It was another of his courtroom tricks: ask an embarrassing question—in a demeaning way—in which there is only one socially acceptable answer. Bonn pantomimed contemplation, but decided not to answer the way he should.

"If he is trainable it shouldn't be necessary." Troy poured himself another two fingers.

"Boys want boy dogs!" Troy shouted the anemic attempt to normalize his son, and perhaps to prove that he was paying attention.

22

As his father dropped in the ice, the man seemed somehow smaller. Shaken. Uncharacteristically pensive. Bonn tried to guess his thoughts. Was he wondering how he had failed? Concerned that further psychological or personality testing was warranted? Did Troy fleetingly consider summer camp—then dismiss the idea as imprudent based on recent events?

The phone rang. "Now? Rupert—we didn't FILE that. Get the district attorney on the phone right now." Bonn left the library. They were done.

~Old Haunts

Three years passed quickly. Henna no longer had a round, soft face. She was growing—changing—much too fast. It was easy to be proud of Henna. She surprised Alvar daily. Henna's face felt like her mother's did at the same age. Henna liked to hear about her mother.

"I called your mom 'Nappi' when she was little."

Henna looked up from her project. Alvar's clothes wore out in odd places. Never the knees, or the seat like her own clothes did, but in parts of his body he used to find his way around, like his shoulders. He bumped his shoulders against parts of the house as points of reference. She sewed patches on his clothes when they became too frayed. It was a rainy day—a good day for sewing.

"Nappi?"

The English equivalent was "button." It was a cute nickname.

"Yes. She seemed always to have a button in her pocket, or held tightly in her fist. Your grandmother scolded her for taking them, but to Nappi it was part of the game—no matter how cross she became, Nappi would always take another when her mother turned her back."

"I like to hear what she was like."

"Your mom was always resilient. It was just after World War Two. There weren't many reasons to play, or to be happy, but she found them. If we didn't have buttons, she found another game—but I liked the button game the best."

"How was it a game?"

"Well, your grandmother would chase her and—"

"Do you mind if we call her Lucrece?" Henna frowned at the sewing. "I know we are related, but she wasn't nice to me. I'd rather call her by her name."

"I understand." Alvar thoughtfully loaded his pipe. "Lucrece would chase Nappi to get back a button. I couldn't see any of it, of course, but I heard it. Nappi would run by with a button in her fist, feet slapping the floor like mad. Lucrece, I think, didn't realize she reinforced the behavior by chasing her, or she would never have done it. I couldn't chase her, but Nappi contrived a way to involve me in the game too. She would busy herself with a book, or some kitchen utensils for a while, until Lucrece became complacent. When she was ready to attack the button jar, she'd pad up to me and whisper something in my ear."

Henna clipped a loose thread from the patch with small scissors. "What did she say?"

"She said 'again.' When Lucrece performed her ablutions, Nappi would make for the buttons. She'd hide one in my shoe, or in my trouser pocket. She never took them for herself. Always for me. When I found one she'd hidden, I'd make a fuss over it. 'Someone left me a gift!' I'd exclaim. Nappi would make a happy little trill in the back of her throat and come hug me around the neck."

Henna swept little bits of thread from the floor. "She whispered to me sometimes too—little secrets I knew were silly but made me feel special. She talked about you a lot, but she never told me about the buttons."

Henna took Mortimer to check for eggs. On the way out she said the dog was turning white on his chin and around his eyes. "His face is gray now, Grandpa. The color of the wolves that pulled Gertie down last winter." The dog lost an eye and two teeth breaking a window to rout the killers. His remaining fangs pierced the skull of a young male wolf. They'd hung the pelt above the fireplace.

Alvar replaced Gertie with two cashmere goats. They didn't give milk, but they were softer to pet and Henna wanted to try her hand spinning wool. Even the farm changed. A trio of black and white Karelian Bear Dogs carved new paths through old pastures and meadows. When they weren't chasing stoats from the chicken coop, they panted on the porch, waiting for enemies. When the dogs crashed from the porch after a forest animal, their noises disappeared as soon as they hit the forest. It was easy to imagine them floating through the undergrowth, their feet barely grazing the ground. Henna said they preferred to hunt rather than eat what she left them. The sweet potatoes, oatmeal, and even the boiled eggs went largely untouched, but each day when he ran his hands down the flanks of the dogs, Alvar thought they seemed more sleek and muscular than before.

The little house seemed so quiet without Henna and the eldest, noisy dog. It felt lonesome, though they'd return with eggs soon enough. Without their comforting mammalian noises, his mind looked for old demons. He reflected on his old life in Helsinki—when both Nappi

25

and his blindness were infants. He had just returned from the un-winnable war. It was a time of momentary relief floating in a sea of terror and hunger. Each small hope of survival was gone too soon—a scrap of meat, a bit of bread—the bones in his hips dug into the pallet they slept on. He slowly starved so Nappi and Lucrece could eat. What he did eat, Nappi gave him. The little girl insisted. He heard her stomach growl even when she promised she was full.

That was a game he didn't miss.

Their terrible game pieces were hollow eyes and bony ribs—creative lies, born of love, traded back and forth. "I'm so full, Papa. You have it. I'll just have to throw it out if you don't eat it." Nappi did what she could. If she found any reason to laugh or smile, she ran to him so he could feel her face. Sometimes she tricked him. She'd hold up a stray cat or a toad where he expected her face to be. She was the only brightness in that dismal time.

While war did horrible things to good people, it turned bad people into monsters. Before they fled to France, he was beaten badly in the bread line. Lucrece sewed him up and read him letters from her mother in St. Germaine. Finally he agreed to the move. Within a month of their relocation, she left him for an aristocrat who considered the war more a nuisance. Money insulated his family from squalor and she joined him eagerly. She was a woman who needed to hear she was beautiful. Alvar didn't tell her anymore.

Lucrece gifted him with her thoughts as she packed her things. "Your eyes are mismatched. You couldn't know this, but you should—one pupil is larger than the other. And oval. You used to have pretty eyes. I remember how blue they were."

She didn't talk about her needs or her dreams. She merely ground away at his damaged parts. After she said her piece, she left without hesitation. For years Alvar wondered if she even paused to look at Nappi. He wondered if she shed a tear. She didn't sound sad. He didn't try to stop her. He blamed himself for failing Lucrece, yet was thankful the woman had a stony heart. If she'd been more human she'd have taken Nappi with her.

"Alvar, war takes and gives what it wants." Lucrece said from the door. "It's finally given me what I've always deserved."

Nappi cried a lot when they packed to return to Helsinki without Lucrece. Without a mother to chase her, she stopped playing with buttons. They left a jar of them behind: Lucrece's only tangible legacy.

26

A friend from the university helped them get settled. Alvar began teaching again, but the school could no longer pay him what it took to live. Nappi paced and pulled at her hair. Sometimes she took his hand away from his pipe to feel her tears. He hugged her and sang old songs. The world never seemed safe, and they clung to each other fiercely. Alvar recalled how terrified he'd been of losing Nappi—his tiny, funny, constant comfort. He wouldn't have gone on without her. He prayed the world would heal so they could. He prayed to live long enough to teach Nappi how to recognize real monsters. He'd lost his faith in The Winter War, but all children had a god, so Alvar prayed to Nappi's. Each night that ended with them together, the bolt slid into the frame of the door, was a gift from Nappi's god. The professor never took gifts for granted.

Then Alvar's worst demons paid him a visit. Alvar was a grunt in the war. Captured near the Karelian Isthmus early in the battle of Summa. His fate was sealed when he shoved a bit of broken radio equipment and a notebook in his rucksack. His commanding officer pushed the items at him after receiving a mortal gunshot to the pelvis. The scholar was following orders. Alvar tried to hold pressure on the man's wound, but he felt bone crunch under his hands and the bleeding worsened. Alvar rocked by the fireplace. He was back again, out in the snow. It always snowed when the memories clawed the haunted man back into their dreaded company. It was The Winter War, after all. He knelt beside the wounded man. The larger man had a warm woolen coat reserved for officers. Officers were issued coats and rifles, but new recruits had to join the effort with what they brought from home. When life left the man's eyes, Alvar saw that the only weapon he had left, a rag tied around a wine bottle full of petrol and tar, was broken. It didn't matter. He was out of matches and the Soviet tanks were far past them now. Alvar slipped the officer's blood-soaked coat on over his thin canvas one and looked around. Hungry, exhausted, alone. Another wave of Russian troops approached. The gaunt intellectual quickly made for the safety of the forest. Resources were scant. Alvar's boots were un-insulated. He paused to roll bodies. Looking for rifles or even a pistol. Finding no weapons to physically grasp, the intellect sat in the snow, slumped and still.

He still had his brain—the petrol bomb was his creation. If he could only reach the trees, he could improvise.

27

Struggling, he rose to his crackling knees, then to his sloughing, swollen feet.

Just move your feet. Start with that.

The months of brackish water and salty biscuits made the reluctant foot soldier slow and weak. Alvar didn't reach the safety of the tree line. The Soviet lieutenant overtook him in a few embarrassingly slow strides. Since Alvar wore his officer's coat, he was taken prisoner. It was the first time in weeks he had felt warm. He waited in relative comfort for days.

"The team will ask you things," said a man who brought him food. "These are the good days for you." Alvar was only allowed two small cups of water a day.

"Can I have more water please?" the inventor asked his mild-faced enemy/provider, polite despite the circumstances.

"When you tell the team," the young man answered, "if you tell them what you know." The team arrived. They brought him to a room. They gave him clean water.

"Officer, we suspect you may know things of use to us." Alvar gave the same replies over and over. After some hours he tried apologetic tones. He truly *didn't* know anything useful.

"You've got me wrong. I'm not an officer. I took my officer's coat because I was cold. It isn't my radio. I'm sorry. I wouldn't know how to use it if it were in working order."

Eventually, Soviet officers called for a man with a hot curved knife. The team held Alvar's arms—his legs. Without drama, the man twisted the knife into Alvar's right eye socket. Another man held his commanding officer's notebook open for his remaining eye to see. The page was a diagram Alvar recognized when they pried his remaining eye open to view it.

"What is this? What other methods have your people planned against us?" Alvar ignored the question. He pressed both hands to his skull. They carried him to a damp room. It was neither wide nor long enough to accommodate his length, so he slumped miserably against a wall. "Your other eye will follow if you don't tell us. It will be a cold knife next time and you will bleed to death from the wound. You will tell us."

Alvar sat in misery. He groped about in the dark and felt a puddle of fluid he hoped was water. He slurped at it in desperation. It wasn't water—it was something vile, but it sustained him. The tortured gentleman moaned until he was hoarse. He didn't know if he could speak. He heard things—and lost what was real. Advanced dehydration caused the unlikely warrior's heart to beat fast. Bile ebbed and flowed—a sour sea, hot and thick—with no visible moon to blame for the stinging tidal misery. The pain roared, mixed with his breathing and Soviet voices. Time passed. Each time he heard steps approach the room, he shook.

He had to act. The way to live was to lie—if they'd believed he wasn't an officer, they'd have killed him already.

He had to think of something.

The diagram. It was his.

The "Molotov cocktail." It was Alvar's contribution to the war. A bit of glass, soap or tar, mixed with fuel. An oily rag tied around it. If set alight and hurled at the hydraulic system of a tank, the weapon sometimes caught the armored demons on fire. If the hydraulics went, the ammunition and fuel tanks followed. Then the beast was ruined. Alvar's petrol bomb required bravery to use. Vyacheslav Molotov lied to the world about the help they provided the Finns. The "bread baskets" they dropped for his people weren't food—they were cluster bombs. Alvar didn't name his invention, but he liked the sound of the name that took.

Molotov lied. Now it was time for him to lie.

If they believed him, it would buy him some time. If he did nothing, death was assured. "I DO know something!"

Alvar shouted the words again, decades later. He shivered by the fire and tore at the patch on his shoulder. The demons always brought him to the same place, but the older his body got, the worse it hurt when he arrived.

They gave Alvar water. He shook badly and spilled most of it. A man poured him more, but kept it out of reach. "What do you know? Tell us everything quickly so you can have all the water you want. You can take a bath if you like. You appear filthy and miserable. All for no good reasons. When you tell us everything, you will help your countrymen. It will shorten their inevitable and futile battles. You could consider yourself their savior. You can save their lives. None of you are fighters. Look. There, you bleed. We will have a doctor look after your wound." The team sat down to take notes. Alvar shakily reported a fictitious and important meeting with some high level German officers. The Finns would receive supplies and trade intelligence at the meeting. It would happen on the eighteenth of

December. Unfortunately—Alvar didn't realize—it was already the nineteenth.

The man returned with a curved, cold knife. With a twist, the man removed Alvar's remaining eye. Another wound, bleeding and despondent, Alvar was dragged back to the small room to die, but decided not to. He ripped a piece from his shirt and forced the makeshift dressing into his eye socket to stop the bleeding. The bookish man heaved from the pain until he lost the precious water. When footsteps approached, the learned, broken man lay quietly so they assumed he was dead. Soon, it seemed, they'd forgotten him entirely. No one came to yank him from the room to shoot him or to pull his body out. The pain was the same, but he'd been through it already. There was nothing left to do but pray. He prayed for water and he prayed for help. He prayed until he lost hope. After a while, he prayed for death, but it didn't come. Instead, Finnish troops pulled him from the tiny room on December 21. By the twenty-third, he was back in Helsinki. A hero. A German optician hurriedly fitted him with mismatched eye prosthetics taken in the Invasion of Poland.

He relived the rest in a more anecdotal melancholy—he was alive and home, but not whole.

He'd never be whole again.

Water was plentiful. Food was scarce, but he could run a hand across Lucrece's belly and feel their baby move inside.

Alvar remembered the rubbery numbness. He would never see his child. He continued to rock back and forth and recalled other sadness, but the sound of Henna's voice jarred him into the present. She and Mortimer were back with the eggs.

"Mortimer got a couple when I wasn't looking, but there were eight left. Enough for a couple of meals." Henna sat on the hearth and cleaned a basket of root vegetables to roast for dinner. The dog noisily washed down the pilfered eggs at his water bowl and then joined Henna at the hearth. He threw his head back and unleashed a low rumble at the wolf skin.

"You got him, Morty. He isn't going to hurt anyone now." It was a game Henna played frequently with the dog: Mortimer would growl at the wolf pelt above the mantle, then look to Henna for praise. After Henna told him how wonderful he was, the dog would nap happily in the warmth of the fire. Alvar envied the simple game. The dog had done his job very well. He'd only lost one eye in the battle.

When Mortimer started the story, Henna sometimes drew it out—until the beast veritably bayed at the wolf skin—but in the end, he always got his reward: the second half of the story, told by the girl, with high praise.

"You bit him in the head, Mortimer. No one else could have done it. You broke the window to save us. You're so brave."

Alvar listened. He loaded his pipe with war-haunted hands. A tear escaped him. He imagined finding a button in the pipe. Although he knew it was ridiculous, he pulled the tobacco out of the bowl to check for one. Henna startled him when she sat on his lap. She washed his face with a cloth that smelled of turnips. She put her hands on his face and felt it with her fingertips like he usually felt hers. She wiped his tears as they poured from his ruined eyes. He'd never told the story of his eyes—no one ever asked.

What good would it do to tell it?

There was no witness to his pain and sacrifice.

He hadn't killed the wolf.

Sure, he had burned tanks and taught others to do so, but how many fathers like himself were inside them? His brain played tricks. Henna became Nappi, sitting on his lap—at this very hearth—many years ago. When Henna spoke, she spoke for them both.

"You did what you had to do, Grandpa. You talk at night. I know your heart. You've always done what you had to do. You're a hero—the only human one I have ever known."

Henna wrapped her arms around her grandfather's neck.

He was wrong. He was whole. Now. After all these years.

He hugged Henna tightly and cried for the fire, for his eyes—for Nappi and Lucrece. For the war and lost time. Mortimer stirred. He eyed the wolf suspiciously, as though it caused Alvar's sorrow, then rose with a groan and rested his great head on the old man's knee. Alvar patted the dog and wiped his cheeks. He was one of the lucky ones. He was alive and here were two creatures that loved him. A peace came over him. He'd changed too.

Henna saw the change in her grandfather. He still talked in his sleep, but it was to her.

He even gave lessons while he slept.

31

~Mother Figure

Raquel had two vices and a constant source of consternation. The source of consternation was her son. After Bonn's evaluation with the psychiatrist, she couldn't feel close to him. Raquel treated her son with distracted disdain. She secretly wished he had never been born.

When Bonn was born she was unable to breast-feed. Troy hired a wet nurse. That changed everything. Her services included diaper changes, childproofing, and twenty-four hour-a-day monitoring of the child. Any sparks of maternal instinct Raquel felt for Bonn were drowned by Audra's ample and milky breasts. Troy liked to watch the baby nurse. Audra didn't seem to mind. Raquel drove backcountry roads by herself most afternoons—an attempt to escape the black cloud of her postpartum depression. She took the corners fast. It didn't help. One evening at a charity auction, a social acquaintance introduced her to her first vice. Cocaine worked much better than racing the Jaguar to lift her spirits. She'd bid enthusiastically on a Chagall to celebrate the discovery of the magic powder. It was only a lithograph, but Troy didn't care. Raquel made some money in her real estate dealings, but Troy's family had deep pockets. Cotton, slaves, wool, paper, coal, now law. Although she disliked Troy, it was a profitable union. Raquel found that liberal re-application of cocaine was necessary, so she became a regular.

Cocaine had side effects, which led Raquel to her second vice. The powder aroused her, but made it nearly impossible to climax. It made her nipples hot, rubbery, and heavy. She pinched them until they became numb, but for a few delicious moments she felt the heat inside the pain. It felt like hot breath on her neck—or strong, warm hands stroking the backs of her legs. Troy didn't know about the habit. He was shocked when Raquel came at him one afternoon. She begged him to do things she'd never wanted before. To Troy, the ordeal seemed rabid and unhygienic. He attributed it to hormonal changes, which never seemed to last anyway. Troy hadn't pulled through for Raquel. Neither had the Hitachi Magic wand she kept behind her jewelry box. One afternoon, Raquel quietly observed that Troy was proficient in causing Audra a moment of sexual crisis. Since they didn't notice her, she said nothing. During Audra's employ, everyone *but* Raquel seemed to thrive: Audra got paid handsomely to have an affair with her husband, Troy seemed to enjoy their clockwork trysts, and Bonn nursed greedily while adorned in a dry diaper. Raquel didn't cope well. She ran through a kilo-and-a-half of cocaine in short order.

One rainy Thursday, she propositioned the family's horse trainer. The man did his best, although his usual rugged charm proved insufficient. Raquel asked him to incorporate a riding crop. He whacked her haunches lightly, but Raquel needed more. She threw the crop and demanded he pull her hair. He pulled harder and harder, but Raquel yelped for more. He pulled until it seemed the woman's scalp would separate from her skull with a sucking noise. Raquel, however, remained unimpressed. Desperate for relief, Raquel ran a fifty-foot extension cord to the barn to plug in her Hitachi Magic Wand. A bin of sweet feed was knocked over in the fray, but Raquel finally saw stars.

Audra stayed until Bonn was fourteen months old. He bit her right nipple shortly after. The wet nurse bled badly. While her nipple healed, she pumped milk from her injured side. She attempted to feed Bonn from her other nipple, but Bonn refused. Audra developed mastitis in her left breast since Bonn wouldn't nurse from it. She believed strongly in the benefits of nursing. She hated to use the breast pump. Bonn would still nurse, but only from her injured side. Audra became cross. She showed him the engorged left breast with a perfect healthy nipple on top, but the toddler pointed back to her injured side. "No, Audra, this one." Audra shook her head, exasperated. What he said next was too much. "Good bite."

Audra gave no notice. To Troy's dismay, she left while he was at work. Raquel didn't tell Troy why Audra quit, but she was glad Bonn bit her. After Bonn and Troy were weaned, Troy focused on his law practice more than ever. Raquel, however, intended to continue her indiscretions—on a more biblical scale. A parade of men serviced Raquel for years while Troy focused on his career. When Raquel told Bonn, "Time for me to meditate," he read in the library while she entertained her guests. By age four, Bonn found he could open the library windows. He crawled out to explore at will. Most days he just traipsed around the side-yard watching the groundskeeper or the horse trainer from a distance. Sometimes his nanny, Frau Hedwig, came with him, but mostly the help left him alone.

Hedwig was not Bonn's first nanny. The first one was a fresh blonde optimist, just graduated from Brown. An energetic French

33

major, Misty attempted to involve Bonn in linguistic exercises, croquet, and calisthenics. Bonn grasped French quickly. He became conversational in just a few days. Misty quit shortly after.

"He isn't right," Misty reported, "He wants to know how to say things in French that are not—well—they're wrong!"

Troy smirked.

What could a two-year-old ask that would cause such upset?

"What things?" Troy asked.

"Dark things," Misty said earnestly.

Misty was unwilling to repeat Bonn's "dark things," and when Troy pressed her, she left.

Had they chosen her too hastily?

Raquel attempted to direct the toddler herself for a week, but found it arduous and stifling. Troy decided to pull out the stops— they'd hire a professional. Troy made some calls and arranged for an English nanny.

Tillie achieved her rectangular shape in only sixty-two years. She arrived promptly on the hour she promised, straight from Brixton. If Tillie carried an umbrella, one would think she was prepared to audition for the role of Mary Poppins, if Mary Poppins wore a men's forty-six-long tweed jacket over her frock. Tillie was physically intimidating. She smelled of lemon furniture polish and mothballs. Her neck didn't articulate. Her nose looked broken. She bent stiffly at the waist to address her new ward and displayed an armored plate of a forehead between her wide set eyes.

"We'll get along fine now, won't we, Bonn."

It wasn't a question.

To Troy Tillie looked like a massive architectural clock with two dials for eyes: one set to London time, one to New York. Tillie reported she typically kept a diary to mark daily occurrences, progress with lessons, bowel habits, and developmental benchmarks. "Is that acceptable, Mr. Maddox?"

Troy had no doubts that Tillie would provide steady order for their son. She lasted a year. The year wasn't kind to Tillie. She shook a bit as she recounted some observations of Bonn. She wanted to give comprehensive, quarterly accounts of Bonn's progress, but Raquel consistently put her off and her journal of observations was missing. Tillie insisted the family seek out professional input from a physician for their child. She couldn't put her finger on the precise problem, she just knew—he was off. Troy was disappointed. Tillie seemed suddenly addled and disorganized. While she prattled on, Troy observed his son quietly turning the pages of a large book: *An Illustrated Field Guide to Birds of Papua New Guinea*. He shook his head.

Bonn was fine.

He just needed more structure.

No one told him to look through the book. The boy had pulled it from the shelf himself.

Bonn re-shelved the book and chose another—a hardbound copy containing pictures of Egyptian scrolls. Troy glanced at the title: *Book of the Dead*. The interior designer watched for collectable, rare books. She charged Troy a modest finder's fee. This particular book arrived recently—part of a retired archeology professor's collection. Troy rarely found time to flip though his books himself, so he was glad Bonn found some use in them. Bonn stopped on a page with a depiction of a bipedal creature named "Opet." The caption described how Opet—goddess of the hippos—was burning some incense. The goddess didn't look like a hippo, more like a bipedal hyena sporting a bridal veil.

It was something a child might draw.

It explained why Bonn liked it—surely he wasn't reading yet.

He was just a good-natured boy who loved books.

There were no kids in the neighborhood for him to play with, or he'd be out there now, running through a sprinkler, or building a fort...

Troy was sure of it.

Frau Hedwig took over two weeks later. The diminutive German could have been fifty, or eighty. She insisted they call her "Frau." She wore thick square glasses with chunky black plastic frames. Her arms seemed much longer than her legs, and she suffered from kyphosis. Despite this, she seemed able to uncurl herself at will, a fiddle-head fern seeking sunlight. She extended her long arms like multi-jointed cranes to reach things even Troy could not. She steered Bonn with her long fingers. She tapped adjustments in his direction like a sheepdog nipped its flock. Frau Hedwig's neck was noteworthy—it stretched out almost horizontally. Her smallish head swiveled slowly at the end of it, like a tortoise pondering each direction carefully before committing to action. Hedwig was previously assigned to a family who perished in a fire while she was out to the grocer.

Raquel was tired of hiring replacements, so she asked some screening questions. "Are you emotionally ready to commit to another assignment, Frau Hedwig?"

Frau Hedwig appeared amused. "Why wouldn't I be?"

"How long did you care for the kids?" Raquel pressed.

"Five years." Hedwig replied stonily. She wasn't a sensitive soul.

Frau Hedwig stuck. Determined to check on the welfare of the nanny weekly in case she became inclined to flee, Troy often asked, "How are things?" or "Doing well, Fraulein?"

The odd woman consistently answered with the same clipped affirmative, "Ja," and then batted Bonn back and forth in front of her like a hockey puck she had utter control of. It truth, Frau Hedwig was terrified of the child and drank vodka throughout the day to cope with the stressors of the job. Frau Hedwig and Bonn quickly reached an unspoken understanding: Bonn expected Frau Hedwig to play bulwark when a parent was around, but she let him have free rein when each momentary scrutiny ceased. She performed the essential functions a nanny should. She bought the child underwear as he outgrew them—and similar tasks, but Bonn was naturally fastidious. There wasn't much to do. He really just needed someone to enable the idea of normalcy, though none existed. Sometimes Bonn stole into Hedwig's room at night to watch her sleep. She'd flick an eye open and see the Alp there. He wouldn't touch her—talk to her—interact with her in any way. He just stood there.

Watching.

Her mother warned Hedwig of "Alps" when she was a child—but now she knew_ ... the elf-like demons who visited in the night? Who could freeze or crush you—paralyze you with fear—play tricks, drink your blood if they wished to?

They were real.

He didn't wear a hat ...

But maybe in the New World it wasn't required of them.

Hedwig remained quiet in regard to this oddity. She was paid very well after all. She learned to act as though she were asleep while she kept an eye out for the little wraith. One night she drifted off, exhausted. She slept soundly until she sensed movement—a small figure returned a pair of her shoes to a bottom drawer of her wardrobe.

It was the Alp.

He padded over to stare at her for a few seconds. She squinted at him through fear-shrouded lids. Although she couldn't see clearly without her glasses, she recognized his movements. He picked up her glasses and looked through them toward the moon. He breathed on the lenses to fog them up, then polished them with the sleeve of his pajama top before creeping out. Fearful to inspect the shoes that very moment, Frau Hedwig lay awake wondering what the demon wanted with them. In the morning she found that the sole of her right shoe had been worked loose at the toe—a razor blade glued into the cavity.

Sharp edge out—a weapon.

She was afraid not to wear them. If this was an Alp-gift, she needed to acknowledge it. Frau Hedwig placed a broomstick under her pillow to ward him off, and that night when she removed her weaponized clogs, she planned to put the heels against the bed frame with the toes facing the door.

A sign, Old World as it may be, to leave her alone.

She wished she remembered more about Alps—*living* with one seemed foolhardy. The elf-demon seemed to ignore the shoes as the day progressed, but that night he was back. The shadowy figure ignored the broomstick, as Hedwig feared he would, and seemed not to notice the shoes placed to keep him away. The tiny devil crept toward her, just inches from her face. Frau Hedwig's heart thumped in her throat. Nearer still. Suddenly, he waved his hand in her face. Frau Hedwig shrieked. She braced herself to be frozen, crushed, bit, or worse.

"Can you get me a small stepladder? So I can reach things myself?" Hedwig opened her eyes.

She wasn't dead.

"Yes. Of course," Hedwig managed. Her creepy, quiet visitor nodded. The deal was done. The trade was accepted. Hedwig lay awake for the longest time. If the boy wasn't an Alp, it would be even more frightening—

But for an Alp, he was quite nice.

Hedwig knew about Raquel's indiscretions. The men arrived like hungry bulls: wide-eyed and optimistic. Raquel broke them. Each lover that slunk off appeared more spooked, rawer than the last. The Alp's mother was not particular about her daytime lovers. Most days pickup trucks parked upon the cobblestones in front of the carriage house, but an occasional sedan delivered her daily ration. Hedwig knew a fuse was lit—she just didn't know which of the freaks was the bomb. Raquel didn't ask Hedwig to keep secrets, nor did she share Hedwig's. Raquel knew about the drinking. Many things went unspoken. The undercurrent of malice never stopped flowing. The riptide just changed directions.

One day Raquel—in a creative mood—poured some of Hedwig's vodka on a light purple pillowcase. She wrung the wet cloth into a tight cone and managed to corkscrew about a third of her invention up a man's anus before he decided it wasn't just kinky.

"Stop! Holy shit—quit that! That hurts like hell!" Hedwig heard the plea for help from the kitchen. Raquel's victim escaped to the bathroom a defeated lavender-tailed donkey and pulled the contraption out too fast.

Terrified and wounded, nauseated and distraught, the opportunistic misadventurer mistook Raquel's bidet for a toilet and threw up into it. Each bout of retching activated the motion sensor, which sent a jet of water forcefully up his nose. The retching and drowning sounds coming from her bathroom aroused Raquel more than when the accountant was in bed with her. After an adequate orgasm, she went to his aid. Raquel sprinkled sugar on his prolapsed rectum, which eventually made it slither back home.

Hedwig watched the big sedan speed away. She wished Raquel would find one that was reliable. One that could handle her.

One day, that woman will bring ruin to us all.

~Morel Day

In the summer Alvar took Henna into the forest. They explored, learned about the world from each other, and collected wild food. Lightning had started a fire the past spring. Several acres of nearby forest burned before the wind died down, and the fire burned out near a brook. Henna didn't know why their walks led them through the charred area every few days—it all seemed dead except for some wildflowers. One day Alvar stopped as they walked through the burn. "Ah. I smell something delicious." Henna looked back to the lush and bushy green living forest.

Did the wind shift?

She started back for the forest, but Alvar bent to brush at the ash with his hands. When he stood he held a mushroom with what looked like a brain on top. Some mushrooms, like *Boletus* were delicious, but this one didn't even look edible. "It doesn't look good, Grandpa."

Alvar smiled. "You can't tell which mushrooms are delicious by how they look." Alvar held the mushroom to his nose. "These only come a year after a fire—today is a morel day." Henna and Alvar left the ashy clearing with baskets and pockets brimming with the treasures. To Henna's young mind, the mushrooms looked as though they were made of ash. Henna felt desperate for answers—life came in so many forms—mycelium, fungal spores, nutrients, even fire led to life. Alvar seemed to know everything about nature. He showed her how to test a mushroom if she wasn't sure about it. She tried it first on a honey mushroom. Henna minced up a bit of it with her front teeth and felt for the sting on the tip of her tongue.

She didn't feel one.

Next she tried a fly agaric, which she knew was toxic. The raffish red-and-white flesh stung just as Alvar promised it would. She spit it out and rinsed her mouth. "All mushrooms should be cooked," Alvar explained. "A person could eat a raw morel, but without heat to break down the chitin, there's no nutritional value in one." A similar looking mushroom, the false morel *Gyromitra esculenta,* could prove fatal if eaten raw—but was commonly eaten cooked. Alvar picked a *Gyromitra.* He held it next to a morel for Henna to see the difference. "If you choose to eat them, it is best to boil them for five minutes, change the water out, then boil them a second time before rinsing and frying them. I think it's too much bother."

Henna was a sponge for information. The girl even learned from the land as she sifted through the ash.

To wildflowers, the ash was as important as rain.

She picked chamomile, bluebells, and other familiar flowers. Henna recited the Latin name of each as her bouquet grew. Though Alvar couldn't see the vibrant yellows and blues, he could smell them—even the ones Henna couldn't. To Alvar, smell was more powerful than his remaining senses. He could remember by smell. Henna chirped with excitement. She brought unknown plants to him. He gave her interesting facts about each to help her remember it. Alvar seemed amazed at what Henna could retain. She seemed hungry for knowledge and refused simple explanations to her questions. Soon, he would realize he was giving the young girl college-level botany lectures.

Alvar began a new lesson. "All things are interconnected—" One dissertation rolled into the next. They covered parasites, symbiosis, osmosis—even the Krebs cycle. Henna was euphoric with new knowledge. Her exceptional mind filed each fact with effortless proficiency. As they left the blackened forest she brought him a new discovery: white flowers that stood in a tuft of green stalks. To Henna the stalks looked like chives.

"Ah," Alvar said wistfully—he could smell the paperwhites well. "Narcissus papyraccous. Six petals. Sweet to smell one, yet fetid in great numbers. They don't normally grow here." Alvar spoke slowly, struck by the memory of Nappi bursting into the house with a fist full of the smelly flowers. "Your mother's favorite when she was a girl. I used to plant bulbs along the brook just to remind me of her. The French used it as an antispasmodic and it's a strong hallucinogen. It must not be ingested directly. 'Narcissus' is Latin for narcissist—one who loves themselves to the exclusion of most things."

Henna stood straight and raised her arms like flower petals. Mortimer peered at the girl quizzically. With great drama she narrated for Mortimer. "The paperwhite waved to the lion-like dog. The flower's weight tore at itself for its tender nature against the brutal breeze, the terrible pull of the sun, the gentle nudges of the moon. Radiant sepals guarded the nestled ovule tucked both with and within style, deep inside—by sun, and soil, and season: 'Here is an egg you cannot have.'" Henna paused to weave about, then stretched her

40

arms back up, high above her head. She unrolled her fingers from tight fists one at a time, as though each wished to show its reverence to the sun, yet was willing to wait its turn to do so. "Anthers quivered quiet apologies to humming visitors from the ends of brittle filaments: 'Too late, you too, too late. Next year. Same time, but a moment earlier and I'll reward your momentum with a meal.' Pipettes celebrated the sun's chemical cocktail—intent? To woo and to placate. From what? From damage done by a passing passerine: I'm OK! Ok. Ok? No. Not enough. I'm—perfect. With its sweet stink it begged the dog—'Please look at me. Please see that I'm beautiful, but never touch. Look now, before I've turned to soil again.'"

Mortimer chuffed and wagged to applaud Henna's performance, then sniffed about, as though he believed there really was an egg.

Alvar laughed. Henna was brilliant. He appeared to marvel at her genius—scientific, artistic—and so much like her mother.

~The Gifted

Bonn got a dog for his ninth birthday. It was a small celebration. Since Bonn didn't eat cake, Raquel asked Frau Hedwig to make vanilla cupcakes with vanilla frosting. Raquel was in a monochromatic phase. She would eat the confections. That week she was in love with all things white. Troy rolled his eyes when he saw the mundane baked goods. Raquel got defensive. "Why shouldn't they be white? Bonn won't care."

Hedwig lit a candle and handed Bonn one of the treats. Troy sang "Happy Birthday" distractedly while Raquel instructed Hedwig to release the retriever. The soft yellow dog burst into the room. He saw the boy holding the cupcake and sat at perfect attention. Troy poured himself a scotch. "You should name him."

Bonn frowned at the dog. "This is a full grown dog. Doesn't he already have a name?"

Troy took a drink and tried to recall the dog's name. "Puppies are too messy—this dog is a show dog. I'm sure he knows some tricks. Life here will be a vacation compared to the rigors of standing correctly and letting people pat his balls down to make certain he actually has two—I'll bet he'd like to forget that life—why don't you give him a new name to celebrate his freedom?" Bonn looked into the retriever's face. He was a good-looking dog. The retriever's eyes flicked from Bonn's cupcake to his face and back. He seemed to want a bite.

"He'll respond to anything you call him. Dogs aren't very smart, Son. You can call him 'Bacon' if you want to. You just have to say it with the right tone."

Raquel glared at the candle. It burned down quickly and might drip on something.

Also, it wasn't white. Hedwig had punctured the pretty cake with a horrible yellow and blue striped candle. She glared at Hedwig next. She'd been very specific—the candle should be white.

Hedwig ignored her, so Raquel glowered at Troy. She couldn't tell him how to dress, of course, but he should wear more white. To Raquel, Troy's teal pinstripe looked so gaudy. If she could, she'd paint the whole world white. She needed a snort. She wanted to coat everything in cocaine—it might make things better. They were all so

42

selfish. Bonn wanted a puppy, Troy probably still wanted Audra. Maybe if she ate the cupcake herself, took a snort, lifted her white skirt for the world and spun like a ballerina, and shot clean, crisp whiteness from her bowels and womb everything would be better.

"Blow out the candle, Bonn!" Raquel yelled with more than a touch of hysteria. Troy startled.

"He's going to," Troy snapped. "He's just thinking of a name for the stupid dog." Hedwig needed a drink, so she excused herself.

Bonn pinched the candlewick to extinguish it. "I'll think of one. I want to get to know him first. A name will come to me." Bonn didn't want to rename the dog. It wouldn't be right to confuse him. A show dog would have papers somewhere. The papers would have his name on them.

"He doesn't look stupid," Bonn added, "he looks hungry."

The retriever shook with excitement. He shifted back and forth on his front paws and watched the cupcake. He whined and willed the boy to give him the treat. Bonn knelt to offer the dog a bite of the cake. The retriever was raised on expensive kibble and broccoli stems drizzled with olive oil—he'd never tasted a baked good. Triumphant and elated, he unhinged his jaws and with a wet-mouthed swipe, took the whole cupcake—candle and all. He ran behind an overstuffed chair to swallow it. Bonn peered over the back of the chair as the dog gagged on the candle. The dog bobbed his head like an oil derrick and clacked his teeth. He stretched his neck out further and further. *Hoark. Hoark.* He took several unsure straight-legged steps to find the right place to vomit. He decided on Raquel's beautiful new white Egyptian cotton throw rug. Troy's phone rang as Raquel rounded the leather chair to rescue the rug. *Hoark.* The dog disgorged his stomach contents as Raquel hoisted and spun him away from the rug. The arc spattered a lower shelf of heavy folios like a Jackson Pollack painting. Troy surveyed the mess as Raquel inspected her new rug for shrapnel. The dog saw a broccoli stem and lurched out of Raquel's grasp to grab it before she could. As the show dog lunged forward, his paws slipped about in the mess. He piled into a glass statue of a woman nursing a baby—a gift from Troy to Raquel when she was pregnant. The glass shattered. The dog, once "Best of Breed" at Westminster, fell onto a stiletto-shaped shard, which pierced his thin, shampoo-scented chest just behind the shoulder blade. Fine pink mist rasped from his nose and a smell of iron filled the room, but he had the stem. Just as he scrambled to his feet to gulp it back down, Troy grabbed his white leather collar, dragged the straight-legged dog to the door, and heaved him outside.

Bonn followed Troy and looked past him into the front yard. The dog ran for the open front gate. He'd reached the relative safety of the road just as the wedge of a Corvette shot him skyward. Troy touched Bonn's shoulder. He knew he should say something. The attorney gave the boy's shoulder a squeeze and took a deep breath, but nothing came to him. The phone in the library rang and he had to take the call. "Send Hedwig out to look at him, OK?"

Troy went into work. Raquel announced it was time for her to meditate. When Frau Hedwig finished cleaning up what she could, she ushered Bonn into the library and shut the door behind him. Of all the books in the room, the thesaurus was Bonn's favorite. It was a paperback, so it stood out among its expensive leather-bound shelf mates. It was not a first edition or fancy in any way. It was a book to be used. Bonn let his eyes wander throughout the room. On a side table, a deck of cards sat protected under a bell jar. They looked like fortune telling cards and in a way, they were. The 1893 World's Fair was a speculative gamble for the elite investors who fronted the money for the exhibits. To thank the patrons who made the fair possible, the most generous patrons were given a deck of the cards. Interesting pictures adorned them—a scandalous belly dancer named "Little Egypt" revealed her wares with a warm smile. A singer named "The Black Patti" wore a dress heavy with medals. One card showed a giant octopus. It was displayed from the ceiling and hovered over a wooly mammoth. Another card had a picture of a sideshow strongman, "Eugen Sandow." The first time Bonn saw the card he was incredulous—he looked like a comic book character. Impossibly symmetrical, he looked to have muscles in places others didn't. He appeared at ease behind the waxy curls of his mustache, though he held impossibly large weights above his head. He was more than an exposition athlete—he was an icon. There were other cards too. The original "Ferris wheel" had a card, as did a huge gun deemed "The Thunderer." When fired, the behemoth used a half-ton of gunpowder to spit a projectile weighing more than a ton. There were fifty cards in all. The strongman card, however, was Bonn's favorite. Bonn's great grandfather, land and slave owner turned coal baron, provided thirty thousand dollars to the World's Fair. Most of the money was used to construct the Ferris wheel—one of the fair's only moneymakers. The fair's organizer asked performers featured on the cards to autograph them for the man, an extra thanks to Templeton Maddox. Even the "Mammoth and Hell-fish" card had an illegible signature. Bonn liked to imagine that conjoined twins held the card out for the mammoth, while the beast signed the card with the tip of its trunk. Bonn flipped through the deck then fanned the cards back into the order his father expected to see.

An old picture of Templeton Maddox sat just to the left of the bell jar. The man looked stern and chiseled. He wore a handlebar mustache. An expensive shotgun was cradled in the crook of one arm. Several limp pheasants hung from a strap in his hand opposite the gun and his foot rested jauntily on the running board of a Duesenberg. The driver of the car, a black man, was slightly out of focus. He appeared to be looking out of the windshield, crying. One hand was blurred on the way to his mouth, as if he saw a horror unveiling itself in front of the car and was prepared to stifle a sob, a scream, or both. Bonn's father took phone calls, smoked cigars, and drank scotch in the library. After he lit each cigar, he seemed to salute Templeton—as if he paid homage to the patriarch and his grand pheasant-killing life. Bonn plucked the Eugen Sandow card from the deck, replaced the bell jar, and slid the card into his back pocket. He took the card with him when he crawled out of the library window each day, but he wasn't quite ready to leave yet.

A framed copy of the Bill of Rights was another of Bonn's favorites. It stood alone behind thick glass just behind the bell jar. Bonn spent many hours in the library admiring "The Amendments." There was a clarity about them he found comforting. The language was plain, but when he brought out the thesaurus and attempted to improve the messages, it was no use. Each word of each line was like a rock. Each rock settled through the fluff of lighter words to provide the most weight to The Amendments. The Amendments worked together to support freedom. Bonn appreciated the time, the wisdom—the vision it took to draft it. The authors couldn't know what the future held, but planned for it regardless. They thought beyond themselves. Since neither his mother nor father seemed able to do so, the phenomenon fascinated him. It was a blueprint for justice and Bonn took it literally. What the nine-year-old didn't know was this: the copy wasn't a copy—rather, it was the *original* copy. Fourteen original copies of the Bill of Rights were produced. One for the federal government itself and one for each of the original thirteen states. The New York copy was thought to be lost in the 1911 fire at the New York State Capitol Building.

Actually, a National Guardsman employed in the cleanup efforts after the fire diverted an armload of papers containing the document to his girlfriend on his way to the basement of the Calvary Baptist Church. The papers were wet but intact. That evening over bread and sausage they hung page after page of stolen parchment up by clothespins in a rented room. The guardsman was illiterate. He didn't know what they had, but his girlfriend did. She took the still-sodden parchment to her bookie father before the young man awoke the next morning. It traveled from bookie to broker. Before it was dry the New York copy rested on the desk of Templeton Maddox. Enough money filtered back to the girl, and she bought a new Knox Roadster. She left the illiterate soldier-boy behind. Trusting the directions of hitchhikers and barkeeps, she journeyed west. She was penniless by Denver. She contracted syphilis while celebrating the sale of the roadster and continued her journey by rail, taking time to enjoy herself thoroughly at each hub. By January of 1913 her syphilis reached the tertiary stage. Her ensuing dementia wouldn't let her remember the fire, or even the car, let alone the damp piece of parchment that kicked off her adventure. Five years later, the last tight-lipped thug who helped funnel the treasure to Templeton Maddox was laid to rest, the victim of an appropriately angry husband. Templeton Maddox enjoyed smoking cigars while peacefully admiring the stolen document for another fifteen years before he died. Speculation was that a poorly extinguished cigar started the fire in Albany to begin with. The idea pleased the patriarch. As the document was passed down, generations of Maddox men were taught, each by their father, to salute the document—with a lit cigar.

Bonn checked his pocket for the strongman card then stepped out through a window.

He needed to walk.

Blackness pushed at Ithaca. A half-hour into his walk, Bonn took shelter from a sudden deluge on the Cornell campus. The stones used to build Cornell looked identical to the stones at the Maddox house. It was a house with a lengthy history.

The stonemasons may have been the same men.

Bonn didn't seek shelter for himself. It didn't matter if he got wet—but the card must stay dry.

He didn't know why, but he needed it.

Bonn hunched around the treasure in an alcove. He knelt to finger the carving on the cornerstone: *Circa 1875*. He imagined Eugen Sandow, there in that spot, tapping the message into the stone. It wouldn't be a regular hammer—nothing about Mr. Sandow was regular—the head of the hammer would be the size of a loaf of bread. The stones would have feared him. The rain let up. Eugen was dry. Bonn put him back in his pocket and continued his walk. He was off campus now. He walked past the sandwich shops frequented by lavender-scented girls seeking pesto chicken salad, past houses. He paused to read the headlines on a newspaper in the front window of a magazine shop. Inside the shop were things to tempt most boys his age: video games, fiery balls of cinnamon to dare your friends to eat, bubblegum in the shape of tiny pizzas, hotdogs in orbit on their own Ferris wheel—tube-meat riders dripping fat-sizzles on the stainless steel field below. The newspaper was the only thing Bonn cared about.

His father was on the front page.

Troy had his arm draped, fraternal and celebratory, around a local criminal. The headline? "Acquitted." It wasn't a surprise. Money always won.

Bonn ducked down an alleyway he had never noticed before. Metal sounds came from a block garage with a flat roof.

Ping-tang. Ping. Ping-tang. Thump.

Metal on metal.

The door of the place was welded to heavy rollers nestled inside an I-beam. It reminded him of a train track. Inside, a short black man in blue coveralls hummed a tune to himself as he squatted by the fender of an old car. He had grease stains on his knees and back, yet a clean white collar jutted halfway up his heavily bearded face. He worked slowly, feeling inside a fender of the car with one hand while he tapped the metal back into shape with an odd flat-headed hammer.

Bonn was fascinated. He didn't notice the black and white dog that watched him from an old couch. The humming and the tapping seemed clean and real. Tangible. Here was a man doing something. Fixing something—creating new from old. The dog exploded in protest of the interloper, and the man jumped as if sprung from a toy peanut can.

"Well there, young man, have you got something for me to fix? I could use a break from this old Goat." The man held the hammer by its head and pointed the handle at the rusty Pontiac.

"Why do you call your car a goat?"

"Ah. That is not my car, son—that's the high school car a rich dude brought me to iron out. Once it looks new again, he'll drive it around and baby it. Never race it around like when he was a young man. He'll probably put it up on blocks and pick the gravel out of the tires before putting it in his nice garage. He'll think about life and mortality and remember the skirts he chased back in 1968." The man put his hands on his hips and smiled at the car, nodding. He was not much taller than Bonn. He held a finger out in front of him and tilted his head, an animated indication that he intended to fully answer the boy's question. "A 'Goat' is a GTO. Manufactured by Pontiac. It stands for 'Grand Tempest Option.' There's a mouthful, huh? In sixty-eight, if you wanted a big floaty car to drive to grandma's house, you bought the Bonneville—but if you had a few extra dollars to buy something less practical, you went for the GTO. A bunch of impractical dudes, who after they go to college call themselves 'aficionados' got together—started calling all GTOs 'the Goat.'" Bonn looked the car over and nodded. The man nodded back and continued. "It's a big pile of metal, but still five hundred pounds lighter than the Bonneville. If you get the idle screw right and have the money to put new tires on it every couple of months, it's a fun car." The man grinned as he spoke. He talked with his hands but rested them on his hips when his mouth was still. "There's a lot to consider—when you, bear with me—by 'you' I mean Pontiac, or me, or yourself, set a goal to get a hunk of metal to whip around faster and faster. Europeans made lighter cars in 1968. They had less horsepower, but less weight." The bearded man pantomimed cornering quickly, but looked wistful. "And maybe a little less soul." He wasn't still for long. He pulled a rag from his pocket and rubbed the nearest of the Pontiac's doors. "Physics, young man—correct observations of the laws of physics are what make certain cars exciting to drive—but soul? Soul is what really makes a car like the GTO."

Bonn liked him.

He didn't speak down to him—he just talked. It felt respectful.

48

The man frowned at the fender he'd been working on and squatted down to feel inside the panel. He looked at the ceiling as he palpated the metal, as if removing his eyes from the work allowed him extra understanding of the car's secrets—as if he looked for divine help while he discreetly searched for the car's soul. "The Goat was a status symbol. Proof of youth and virility—silly huh? I'm thankful for it actually. The phenomenon has kept me in business. These days women want a dude who drives a BMW—or she just buys *herself* one. Took all the fun out of the mating ritual, if you ask me—another bit of Americana lost." His eyebrows shot up. He tapped confidently at the fender for a while. "I'm a throwback. I'm a machinist by trade, but I found my niche in bodywork. I see a day coming when no one will bother with the old ones. Soulless, fast little efficient cars will pop out of a machine—wreck one? No big deal—just dump the parts in a funnel on top. It'll make a new one, at a subsidized cost. No need for people to tap it into shape again. They'll be disposable just like the cars." He paused to tap at the fender again. "For now, though, the 'Goats' come to me and Tidbit. No more drive-ins—no more drag races." The man wiped his hands on the rag. "The folks who bought these cars new? And really drove them? Never sold them. Those are the folks that hope if I tap their 'Goat' back in shape it'll bring back their vitality too." He made a low whistle and picked a rock out of a tire with a screwdriver. "So we are a whole bunch of throwbacks—just passing around money and dreams."

The black and white dog inched her way toward Bonn. Her lips quivered. She laid her ears back. The man shook his head at her. She froze in her crouch and waited for him to have a change of heart. He might revoke his disapproval and give the command to attack after all, so she'd stay ready. "Tidbit? Are you planning to kill and eat this young man?" Tidbit flashed her eyes toward her master but kept the wedge of her head pointed at Bonn. "Would you consider, as an alternative to murder, going to check on the puppies while I get lunch?" The dog seemed to smile. She wagged. She looked at the man with soft-eyed adoration, then perked her ears, tilted her head, and swept her tongue quickly across both sets of whiskers, as if saying, *You said you'd check on lunch. Did you forget?* The curious man held his hand out to Bonn. "Manny Tott."

49

Bonn shook Manny's hand without reviewing the rules for doing so. "Bonn Maddox." Bonn watched the dog disappear behind a worn-out couch. "She looks like a Border Collie."

"You know your dogs, Mister Maddox." Tidbit poked her head out in a menacing relapse, but Manny shot her a look and she disappeared again.

"I prefer you call me Bonn."

"And you can call me Manny," A buzzer went off behind some metal shelves brimming with odd-shaped cardboard boxes. "Excuse me. I've got a kidney pie in the oven. I'd better tend to it for a minute." As Manny walked, Bonn couldn't see his knees bend. He couldn't tell if the man actually had knees—his coveralls were loose and the legs were rolled up. "She won't bite you," Manny's voice came from behind the shelves. "Not unless you try to pick up one of her puppies." An oven door creaked open and banged shut again. "She pushed out a litter so big they're hard to count—a whole school of pig-fish." Bonn looked around the shop.

There were so many tools.

Not just hand tools—complicated tools too, as if Manny made new parts for cars if he couldn't fix the old ones. Bonn looked into a tin coffee can full of what looked like big flat washers. Manny emerged holding a pie with the detailing rag. It steamed from its thin silver tin. "That is hot." He dropped the tin onto the oily workbench and wiped at his hands with the rag. "She stares me down too. When she gets bored mostly—even before the pups. When I don't give her enough to do, she looks for odd jobs. It isn't fair to her, really. She should be out nipping sheep. Maybe we'd all sleep better if she could do that a couple times a day." Manny whistled as he cut wedges of the kidney pie and shook the sticky food onto coffee filters. "She's good company for the most part." Manny paused to frown in thought for a moment. "Well, not when I let my beard get too wooly. I think when I hunker down to work on these old Goats she might think I'm a sheep." Tidbit tilted her head and perked her ears. She stared hungrily at the molten pie. "In a minute, girl. It's still too hot."

"I had a dog," Bonn said. "It's a weird story, but technically, I had a dog once."

Manny turned from the bench with a furrowed brow. "Hmm. The 'had' part doesn't sound too good."

The smell of hot beef kidney broke Tidbit's resolve. She jumped to grab a piece from the bench, then backed away from the fallen treat to lick her scalded lips. She took a step forward to paw at the coffee filter then reconsidered and sat down with a groan. "I told you it was hot, but you can make up your own mind."

Manny even talked to the dog like she was his equal.

Bonn never met anyone like him.

"I'm so rude. Bonn, have you had dinner?"

He thought for a moment. He'd not, in fact, had dinner. Tidbit circled the wedge of meat pie and lunged in to test it.

"I haven't."

"Well, are you in a hurry to get something fixed or should we eat first?"

"I don't have anything to fix. I just heard some pounding noises. I'm sorry I bothered you at mealtime. I should get going, Manny. It was very nice to have met you."

Manny scowled. The repairman shook his head with a sigh and cut another wedge of the pie, tapped it onto an improvised plate, and pushed it into Bonn's hands. "I can't, in good conscience, let you out of here hungry. I couldn't look myself in the mirror knowing I had all this and you left here with an empty belly." Manny served himself last. He flipped a couple of buckets upside down for chairs. He sat down on one, using the couch like a table. Bonn did the same. "What happened to your dog?" Bonn recounted that morning's events between bites. By the time he got to the Corvette, Manny's mouth hung open—he bowed his head low and shook it. His shoulders shook next and the man pulled a handkerchief from a pocket and blew his nose. Bonn couldn't be sure, but it appeared that Manny was crying.

Manny threw his head back and belly-laughed. It sounded deeply off every flat surface in the shop. "Bonn…" Manny paused to catch his breath "…you've had the worst birthday I've ever heard of. I apologize for laughing, son. I know you aren't fibbing to me. What a gruesome, terrible story."

Tidbit, caught up in the spirit, did a Cossack dance. She lowered her butt and spun her tail like a propeller. Paws held high, she performed some jumps and side-hops before giving Bonn an arm-lick. She finished with a whisper-bark and ran behind the shelves to peer through the oven glass in case another pie hid there from them. Manny regained his composure. He wobbled straight-legged to the oven and opened the door for the dog to see that it was empty. Tidbit returned and leapt onto the couch with a defeated look.

51

Manny found a small jar of salve and picked Tidbit up like a baby. Tidbit licked at Manny's beard while he rubbed the medicine into each of her several pairs of sore nipples.

"A couple of the pups have the sire's head. He's a Pit." Manny recapped the jar and scratched the dog's belly. "The teeth on the block-headed ones came in quick—they're tearing poor Tidbit up." He put the dog on the floor, but she spun and put a paw back on the seat of the couch to ask permission to jump back up. "Most of them have little panda looking bodies like Tidbit here, only chubby. Whatcha think, Tidbit? Are you going to let your new friend see your pups?"

Tidbit dropped her ears, but panted a tired consent and disappeared behind the couch. Manny knelt on the couch cushions and peered over the back of the couch like a child. Bonn joined him. Tidbit gave a long-suffering sigh and settled in to nurse the puppies. One puppy did look like a tiny panda bear. It rolled out of the fray via the kicks of her larger littermates. Manny shook his head. He stuck a leg out for counterbalance and leaned over to pluck up the small creature. "Hold her for a minute, would you?"

The squeaking puppy quivered in Bonn's hands. He lifted back her lips to see if she had teeth and she tried to nurse on his fingertip. Finding no milk, she bawled a high-pitched complaint. Manny returned with a rubber glove full of warm milk. He took an awl from the workbench, poked a hole in the smallest finger of the glove, and offered it to the puppy.

"I know, I know," Manny started as the tiny puppy found the contrived nipple, "Mr. Darwin wouldn't approve, but I believe the Lord put her here with me so she could have a chance. Tidbit buries her in the laundry when I turn my back. You can poke fun at me if you like, Bonn, but I'm an old softie. I can't help but to try to keep Jelly Bean here going."

An old black Bakelite phone on the wall of the shop rang. Manny ignored it.

The little panda-dog nursed until the glove was empty. The other puppies were already asleep, and Manny rearranged them so that Jelly Bean could warm up between them. He tucked the block-headed puppies behind Tidbit so both Jelly Bean and Tidbit's nipples could get a break. Tidbit seemed to understand the strategy and gave Manny an appreciative wag. As Manny inspected his puppy-sorting job, Bonn felt an odd calm peace come over him.

What was this sensation? He'd never felt like this before.

Words from the thesaurus flew at him—

Bucolic? Content? Serene? Tranquil? Happy? Was this what happy felt like?

"Would you like to take one of the pups home with you? For a birthday present?" Bonn nodded his head. Manny smiled. "Good. Pick out the one you want." Bonn looked at the squirming mass for a moment.

"May I have the little one? Jelly Bean?"

Manny smiled. "I want good homes for all the pups, but I want the best for little Jelly Bean. I hoped you'd pick her." Tidbit seemed relieved that Jelly Bean was leaving. They both watched Manny as he packed up a small bag of supplies. "Tidbit," Manny said with a chuckle, "now you won't have to perpetrate a backhanded murder when I'm not looking." Manny wore an appreciative squint. The fingers of his right hand stroked his beard thoughtfully as Bonn removed his belt and constructed a way to carry the bag hands-free. Rolling the top of the paper bag over his belt twice, he put it back around his waist over the belt loops. It was a solution that would allow both hands to support the wriggling puppy. Manny nodded approvingly. "Stop in anytime you'd like, Bonn. I hope the rest of your birthday is boring."

Bonn gave Manny what could only be described as a haunted look. When he spoke, trying to interject some feeling, it was even more awkward for the attempt.

"Me, too. Thank you for the puppy—and the pie." Bonn cradled Jelly Bean underneath his chin on the way home. While Manny packed the bag, he had said, "Most people wouldn't consider a mutt-puppy a good birthday present—"

It was nonsense. The puppy? The shared food? The polite conversation? It was the best day he'd ever had.

~Wolfsbane

As the season progressed, black tree trunks were the only evidence of the forest fire. The ash was covered in lush green growth. Henna left the forest with a bonanza each day. Once the baskets were full of edibles, she picked flowers. The sun was out and the birds chirped happily over full stomachs, but something was wrong. Alvar bristled. Henna stood in front of him, holding something.

A flower.

Alvar couldn't place it by smell. She was too quiet. It was unlike her. There were guidelines in wild-crafting, and Henna only got quiet when she strayed from the rules. A sense of dread came over him. "Is it a single purple flower?"

"Yes," Henna chirped, amazed. "It looks like an angry little robot." Alvar smacked the flower from her hand, scooped her up, and sprinted with high blind steps toward the sounds of the brook.

He'd warned her not to pick or touch plants that grew alone until he could help her identify them.

He clamped her small frame in-between his knees in the water and scrubbed her hands, then her face—and then both his and her hands again. "Friction is enough. If you don't have soap, rub hard, Henna. Friction cleans better than soap." Henna looked dumbfounded. It appeared that she might cry. "I will explain, but first this." He shook his head, muttered something, picked her back up, sidestepped upstream, and began to wash her hands a third time. Their hands felt raw and hot despite the cool water. Alvar finally relaxed. He sat on the mossy bank of the brook to catch his breath. He wiped at his face. "You know not to try the mushroom trick with flowers, don't you?"

"Yes, Grandpa," Henna answered gravely. Her voice told him she didn't understand why he was angry, but he wasn't angry—he was terrified.

"I know that trick is just for mushrooms."

"Did the flower look like it had a little dark-purple hood?"

"Yes, Grandpa." The tears came on hard. "It was so pretty. I'm sorry I picked it. It grew alone. I should've asked you first." Alvar heard the choked emotion behind the girl's speech—she'd never been in trouble with him before. She knew this was serious. "Are we going to die?"

"No, not today, at least, but we had to wash our hands. That was northern monkshood." Mortimer joined them on the moss. He had something in his mouth.

Dogs carry horrible things around if they get a chance to. Dead things. Some roll in the putrescence, while others mouth-carry their gruesome payloads, not sure what to do with the rotten treasure, yet also not willing to swallow it. Mortimer wagged. He spat a rotten blue jay out with a plop. The bird's head flopped loosely onto the toe of Henna's shoe. Suddenly the dog seemed to realize how bad the offal had tasted. He rubbed his muzzle back and forth on the clean moss and scraped his tongue across his teeth as if trying to remove peanut butter. The bird must have been inside, or even under something. Mortimer seemed relieved to have the black tissue and damp feathers out of his mouth. He waded into the brook and took a long drink. The smell of death clung to all of them the rest of the day. Alvar knew he couldn't protect the girl forever—he'd have to teach her everything he knew. It was a rude introduction to toxins, but Henna would *never* forget wolfsbane.

~Guttural

Bonn didn't want to risk dropping Jelly Bean climbing back through the library window, so he headed for the front door. A flatbed Dodge seemed out of place in the driveway.

It looked like a tow truck.

Bonn let himself in and started for the kitchen to warm up more milk for the puppy. Screams came from the rear of the house. Bonn put Jelly Bean in a sunny corner of the kitchen and went to investigate. They weren't quite screams—some muffled noises were intermingled, but none of them sounded normal.

Glottal? No—guttural.

Bonn neared his parents' room. A full-blown shriek startled him. He snatched up an ancient brass-headed putter Troy kept at the end of the hallway.

It was his mother.

He burst through his parents' bedroom door. A giant naked man straddled his facedown mother. Her thin wrists were held behind her in a gorilla-sized fist and the man choked her with the other hand. Bonn swung the putter without thinking and the century-old brass head unceremoniously married the man's brain with a sound announcing crushed bone and wet displacement—the sound of punky wood pierced with an axe on the first morning of a frost, rudely visiting a groveling pocket of worms within. *POCK.* The man collapsed and rolled sideways. He made snoring noises. One leg pin wheeled as if riding an imaginary bicycle. Raquel sputtered. She rolled away from the man and parried her Magic Wand to hide her celebrated privates. Jets of arterial blood hissed from the head wound onto her white linen sheets. Events slowed for Bonn. His mother stood beside the bed and looked at the man, then at the blood. The Magic Wand was no longer shield, nor rapier. Raquel worried less about modesty each moment. "What have you done?" The man's leg stopped circling. He lay motionless.

I killed a criminal.

Raquel tore about the room and found a white robe. She held it in front of her, but didn't put it on. "Bonn, go to the damned library. I need to think." Bonn pried the putter out of the dead man's skull and wiped the gore off with his shirt. On the way to the library, the boy put the relic back where Troy could find it when he practiced putting down the hallway.

Jelly Bean was where he had left her. Bonn brought her to the library with him. He laid the puppy on the soft white rug then put Eugen Sandow back under the bell jar with the other cards. Templeton grinned at him from the Dusenberg, but Bonn ignored him. The boy inspected the face of the chauffeur for a resemblance to Manny but didn't see one. Jelly Bean wriggled. The puppy squeaked hungrily. Bonn held the tiny warm mammal to his neck. He crooned to the runt like Manny had. She grabbed his earlobe with tiny needle-teeth and tried to suck it. Bonn pulled the rug beneath the Bill of Rights. He sat, admiring the curves of the script. He read the Fifth Amendment to Jelly Bean aloud, since it seemed appropriate.

Raquel appeared, clothed, in the doorway. Blood trickled from both nostrils. It mixed with the cocaine that caked her upper lip. She pointed a pistol at him. Bonn ignored the gun. He held Jelly Bean up for his mother to see. "Her name is Jelly Bean. A man downtown gave her to me." Raquel's gun hand shook. Bonn tucked the small dog back under his chin and stroked her ear with a fingertip. Hedwig crept behind his mother, her long neck pointing her odd head toward the pistol.

"I called to report the intruder," Hedwig chopped nervously at her words. Her accent thick, fearful. She spoke slowly, as if hopeful that the torque of her carefully chosen words would turn the gunwoman's head. "The police—are on their way here—to help us." Raquel lowered the pistol. She wiped at her top lip then pinched her nose. She discovered the blood and looked at it on her fingertips.

"You," she whispered into the room, "you've killed us all."

Hedwig kicked the razor into the back of Raquel's knee just as Raquel raised the pistol. A shot rang out. Bonn dropped. Another shot followed. The world was gone for a while then Hedwig was beside him. She held something against his head. When she spoke, it was in a croaking voice that made sense. She'd always seemed like someone who would croak. "She perforated us both, but you might make it. I'm going to hold this on your head as long as I can, little Alp. If you wake up, you hold it tight, because I won't be here long. You knew? Didn't you? Thank you for the shoe. I tried, little Alp—I really tried."

Raquel stuck the gun in her mouth on a back road she knew well. If she wasn't losing so much blood from the back of her leg, she would've killed Troy at his office, but she felt woozy and didn't think she could walk. Raquel breathed for a while after she pulled the trigger. At first she thought she'd missed, yet she couldn't see or move her arms. Lucid thoughts kept her company until the swelling breached her brainstem.

This serves Troy right.

That puppy looked like a panda bear.

She wanted to sleep.

~Give and Take

Vieristä was an unusual day for presents, but Alvar intended to make the holiday special for Henna. It wasn't a holiday the girl had celebrated in Connecticut, so the old man decided they could make some traditions of their own—they could enjoy the day however they pleased. As soon as his granddaughter awoke he gave her a hand-woven basket and a folding mushroom knife. The small knife had a curved blade. The brush on the opposite side could be used to clear debris from each mushroom before placing it in the basket. They took turns breaking star-shaped gingerbread in one hand. It was an old tradition, not one of their own devising. Alvar's star broke into a dozen pieces, but Henna's gingerbread broke into three. Henna smiled.

"Shh!" commanded the girl as she placed each piece carefully in his hand. By doing so she gave him the wish. He couldn't disapprove, or the wish be lost. Alvar shook his head, smiling.

She remembered the rules.

He shut his eyes tight, held a finger to his temple so she knew he understood, then ate each piece carefully so the wish could come true. The past few months, they'd foraged for all they ate or used—medicinal plants included. It was an epic lesson. Henna seemed to love the challenge. In late summer and fall they lived well. After the snow fell they resorted to eating dried and canned stores, but they still walked each day. They'd stop to dig, to sit—to listen to the forest. Henna's formal schoolwork was placed on hold during berry picking season, but during the long, cold days of winter, the lessons lengthened again. Both of them had become lean—focused.

Henna readied herself for their morning walk. She paused to watch her grandfather as he slowly sipped his tea. When she asked him about the walk, he'd sent her to find Mortimer's pack baskets. The baskets functioned as saddlebags. Henna brought them from the barn although it seemed improbable that they would find much to harvest. If they found anything to bring home out there in the snow, it would likely be something small. There wasn't enough sun to feed them yet. Certainly they wouldn't find anything so big it required

Mortimer to pack it home. Mortimer lay by the fire, his age was showing more each day. Sometimes he skipped the walks. He'd eye the wolf and puff out his cheeks, as if saying, *I have to stay here. To watch him.*

The sight of the pack baskets excited the dog. He momentarily forgot the wolf and sprang to attention. He panted with a wag, turned a tight circle, and happily poked his nose into each basket. Henna strapped them on and he lapped water from his bowl and ate the eggs he'd earlier ignored. Chicken eggs were off limits for humans during the yearlong foraging exercise, but the chickens laid them anyway. Mortimer seemed tired of them.

Alvar lazed by the fire and loaded his pipe. "Can you boil more water for tea please, honey?"

Something wasn't right. Mortimer watched Alvar for a few minutes, then perked his ears and loped to the door—he waited there and listened but didn't scratch to go out.

Someone approached?

A knock at the door confirmed it. "I'll be back in a moment." Alvar made his way quickly to the door and slid outside. A woman's voice mumbled something. Alvar laughed a lighthearted laugh. He came back alone, but held two bulging cloth sacks. He placed a sack in each of Mortimer's baskets and slipped on his coat and boots. "My wish came true."

Mortimer loped down the path with purpose. Henna felt woozy from anticipation. She tried to estimate the weight of the bags when the dog stopped to poke his head in a snow bank, but she couldn't. Everything seemed surreal. She could feel the cold in her nose when she took a deep breath, so she knew she wasn't asleep. Mortimer emerged from the bank a snow-dog. He blinked and smiled at Henna, young and playful as ever. He sneezed to clear the snow from his nose and bounded ahead as if the baskets he carried were empty. Alvar seemed pleased. He whistled as they moved along the path. Henna knew it was no use asking him what was going on. She'd have to be patient. It was still early. The sun wasn't up yet. Alvar and Mortimer waited on Henna as she picked her way along the path in the faint blue-white moonlight. Her stomach rumbled. The gingerbread wasn't a filling meal, but it was a nice treat after the months of wild food. She thought of the buttery eggs Mortimer ate. Her stomach complained even louder.

In a small clearing sat two chairs and a blocky table carved from packed snow. Reindeer hides sat atop each chair. Soft fox-fur blankets lay neatly folded on the snow-table. Three large logs sat on end, partially split and on fire—each log burned from the top. In the low light, they looked like smoldering stars. Crystalized branches of nearby trees sparkled like fireflies frozen on ice-perches. Mortimer understood. He sat by the blocky table and wagged as Henna unloaded the baskets. Alvar held his hands over a log to warm them. "Can you show me to a chair?" Henna helped her grandfather to a snow-throne. The forest was so still in the cold. Smoke curled in sweet ringlets from the logs.

It felt like a dream.

Alvar covered himself with one of the furs. "OK, let's see what kind of forbidden breakfast we have in those bags." Henna pulled the end of a bow and loosened the drawstring.

It was treasure.

"A little blue iron teapot, Grandpa!" A small jar of birch syrup was nestled inside the pot, wrapped in cloth. Henna packed snow into the pot and placed it on a log. Next came an iron skillet with a lid. The skillet was also blue. When Henna took the lid off, her stomach tumbled with urgency. "Butter, too." Henna discovered a third pot, a jar full of batter, wooden forks, knives, plates, a carved wooden spatula—and two cups with tiny seahorses for handles. She placed the skillet on a log and opened the tin of butter. She checked the teapot and packed in more snow. It melted quickly. She placed a bundle of sweet smelling tea leaves tied with string inside the pot to steep. She poured the syrup into the second pot and placed it on a log. When butter danced in the skillet, she poured the batter in and replaced the lid. While the pancake cooked, Alvar smoked his pipe. Henna happily stirred and checked on the food then set the table. She eyed the second bag, but wanted the magic to last, so she made herself wait to open it. She poured tea for them both then sat to wait while the cake cooked. Alvar sipped his tea.

He chuckled, mirth spilling from him flavored by his own excitement. "Open the other one, you silly goose."

Henna ran for the bag. "Grandpa—a knit hat! So soft—I can't tell what it's made from—some sort of wool? Softer than wool." Henna removed her old hat and pulled on the new one. A small box with a ribbon held a carved wooden comb. When she opened the box a beautiful smell escaped. "Grandpa it smells like—like perfume." She held the fragrant comb to his nose.

Alvar smiled. "Sandalwood."

"Wood can smell like this?"

"Wonderment lurks at every turn in this big world, Henna—if you watch for opportunities. If you recognize them." There was more in the bag. A leather-bound journal, pencils for sketching, field guides— even a book on Latin. The last item she pulled from the bag was wrapped carefully in brown paper and tied with string. It was a plain wooden box painted black. Henna couldn't figure out how to open the box. Wordlessly, she placed the item in the old man's hands and watched his fingers. His knuckles were thick. His hands were strong and quick. He slid a wooden bar along the bottom of the box to unlock it. Inside sat several small glass bottles with heavy silver caps. Henna screwed the top off of a bottle. It was empty. She tried another—

Empty.

Inside each heavy cap sat a thick rubber stopper. Could something have leaked from the bottles? "They are empty—what are they for?"

"Tinctures." Alvar had a serious look on his face. He frowned down at his pipe. "Wonderment is not alone in the world, Henna. Some of the world is wicked. I'm going to teach you many different things from now on. Some of them may never prove useful, but they are things you should know. It is my job to prepare you for anything." They were quiet for a few moments while Henna looked over the bounty. Alvar loaded his pipe. "Viestra commemorates the three 'Wise Men.' Since I am only one man, I have a lot of catching up to do." They feasted on pancake. With her belly full, Henna felt cold. She sat on her snow-chair and pulled a fur to her chin. The cake tasted floral—

What was in it? Apple powder? Vanilla?

The pancake was like a custard—a filling meal. Even Mortimer got some. Henna sipped at her tea. It was dark and intense. It smelled like her grandfather's pipe tobacco before he smoked it. There were so many new tastes and smells. She thought about what her grandfather said about opportunities. She clenched the fur in her hands and closed her eyes. She smelled the sweet dry smoke, the evergreens, she smelled her grandfather's pipe tobacco, the tea, the cake, the syrup. The rich butter. It was a special day. She wanted to remember it. Mortimer dozed at her feet until the bear dogs chased a moose through a nearby thicket. He opened an eye, but didn't lift his head.

"He isn't going to live much longer is he?" Henna asked.

Alvar puffed at his pipe. He'd always refused to weave a falsehood for her—temporary reassurances were always unfair.

"No. He's older than he should be already. Sometimes dogs and old men seem very vibrant just before they let themselves die. You don't have to worry about me yet—I feel old and tired and sore today." Mortimer groaned and lifted his head. He gave his long tail a slow fanning wag, but winced with the effort. He looked back toward the tidy stone house. He puffed his cheeks, waiting for Henna to tell "the story." He chuffed, then aimed a low howl at the mantle-wolf. Henna patted her lap, an invitation to cuddle the dog while she finished the story. Eyes half closed, Mortimer rested his massive skull on the girl's lap. She rubbed the base of his ears while she recited her half of the legend to him.

Alvar frequently heard things neither Henna nor the dog could. He looked deep into the forest, as though he heard the wolves howling back. Henna wondered if wolves told stories too.

"I've got one last thing for you." Alvar pulled at a string around his neck and handed it to Henna. A gold ring dangled at the end of it. "It's your mother's wedding ring. You should have it." Henna held the ring in her palm. She turned it, read the inscription, and held it to her nose to smell it. The ring smelled like Alvar, of course, not her mother.

"How did you get it?"

"Lucrece had it. She gave it to me the day she brought you up."

One of the only decent things she'd ever done.

Henna slipped the string over her head and dropped the ring inside her shirt. The weight of it was comforting. It was the best present of the day. Her mother seemed more tangible. After the baskets were re-packed they seemed too heavy for Mortimer. Henna split the smaller items up between the two baskets, but slung the bag full of cookware over her own shoulder. She felt for the ring against her chest.

It was there.

They left the hides and blankets for Alvar's accomplice. The sun was up. They made good time walking home.

While they were gone, someone put a moose roast in the pot to cook. A strange basket sat on the table, conspicuously overflowing

63

with fresh bread, tins of pudding, more butter. With no cooking to do, Henna laid a quilt by the fire for Mortimer. Alvar sat nearby to share the warmth. The dog groaned happily as Henna ran her fingers through his ruff. Flying embers didn't wake Mortimer anymore, so each time Henna heard the wood pop she checked his fur. Mortimer whined. He tried to get up, but couldn't. Henna brought his water to him. After a long drink he looked up at the mantle-wolf.

Henna expected him to start the story, but he didn't. Instead, he looked at her with grave expectation. "It's OK, Mortimer. I'll watch him. I won't let him get away with anything."

Mortimer seemed satisfied. He laid his head to rest for the last time. Alvar and Henna dozed in shifts. When the dog stopped breathing, Alvar woke Henna. They held each other, petted the still—regal beast, and cried.

~Dead Reckoning

When the state trooper pulled over to offer assistance to the driver of the oddly parked Jaguar, he didn't expect a crime scene. When he discovered Raquel, he radioed it in. The car was locked. Although the woman was obviously dead, protocol indicated he feel for a pulse. He used his lockout kit to open the door and pulled on a rubber glove. She was pulseless.

Obvious suicide.

A small revolver lay in the front seat next to her limp hand. She had an exit wound on the back of her head, with no visible entrance wound—most likely she put the barrel in her mouth. A VHS tape sat on the passenger's seat next to the revolver. It looked like pornography. The trooper backed up to look at the expensive car.

Pretty woman, expensive clothes. The tape didn't fit. Could be more to it.

He eased the door shut carefully and returned to the cruiser to wait for the team. Dispatch crackled to life over the radio. There would be a delay. All local units including EMS were called to respond to an address in Cayuga Heights.

A few days later, two homicide detectives finalized their report after one last interview with Troy Maddox. The exit interview was a formality, but considering the widower's status in the community, they wanted to seal this one up tight. Troy Maddox entered the meeting with red eyes and shaking hands. He hadn't slept in days. He was starting to hallucinate.

"Hello, Mr. Maddox. Let me start by extending our condolences for your loss—"

"I know the routine. Save the small talk. Let's get on with it. Who was the man?"

"Local tow truck driver. Retired porn star."

"Porn star," Troy repeated. He scratched at his face where a grizzled beard born of self-neglect took hold. "A porn star was in my house."

"Yes, sir. Our investigation indicates he was in a British film." Troy leaned back in his chair and studied the false ceiling. The irregular holes in each tile differed from one to the next. He wondered distractedly how they made them.

Did a little machine make the holes? Did a person have to do it? Is that where I'm headed? To poke little holes in damned ceiling panels?

The senior detective stood and poured Troy some thick black coffee. He tried to hand it to the attorney, but Troy ignored the gesture so the man set the cup on a nearby table. "What film?"

The junior detective spoke. "Trencher's Cafe."

"Is it a film with a plot?" Troy was near his breaking point. He was suddenly aware of his own smell—cheap cigars breathed from a dirty mouth, but with a tinge to it ... like when the weird kid in second grade crapped in the sand under the slide after gorging himself on pot roast, boiled carrots, and a shot of Aqua Velva.

"Yes, sir, a loose one." Troy noticed the coffee and held the cup in both hands to take a drink. He slid back in the chair and spilled most of the cup on his shirt, but swiped his mouth with a sleeve and carried on.

"What's the plot?" The senior man stood. He rummaged for paper towels. He held them out for Troy, but Troy wouldn't take them.

"Sir, I'm not certain that will be helpful."

"Who is this meeting for?" Troy shouted at the ceiling. "Are you attempting, feebly, to provide me with the illusion of closure, or are you here to give me a sponge bath?" The junior detective raised his eyebrows and looked to his mentor. The older man nodded the go-ahead.

"To summarize, the man killed in your home played a line cook—short skirted waitresses serially begged to have variations of dirty sex with him, plying him with their tips. He was a horrible actor, but he nailed the big penis requirement."

"Of course he did." Troy poured a little coffee into his mouth, more down his shirt. "But he was only in one film. Why is that? What led the prodigal penis to my house by way of a tow truck?"

"He gained a lot of weight celebrating the film's success. He let himself go and couldn't get any more work."

"In England." Troy clarified.

"Correct, Mr. Maddox." The junior man shrugged at his partner, and the older man took over. "So he came to the United States, attended a trade school, and was placed at an import service shop driving a tow truck."

"And that's where he met Raquel, my dead wife."

"Yes, sir. That's where they met. He towed her Jaguar. They became—friendly."

"Who told you that? He's dead. She's dead. Who are the sources? I want some specifics. You guys write things down in little notebooks and run out of ink on the quotations alone. Take one of them out, flip to a page that's germane—help me understand how my wife met this dirt bag." The junior man did as he was told. His partner chewed a pen and studied his shoelaces. Troy watched the stressful dynamic unfold.

This wouldn't go well for them. It didn't matter what they said. He didn't want closure. He wanted blood.

"Sir, let me preface this by saying—"

"Random. Turn to a page at random, look for quotation marks, read."

"OK." The junior man scanned desperately and flipped through the book.

"Don't screen the quotes, detective. Read one. At random."

"Yes, sir. OK. This one's from a co-worker, Leon. 'Tony told me the gal could suck a dime bar out of his molars from across the room.'"

"The gal being—my dead wife, Raquel."

"Yes, sir. Raquel Maddox."

"What the hell is a dime bar?"

The senior detective winced.

Did he recognize the unlikely catalyst?

He was fueled to immolate the department—the damned candy bar was the tripwire he needed.

There was nothing for them to do—he wasn't going to un-ask the question.

"A candy bar. Spelled D-a-i-m—they're from the UK." The younger detective volleyed, eager to help.

"No—I'm sure he said 'dime bar.'" The senior man shot a warning glance at his partner. "It's D-a-i-m though. It's like a Heath bar."

Troy nodded, bent forward, pushed his fingertips into his gritty eyelids. "Thank you. I appreciate the measure of suction my wife could apply, foreign or domestic." The detectives exchanged sheepish glances. "Continue with an urgent sense of thrift as it relates to similar minutiae." Troy ran his fingers through his unkempt hair and looked back to the ubiquitous holes in the tiles of the false ceiling.

I followed the formula. I did it all right. I shouldn't be here. I'm ruined. This will affect my client base. I'm the town cuckold. An obese tow truck driver was my replacement in our marital bed.

The senior detective provided a judicious summary.

Almost there.

The younger detective chimed in. "The boy may need counseling. He cleaned the murder weapon off with his shirt. Children frequently develop lapses in memory to deal with extreme situations like that." The senior man sucked in his breath—a fearful sound that Troy recognized.

Got them.

Troy stood. "You think so? Write a name down. Write down the name of a person on Earth who can help my son with the troubles he'll accumulate over a lifetime by cleaning off a putter with a shirt. Maybe there's a team of psychiatrists you know that specializes, say, in that, sure—but also, being shot in the face by your mother?" Troy walked to the coffee machine. He picked up the carafe. "You think when he wakes up, if he wakes up, that a phalanx of therapists could get him to the point where it's all cool?" Both detectives shook their head. The junior man held his breath. Troy held the carafe aloft. "This? This is the worst coffee I've ever had." He tossed the carafe into a plastic garbage can. "I'm going to go take a shower, shave, brush my teeth, put on a four thousand dollar suit, maybe the shark-skin shoes—I'm going to call my office, have eight of my associates meet me for a briefing, then march that parade of rainmakers in to make a personal visit to your captain. By the end of the day, one of you'll be brewing that filth for the other one. You can drink it from chipped little cups at your new desk jobs."

Troy put the house on the market immediately. He didn't expect it to sell quickly—the required disclosures assured that. A caretaker maintained the mansion. Everything of value was put in storage in a secure part of the office. Since the office also had a living space, Troy moved in for a few weeks. Word traveled. Troy felt pressed to reinvent himself somewhere before business dropped off.

What a disgrace—everyone knew what she'd done—what she was. Reputation was everything.

Bonn surprised everyone. He awoke despite his critical injuries. Surgeons and neurologists murmured amongst themselves—

A millimeter here, a millimeter there, the bullet should have killed the boy.

The bullet carved a trough through his son's left cheekbone. It took off the top of his ear. He could see, but his left iris lost its pigment. Some days it looked white—others it appeared a dusky, dead, blue-gray. When his hair started to grow out, some of it was white too. Around the scar. He walked fine—he could move his arms—but Troy couldn't bear to look at him. Bonn took the little mutt for daily walks. The dumb animal wasn't house trained yet, so the office stunk. In a flash, everything good, it seemed—was gone. Troy asked Bonn if he was eating. Bonn said yes. Troy drank a little less, bathed regularly, and grew obsessed with boats. Bonn asked about Hedwig, but Troy changed the subject.

The kid had been through enough already.

"She's fine, Son. She quit, though. It was all too much for her. She told me she'd look in on you one day soon—hey, do you like boats?"

Troy bought a 290-foot yacht—sight unseen. The vessel had disclosures of its own—a diving accident in the Bay of Bengal. The accident involved a swimming elephant. Two women were dead. The owner, a sheikh, wished to sell quickly for superstitious reasons. The asking price was $80,000,000.00—less than half the ship's worth. The purchase price included two years of the crew's salary and delivery. The original name of the ship was sensitive information, but Troy liked the new name. The *Élan Petite* required a staff of sixty-five. It could accommodate thirty guests in opulence. It had all the necessities: jet skis, helipad—swimming pool. A 55-foot catamaran speedboat served as a tender in shallower waters. Troy started to take better care of himself—the new start was something to look forward to. Troy decided to set up shop in Grand Cayman.

Élan Petite—it had a ring to it.

The name suggested there was a larger *Élan* cruising about somewhere—perhaps a 400-foot behemoth. Since Troy would live aboard the ship, new clients visiting the Caymans would appreciate his sensible nature. "The boat's pristine," the broker promised. "You're going to love it, Mr. Maddox."

When opportunities knocked, he answered.

Troy arranged for Bonn to attend junior boarding school in New Hampshire. "You're going to love it in the islands, Son. When you visit. There's world-class golf and a warm ocean. We can even ride horses on the beach."

69

Although Bonn seemed indifferent to horses on beaches, he took the news well.

70

~Different

Bonn packed for boarding school while Troy explained the trust fund. It would pay for everything Bonn might need so Troy could focus on growing his new clientele from the Caymans. The caretaker would drive him to the school in New Hampshire. Troy seemed to have arranged for everything.

"Pack light," was the last thing his father said to him before he left. There could be worse parting advice. Troy's partner in the local firm agreed to manage Bonn's fund. He knew Rupert's number, but slid the man's business card in his pocket with Eugen anyway. On the way out of town Bonn stopped to see Manny. His friend promised to take care of Jelly Bean. He even invited Bonn to keep some things at the shop if he wanted, but he still seemed surprised when the caretaker carried the heavy-framed Bill of Rights into his greasy shop.

Linda brought a casserole and they ate. She and Manny never had children, but she loved them. Linda was a tall, fine-featured lady—a gracious hostess. After the meal she gave Bonn a long hug. "Please come and visit us." Manny and Bonn said their goodbyes next. Manny teared up. Bonn wondered at his friend's raw emotions.

Should he say something?

Instead, he handed him the old deck of cards. The words came to him as the mechanic flipped through the deck.

He must think it an odd gift.

"Manny, I want to thank you for taking time to get to know me. You and Linda are the most genuine people I've ever met." They clasped hands. Manny held on for a long time. The handshake felt paternal—fatherly, but like a real father shook his hand. Not Troy.

Manny admired the framed document. "It's good you're leaving something here, so Jelly Bean knows you're coming back." The boy nodded and looked at the puppy. "Are you going to spend all your breaks and vacations on that fancy boat, or would you consider coming here? You know what it's like here—common food, lots of laughs—we'll stay up late and fix up old cars every night. I can't compete with a big boat, but I'm sure gonna miss you."

Tidbit circled Jelly Bean. She had different smells on her. She seemed big and healthy. Tidbit smelled Bonn on the puppy too. She wagged and bowled the puppy over with a playful lick. Jelly Bean sprung to her feet and bit the skin on her mother's throat with a jubilant growl. Tidbit allowed the puppy to menace her and panted happily.

"If you decide you don't like boats, you could spend some time here with Linda and me—we'd sure be glad to have you."

"Thank you, Manny. Really."

Manny pulled Bonn into a bear hug. He spoke softly. "You know, son, sometimes people just say things. A thing they think they've got to say, but everybody who hears it knows they don't mean it. I mean it. There's a place for you here if you want it." Bonn closed his eyes tight and hugged him back hard.

"I'll see you at Christmas break then. Save some things for me to do—I don't want to loiter." Manny smiled. He'd watched the boy try so hard to speak with feeling. He still couldn't do it, but he sure tried. He wondered what it was like inside the boy's head. Bonn seemed to know he was different.

It didn't matter. The kid had heart. He'd do big things. He was sure of it.

Jelly Bean pulled on the cuff of Manny's coveralls as the town car rolled down the alley. Linda stooped gracefully and picked up the puppy. She cried, but still smiled in the way that always made her look extra beautiful. Manny took a deep breath and surveyed the dusty shop. He paused on the framed document.

They did a fine job aging the reproduction.

The edges were wrinkled. The yellowed dappling must have been achieved with some chemical—there were water stains too, which seemed like overkill, but the effect definitely worked. "Looks pretty authentic." Linda put the puppy down and stood before a poster of a Vargas girl.

"That thing is lewd. Let's put Bonn's picture up here instead." Manny hung the document in its new place. They held hands on the couch for a while. Linda spoke first. "You know, it brings sort of a sophisticated air to the room."

Manny nodded. "Someday he'll want it back. Then I'll put my girlfriend back up where she belongs."

72

Linda smiled. "I'll be sure to store her somewhere real safe." Manny and Linda talked about Bonn for at least an hour. He'd been dealt a bad hand with the silver spoon, but he didn't seem to choke on it.

Everyone else did.

After dinner, Linda had an epiphany. "He isn't afraid, Manny. That's it. The boy isn't afraid like normal people are. I'm not saying he's bad, I'm not saying he's crazy—I saw him with the pup. I know how he is with you, but that's the thing I couldn't put my finger on. That's how he's different. Terrible things have happened to that boy, Manny. He isn't just dealing with it all extraordinarily well—he doesn't have superior coping skills. He isn't dealing with it at all. He's like a fearless, matter-of-fact little machine. Some of that he needed to survive his terrible family, but some of it he was born with."

Linda was right. No doubt about it.

The dead retriever—on his birthday no less—the murder of his nanny, his drug-crazed mother shot him in the head before she'd offed herself, the selfish absentee father. Little Bonn just kept ticking away, one eye white, a white shock of hair framing his clipped ear. Bonn was in the hospital for a week after he was shot. Manny wondered why he never came back. It seemed odd. When he showed up with his head shaved and scarred up, Manny had been aghast, but Bonn just shrugged. "My mom shot me."

That's what he'd said.

He said it like Manny might ask, "Pass me that wrench." Manny couldn't even remember his reply. Whatever it was, it wasn't enough. They had a good couple of months after that, when Bonn came by every day. One day, though, Bonn saw a floor jack tottering when Manny removed a wheel. The boy reached to steady it, but the car fell. It trapped his hand. Manny was nauseated and frantic when he realized what happened. He rushed to free Bonn's hand. Even Tidbit stood by, barking and nervous, but not Bonn. Bonn stayed calm. He patted the dog with his good hand until the weight was off. He continued the conversation they'd been having about carburetors.

As if nothing terrible had happened at all.

When his hand was finally free, Manny ran to get ice. And Linda. He was too upset to drive. When he returned, Bonn was mashing on his injured hand. "I feel some crunching. The first metacarpal's broken." Linda drove them all to the emergency room. The physician confirmed Bonn's suspicion. Manny watched Bonn as the physician realigned the bone. Bonn didn't grimace or wince—he just watched. "Do you feel this young man?" the physician asked.

"Yes," Bonn replied. When Troy finally arrived, the physician gave Troy an odd look.

"Humor me a couple minutes, Mr. Maddox." He jabbed a pin into the bottom of Bonn's foot. Bonn's breathing remained steady. He didn't pull away.

"Why did you do that?"

"I wanted to make sure you could feel pain. Did you feel that?"

"Yes."

"You didn't react normally. Some people can't feel pain. It's a rare condition, though—are you sure you felt it?"

"Yes."

"What did it feel like?"

"I'm not certain what you mean. It felt like you pushed a pin into my foot."

"But you didn't react."

What Bonn said next gave Manny a cold shiver down his spine.

"What's the correct reaction?"

~Polymath

Alvar ran out of lessons for Henna. By age thirteen, it was clear that Henna was a prodigy. Alvar drafted a letter to the dean of the University at Cambridge:

> Dear Sir,
>
> A correspondence from a pleasant hillside in the north of Finland.
> My granddaughter has been my ward for the past nine years. Although I'm a learned pharmacist, chemist, and naturalist, her young mind is no longer sufficiently challenged by what I can provide her—I assure you, she is a phenomenon. Henna exhibits eidetic tendencies—she is a gifted painter— with her knowledge of physics, chemistry, languages, and the natural world, it would be shameful for me to keep her my secret. With access to microscopes, telescopes, linguists, the equipment and minds inherent to an institution such as Cambridge, I have no doubt her mind will bloom at an even more accelerated rate. Please reciprocate my correspondence. Imagine adding Marie Curie to your roster of alumnus and allow this young polymath to outgrow your gardens as well.
>
> Warm Regards,
>
> Alvar Takala

The letter was shared via university channels. That spring, Henna was invited to attend interviews at École polytechnique fédérale de Lausanne, on the shore of Lake Geneva. To Henna, the interview seemed informal and rambling. The head of the physics department and a famous chemist met with Henna first. The chemist couldn't stop smiling. Soon the small group moved to a conference room. More people arrived. People brought in urns of coffee, bread with small bowls of sweet mustard, chocolates. Everyone seemed well dressed. Polite. Reports of the gifted prodigy traveled across campus: "Come meet the genius—they are serving lunch." Things settled down when food was placed at a large round table. A dozen people spoke to each other in several languages. No one in particular seemed to be in charge. The chemist returned. Introductions were made, platters of pickled fruit placed on the elegant table. Plates of perch, potato cakes, cream tarts were served. French seemed the most common language, but some spoke German, Italian, English. A professor of theoretical physics asked Henna in German, "How many languages do you speak?" Everyone listened for her answer, which she gave in Latin.

"I'm fluent in nine languages." The woman clapped and gave a pleased smile. "Nine? Wonderful—why, though, did you answer in Latin, if you understood my German?"

Henna gestured toward Alvar, who sipped coffee in a chair by the door. "My grandfather taught me it is most polite to answer a question in a language common to the greatest number of listeners. It appeared that each of you stopped for a moment to listen."

A beaming professor of linguistics asked in Portuguese, "Why Latin and not English?"

"Most of you have already spoken to me in English. I hoped to practice my Latin a bit on this trip and I've guessed Latin is a language we all share."

The group insisted Alvar join them at the table. He said that coffee was enough, but a plate of food appeared in front of him, regardless. The man who brought it took a moment to describe the contents of the plate, as they would relate to time on a clock.

"Professor Takala, a fillet of perch sits at five o'clock, a cream tart rests at nine o'clock. A small assortment of cheeses and fruits span the other hours. Would you like more coffee?"

Henna never considered her grandfather's title, but it was correct. As Alvar visited with the academics, she was reminded how amazing he was—he was humble and funny. Though he chose to live alone above the Arctic Circle, he maneuvered his silverware and napkin with class. He was a quiet gentleman. He made people feel good about themselves, but steered most topics back to her. The meeting continued another hour. Finally a lady asked a question from the official interview form.

"Why would you like to attend EPFL?"

Henna answered truthfully. "Although the lunch and conversation have been very nice, I'd like to see the school's library. Perhaps tour any labs I would be allowed into. If it's not too much bother, I would feel more comfortable answering your question afterward."

She was admitted that fall on a full ride scholarship. She would be the second youngest to gain admission to EPFL to date, but her knowledge of the sciences was already at a post-doctoral level. Her options were staggering.

Alvar missed Henna terribly. He worried day and night.

Did her door lock? Was it a thick door? Was she on the first floor? Who would she call if she lost her key? What if that person didn't answer? Was she ready for this? Was he?

He smelled things she left behind. A sweater—a hairbrush. He still spoke to her despite her absence. He couldn't help it. He considered a telephone, but the logistics were impractical. There were no phone lines—or even electricity for miles. One day a box arrived from Switzerland. It was a book on philosophy adapted to braille and a small electrical device with earphones to teach him braille and a small box of chocolate. Henna left a tip for the postal clerk, who read the accompanying letter.

He hadn't read anything at all since the war.

> Dear Grandpa,
>
> It's time for you to catch up. This technology exists. You should have it. The registrar is a bit of a brood-hen. She has taken me under her wing, attempted to organize chaperones,

77

meals, other similar nonsense. They celebrate, yet are certainly unsure of me. I wish I were a bit taller. With sunglasses on, my age may not be so evident. Maybe I will grow a bit more this summer? I can only believe the chlorophyll can aid my egress from under the threshold of Ms. Ebersold's pendulous embrace … although pleasant enough, I would prefer my privacy.

Love, forever your garden perennial,

Henna

Henna was right. It was time to rejoin the world. If she was that brave, he could learn a bit too.

Without Henna to cut the brush back and clear the springtime roots from his usual paths, Alvar began to fall. He used a stick to feel his way about the little homestead, but he frequently felt short of breath. The lady who helped with his mail stopped in to help frequently. She brought him a pie now and then. She thought he should stop smoking. He'd known Akka for years—she was his accomplice each Vieströ. Akka was right about the smoking, of course, but he'd already smoked so much.

What good would it do him to quit now?

When Akka brought him a box a week later, he told her he'd burned his pipe in the fireplace. "Good. You'll live longer and be able to eat more pie. Would you like some help with your parcel? I might be as excited to see what Henna has sent as you are." The years spent with Henna seemed to have passed in just moments. He didn't feel eighty, but he was.

Maybe he'd live to be really old—just to see how things turned out.

"I'd like that. I'll make us some tea." Akka watched Alvar stoke the fire, hang the kettle. She waited for him to sit beside her before opening the box.

"You know, Alvar, I'm almost seventy, but I find myself amazed about at least two things every day. You'd think a person my age would run out of amazement, but I don't seem to." Alvar reached into his pocket for the pipe and then remembered it was gone. He sighed. He wondered what to do with his hands while he sat. "It's the surprises that keep me going, I think."

Akka opened the box. Inside they found a tiny tape recorder. A dozen tiny tapes. A few packages of batteries for the device. Alvar poured the tea while Akka read the instructions for the recorder. One of the tapes was marked. She put it in the device to play. Henna's voice was strong and confident. The little device fit into his hand perfectly. When Henna's recording ended, he put it into his pipe pocket. Over the months they stayed in touch that way. Henna asked him to send her some dried mushrooms, to tape his voice next to the brook—he asked her to describe the buildings and the laboratories she studied in. One day he sat by the fire and spoke into the recorder. He described the contents of the stew pot and then told Henna stories about her mother.

At the end of the school year Henna came home to visit. Tall, her neck frequently wrapped in a silk scarf, she was becoming a woman. The smell of an expensive bouquet caressed the air behind her. She had discovered perfume. Excitedly, Henna caught him up on her studies and theories. As she talked he felt past her scarf to her face.

Beautiful.

He pulled his hand back, but she retrieved it. While she told him about extremophiles, Henna traced his knobby knuckles. She'd received a research grant to study them. The world awaited her. He had always known.

"I've missed you so much, Grandpa. I feel like an odd transplant from the garden outside. I feel as though I stick out at the university. Like I stink it up? Like a paperwhite." The girl joked, but there was sadness behind her words.

"No," he reassured her, "you were a transplant even here. You were always destined for bigger things. That isn't sadness—it's your responsibility to realize your potential. When Lucrece dropped you off here years ago, you were wild, but you were already you. I only watered you. You *are* sort of a wild perennial—you keep coming back." They laughed, drank tea, and ate small bits of chocolate until late in the evening.

"Let's go for a walk in the morning. I need to smell the woods." Alvar nodded and tucked the girl in like he always did, with a kiss on the forehead.

79

~Mississippi

Curfew was enforced at the boarding school so Bonn got creative: At 2:08 AM each day he climbed from his dormitory window. He jogged back onto campus a few minutes after 6:00 AM as if he'd just gone out for a short run. A cluster of old maples in the center of town provided cover for his experiment. Bonn spent hours in the canopy of the second tallest tree. Getting himself comfortable in the tree was improbable, but stability was crucial. By 3:00 AM Bonn dangled, prone, from a sling in the tree. The sling needed a spanner of sorts—it compressed his ribs proximally.

If he couldn't breathe smoothly, it would affect his accuracy.

Bonn practiced for weeks in the tree. Each day he took notes, made adjustments, and watched the town wake up. Bonn measured the distance from his pupil to the ground with a string weighted on one end, a knot tied at one-foot increments. Sixty-eight knots bumped through Bonn's fingertips before the weight touched the ground. He untied the hitch in the line that suspended him. Employing sailing blocks, pulling smoothly, soon he rested at an even seventy. From the new vantage point he had clear lines of sight up two streets: one at his ten o'clock, the other at his three o'clock. Bonn held a willow branch in lieu of a rifle. He alternated his aim down each corridor and took notes on stability. His spine limited motion more than anything else. Stability suffered when he compensated his aim with head and neck movements. One of the two blocks from which he hung gave a tiny squeak as he swung side to side. Frowning up at the pulley, Bonn scrutinized the system. Despite the second attachment point to the tree, he still swayed a lot—even with normal breathing. Bonn considered a third attachment, but dismissed the thought quickly.

Simpler was better.

The light breeze and leaves combined with the low light provided ample cover. Bonn wrote terse notes in a small notebook:

1. Transfer weight from chest to knees.
2. Prussic-adjusted rifle rest?
3. One corridor. Minimize. Focus.

If he did his homework, he wouldn't need multiple corridors.

4. Timing.

80

By 5:00 AM it was functionally light.

There—movement at his ten o'clock.

Bonn peered down the length of the branch toward his target. The terminal bud on the straight green stick served as a primitive sight. Bonn trained the oblong bead on the chest of an early riser.

A woman.

As she approached, he made out more details. Her silver hair was piled loosely atop her head. She wore blue slacks and a red windbreaker. At approximately 400 meters, he saw that a small dog oscillated at the end of a leash the woman held tight against her hip. She looked as though she smelled of pie dough and furniture polish.

Close enough.

Bonn frog-kicked to simulate a rifle blast.

Click.

One Mississippi.

Bonn swung in the sling and experimented with maneuvers to stabilize himself. He saw silver hair through the leaves, but a follow up shot wouldn't be possible if he needed to make one—not for several seconds. In a flash he recalled his last embrace with Manny. His friend's beard had smelled of fresh laundry. And motor oil.

Two Mississippi.

Leaves blocked his view. Bonn peered through a gap in the branches at a point on the sidewalk where he expected the dog to emerge.

Three Mississippi.

The dog was visible for a moment and then disappeared behind a tasteful refuse bin.

Four Mississippi.

The tiny red head of the terrier emerged from behind the bin. The dog paused to consider what was either an old piece of sausage or a pile left by a previous dog. The lady jerked the leash. She took a wide berth around the treasure. For a moment the dog strained to achieve the prize while the woman walked in an arc around it. It reminded Bonn of an architect's compass. The dog's brain served as the needle—the pivot point. Bonn shifted slightly, placed the tree bud over the terrier's static head, and squeezed the imaginary trigger.

Click.

Bonn propped the branch into a fork of the tree. He wrote in the notebook:

Follow-up shot too slow without tertiary stabilization.

~Shrikethrush

The university was just what Henna needed. The chemistry department had incredible resources. She found the unknown so exciting. Chemistry explained the world. There was so much other people already knew—or thought they knew—she pitied those who couldn't collaborate due to large egos or personality defects. They would lose so much that was recently vetted—even replicated—by appropriate use of the scientific method. She was drawn to mathematics and physics as well as chemistry. She spent the balance of her precious time in the conservatory. The campus conservatory held tropical plants she'd only seen in books. The floor plan resembled a cartoon-sun. Triangular rays radiated from the central sphere in even jags. The main room was an immense glass dome. It contained tropical trees, ginger plants, ferns, lilies, and other exotics. Inconspicuous heaters warmed certain areas when the sun went down. Henna found the humidity and the foliage in the dome cleansing. She used the area to center herself. Although there was a dedicated study area near a pool of water, Henna preferred to explore the huge dome. She quietly walked the paths and marveled at the diversity of life.

One day she squatted to look inside the water jar plants she saw—without fail—a different tiny frog peering back at her each time. The triangular wings that radiated from the main room were dedicated to specific areas of research. Although it seemed unlikely, each researcher's clothing—and even behavior—seemed affected by the wings they frequented. Some of the people seemed more captive than the animals. The rat researchers loved white coats. Most of the primate researchers were women. They preferred yoga pants. Tight tee shirts with droll messages. The few male researchers dedicated to primates showed a penchant for corduroy. Frog researchers as a whole wore leather. It also seemed you weren't allowed to be a frog researcher unless you had visible tattoos. One afternoon a tall, handsome man emerged from the frog wing holding a camera and a small plastic box. He donned gloves and removed a beautiful tree frog from the box. It had cobalt legs and a yellow horseshoe-shaped mark on its head. He gently placed the frog inside a pitcher plant. He took pictures of the animal with the camera. Henna drew near. The man wore jeans and a simple sweater. He didn't appear to belong to the frog tribe. "I haven't seen a frog like that before."

The man smiled. "Dendrobates tinctorius—the 'dyeing dart frog.' I'm taking some shots out here for a field guide. I don't like the lighting in the lab. It's unnatural." The man paused to laugh at himself. "It feels much more natural under this glass dome, kneeling next to a plant that's 1700 miles from home, don't you think?"

"Oh yes, much." Henna smiled and stooped to look more closely at the frog inside the plant. It seemed to be enjoying the field trip and blinked serenely back at her.

The tall man pulled out the legs of a tripod. "Have you been inside the lab?"

"I haven't." The man adjusted the lens of the camera. He clicked a few pictures then donned a new pair of gloves. He coaxed the reluctant amphibian back into the box. "It's an interesting collection—come see it if you'd like." Henna followed the man through the heavy glass doors and watched as he released the frog into his usual enclosure.

"I'm Stephan."

"Henna. Thanks for inviting me in."

Stephan pointed at the dyeing dart frog. "The pumiliotoxins in those little guys aren't very potent, but it can still make a person feel sick if you hold them when they're mad." He walked down the aisle, pointing out specimens as they went. "Phyllobates are way hotter—sorry, that's science geek for 'efficacy of poison or venom.' Anyway, they excrete an alkaloid…" he paused at an enclosure containing a tiny golden frog "…this one in particular." Henna read the Latin name—*Phyllobates terribilis.* Stephan grinned at her—he wasn't as young as she was, but his height could serve to mask his youth.

He probably wasn't more than twenty.

"'Terribilis' sounds so much more exciting than 'golden poison frog.' They're an important species to indigenous hunters in the Columbian jungle. They scald the little guys and smear frog juice on the tips of darts and arrows, but in captivity they lose their toxins. Without a varied diet of Columbian beetles and jungle ants, they aren't quite so 'terrible' after all. Most of the researchers in here are studying indicator species of frogs, but I'm most interested in the toxins. Did you know the university is putting in a toxin wing? Dedicated solely to venomous and poisonous species? I'm really excited about it—I hope to be a part of that."

Henna thanked Stephan for the tour. She rushed to the library. She found a book titled *Neurotoxic Taxonomy* and skipped her afternoon classes. An entire chapter in the book was dedicated to *Phyllobates*. She studied the chemical chains formed by steroidal alkaloids and wondered at the diversity of creatures that made the toxins. When toxins themselves were broken down into groups, an astounding diversity of animals used similar toxic defenses. Henna leafed through pictures of toxic beetles, pausing to commit each common and Latin name to memory. Astonishingly, there was even a chapter on birds—some birds in Papua New Guinea ate toxic beetles. It didn't harm them—instead the toxins accumulated in each bird's skin as a measure of defense. Some were colorful like the beetles they ate, but some didn't broadcast their defenses at all. An unassuming mouse-colored bird had a great common name, "little shrikethrush." The plain little bird seemed to look at Henna from a smooth tree trunk. Her very blandness made her more beautiful. Her shape was a perfect bird shape. She was a self-assured looking creature. She didn't need flamboyant colors to advertise the deadly batrachotoxin stored in her skin.

She was perfect.

~Freak

Bonn guessed all boarding schools were about the same. Prestigious names and astronomical tuitions convinced wealthy parents to send busloads of kids. They were prepped for political posts. For elegant jobs, white collar lives. Each student looked forward to a top college placement and eventual high earning potential. Even the rebel kids sent to the school—by parents tired of their rebelliousness—rebelled in conformist ways. Bonn scanned the dining hall. He was the only boy who didn't wear his collar up. He didn't wear 'boat' shoes. He was the youngest boy. Usually no one paid any attention to him, despite the eye, the ear—the scar. People were socially complex, but they were still just animals. Although sharks are socially simple animals, they share some traits with humans. For instance, sharks frequently give a test bump before they commit to a full-blown attack on their oceanic quarry. One would-be "shark" decided to test Bonn after the dinner bell sounded one evening. He threw a fake lunge-punch to make Bonn flinch, a move his crew had recently seen on TV. The pubescent anticipated waves of laughter from his friends. What the preppy didn't anticipate was Bonn's reaction. Bonn tucked his chin and stepped *into* the punch, forehead first. The kid grasped his injured hand. He involuntarily threw his head back in anguish. Bonn punched the boy in the trachea, quickly finishing the fight.

Bonn offered a handshake to the nearest of the bully's posse. "Bonn Maddox." The boy nervously shook Bonn's hand, but didn't offer his name. "Always tuck your chin when someone throws a punch at your head. The frontal bone can take an incredible impact, but facial bones are fragile. Trust me, I know." The boy's hand felt limp and damp. The kid had no idea what to do. "Your hands sure feel soft—and very clean." The boy tried to shake loose of Bonn's hand, but Bonn held tight. "I'm here to study. Are you here to fight? If you are, we should get it over now."

"Nuh—no—" stammered the terrified boy with soft hands. Bonn released him and surveyed the rest of the boys. None were capable of eye contact. The boy on the floor managed a few raspy inhalations but remained in the fetal position. "My guess is that none of you can fight worth a damn. It's a shame you need to school together for safety, but I get it—safety in numbers." Bonn squatted to peer at the downed boy. "A whole school of limp fish." Bonn hooked a finger inside the bully's cheek. He hoisted the bully's head aloft by the tender flesh to send the point home. None of the boys made a move to help their friend. "Let's keep the glass between us, fish. I'm not one of you."

The school's administrative secretary poked her head into Dean Creed's office. He raised his eyebrows. "Yes, Margaret?"

"The bully called his parents. His dad is on line one." Creed noted that the woman looked giddy. Gleeful. Theirs was a quiet school, usually bereft of intrigue. He guessed that the secretary would waddle back to her desk and put her phone on speaker with the volume down so she could listen in. Creed nodded and peered at the blinking light. He had reviewed the tapes a dozen times. He pursed his lips.

"You may stay and listen, Margaret, if you wish to do so." Margaret grinned and leaned against the old mahogany molding surrounding the doorway. With a sigh, he pressed the button. The bully's father, mayor of a Midwestern city, was enraged. Creed listened to the man for a while. His oral diarrhea was truly impressive. Finally he'd heard enough to establish how to deal with the man.

"Sir, I'd usually be receptive to your boy's plight, however, I must interject—boys sort things out here. On their own. Furthermore, I know your son. He's an ass. He'll never be chief of state. He practices intimidation more than he studies. The little bully was bound to find someone he couldn't intimidate. The Maddox boy sits alone, eats alone—gets perfect grades, uses perfect syntax. His father is an attorney. A good one. Troy Maddox recently donated four million dollars to the school, which we intend to use to put in a state of the art computer lab." The mayor fell silent. Creed tapped a finger on his glass desktop, waiting for a retort. None came. Margaret shifted her heft back and forth unhappily—as though she'd been hoping for more excitement.

"Sir, would you consider contributing to the school's upgrades? Our closed circuit TV system should be expanded. We couldn't quite see the sneer on your son's face when he picked the fight with the Maddox boy." The mayor cleared his throat but said nothing. "Did you know the Maddox boy was granted early admission to the school? Your son is five years older. He outweighs the Maddox kid by forty pounds."

"I'll talk with my boy," snarled the mayor. Dean Creed smiled and disconnected the call.

"That's as far as it goes, Margaret." Margaret tilted her head at him like an overfed parrot looking for the right word. "Margaret, that is as far as this will go. Do you understand?" Margaret nodded, wounded. "You may return, please, to your desk now, Margaret." The woman creaked off with a scowl. Creed leaned back in his chair and studied his credenza.

It had better be as far as it went.

The computer lab opened the world to Bonn. He was a natural. When the school purchased the license to access "Usenet" Bonn was overwhelmed with information. Most of the posts were about computers themselves, but some historians and other enthusiasts started newsgroups to share information. Bonn was surprised to find he wasn't the only Eugen Sandow fan. He took furious notes and filled notebooks with references on many topics. Bonn was most obsessed with Sandow's physical accomplishments. Though the man was a ribald showman, he was very strong. The grip strength alone it took to achieve some of his feats of strength seemed implausible. He studied the fair photograph of his idol often. Sadly, the man died in his fifties. If he hadn't burst an aneurysm, he'd be 113 years old, but Bonn imagined him tall and proud in his dotage. Rumors existed that complications from syphilis were his actual cause of death, but Bonn couldn't imagine that a mere infection brought down his hero.

In the evenings Bonn visited the gym. He focused on calisthenics and bodyweight exercises. Soon he could walk the length of the basketball court on his hands. He studied nutrition and saw incredible gains. He cranked out one-armed pushups. Bonn's classmates obsessed with free weights could do them too, but when he added one-armed pull-ups to his routine, the free weight guys were impressed. He wasn't just strong.

He was a freak.

~Old School

Henna's last year at the University she brought Alvar a cellular phone and a small solar phone charger. He memorized the positions of the numbers and grumbled a bit.

"I'll only use one phone number. Let's not make a big fuss out of it."

Henna programmed her own number into her grandfather's phone along with some emergency numbers. Henna's own phone rang while she cleaned out the barn. "Hi honey," Alvar said from a few yards away. "I think I like this thing."

Henna completed her doctorate in chemistry and returned to Switzerland to defend her second thesis—a biological science doctorate. A toxicology fellowship awaited her in Edinburgh when she was ready—the world was full of opportunity. She worried about her grandfather. He was so alone in the mountains. She scouted out some areas in the suburbs of Edinburgh that Alvar might like, but he assured her he was fine where he was. He wasn't forgetful—he was just slower each time she saw him. He'd kept all the tiny cassette tapes from her first years at school. He had them arranged by date. Now they had cellphones. Even though this was progress, Henna felt nostalgic. Tearful.

Everything seemed to change. Nothing stays the same.

Henna drove Alvar into town in her rental car. He needed some things. A paring knife, a new whisk broom, paraffin. She marveled at the simplicity with which her grandfather lived all these years. When they couldn't find a wooden handled knife he grumbled some more. "Plastic. Everywhere now. Plastic. Solar phone charger? Plastic. I don't want plastic in my house. It doesn't feel right." Thankfully, an outfitters store supplied carbon steel boning knives with cork handles. Alvar smiled. "This is more like it." Alvar insisted on paying for the purchases. She marveled at him. His back remained straight. He was still tall. Alvar, the survivor. Alvar, the hero. She couldn't fathom the patience and the energy it took to let her burst into his quiet existence. He'd earned the right to be a hermit. She felt certain that dealing with her hormones and her menses hadn't been easy for the man, but he'd done it all so kindly.

He was a gentleman.

She watched him fiddle with the phone. He ran his fingers over the keys as a drill. He hovered over the keys to call the phone Henna carried and turned to her self-consciously.

"How do you carry your phone?"

"I just toss it in my satchel, with the ringer up so I can hear it."

"How do men carry them?"

"Some men put smaller ones like that in their pockets." Henna watched as Alvar tried the phone in his right pants pocket, then his left. He furrowed his brow. He already kept things in his pockets. It wouldn't work.

"How about a holster for it?" Henna found a store that sold phones. Alvar bought himself a case that slid onto his belt. He adjusted the phone in the case and did some dialing and answering drills as they left the store.

"Grandpa—puppies!" On the sidewalk sat an apple box full of puppies. Paws and faces poked out the top. A woman in a folding camp chair stood to begin her sales pitch.

"We have a deep-chested Chesapeake." She hooked her thumb over her shoulder to indicate the big-headed waterdog in the back of an old truck. "He took a liking to my friend's Labrador." The dog yawned. He unfurled his tongue like a cartoon red carpet. *Row, row, raow.* The lady pursed her lips and scowled. "He denies it, but I saw him. He's a big talker, but a poor historian." Henna dipped her hand into the box and let the puppies maul her. Alvar walked to the old truck to pet the Chesapeake. "If we place the puppies in good homes, my friend promised not to sue us for child support. No takers yet. When people see how big Olle here is, they balk. You have pick of the litter."

Henna counted five happy faces looking up at her, tongues lolling. *Yowp.* Olle wagged and kicked a leg happily as Alvar scratched his ear. Alvar joined Henna at the box and felt around inside. The puppies followed his hand like moths to a light. He had a distant look on his face. Most of the puppies nipped, tumbled and roughhoused, but one sat calmly—waiting his turn. When Alvar's hand came close, the curly faced puppy gave him a joyful lick and threw his head back in a gleeful howl. *Raow!* A smile spread over the old man's face.

"There's another talker in there."

The puppy sat on Alvar's lap on the way up the mountain. Alvar pulled out his phone, but not to practice drills—he let the puppy sniff the device. When the puppy fell asleep he felt his ears, his legs, his paws, then smiled and reached for Henna's hand. They held hands the rest of the way home.

~Barn Find

Bonn visited Manny on all his school breaks. Business boomed for Troy in the Caymans. Bonn didn't talk much about his father. He never went to visit him. By the time Bonn was fifteen, Manny swapped the old couch for a hide-a-bed so Bonn would be more comfortable. They stayed up late when Bonn came home. They fixed up old Chargers, Mustangs, a Barracuda. Manny taught Bonn to use a machine press to make hard-to-find parts. One summer evening as they repacked the bearings on an old rat-rod, Troy called to wish Bonn a happy birthday. Since his hands were greasy, Bonn put the shop phone on speaker. Manny shook his head sadly when Bonn hung up.

"Son, I know when your birthday is. It's not today. We've still got another three weeks."

Bonn rolled a bearing between his fingers. "I know." Manny shook his head, but kept his feelings to himself.

The man doesn't even know when his own son's birthday is.

Well, Manny thought, he intended to make the day special.

For Bonn's sixteenth birthday, Manny and Linda took him to Seneca Lake. A reclusive old farmer willed his immense car collection to his daughter, who intended to sell them off quickly. Manny showed Bonn the advertisement in the paper. "Dozens of classics for sale." Ever since Manny read the ad he'd dreamed of Fastbacks, Stingrays, other possible treasures lying fallow in the fields, eagerly awaiting his help. He intended to let Bonn pick one out—they'd fix it up together. It'd be Bonn's car. Manny became animated as they neared the farm. He had the door of the car open before Linda turned off the ignition. He sprung from the vehicle with purpose and disappeared among the neat rows of cars.

Bonn and Linda walked the rows slowly. They paused to admire an old Cadillac. Linda told Bonn a story. Bonn ran his finger along an ostentatious tail fin. Manny returned to excitedly report his discoveries. He rambled on about curb weight, horsepower, torque. Linda watched her husband proudly. Then she felt sad. Bonn was grown-up. Once he enrolled in college he might stop coming home altogether. Manny needed one last summer with the boy. A carefree summer. To tinker with old cars, to stay up late and tell stories.

Although Bonn would certainly fill out a bit more, he was already like a forklift. Linda saw Bonn move even the heaviest parts in the shop with relative ease. Manny bragged about him like he was their boy.

An irascible-looking woman trudged from the farmhouse in a bathrobe and mud boots. Her greeting was clipped.

"Anything you like? Going to auction day after tomorrow." Manny pulled Linda toward a barn. The doors were open. More neat rows of cars covered with canvas tarps were inside—cars special enough to store under the big roof of the building. Manny read the shapes that lay beneath each fabric. His breath quickened. He felt heady. He pulled covers back with reverence. Linda laughed as he fondled grills and assessed aged undercarriages. Bonn excused himself to make a phone call. Manny peeled a corner of a tarp back. If he was right, this was a—

He was right. A '69 GTO convertible. The Goat of all Goats.

Manny teared up. He whispered to Linda, "The Judge." Manny yanked the rest of the tarp off and allowed himself to be pulled into the orbit of the legendary car. The trim was intact, but the body needed work. Manny sucked air through his teeth nervously. He squatted to inspect the "ram air." He fingered the husk of a dead wasp and admired the intact chrome emblem on the old Pontiac. "How much for this old GTO? She's in kind of sad shape." Manny looked around for Bonn to make sure he approved, but the boy had his back turned. The woman adjusted her glasses and fiddled with her hair. She squinted down at Manny, cracked her gum—took a moment to re-tie the belt on her thick blue robe. She cinched the belt deep into her doughy middle in a serious way, a dramatic gesture. An obvious necessity to prepare for a successful negotiation.

Bonn hung up the phone. "We'll take them all."

The woman's gum fell from her open mouth. She stared down at it, as if the gum had spoken, but didn't stoop to retrieve it. "How much you offering?"

Bonn dialed the phone and handed it to the woman. "Why don't you think of a price? Tell the man that answers this phone that I've agreed to it. When you hang up, we will shake on it. We will send some car haulers up in a few days to disburden you—unless the farm is for sale too." Bonn made eye contact with Manny. His mouth hung open as well. "That would certainly make storage easier."

"Son, what are you doing? We came up here to buy you an old car we could fix up together. You can't buy all these cars—" Manny gave

Linda a terrified look, imploring her for help. She looked confused but entertained and remained quiet.

"Don't you have to ask you dad for the money?"

"My dad was killed last week." Manny and Linda froze. Bonn shrugged. "Tropical storm." Linda held her hand to her mouth. Manny felt his head reeling. He sat, abruptly, in the dirt. Bonn sat next to Manny and spoke in a hushed tone. "You can fix these cars up and sell them—stop bidding on renovation jobs. You grumble about deadlines, Manny, but if the cars are yours there aren't deadlines." Linda helped Manny to his feet. They looked together at the rows of cars. There must be nearly a hundred. Although neither of them would admit it to Bonn, times had been tight. Manny was in shock. He dusted himself off. He walked the rows. He pulled covers off. The last two were Shelbys. The woman approached them like a shoddy automaton. She shook Bonn's hand.

The deal was done? It actually happened?

Bonn smiled. He followed the rules for a proper handshake. "Is there a burger place nearby? It's my birthday."

"Lunch is on us," Manny said quietly.

Lunch is definitely on us.

~Just Right

"Perfection is achieved, not when there is nothing more to add, but when there is nothing left to take away."
~Antoine de Saint Exupery

Henna bought her own place in Edinburgh. Before the building was converted to lofts it was a warehouse. Before that, it was a candle factory, a butcher's quarters, grain storage. In the deeper past it housed a successful felter. Recently rezoned, resold, internally renovated, Henna was the first person in over a century to live in the building. Massive renovations weren't new in the city. Over the centuries political shifts changed the skyline drastically. Some projects evolved so swiftly that people's homes and businesses were literally buried by progress, though still occupied.

The loft retained one feature: the floor of thick old heart-pine. The age-worn patina spoke to nearly two centuries of hard and varied use. Henna didn't intend to disrupt the space more than necessary, so she hired a cabinetmaker to build a small functional island in the middle of the loft. It contained everything she really needed. Henna never intended to own more than the cabinets could contain. On the north side of the built-in, a solid-looking refrigerator winked a blue LED toward the harbor window. A deep German nickel farmhouse sink grounded the counter. Henna had a fold-down cutting board and a small drawer to hold utensils. The small blue teapot Alvar gave her in the woods years ago rested on a single gas burner. The east side of the built-in held a small room containing her water closet and a small sink. A sliding shoji door, decorated with flowers she'd collected and pressed while on holiday in France, hid the room. The south side held a Murphy bed with soft white sheets and a quilt she'd sewn as a girl. The west side held a vast bank of cedar-lined drawers. They rose from the floor to just below the deep crown molding that capped the structure. An oak library ladder was installed to access the upper drawers, which contained Henna's clothing and other belongings. A marble mantle interrupted the drawers at eye level. Henna had found it at an architectural salvage store. It had a wide copper sconce along the back, which reflected the light of mismatched beeswax candles. When lit, the effect reminded her of her grandfather's fireplace in Ruka, but without the hassle of a chimney.

Henna left the tall windows unfettered. She enjoyed the natural light. The building itself was tall. Her loft sat on the top floor. She didn't suffer a lack of privacy—in fact, a massive copper bathtub sat near the windows facing the harbor. While Henna bathed, a grim gargoyle hunched under the eave to keep watch. He was original to the building. To Henna he appeared part bird, part goat, and part cat. He had large human feet and hands. The stone creature still functioned as a waterspout during a downpour. She enjoyed sitting in the tub when it rained and soaked frequently. Head relaxed, eyes half closed—it felt meditative. She liked to watch smoky drips of dew fall from the tip of the gargoyle's beak-like nose. The creature lost a horn to the scaly grip and acidic excrement of aeons of pigeons at rest, but he looked good with his remaining horn. She considered naming the gruesome figure, but couldn't think of a name that suited him. One crisp fall evening she opened the window. Tub-fresh, bare-chested— she leaned out to touch the little monster's face.

Then she painted his toenails. He looked happier. He remained nameless, but now he was truly hers.

The only other fixtures in the loft were the small bronze coat hooks just inside the door. Henna labored over whether to place one or two hooks. She chose two, after some deliberation. One sat slightly higher than the other. And crooked. Initially it bothered her, but the imperfection grew on her. It added the warmth of character similar to hand stitching or a well-adapted three-legged dog. The remainder of the loft was uncluttered space. Her *tabula rasa*. If filled with things, it would become imperfect. She neither neglected nor took the space for granted. She frequently danced alone in the loft, thoughtless and free. On warm days she picked sun-warmed spots on the hard pine floor to stretch—to breathe—to contemplate the history of the wood beneath her. The oil spilled, love made … the tears of loss, the glow of fortune.

Although just eighteen, Henna projected wisdom. She had striking green eyes. She left her strong dark eyebrows alone. She had her grandmother's high cheekbones and a strong jaw that swept to the graceful point of her chin. She kept her soft dark hair short, only bothering to run her fingers through the natural loose curls after she conditioned in the tub. She didn't require makeup, which was fortunate. She wouldn't wear it even if it were necessary. A small tin

96

of lip moisturizer that she'd made from the forest in Ruka sat near her toothbrush and floss. She rubbed a little on her full, soft lips before folding the Murphy bed down at night. The toenail polish was a gift from a friend at the university. She only used it on her gargoyle.

Henna's loft reflected how she wanted to live her life: light and happy. Her education allowed her to choose her destiny. She telephoned Alvar daily. He frequently told her, "Only befriend those who offer encouragements instead of advice." Henna traveled voraciously. She moved light and fast, not just in the city, but also throughout the world. Henna sought organic goods. She brought home amazing things—exotic fibers, mushrooms, resin—many interesting things found their way into her wardrobe. Since she made her clothing, it fit perfectly. Henna's youth and mobility were of great benefit to her research. She didn't suffer from practical considerations. If she wanted to go somewhere, she simply went. Sometimes Henna traveled for months on end. She trusted her instinct. She made the world her playground.

A worn leather satchel was all she carried on any trip. Henna packed simple yet elegant garments. By adding a scarf, a wrap, or some wool leggings, she could morph from an elegant Scotswoman out at the theater to a Moroccan market-goer in moments. A coat hung from the lower hook near the door. A fashion conscious observer may assume it was a smartly cut Barbour—in fact, Henna knit the coat. The hood could be worn up in the rain, but became a cowl that wrapped upon itself when not needed. Tagua nut buttons formed squat hourglass shapes. The coat appeared double-breasted at times, or with a few adjustments flowed open. A gossamer liner held baffled chevrons of fine goose down. A baleen pin threaded through two carved horn loops at the neck when weather got really bad. Although the coat could appear plain and casual, or sophisticated and serious, the hidden pockets were Henna's favorite features. Henna frequently carried small bottles of tincture or vials of powder. Henna felt powerful with the coat on. Almost—impenetrable.

She felt like the shrikethrush.

Henna pulled on her boots and draped the coat over her shoulders. She slid aside the heavy elm door and rode the elevator to the ground floor. Today she carried enough toxins to dispatch the occupants of two popular London pubs at peak hour and a South American soccer stadium during finals and all the people of Brest, France combined. She had no plans to do this—

But she could.

~Plenty

Rupert Trembling worked for Troy Maddox for decades before Troy went to the Caymans. He knew the man well. Troy's partner expected Troy to need a new start after the craziness with Raquel, but he didn't expect him to thrive so quickly in the islands. Troy called him a week after he left. "Rupert, this place is what I needed. Money is falling in my lap."

Troy proved to be a master of reinvention. Rupert reflected on the man's resilience, but was a bit shocked by the details Troy shared with him. "I started taking growth hormones. Poke fun if you like, but I'm firming up and feeling young. I even grew out a three-day beard. I don't know why I packed suits when I came down. I've thrown them all out. No one wears them here." Grand Cayman was brimming with poolside beauties and mobsters. He'd discovered "boat parties" and even hosted one of his own on the ship. Troy's first big client brought along many potential clients as guests. Word of mouth was everything. "It's more efficient than time spent on the links, Rupert. Less plaid too."

"Don't you miss golf even a little?"

They used to play eighteen holes each weekend.

"Nope. I've traded golf for tanned breasts and drug lords. Drug lords, Rupert, are much better company than golfers." Troy told him he'd purchased a small fleet of jet skis for the girlfriends and families of clients to ride while he set up "tax havens." Troy didn't share any details about actual business, but Rupert guessed he was laundering money. Troy asked about Rupert's family, as he usually did, then got around to why he'd called.

"I know I left a hole there, Rupert. It can't be filled by me. It'd be best for us all if the locals thought I'd sold out. I've hired a couple guys to help. They're machines. I don't want to tell you too much about them, but don't be afraid to work them. Throw whatever you want at them. You'll see results. They work fast. I'll pay their salaries on my end. And Rupert? I know you worry, but you can trust them."

Troy was right. Rupert didn't trust them, but the men were workhorses. Somehow Troy was using the firm to legitimize his dealings in the Caymans. If the firm had been turned into a front for something else, at least it was a working front. The men mowed through legitimate busywork quickly and efficiently. They didn't have big egos, and they didn't put anything off. "Machines" was an apt description, but they were more than that—they seemed like—connected guys. High-profile types. He didn't know who they were connected to, but they were certainly a part of a larger machine somewhere. With the new men at the office, Rupert was superfluous to daily operations, which was fine by him. He came in as late as he wanted. He cherry-picked his clients.

Business surged ahead regardless.

The tropical storm that killed Troy wasn't even a notable one—really just a weekend side note on the news between commercials for toothpaste and sexual enhancement pills. Rupert learned more details from the insurance company. The swell hit the *Oyster Bar* broadside. Rupert stopped to shake his head.

The original name of the boat was better.

It listed heavily to port. An unusually shallow trough followed. Troy went to look over the side and the boat bottomed out on the reef. Troy didn't drown—he died from traumatic impact. Witnesses said he fell from the ship headfirst into the reef when the boat bottomed out. The reef pierced the hull of the ship and it took on water. Guests fled to shore on jet skis.

It wasn't the glamorous death Troy would have chosen.

Rupert reviewed the paperwork detailing Bonn's trust. He was the fund's administrator. Troy drafted the papers years ago. For his troubles, Rupert would receive three percent of the net worth of the Maddox estate. Rupert knew Troy did well financially—he worked, not because he had to, but because that's what he did. The Maddox family never seemed to sell things, but they didn't allow assets to lie fallow either.

Once Troy had invited him for a weekend of upland game hunting in Texas. Rupert wasn't the only one invited. An ambassador from South Africa attended, a lumber executive, several oil executives. The lodge was posh. They ate seared buffalo steaks encrusted in lavender with Armagnac. Crab omelets were brought in a silver steam tray into the field for the men at lunchtime. Wild game sausages adorned with bits of citrus peel were punctured by tiny hand-carved wooden pikes. A Model A Ford, restored as a mobile bar, accompanied the men on their hunts. The topless driver and bartender, a doe-eyed nineteen-year-old from Galveston, wore the cloche of a flapper, jodhpurs, and Italian riding boots. She would receive enough tips to pay her tuition at Stanford for the coming semester. Ceviche was served beneath the heads of large African animals—each spot prawn, the lime-brined crown jewel on each flute, still held the sheen of life. Top shelf liquor was served to the fat-cats on a massive veranda. The sun set in exclusive tones of crimson and honey, like a cocktail from the menu. They sat in hand-carved plantation chairs. A beautiful woman with an Australian accent offered cigars and described the next day's hunt. High stakes poker games followed for those that chose to join. Men spoke of things foreign and wondrous: boxlock rifles, elephant polo, an anecdotal account of an ambergris smuggler. Rupert wondered how Troy knew these people. Troy seemed very at ease in that environment. He acted as if he owned the place.

And in fact—he did.

With a sigh, Rupert dug into the pile of papers. It was time to find out exactly how well Troy had done. The first document reviewed the sale of the Maddox house. A French actor saw the for sale sign during a morning run. Being an A-lister, he wasn't the least interested in the disclosures, although his depressed-looking daughter loved the dark past of the place. The anthropology major gave her father a nod. The sign came down. Rupert picked up the report of Troy's death.

Thank God the boat was insured. It was a total loss.

A light on his phone flashed. Rupert picked up the call. "Hi Rupert. Listen, I'm in a field full of old cars that I intend to gift to a friend. When I call you back in a few minutes, you'll hear the voice of a startled woman. She'll quote you an astronomical number. I'd like you to round her down by twenty percent since she's been a bit rude, but agree to the sale."

"Ok, Bonn—will do."

"Thank you, Rupert."

"A field full."

Rupert fully expected the kid to blow his inheritance on odd things. The call didn't surprise him one bit. Bonn had no restrictions on how he could spend his inheritance. He'd probably buy a jet next—or take on a drug habit like his mother. Those details weren't Rupert's to monitor.

Troy's assets brought from the boat included some oddities. Many of them couldn't be easily explained.

Lucky thing—so far no one came looking for explanations.

The salvage team shipped Troy's safe back, unopened. Either the behemoth was waterproof or it was never submerged because the contents were dry. Rupert dialed the combination on the gleaming wheel and pulled the beast open. Although he was the man designated for the job, he didn't like looking through Troy's things. It felt much too personal. Rupert shrugged and removed an expensive aluminum briefcase from a suede-lined shelf. Inside the case rested a collection of Victorian-era jeweled daggers.

Odd.

Rupert frowned and closed the case. He inspected the bill of lading. The safe was, of course, from the *Oyster Bar.* He kept the combination to it in his own safe like Troy had asked.

Why would Troy own items like this?

It didn't make sense. He pulled two heavy black polymer cases out next but left them on the floor.

He'd start with paperwork.

He removed a brown leather file case and opened it at his desk. The first section contained deeds. One for a golf course in Colorado. Two more golf courses on Maui. Rupert opened the next file. An eclectic stack of bearer bonds thicker than a 1950's JCPenney catalog was nestled inside.

This changed things—it might be difficult for the boy to spend all of Troy's money after all.

Rupert needed new bifocals. As he leafed through the case, he appeared to be nodding slowly as he shifted his gaze between lenses. Hundreds of banks in Wyoming, Colorado, and Nebraska were listed on a ledger—an account in each bank held the exact sum the FDIC insured. An investment algorithm paper-clipped to the ledger outlined the strategy. Each account bore interest—when the interest grew fourteen percent over the insured amount, a new account in a new bank was opened. None of the accounts were in Troy's name. They all belonged to the trust.

Troy didn't pay many taxes.

Someone managed these accounts. The ledger outlined dates new accounts were opened. Every FDIC monitored bank in Kansas, North Dakota, and Montana also had an account.

Line one lit up again on his desk phone. Rupert pushed the speaker button. A woman's shrill voice made him wince. "Hello? Is this a joke? A kid here just said he'd buy all of the cars I've got for sale here at my farm. Said I could name my price."

"Yes madam. What is your price?"

"Well, there are 104 cars here. Some are worth more than others. Some don't have engines. If I said I want $25,000.00 a car, what would you say?"

I'd say you were dreaming.

Rupert did some quick calculations. "Can you provide me 104 vehicle identification numbers?"

"OK, no—there are ninety-six cars. It would take me all afternoon to write the numbers down." Rupert tapped different numbers into the adding machine.

Twenty percent for being rude, five percent for being dishonest.

"I'll draft a check for $1,800,000.00. Would that sufficiently offset the chore? It'd save you years of lowball offers. Take it or leave it."

"One mill … yon … One point eight? I'll take it."

Rupert disconnected the call. Although the figure was a drop in the bucket, his stomach didn't feel right.

His home cost less than an eighth of that.

He stood for a moment and wiped his glasses clean with a handkerchief. He struggled to understand the depth of wealth contained in the safe. It held only a portion of the funds eventual worth. It didn't feel real. He held the glasses up toward the main office, where the light was better.

Clean enough.

He paused to watch the new men. They worked steadily. They moved quickly, yet only seemed able to move one body part at a time: first an arm, then a head. They looked more like stop motion animations than men. Rupert sat. He rubbed his temples to clear his mind and returned to the files. He reviewed another deed. One for a casino.

A casino?

More deeds. A manufacturing firm in Singapore. Apartment buildings in Prague. Rupert sped through the files, overwhelmed. The only way to estimate Bonn's inheritance was to sell everything. Until that happened, a sum would remain theoretical. It seemed Troy excelled at the silent partner gambit. Another ledger showed holdings in hundreds of medium-sized high-growth companies. He'd made a mint on IPOs. Normal people didn't get to buy IPOs.

No wonder Troy was constantly on the phone.

Things became surreal. The safe seemed to swell. It was a library of wealth. The trust owned a cattle ranch in Idaho and another in the

Black Hills, complete with mineral rights. The attached quitclaim was signed in 1958. That put Troy in his—teens?

Thirteen. Troy bought a ranch at thirteen?

The attorney leaned back to survey the documents and assorted treasures that littered his desk. Here was a legacy of wealth to make Midas feel impotent. He had no idea how to proceed. Three percent of this was his.

He'd need help. His glasses were smudged again. He needed fresh air.

Rupert headed for the window but stumbled over one of the heavy black cases.

Might as well open them.

Rupert stooped to lift one onto his desk.

It was heavy.

Each thick hasp opened with a dull thud. He swung the lid open.

Cash.

About fifty pounds of hundred dollar bills. He felt nauseated. Rupert stooped to open the second case where it sat on the floor.

More cash. Identical to the first.

He really needed that air now. Cash meant danger.

Cash brought questions.

The cases shouldn't be in his office. Rupert felt like he was choking on money. He opened the window and took some deep cash-free breaths. He looked nervously into the main office. The new guys continued their jolting movements. He tried to imagine them kicked back on that veranda in Texas. What would they drink when they leaned back in their chairs?

They wouldn't.

They didn't seem capable of kicking back—or even slowing down. If you offered them a plantation chair, they'd probably sell it. Though he couldn't decipher content, he heard the inflection in their voices as they worked. Each hiss and roar the men uttered into their headsets seemed perfectly metered.

Not too little. Not too much. Just right.

Rupert daydreamed he was at home, sitting in his chair by the window, reading his granddaughter *Goldilocks*.

That towhead enjoyed such a nice resolution.

Though his granddaughter always demanded he re-read the book at least once, it was always a clean ending.

Predictable.

Step 1: Girl raids abode of apex predators.

Step 2: Girl messes things up.

Step 3: Girl makes a clean getaway.

Step 4: Repeat.

As if on cue, one of the new men returned his gaze.

Ryker?

He was slightly shorter than Rickard. Otherwise, it was hard to tell them apart. The man held eye contact with Rupert and tilted his head with a precise chop, like a bird of prey might investigate a subtle movement in the grass, wings at the ready. He reached to the keypad on his phone without looking down at the device. Rupert was startled when line one lit up. Ryker's tongue seemed to snap in and out as he spoke. "Let's visit."

To taste the world for heat? For blood?

The taller man stood and removed his headset. Rupert's nausea worsened. He felt the glands under his tongue squirm and pulse. His diaphragm began to spasm.

He was a good man. He hadn't done anything wrong. He was now the senior partner in this thriving law firm. Why did he feel like crawling out the window and running for his car?

The men approached Rupert's office. They tilted their heads with choppy motions. They considered the door like confused birds. Rupert felt exposed. Vulnerable. Ryker's lips moved. Rupert realized he was still holding the telephone—

Frozen—like an idiot.

"We'll sort it out. Unlock the door. We'll explain." Rupert recognized the clipped accent as German. He considered leaving the door locked, maybe even hiding, but that seemed juvenile. He was already standing up gawking at them through the glass door. Troy said he could trust them—trust them to do what? Should he trust Troy? A German accent?

They'd explain what?

Rupert unlocked the door. Rickard slithered into Rupert's chair while Ryker closed the heavy black cases full of cash and stacked them by the door. The taller man tapped buttons on the Danish phone system that would send all outside calls to a pleasant digital voice. The voice promised eventual satisfaction if only the caller left a number.

~Intuition

Henna became the Jane Goodall of the venomous and poisonous. Shortly, she was offered the chair in the toxicology department at the university. Since she wasn't required to lecture as the chairperson, she spent most of her time traveling. The university granted her some space to compile a modern cabinet of curiosities in return for writing grants and publishing research. With access to lab equipment, secure spaces for live and frozen specimens and a steady income, Henna had it made.

In the field Henna trusted her instincts. She watched for clues. When none presented themselves, she became quiet. She listened, watched for something to present itself. It was an art. She learned the technique from her grandfather. Intuition, Henna knew, was inside everyone.

Most people just ignored it.

Alvar had always encouraged Henna to trust her intuition, yet it was a bit like a divining rod: if she were pressed to explain how she made decisions, it would sound too mystical for non-believers to grasp. When barriers presented themselves, she didn't rage—she became fluid. Solutions waited when she became receptive. When her mind relaxed. It's important to have a goal, but imperative to recognize an opportunity—

Opportunities visited only those who were receptive.

A team couldn't achieve what Henna accomplished alone. A team would break for coffee. A team would argue, seek out romances and drama. Egos were barriers to progress. A team was a machine. At idle that machine sounded like static to Henna. She couldn't focus around static. But alone? Alone Henna was a dynamo. Soon her ability to recognize opportunities opened the entire world to her. She collected toxins and stories—some of the most scientific minded adults in the world were social toddlers and the stories made eventual collaboration easier.

Australia was particularly fruitful for both. Her goal was to collect live blue-ringed octopuses. She needed Tetrodotoxin (TTX). The beautiful little *Hapalochlaena maculosa* had it. Initially the species eluded Henna, but she befriended some local spear fishermen on Fraser

106

Island who promised to keep their eyes open. When it came to the ocean, Henna thought, scientists should always start at a bar.

Fishermen knew where to find things—especially the nearest bar.

Fishermen discovered a live coelacanth in 1938. The fish was long considered extinct. Thousands of fossils of the creature existed, but then one day, a fresh one was dragged on board a boat deck. Fishermen said, "That's something different." The captain of the boat took the initiative to notify a local museum official, who consulted her friend, an ichthyologist. Along the way, each person to see the fish knew it was special, but it was the museum official that was honored in the naming of the find—not the fishermen. Granted, Ms. Courtenay-Latimer gave the coelacanth a ride in a taxicab. She did have it stuffed to preserve it, pending scientific review, but it was fishermen who recognized the prehistoric lunker. *Latimeria chalumnae* would likely be *"Goosenia" chalumnae* after the Captain of the boat, named Goosen if Ms. Marjorie Courtenay-Latimer hadn't spent time befriending fishermen. Fishermen who knew she wanted to see something interesting.

Henna was about to purchase a ticket to New Zealand when one of the spear fishermen called her. He had three live blue-rings and a bucket of beaked sea snakes. He promised to bring her a box jelly. He'd sent a group out to look for stonefish. Henna smiled. The fishermen at the bar were certainly drunk, but they were good listeners. For the price of three rounds of beer her bounty exploded.

Henna stayed on the mainland for three weeks. She kept a courier service busy around the clock, shuttling live specimens back to Scotland. With the fishermen scouring the ocean for her, Henna took time to hunt specimens on her terrestrial wish list. She collected a pair of aggressive eastern brown snakes, *Pseudonaja textilis*. They carried textilotoxin, a presynaptic neurotoxin. She hunted and was eluded by the inland taipan. *Oxyuranus microlepidotus* had both presynaptic and postsynaptic toxins. The snake was extraordinarily lethal, yet famously easygoing. The most lethal known venomous snake was a peaceful snake—nothing to prove to anyone.

Nature did have a sense of humor.

Henna's last night in Australia she used a technique called "road hunting." She drove the few asphalt roads on the map of South Western Queensland just before dark; cold blooded animals living near the dark tarry highways seek them out at night. The roads stayed warm for hours after the desert cooled. The road was thick with snakes that took advantage of the heat. Henna remained optimistic that she'd find an inland taipan. She drove the rented HiLux slowly. She turned on the high beams and let her mind relax. As the sun set and the desert sands cooled, she willed the snake to seek the heat of the road.

There.

Henna leapt from the truck to inspect the first snake of the evening. Not a taipan—a desert-phase death adder. Henna used a long hook to manipulate the fat orange snake into a pillowcase. Once inside, she tied the top closed and placed the snake inside a large plastic tub. Fifty meters down the road she came across a red-naped snake. She handled it gently with the hook but didn't collect it. The snake's venom was both mild and common. Next came a bandy. She admired the black and white snake but left it undisturbed. Henna learned road hunting in the Anza Borrego desert. She'd used the technique successfully in Mexico and Columbia. She was never disappointed.

What a variety and density of animals.

Before long, Henna didn't get out of the truck to identify the cold-blooded menagerie. To explore the most area, she stayed in the truck unless she saw an animal to collect or one that would likely be hit by a car. Henna slowed to identify a woma, then sprung out to photograph a curl snake. As she put the snake in a pillowcase, she saw movement a few feet away.

An eastern tiger snake.

The thick reptile was road-warm and grumpy. It took a while to get it in a pillowcase. The moment she tied that pillowcase shut she saw something else in the road. Something big—ambling toward her. Henna stepped into the HiLux and backed up. She focused the headlights at the newcomer and sucked in her breath—an enormous perentie! A Stimpson's python dangled, half swallowed, from the monitor's jaws. The lizard noticed the truck. Head high, it ran off the road. It wanted to swallow the rest of the snake in peace. Without the benefit of a tranquilizer, the two meter long perentie would be a handful, but Henna felt up for it. She strapped her satchel tightly across her left side to protect her from the monitor's long tail and aimed the headlights at the monster so she could see well in the battle to come. The monitor stopped a few meters off the road. It worked hurriedly to gulp down the snake. Henna approached from behind and jumped on top of the lizard. She forced the beast's right rear leg straight and pinned its body with her knees. The monster smelled of rot and dust. If it bit her she was in trouble.

It worked.

The perentie could only lash its tail to the left. The satchel took the brunt of the impacts and she pinned the animal's long neck to the sand with her left hand. The lizard struggled to bite her, but the python was in the way. Henna quickly collected the biofilm scrapings and saliva she needed. When the animal stopped struggling, she released it. Henna encountered monitors throughout Indonesia and Asia. The samples from the perentie could be compared to the others. It was a good night. The inland taipan gave her a reason to come back.

When Henna returned to Edinburgh, she set up permanent enclosures for each new addition. The trio of tiny octopuses was amazing to watch. They were so intelligent. She hired a grad student to log the animal's behaviors. She hoped the colorful invertebrates would breed in captivity. Two of the three were females. Since their lifespan was only two years, providing a breeding environment was a top priority. She would study TTX levels in each generation, to measure if the species lost their defenses in a captive environment. Henna didn't organize her collection by species—she organized species by toxin. Each blue-ring was roughly the size of a chicken egg. They studied their enclosure methodically. Henna imagined the intelligent trio formulating an escape plan as they surveyed their neighbors. The TTX-laden moon snails were unlikely accomplices, although the snails did have the sense to migrate as far as they could from the octopuses. The octopuses next focused on the nearby comedians of the TTX collection, *Taricha granulosa;* the male rough-skinned newts staged slippery Greco-Roman struggles to impress the female newts, but promptly forgot about wrestling when Henna tapped some crickets into their vivarium.

The octopuses seemed to conspire in a huddle. They quietly reached consensus—they were on their own.

Henna kept some of her TTX collection in the laboratory deep freezer. Starfish, worms, puffer fish—she was thrilled to bring live animals home, but there was only so much room. Henna smiled at the blue-rings. When she'd bought drinks for the divers at the open-air bar on Fraser Island she told them a story about a dragon. She'd scraped biofilm from the teeth of a tranquilized Komodo dragon. When she got to the exciting part of the story, one of the fishermen paused to throw his half-empty bottle of beer at a dingo that sniffed at Henna's satchel.

Life was strange.

Her audience hadn't realized it, but the dingo story was better. The divers stayed and drank more. They exchanged contact information. The octopuses hadn't cost her a dime.

She probably had the dingo to thank.

Henna checked the time. It was late. It was a nice night, so she decided to walk to her loft.

Henna passed a bar on the way. A student she recognized from the university stood smoking outside. He was inebriated, but polite. She spoke with him for a moment before moving on. Then, no longer polite—

"Come back. I'll buy you a drink."

"No. Thanks." Henna walked faster.

"Oh. She's too good to drink with me. Are you? Are you too good?"

Henna moved faster. Most of the businesses were closed. She jogged. He jogged.

She ran.

He ran.

Henna held on to her satchel and sprinted. Her lungs burned. She heard him falling behind, but he didn't stop. He wasn't just trying to catch up—he wanted to harm her. She dodged some people on the sidewalk in front of another bar. Two guys and a girl. She spun. "That guy's after me. Please help me!" One of them laughed, but one—maybe a bouncer—didn't.

"You don't know him?" The guy was almost on them. Henna ran. The bouncer yelled after them but didn't—or perhaps couldn't run. His footsteps closed in. A Middle Eastern man opened the door of a car nearby. Henna ran for him—

"Help me! Please! Can you help me?" The man got into his car quickly and locked the doors. Henna raced by the car. He avoided eye contact.

Just feet behind me. He's going to catch me.

She dropped her satchel and flew down Fleshmarket Close. She had her keys in her hand and fumbled with them to contrive a weapon. She bounded, terrified, down the stairs.

"Help me—please someone—help me!"

A woman in a garish dress heard her. She was already headed up the stairs, but now she bounded up—the roar of a Berserker barely preceding her mass—four stairs at a time. The woman grew as she came closer. She left no doubt regarding her intent nor destination. Suddenly she pulled off her hair and tossed it behind her. Henna blinked.

A wig?

It wasn't a woman at all. It was a very large man in high heels. He passed Henna like an elephant in musth—momentarily crazed—enraged enough to stomp a usually beloved mahout into the earth like an unlucky man-seed at planting time, only this was not the mahout.

This was the enemy.

She was pulled toward him for a moment as he displaced the dank mineral air in the alleyway, the vacuum a taxicab creates when it has sped by too close. A body hit the stone steps just behind her. Henna collapsed against the wall. The drag queen was easily over seven feet tall in the heels, but with the wig off, he was nothing but man.

"Get off me, you nancy!" The drag queen knelt on the guy's head. Somehow he'd incapacitated her aggressor with the fingers of just one hand.

"See? That isn't nice." The enormous cross-dresser adjusted his chest. He'd lost a breast sprinting up the stairs. "How far did he chase you? His heart rate is about 160."

Henna shook her head, too out of breath to answer.

"Bugger off, queenie!"

The tall man's beautiful face changed. "Well, let's slow you down a bit."

Finger bones cracked. The guy struggled to fight back, but it was like fighting a living monument. The man in drag picked Henna's would-be assailant up like a rag doll. He pinned him against the stone wall with a forearm and drove his knee up, delivering devastating blows to the drunk's ribs. He tilted his head—a lion assessing damage he'd done to an unfortunate jackal. He palmed the broken man's face as easy as a softball and eased him to the steps. "Are you done now?" The man couldn't talk. He curled and moaned. "Silly bloke," the man offered with a London accent. "The dress always fools them—they don't think us girls will fight, but we always do."

"My bag. I dropped. My bag." Henna managed.

The tall man swept his fingers across the downed hairpiece to fix the part but didn't put it on. Instead, he offered Henna his arm. "Let's go get it."

After they retrieved Henna's satchel, the man walked her the rest of the way home. He was a Krav Maga instructor. He'd just moved to Edinburgh as well.

"From a little town near Lake Geneva."

"Wait a minute..." Henna looked more closely at his face "...the frog guy? Did you study in Lausanne?"

"Yes—"

"I know you. Dendrobates tinctorius? Stephan?"

It was him.

Stephan accepted a teaching job in Edinburgh when he wasn't invited to participate in the toxicology program at EPFL.

"You're that girl? Sorry—that sounded incredulous. And you're obviously not a well—a girl—it's just that, well, you've grown up."

They stood outside Henna's loft. They talked for a long time. Stephan held his wig in his hand. He gesticulated with it like a man holding a football after a winning game. "They're growing the department here. The toxicology department I mean—I've got an interview with the new chair of the department next week. Professor Maxwell, I think. I haven't met her yet, but I'm praying my interview goes well—I don't mind teaching, but I love research."

"I'm sure you'll get it. I'd bet my own money on it."

"Thanks. That means a lot. Listen, I've been dominating this conversation. You're also at the university? What department?"

"Yours. I'm Henna Maxwell." They laughed until they had tears in their eyes. Stephan invited her to his martial arts gym and wished her good night.

"We meet Mondays and Wednesdays—late Sunday nights. It is a good workout. Everyone's welcome."

Henna went on Wednesday. The two became fast friends. Stephan taught Henna how to fight dirty, and she taught him to write grants. When Stephan wasn't impersonating Marilyn Monroe, he was a regular badass. He was stoic when others were around, but when they

112

were alone, he was a comedian. He loved to impersonate lab animals. He assigned each one a hilarious voice and did accents well. The blue-rings spoke with an Irish brogue and had frequent arguments with the cockney-voiced newts. The moon snails replied to all inquiries with "scissors please" in an East Indian accent. When he channeled one-liners for the animals, Henna laughed like she never had before. He joked that they didn't want to share her with him.

The male blue-ring was particularly jealous.

~Fork-Tongued Children

Rupert closed the office for business while the snake-eyed Germans sold assets. The men wrote figures on a dry erase board for Rupert. His only job was to add numbers—the Germans did everything else better than he did.

He never saw them eat. He doubted if they slept. When the business day ended in the United States, it opened in Asia. The men worked tirelessly. They did big business in the middle of the night, perhaps even better than they did in the daytime. Each asset was sold without ceremony, but Rupert noticed that the stoic duo did have small personal rituals. When Ryker sold a large asset, he stood and stretched his lower back. Rickard rewarded his financial heroics with a new piece of chewing gum. Rupert just tried to maintain by drinking pot after pot of coffee. He kept a running total on an adding machine, so if he made a mistake he could fix it. The Germans drank filtered tap water out of coffee cups. They'd even brought the filter with them. Rupert felt very out of his league. Troy said he'd recruited the duo straight out of MIT—come to find out, the men weren't even lawyers.

They were wizards. The gray matter equivalents of planetary gears.

While Rupert watched, Rickard pulled up a high dollar auction on his monitor. His fingers flew across the keyboard. An illusion was born. It appeared as though a crowd of international investors bid on the fleet of Asian cargo ships, though only one investor in Singapore was logged on to the auction. Rickard pointed Rupert to a digital clock on the screen. Minutes passed. When the clock ran out, a banner above the auction read: bid complete. Rickard dialed a phone number on his headset and placed a confirmation call to the buyer. Rickard congratulated the investor and read a confirmation then gave instructions on how to transfer funds electronically. He opened a piece of gum. He waited to pop it into his mouth until the funds posted. He placed the old gum in the new wrapper. He folded the foil-coated paper elegantly around the refuse as if it were museum-grade origami and opened the next auction.

Ryker stood. He sipped water from his cup and wrote a figure on the dry erase board. The golf course in Colorado sold for $11,000,000.00—forty percent above the projected goal. In minutes,

Rickard liquidated the ranch in South Dakota. Hundreds of millions of dollars an hour were posted to an account, and they'd been going for days. Rupert secretly nicknamed the duo "R&R" however when the job was done, he doubted they'd kick their feet up on a beach and lie low. They were the variety of men who created movement in underworld finance.

He imagined them tucked into a glass building. They would choose a place with a nice view so they could ignore it—perhaps somewhere in a city overlooking a historic bridge. They would amuse themselves by hacking government files. Once that became tiresome, they would perfect teleportation. Rupert imagined Rickard whistling minty breath into the oval office as he rolled up the big blue rug, tossed it on his shoulder, and beamed himself home. They might use the pedigreed rug for a shower mat and stand barefoot on the icon while they dabbed at their scaly bodies freshly soaked in stolen French spring water. Rupert shook his head. He'd lost any misconceptions of normalcy quickly. Nothing was anymore. Even the numbers on the adding machine didn't seem real. What was he to tell his wife? It was like monopoly money, with dozens more zeros. Shouldn't he be happy?

Three percent of the total was his. He didn't feel happy. He felt terrified.

Twice in the past week Ryker used a satellite phone when money wasn't transferred by an agreed time. Who in the hell did these guys call for help? Rupert didn't want to know.

The sooner they were done, the better.

Two days later, a third call was placed on the satellite phone. Ryker made cold, direct eye contact with Rupert while he dialed; a protective, primordial film seemed to ooze toward the man's pupils, stopping just short of each feral void as the apertures adjusted, finely tuning information: the attorney's distance, potential burst speed, and willingness to engage. He spoke in a language Rupert didn't recognize. When he finished the call, he blinked at Rupert slowly. He then spoke to the older man as if he were a child. "The most effective parenting allows one warning for misbehavior."

Rickard nodded. He put his call on hold to add his two cents worth. "Followed by severe consequences if the misbehavior isn't corrected."

Ryker's eyes never left Rupert. "One warning." Rupert felt a cold shiver. This was no anecdotal lesson—

This was his one warning.

He hadn't done anything he knew of that seemed satellite phone call worthy. Perhaps the Germans decided to give him a warning first. Rupert doubted Ryker would call anyone if he messed up. They'd surely handle local problems themselves. He imagined the Germans emerging from a leathery clutch of cobra eggs. The man-snakes entered the world seconds apart. Each slit his way to fresh air with a stiletto egg tooth. Back-to-back, hoods open, they swallowed their emerging siblings one by one. Each victim became a limb. Soon, they sat alone—armored golems.

Fork-tongued children.

In nine days, it was done. Each man watched a monitor as his respective three percent was transferred to an offshore account. Ryker went to retrieve the water filter from the kitchenette while Rickard explained Rupert's account. As a favor, they'd started a company for Rupert. An insurance company. "Malay Industrial Qualifiers" would be based in a skyscraper in Johor Bahru. The building would have sixty-eight stories. The foundation work alone would take two years to complete. After year eight, when the project was complete, the insurance company would stop taking construction losses. Rupert would declare bankruptcy. He'd sell the building for a premium, however, as it was a booming region. As sole owner, Rupert would pay himself a monthly salary of $510,000.00. To legitimize this income, he would attend quarterly meetings by telephone and fly to Malaysia once a year. On March 29 of the ninth year, a new construction project would be explained and his monthly salary would increase to $2,102,000.00.

Ryker returned from the kitchenette. He wiped down the water filter and put it in his briefcase. He handed Rupert two Irish passports. One had Rupert's picture inside, but the name on the document was Aaron Musselli. Rupert flipped through the passport. His Irish doppelgänger was well travelled: he'd been to Paris, Amsterdam, and Chicago in the past year. The second passport was for his wife. She had more expensive taste. In addition to the trips she took with "Aaron" she'd visited Fiji, Barbados, and Las Vegas. Rupert didn't ask why his fictitious last name sounded like a Swiss cereal. He didn't ask why the passports were Irish. He knew the identities were necessary to insulate him from paper trails—to protect them all from big brother's helpful oversight.

This was the new normal. This was how it worked.

Rupert watched for the correct moment to thank the Germans, but coffee cups in hand, the men left without a word. Rupert looked out the window. The Germans slid into a rented Tercel. Each man buckled his seat belt before the car cautiously entered traffic. Alone at last, Rupert felt amazed. The number at the bottom line of the adding machine was absurd. He subtracted nine percent, then shook his head with smoothly accelerating incredulity. The Germans were magicians. Bonn Maddox was worth several hundred billion dollars, yet as far as the State of New York was concerned, Bonn would only receive $3,825,633.00 a year for the next twenty years—the sum of Troy's documented estate.

The house. The ship. Troy's retirement fund and life insurance.

The boy had immediate and unlimited access to the fund.

It was staggering.

Rupert looked at his desk phone. Besides Bonn, there hadn't been calls for days.

No messages.

Rupert would have to hire some lawyers to keep up appearances … or would he? Why not sell the building and farm out any existing business? Maybe he'd relax a bit. He wondered what Malaysia was like. Maybe he and his wife would actually go to Fiji. Rupert pulled the phone onto his lap. For the first time in his life, he swung his feet onto his desk. His old oxblood penny loafers looked good up there. He'd taken them to be resoled many times. Although the current fashion was loafers without socks, Rupert wore them.

He always would.

Rupert bought the shoes thirty-one years ago—the day he graduated from law school. His daughter was only a month old at the time. The shoes were a big expenditure back then. Rupert leaned forward to pull a baby food jar out of a drawer. It was full of pennies. On New Year's Day each year he'd pried the old pennies out of the shoes with a letter opener and put them in the jar. He'd shine the shoes then put sparkling new pennies in. The jar still had the label on it: *Blueberry Buckle.* It had been his daughter's favorite. After the shoe ritual each year, Rupert cut loose in his own way. He took one drink of cherry liqueur. He was a simple man—

A superstitious man.

Superstition and routine served him well. Though it wasn't January, Rupert pulled out the bottle of Heering and removed the cork. He took a drink right from the bottle and shook the penny jar.

The coins gave a nice rattle.

Rupert sat the jar on his desk and looked back to the phone in his lap. He felt the alcohol already, the oily warmth seeping comfortably throughout his brain.

It was so quiet now without the Germans here.

Rupert took another pull from the bottle to celebrate their absence.

No matter. He'd take a taxicab home.

He let his eyes drift from the keypad on the adding machine to the keypad on the telephone. Absent minded, he tapped Bonn's annual trust fund revenue into the keys on the phone. He was good at word jumbles. Now he'd have time to do the one in the paper every day. He tried to spell something from the letters corresponding to each number. 3-8-2-5-6-3-3. Rupert shook his head and grinned.

It was obvious.

3-8-2-5-6-3-3 became F-U-C-K-O-F-F. R&R's message to the tax collector.

The "Tax Man" would never be privy to Bonn's actual wealth.

~Mantle-Wolf

Henna was headed to Diego Garcia. From the airport she called to check on Alvar. He was fine. So was the curly-faced puppy. The cashmere goats had multiplied.

"The kids are earmarked for a lady nearby. She has a spinning wheel." Alvar sounded vibrant. Involved. He had projects. He'd traded the goats for beehives. "I'm going to put up some wildflower honey. Lots of beeswax. Do you want me to send you some wax? I'm anticipating about thirty kilograms."

"Save some for me there, Grandpa. If you keep it in slabs, we can filter it together when I come home."

He sounded young again.

Clear—like the man who'd taken her in nineteen years ago. Alvar was a gentleman. He'd never press Henna to visit, but he sounded happy that she'd declared a possible visit on the horizon. He sounded lighthearted. "You said you were at the airport? A grand adventure, I hope."

Henna explained. "Renegade fishermen on the outskirts of Diego Garcia have been dragging everything up from the seafloor. I read an article about sustainability and in one picture I saw a species that isn't in books yet."

"Renegades, huh?" The lightness in Alvar's voice was gone. "Diego Garcia is remote enough. I don't like the sound of 'outskirts' at all."

After an uncomfortable pause, Alvar forced some levity back into his voice. "I'll be excited to hear about the discovery, though—I guess most remaining discoveries are in some 'outskirt' or another." Something seemed off. Henna couldn't place it. She considered asking Alvar if she shouldn't go. She didn't know much about Diego Garcia aside from the island's military history. Henna hung up unsure about the trip. Her intuition told her to cash in the ticket.

Go home. Take a bath. Sit down at a hotel for a full Scottish breakfast. Sip mineral water the rest of the day. Poke around a bookshop.

But why shouldn't she go? Diego Garcia was now a military atoll. In her pocket she carried a fax, which granted her permission to collect any unknown species from the marine protected area. She knew fisherman—they had a code. She'd be fine, wouldn't she? She called Stephan, regardless. If Stephan felt she shouldn't go, she wouldn't go. Her phone rang. It was Stephan. "I was just getting ready to call you."

Stephan was in a joking mood. "I have a checklist we should review before you board. Ready?"

"Yes."

"Hand sanitizer?"

"Check."

"Jaguar-print panties?"

Henna laughed. "Going commando, mate—no laundry services on boats." Usual banter followed. Henna congratulated Stephan on his recent grant. He brought money into the university now.

"I'm going to write one while you're gone. I think we'd benefit from some of that coffee that's already traveled through an elephant before they roast the beans. It's expensive, but now that I'm getting good at this grant writing thing I should test myself." Stephan didn't offer warnings. He was nothing but encouraging. Henna felt better.

He'd know if something bad awaited her.

Henna was no martial savant like Stephan, but she felt confident in the failsafe techniques he'd taught her. Quick fight-enders. They routinely did drills. Stephan tested her skills with random attacks. The first time he'd done it, she got angry. "I wasn't ready!"

Stephan smiled. "We never are. That's why it's called 'defense.' When you're truly ready it becomes offense looking for a reason to justify itself as defense. I can teach you offense, but you're really organized. It may feel a bit more like premeditated murder."

He was right. Random was better.

Sometimes she was bested. Sometimes she fended him off. She always learned. Stephan insisted she counter his attacks with full contact. When she did well, he needed ice packs. They traditionally ate gelato and watched old black-and-white movies while he recuperated. It felt brutal, but Stephan was a hardened man. He could take it. It allowed Henna to learn how to actually fight, but in a safe environment. Of gifts to give another person, there were few greater.

Stephan signed off without giving her an ominous warning. Henna dismissed her hesitations. She was quite early at her gate. She dozed off. She dreamed of Mortimer and the mantle-wolf. In her dream the wolf skin came alive. It peeled itself from the wall and dropped onto Mortimer's dead body. The large dog absorbed the skin of his conquered foe. A hybrid beast arose, gasping dead, fetid breath—breath hotter even than the fire licking at the hearth. Embers glowed on each matted tip of the creature's mane. As the hellhound turned to face her, the glowing firebrands became the heads of venomous snakes. Adders and vipers hissed hatred and vitriol in every direction. Vestiges of Mortimer were gone. The beast's jaws yawned open. Its great glass teeth clicked and foamed. Its face grew longer. It appeared part wolf, part Komodo dragon. Foam spittle churned from the demon's mouth in jagged coughs. The wood skinned floor beneath the wolf was blackened. The foam was acid. The floor hissed and fell away. A necrotic maw opened in the crumbled earth beneath. The thing scrambled for purchase. It was Mortimer again. He struggled to claw his way to safety. Mortimer fought the beast from inside his corpse. The lion-dog looked plaintively at the spot above the mantle where the wolf pelt should be, then turned to Henna, frightened.

He was losing.

He panted and whined. He was exhausted. In a last great effort, he pulled himself from the hole and turned to look at it. He wagged a moment, then shook his mane. The firebrands spread. He began to burn. The heads of the snakes bleated like sheep and struggled to escape the flames. The snakeheads birthed themselves from scaly hair-stalks to become fire-bees—

"Gate 64 now boarding."

Henna sat up. Heart racing, mouth parched—she tasted fear and blood in the back of her throat. It took her a few moments to realize there was no monster. People jockeyed for position in line.

Get up and move.

Henna closed her eyes. Mortimer remained. He wagged at her from the backs of her eyelids, like an overexposed negative in various tones of red, orange, and pink. His fangs were broken glass. He puffed out his cheeks and looked at the mantle, telling the first half of their story. Henna followed his gaze to the mantle and saw herself hanging there. Her own skin. Pale, mottled leather—hollow eyes, small—her skin from childhood. Dirt from the garden wedged beneath her fingernails—one hand clutched a paring knife. Curly soft hair floated like dandelion fluff above her rancid blue-black scalp.

The attendant called Henna's row. She stood to board the plane. As she entered the jet way, she felt committed. People bumped into each other as they shuffled along, looking forward to the comfort of seats they'd soon realize were too cramped. Henna felt tired. She

121

found her seat and buckled herself in. She needed to close her eyes again, but didn't want to return to the dream.

It wasn't real. It wasn't symbolic. It was just stress. Doubt.

She suffered an amazing imagination. The dream was just that, wasn't it? Stress, combined with imagination?

Not a premonition.

The plane took off. It gained altitude and leveled off the way it should. Henna started to relax. She meditated a bit to clear her mind. She focused on the thought of a field—a light breeze waved neat rows of meadowsweet. Nothing bad lurked out of view. There was no wolf.

But there was.

He waited for her to go deeper. He waited for her muscles to freeze so she couldn't escape, then he eased his glass fangs into her meat and the hole took them. When Henna fell into the abyss, she fell with the wolf. They fell together through the hole in the blackened skin-wood floor, and they landed together in her grandfather's hut. No longer a woman, Henna was a jumbled pile of bone and sinew. The blackened soft skin of the blue jay bounced from the pile and stuck to precious things. She watched the wolf paw through her rotting self from a shelf nearby. It was a real wolf. It sorted through her putrid parts as though he revisited a kill. The wolf turned from the task, mouth full of her, to glance at her shelf-self. He gazed at her as he chewed. He had her grandfather's glass eyes. When he spoke, it was Alvar's voice.

You promised me. You promised me you'd watch him.

~Evolution

College courses would achieve portions of Bonn's goals, but not all of them. New York City had the most resources to hone his other skills, so that's where Bonn went. He didn't declare a major, but studied physics and engineering. Bonn didn't care if he graduated— he simply wanted the knowledge. He sought out extreme fitness and improved his machinist skills. Bonn knew where things were headed for him. He watched the news. Murderers and rapists were acquitted at accelerating rates. These were not hidden stories: James Porter, known fondler, rapist, Catholic priest, amassed 160 or more victims. He bumped against the law for decades. The law ever-so-gently—so fairly—with fashionable kind civility bumped back, but didn't remove him from the public for long. A few months here, a few years there, then back again.

Massachusetts, Texas, New Mexico, Minnesota. He's reformed now. OK, not then, but now. Now he's reformed. It's truer because we said it twice. We are sure this time. Whoops, we were wrong, but now we are certain. Certain is a bigger word than sure, so rest assured, James Porter is not a danger any longer. We are certain, and our specific certainty we have reached, at this particular time, is indelible. Stop diddling kids, James—you are making both the system and the church look bad.

They could have killed him on the spot—either the system, or the church. It had been done before. That Porter made it out of Texas alive was amazing.

Could have? They should have. One was enough—160?

Mothers killed their kids and blamed it on hormones. A man ate some junk-food, so a premeditated murder was downgraded to voluntary manslaughter. These were hugely public cases. Police? Many times found above the law. Reports discounted. The uniform shielded even those who didn't deserve to wear it. They were still criminals, left to act outside the law without repercussion. Many for decades. Bonn intended to *be* that repercussion. Hell, he intended to be proactive. No one else was going to do it. He reached his tipping point early. He had attended celebrations intended to laud his father's grasp of that one loose legal thread. The legal system failed true citizens every day. Lawyers like Troy played dirty games to get their clients off. Judges and lawmakers were too afraid to uphold the law, unable to focus, too removed from crime to remember what mattered. Bonn knew—only one thing mattered.

Justice.

Maybe he wouldn't make big differences at first. It would take him some time to get up to speed. He could play dirty too, but the time for games was over.

Bonn walked through Central Park often. He liked the trees. He liked seeing people walk by, yet the idea of interacting with any of them was distasteful. He didn't need people. He didn't feel like a person himself—more of an extension of the Bill of Rights.

A living extension.

One fall day a family walked ahead of him on a trail. A whole family. A mother and father marched arm-in-arm while a small girl ran zigzags out front. She called each discovery back to her parents. Although she had the speech of a toddler, she explored with utter confidence. Bonn slowed his pace to watch. The girl picked up a stick. The mother called out, "Be careful." The girl wasn't careful. She ran with her wand and swung it very close to her eyes while she did. The man surged ahead and grabbed it and broke the sharp pieces off. When he gave it back, the tiny adventurer held it aloft and ran triumphantly. The couple laughed. The girl seemed to have—even to *be*—pure joy. She had a gentle father and a mother who cared if she got hurt. They let her take calculated chances. They had found the sweet spot that left her spirit intact.

It was the perfect way to learn about the world.

Bonn was now close to the family.

Too close?

The man saw him and gave his wife a tap on the hip. Without fanfare, he gracefully stepped in-between Bonn and his family. He managed a smile. "Good morning." He had curly hair. He wore his mustache exactly like Eugen Sandow wore his.

Bonn nodded. "Good morning."

The man seemed like a perfect father. A good husband. He would protect his family. He cared if his wife was happy. He inspired glee in the tiny girl. The epiphany buckled him: Bonn had nothing in common with Eugen Sandow. He was nothing like him. Sandow was a show boater. An exhibitionist—some even speculated he was bisexual. Bonn didn't identify with any of that. Bonn gave a wide berth to the family. He sped up so the Sandow lookalike could relax. He later pulled the card from his pocket to look at Eugen. He felt nothing. The usual and euphoric comfort, the idea of the man as a shield worthy of worship, the photograph proof that the marvelous ideal had ever been real? The feelings were gone. He was just a man. A man he wanted to be nothing like. In a moment of rare introspection, Bonn realized he'd tried to turn Sandow into his father—back when he'd needed one. Manny, however, had been like a real father to him. Manny and Linda were both gracious. Kind. Gentle and funny. Supportive. Consistent.

They were what every child deserved.

The realization fresh, Bonn did something he never dreamed he'd do. He folded Eugen Sandow in half and shoved the card in his wallet as if it were change from a street vendor.

That would've made Troy furious. He'd have come unhinged.

Bonn had Manny and Linda. He'd care for them.

He didn't need Sandow anymore.

When Bonn wasn't studying, he exercised. Bursts of intensity throughout the day seemed most effective. He varied movements so his body couldn't become accustomed to any one thing. The city had every type of gym Bonn could imagine. Some useful and some not. Bonn harvested techniques from many sources, but preferred to practice alone. Kendo taught him timing: when one struck was more important and the item *with which* one struck mattered little. Kung fu taught him speed. In addition, it offered techniques to harden his body. Both Kendo and Kung fu bordered on religion for its practitioners, however, but Bonn didn't seek religion. He didn't trust those who took their own religion too seriously. Faith was different. It was more like optimism, and Bonn had plenty of that. Boxing was good burst exercise, but there were lots of rules. Bonn didn't want to be "a boxer." Once he realized the best way to knock out your opponent was to cheat, he quit. Cheating made sense when your life was at stake. Cheating was smart. Rules wouldn't get him where he was going. In the darkest times, those who walked away were the ones who won quickly.

Efficiently.

He wanted tricks. Judo had a lot of them, so he studied it extensively.

Bonn took one Tae kwon do class.

Kicking things seemed inefficient.

The grandmaster had an obvious need to stroke his own ego. He attempted to dominate the fit newcomer to impress the regular students. Bonn followed his instructions and dutifully held a pad out for the man to demonstrate a spinning back kick. Then, just as the instructor started his spin, Bonn stepped in low and fast. He put his shoulder into the man's groin and hoisted him for a moment, then took him to the mat, hard. His opponent attempted to escape, but Bonn choked him unconscious.

When the man awoke, he was both humiliated and furious. "You cheated! There are rules in this discipline. There are methods. You think you're ready to spar with me?" Bonn stood quietly while the man adjusted his uniform. "How dare you. This is my gym. My rules. You want me? Let's go!"

The more the grandmaster ranted, Bonn realized, the less he had to learn from him. This was no battle-worn soldier. This guy smelled nice, sort of floral. Still, there might be an opportunity to learn something. If the guy had a trick, he'd use it now.

"OK," Bonn said in what he hoped was a deferent tone. "Let me know when you are ready."

"Ready for what?"

"Ready for anything. Ready for me to attack you. Get yourself ready. Let me know when you are. It's your gym. Just give me a nod, or a bow, or whatever makes you feel prepared for what's to come so I know when we've started."

The man fussed about. He put in a mouth guard. He jumped up and down. He stretched. He walked back and forth and popped his hands in and out of fists. It became apparent he was unable to formulate an attack, so Bonn baited him. He turned his back to the man and yawned. The Japanese hero Miyamoto Musashi might use better techniques to get inside an opponent's head, but Bonn couldn't think of one offhand.

It didn't matter. The grandmaster had lost already.

He'd let his own fear, his own self-doubt in. In addition, he had needs. He needed to save face in front of his students. His reputation—his very livelihood—depended on how the next few moments played out. Bonn, however, had something to gain if he lost the contest. He lay on his back and slid his hands behind his head. The students looked pensive and tense.

126

"Tae kwon do is an art form!"

That sounded like a disclaimer.

The students had honest faces. These weren't Olympic hopefuls, just people hoping to learn some defense skills.

It was a shameful charade.

Shortly, the gym owner would prove himself an impotent blowhard and they'd realize the time they'd wasted. He pitied them. They sought empowerment, but found this charlatan—glad to take their money. Pleased to bully them in scripted ways.

"Stand up! You need to leave!" The instructor seemed adequately enraged, so Bonn stood.

"It's your gym. Let's spar on your terms."

The man leered. He adopted a silly stance. Bonn threw a slow and sloppy right-handed haymaker. Most choreographed attacks in martial arts classes began with similar nonsense moves. The man stepped left and performed an inside block. Bonn's right kidney was exposed. His foe attempted a right-handed jab. In a flash, Bonn had the man's right wrist in a lock. He yanked down sharply, then up and to the side, then stepped back with his right foot and pivoted hard toward his adversary with his left leg, driving his left palm into the man's right elbow. Once contact was made with the elbow, Bonn slammed his rival facedown on the mat. The stunned man tried to turtle. He pulled his left arm in to protect his neck and tucked his legs beneath his body so they couldn't be used against him. Bonn shifted his left hand up to the man's shoulder and released his grip on his wrist. He shot his arm under the man's chin and grabbed the collar of his uniform. He stepped over the immobilized man's head with his right foot and used his arm for leverage. He choked the man-turtle until he became limp. When movement ceased, Bonn placed him in recovery position. He watched closely until he began to breathe again. "I guess I've got the hang of it." The speed of Kung fu, the techniques of Judo, the strategy of Kendo ... Tae kwon do, however?

Useless.

It was not, however, wasted time. He did feel inspired to read more about Miyamoto Musashi. The drooling black-belt on the floor may have performed better if he hadn't been enraged. Today he learned something about fight psychology. Bonn considered the crumpled man and glanced at his stunned classmates. Inspiration came soon enough. He removed the man's garish black belt.

Bonn had no interest in posturing or a gentleman's battle. He didn't intend to learn a new "art form."

He hog-tied the grandmaster with the showy belt. Once finished, he waved the students over to show them how to untie the knot. Two students, both boys, wore grins ear to ear. One had a hard time containing laughter. "When should we untie him?" Bonn regarded the small boy. It was likely the child was sent here by parents hoping to encourage an intact self-esteem.

"Whenever you like. If left to me, I'd wait until he verbalizes something approximating humility." The boy blinked and smiled so big Bonn could count his teeth.

"Judo's kind of fun," Bonn added. "Go try it out."

~Homesick

On a layover Henna reread the article that inspired her trip. An advocate of sustainable fishing practices wrote it. The article argued that though cumbersome, the need to establish an infrastructure to successfully police protected waters was crucial. Many marine parks had poorly defined borders. Add a lack of consequences for lawbreakers? A free-for-all. Diego Garcia was only one example of the all too common problem. The British Indian Ocean Territory administration in London frowned upon commercial fishing near the military base but didn't take action. Soon they might declare the atoll and surrounding areas entirely free from commercial fishing, but neither UK personnel or US troops were prepared to patrol the waters. Since boats came from as far away as Zanzibar, it would be difficult and expensive to enforce a ban. Many of the Chagossians evicted from Diego Garcia in the 1960s found work fishing. They knew the waters. After all, they used to fish the area to subsist. Since they couldn't come back to the island itself, they came back to their waters in boats. Big boats. With big ice machines. Boats that carried metric tons of exotic seafood away on ice.

Hungry mouths don't ask questions.

Henna studied a picture captioned: Bycatch in Uncertain Waters. A dark-skinned fisherman posed with a shallow basket brimming with sea life. One of the snails, a fish eating species, appeared to be an enormous *Conus geographicus*. It wasn't, however.

It was something new.

Well, new wasn't correct—the Chaggosians probably had a name for it. It was, however, not a species known to the scientific community. She couldn't clearly see the pattern on the shell, but it was certainly a *Conus*. It looked longer than typical—and darker.

Recently, some of the boats led to the atoll by the ousted Chagossians began dragging heavy iron bars over the seafloor. It was wrecking fish habitats. Everything the bar pulverized floated into a fine mesh net. Sea turtles drowned by the thousands. The article had various photographs of fishermen posing with drowned turtles. In a particularly distasteful one, a young man sat astride the wide back of a dead hawksbill like a bronco buster—he looked happy. He smoked a cigarette while he dug his heels into his majestic victim. Though illegal, the turtle would bring a premium on the black market. This type of gruesome picture was the spark environmentalists needed. It woke up the public. A toll-free number allowed wealthy, sympathetic callers to pledge money to stop the practice. It was a grassroots operation. When Henna called the number, the author herself answered. Henna made a donation and kept the woman on the line for a while.

"There's a picture of a man holding a variety of bycatch in a basket. One of them is a cone snail—"

"Yeah—one of them zapped a guy when he stuck it in his pocket. Served him right." The turtle advocate paused, perhaps worried her enthusiasm for a human death wouldn't be well received. "He died quickly," she added in a solemn voice. "Who'd you say you were again?" Henna provided an alphabet of credentials. The woman brightened. "You think the snail's a new species? This is great! If it's rare I'll showcase that in a follow-up article. Would you stay in touch? I want to know what you find out. What if the snails hold the key to a new medicine or something? If that's the case, they're robbing us all."

Henna promised to stay in touch. The exuberant woman told her what she knew about Diego Garcia and the surrounding waters. She even gave Henna a place to start. There was a building in Malé where non-Muslim fishermen cut loose. It wasn't a bar—the local religion didn't allow them—but it was a good lead. Malé was the nearest port to have a boat serviced if anything malfunctioned.

Fishing boats always malfunctioned.

Each plane Henna took on the way to Malé was smaller than the last. She was glad to stretch her legs when the last one touched down. Henna found the building the woman told her about without much trouble. It was blue with a flat roof, just off the boat harbor. A young man sat on an empty crate by the door. He held a book. Henna suspected he was a gatekeeper of sorts. Since alcohol was banned in the Maldives, the tropical speakeasy needed a lookout.

"Salaam," Henna offered. The man startled. He was much younger than she thought. More boy than man. He looked up and then quickly looked away. Henna tried to guess his thoughts.

She obviously wasn't Muslim, so she may be there to drink, but she could also be a spy. If she were a tourist and he let her in, other tourists would soon overrun the place. She'd be the only woman in the bar if he did let her in. That made him nervous too. What has he got to lose?

130

Since he didn't know how to proceed, he employed a technique used by administrators worldwide: he ignored her. Henna spoke to the boy in Arabic. "I need a boat headed to Diego Garcia." He peeked up at her curiously out of the corner of his eye.

White tourists don't speak Arabic.

Henna stood tall and squared herself to the boy. He was a poor boy who spent too much time in the sun because he had to. There were obviously conditions she didn't meet to be allowed inside the building, or he would've let her in already. Henna let her mind relax. Like most problems, this was simply a puzzle. The boy looked Indonesian. He wasn't local. If he were local, his neighbors would ask him why he lingered here. She doubted he was Muslim. Henna looked at the boy's book. It was written in Arabic, but the binding was pristine.

Was the book a prop? Ahh. He can't read.

Henna spoke in Indonesian. "Do you miss home?"

Bingo.

His eyes flew wide. She'd correctly guessed his nationality. The boy began to sweat. He was clearly terrified. He forced his nose toward the middle of the book and turned his head side to side with furious exaggeration.

I'm reading, lady. I can't be bothered. Leave me alone.

Henna looked toward the harbor for a moment, then back to the boy. He glanced at Henna but kept his face sheltered inside the book. Then, almost imperceptibly, he nodded.

Yes. He missed home.

The boy's guilt-laden eyes darted about, as though punishment raced toward him, but he couldn't see it yet. Henna nodded back discreetly. "I need to find a boat headed to Diego Garcia. Is there anyone inside that can help me?" The boy nodded tentatively. He looked at the door and back to Henna. He frowned.

He wanted to help, but he couldn't.

"Do you know someone inside who has such a boat?" The boy's frown spread. He let the book drift down to his lap and his shoulders drooped. He nodded with unmistakable melancholy. There was nothing left for him to do. He shrugged his shoulders and opened his mouth.

Someone had cut out his tongue.

Henna nodded sadly. His meaning was clear.

He couldn't help if he wanted to.

131

The boy had taken risks to interact with her.

It was time for her to take one.

With a deep breath, Henna stepped past the boy and went through the door. The boy didn't try to stop her or follow her. She stood in a hallway of sorts. Rudimentary diving gear hung from hooks on the walls. A sour mildew smell hung in the room. Henna heard voices. A door was cracked open at the end of the hall. Slurred speech and laughter came from the room beyond. She walked through the door with confidence. It was dim inside. When her eyes adjusted, she saw an open chair at a table. She sat and nodded greetings to the men who gawked at her. There were two small tables in the room. Bottles of bootleg alcohol sat in the middle of each. A muscular man in a faded orange tee shirt approached her. He wore jeans rolled up to his knees and dingy white sandals.

"You must be lost," he said in English. "Come outside. I'll give you directions to your hotel."

Henna ignored his offer. "I'll buy a drink for everyone. I'm looking for a boat headed to the waters near Diego Garcia." Henna tossed £100.00 on the table. The climate in the room changed. A dirty glass was placed in front of her and she sipped the foul fluid politely. After a few minutes a short dark-skinned man in swim trunks and a sun visor spoke in his awkward English from the other side of the table.

"I take you. We do not land in Diego Garcia, but we fish nearby. It is expensive passage. What do you pay for this?"

"£400.00. I want to see the boat first."

"£700.00. You have private place on the boat."

"£500.00. I keep any specimens I want from your bycatch." The man smiled. He had uneven gold teeth. He approached and poured Henna's glass full of the evil alchemy resting in the nearest bottle.

"We drink to £500.00, but you bonus me a per-sample fish fee—twenty for big fish, ten for small fish."

"Snail shells," Henna countered. "Ten for each."

"No." The gold-toothed man poured his own glass full, "All shells twenty. Big fish fee." Henna struggled to down the drink. The short man tossed his down easily and poured even more into each glass. "Boat is nice. Nicest. Big. Safe for you. You pay now." Henna shook her head and stood to leave.

"We drank to the agreement already. I'll pay your captain after I see the boat. The drinks were on me so don't look for an advantage." The man frowned. The blood vessels in his neck bulged.

"Wait at dock. Freezer done soon. You pay me. I *am* captain." Henna made it outside before she vomited. The caustic liquor burned her again on the way out.

The boy was gone.

She walked awhile and found a woman selling bottles of water. She bought four of them and took greedy gulps from the first bottle. She tucked the rest into her satchel and made her way to the dock.

The man with the sun visor waved at her. "The freezer fixed. This is it. You see it? The boat. You pay now."

Henna stepped onto the rusty hulking vessel. The boy with the book was there. He held his hand out for her bag. Henna smiled but kept her satchel. The boy shrugged and let his arms hang limp. He looked at the deck as if wondering what to do. She pulled the captain's money from a pocket and paid him.

The tongueless boy led her to a small, light green room off the galley. A thin, stained mattress had been tossed on top of crates containing breadfruit, coconuts, bags of rice. The door had a lock on the inside and a vent in the ceiling. Henna nodded to the boy.

"It will work." Next, he showed her the head, usually reserved for the boat's kitchen staff. It was surprisingly modern. She turned a fixture. Clear water flowed into the stainless steel sink. The toilet had blue chemicals floating in the water. For a toilet used by fishermen, it looked clean.

"Thank you." The boy straightened for a moment. He gave her a small salute and a grin. As he walked away, however, his shoulders drooped and he appeared tiny—a mute orphan off to accept a beating. Henna locked the door to the head and ran the water in the sink. She held her hand in a scoop and tasted it. Her sinuses stung. Her eyes teared up. The water had too much bleach.

Better than none I guess.

She spat out the water, but refilled the empty bottles in her satchel anyway.

Should have bought more.

Henna took some deep, even breaths. She still felt woozy from the alcohol.

If she hadn't thrown up, she'd be in worse shape.

A deep horn sounded. The ship inched free from everything solid, from everything trustworthy. Creaking and thrumming sounds filled her head as she made her way to the storage room. Once inside, she saw that the lock was broken. She took some cord from her satchel. She tied one end around the door handle. A thick black pipe ran up the wall behind the boxes of breadfruit, and she looped the cord around it. She finished the improvised lock with a trucker's hitch. The smell of diesel exhaust came from the air vent. Henna's head felt brittle. She felt like she'd swallowed broken glass; somehow the jagged shards now rested just inside the back of her skull. Henna focused. She needed to think of something pleasant. Had this been a mistake?

The diesel fumes. They drowned the sting of the bleach.

It was all the optimism she could muster. Henna untied the hitch and opened the door. The fumes were everywhere, so she tied herself back in. Reaching into her satchel, things seemed backwards. As if even the piece of familiar luggage was playing tricks.

There.

The sarong had been in plain sight. Wrapped around the water bottles. Puffing out her cheeks, disgusted and woozy, Henna cast the thin layer across the filthy sleeping mat like a bait net and collapsed. The world spun. A thrumming drone increased as the big boat picked up speed.

Sleep would come quickly if she let it.

Henna hoped the wolves would leave her alone. She couldn't smell the fumes anymore and felt her guard dropping. Each blink stayed on a little longer. The ship's big engine slowed to a cruising speed. It settled into a deep iron heartbeat.

Maybe the sound would scare off wolves?

It was a very big boat. The *African Queen* would fit in the boat's kitchen. She'd watched the old Humphrey Bogart movie with Stephan. She wished he were here now. She pictured Stephan in the Maldives' clear waters. He had his shirt off. The imaginary Stephan pulled the boat into the Indian Ocean behind him, just like Humphrey Bogart did in the part of the movie when you thought all was lost. Stephan grew. Soon he was big as the Colossus of Rhodes. He casually pulled leeches the size of potato cod from his chest. He called back to Henna over his bus-sized shoulder. "It'll be OK, old girl. Nothing we can't deal with here." He continued to grow. As the water became deep, he grew proportionally. "Just a spot of trouble on the horizon, but we'll emerge from this just fine." Stephan was now a skyscraper-sized man. His voice drowned out the sound of the boat. "Could you heat a spot of tea for me? I'm catching a chill here in the depths." The boat grew too. Stephan turned to glance back at the vessel. The whiskers on his chin were the size of old growth redwood stumps. His eyes were not his own. His pupils reminded Henna of her blue-ringed octopus.

"Just a touch of Earl Grey, old girl. That should do the trick."

~Marauder

Bonn met the Germans for coffee, though none of them drank it. He'd known the men for years. They always looked the same. His father had usually met with them behind closed doors. Troy's whispers had been audible, their hissed replies less so. It had never occurred to Bonn to question their loyalty. It was as though he had inherited their ill-defined services as a part of the estate. They were reliable men; the types, it seemed, you could pay with meat, though not by hand. Polite distances were observed in the relationship. They had access to a large account, and claimed their fees fairly—without the need to ask. It occurred to Bonn that he had heard Troy raise his voice with Rupert, had yelled loudly, in public no less, at his mother, and even berated judges in aggressively ambiguous tones in their own courtrooms … but his father had always presented these men an unnaturally respectful version of himself.

If you are to place your head in a lion's mouth, it is best to know you are on good terms.

Ryker handed him a portfolio. Bonn flipped through the pages. The men did great work. Though their methods were unusual, he trusted them. Each page in the binder had a picture and summary of a property he owned in the city. The Germans did the research and made the purchases, but Bonn liked to know what he owned. They bought real estate throughout the city: industrial spaces, office buildings, warehouses—the Germans didn't buy anything smaller than 15,000 square feet. Rickard slid a folder across the table. Five new listings they hadn't acted on yet. These were residential buildings. Bonn wanted one he could rebuild.

One stood out. A recent fire led the city to condemn the 168-unit apartment building on 79th. The insurance company had the owners wrapped up in court. Without the insurance money, the owners couldn't afford to demolish the building. Quotes on demolition costs exceeded the worth of the building pre-fire. The owners were desperate. The city insisted the building be razed within a month. They'd be lucky if they recouped their court costs.

"Let's go for it. The location is right. This is the one. If the owners aren't dirt bags, let's intervene for them with the insurance company. No reason for them to lose their shirts while we profit."

136

Bonn wrote some notes. The Germans nodded approval. Ryker pulled his headset on and followed Rickard out.

He would own the building before the Germans got on the subway.

Bonn's phone rang. It was Manny. There was an edge to his voice.

"Listen, son, these cars have sold like hotcakes. I sold both fastbacks to the same guy. A history buff. He came back with an old Indian Scout he wanted me to restore. It felt rude not to agree to the job. The guy hangs around the shop a lot. He's obsessed with your Bill of Rights replica. Came back in just yesterday, said he wanted pinstripes or some nonsense. While I talked him out of it, he whipped out a magnifying glass. He stood there and said 'uh huh' and ignored me while he inspected the edges of the thing. I told him I'd paint the car pink with a metallic flake and he got real excited, but not about the car. He wasn't listening to me at all—just muttered something about the correct era."

The distress in Manny's voice was palpable.

"I tried to redirect him, but he wouldn't hear of it. He even tried to photograph the thing. I stopped him. 'No photos in the shop,' I said. I kicked him out. I told him I was late for something. You know what though? Mr. Persistent came back today. Didn't give a reason. Didn't talk much at all, in fact, just loitered about. Paced back and forth. Eyeballed that replica. I didn't know what to do. He talked to himself a lot and got sweaty. He finally left on his own. I thought I was done with him for the day, at least, but not so—after lunch he called me. 'I think you have the missing New York copy of the Bill of Rights.' He told me it supposedly burned up, but he's sure I've got it. What should I do? He really believes it. I'm getting jumpy. I'm afraid he'll call the feds—say I've been eating bald eagle or some such nonsense—get me arrested, so he can break in here and snatch it."

Bonn thought for a moment. "He's probably right." Manny uttered a small groan.

"My father's ego wouldn't have allowed him to hang a mere replica in his house. It probably is the New York copy."

Manny was speechless. Bonn felt a tinge of guilt.

His friend's troubles were his fault. The original New York copy of the Bill of Rights hung in his greasy little auto body shop.

"Do you still have the Vargas girl?"

Manny replied shakily. "I think so, yeah. If Linda didn't throw her out. I've missed her dearly."

"I have too. Let's do this—put her back up where she belongs and stick the Bill of Rights in the trunk of the Marauder."

Manny had relief in his voice already. A change of subject was just what he needed. "It'll certainly fit in the trunk of that ugly thing." Bonn recalled the consternation in Manny's voice when he had told him the Marauder was the car he liked.

A barn with a Shelby? Half a dozen Plymouths? And you picked out a beat up Mercury Marauder …

It had been hard to convince Manny about the Mercury.

Son, I don't even want to restore this car. The best thing we can do is sell it 'as is' to some kid who doesn't know better.

His reply had been simple.

I like it.

Manny begrudgingly agreed to the project, but the body and fender artist was obviously disgusted each time they opened the hood.

Bonn, if we are going to overhaul a rusty engine block, cracked hoses, missing belts, and chrome the thing up, we should be working on a car with the stock 429. We could even drop a crate engine in it and be done with it—a seven liter. A 427.

No. It'll look good black-on-black. We'll tune it up, but leave the rust. Just hang some white fuzzy dice on the rear view. That's what I want.

Manny had crossed his arms and fumed. It was the closest thing to an argument they had ever had.

Finally, Bonn said something Manny understood.

I don't want to drive something fancy. I grew up with the best of everything and nothing worked out. I want a car that's been around long enough to rust. It'll comfort me.

Manny began to soften. He'd understood then. It wasn't about the car.

Marauder—

He had added as he leaned down to wiggle the loose tail pipe.

I like the name.

Manny had nodded and tucked a fresh toothpick into the corner of his mouth. He chomped on the little sticks of wood each time he ruminated on a new problem. Manny had always wanted much more for him than Bonn wanted for himself.

Manny pulled the Bill of Rights off the wall and set it on the couch.

OK. Time to hide this thing.

138

He looked around in the rear of the shop for the Vargas girl. He hoped Linda hadn't thrown her out. It didn't matter how priceless Bonn's document was—the girl was nicer to look at. He found something rolled up in a drawer, held by an aging rubber band. "There you are." Manny unrolled the poster and pushed thumbtacks in each corner. He stood back and smiled. He'd never found the silly thing erotic. He just liked the era it came from and enjoyed razzing Linda too. She was good at playing along. He was a lucky man. He was an odd, wooly little perfectionist, but Linda loved him anyway. In the love department, Manny won the lottery. He knew it. He'd wait until Linda came down for lunch tomorrow. When she noticed the bombshell was back, he'd act surprised—

Lady, you've definitely got the right to bear arms.

Manny carried Bonn's document to the rear of the shop.

It looked different these days.

Bonn surprised Manny and Linda one summer. He bought the property behind Manny's garage and sold it to them for a dollar. A massive rolling door was now where the oven used to sit. It led to the new shop. The addition was built with several dozen shipping containers. Two banks of twenty footers, four high and five across, served as both walls and storage. Bonn bought a hydraulic lift to allow easy access to cars and motorcycles inside the containers that weren't on ground level. Eighty-foot-long I-beams were welded on top of the containers. They supported a warehouse-sized attic. The shop had everything he could dream of. Chain hoists, lifts, floor drains—even a dedicated painting room. If they chose to, they could build a car from scratch here. Bonn had things delivered almost every week. The latest addition was still in a heavy crate by the back door: a CNC machine.

Computer numerical control. What a mouthful.

The machinist sucked his breath in nervously through his teeth. Manny promised he'd wait to unpack the expensive toy until the boy came to visit. Bonn wanted to play with it together. Manny's growing collection of hard-to-find car parts was housed in the top of the building. Parts were organized by make, model, and year. It was like a muscle car parts museum. He and Linda traveled quite a bit now that they could afford to. When Linda went shopping for clothes on a trip, Manny hit the junkyards. He'd shipped parts back home from at least a dozen states now. In truth, Manny hated to mess up the new addition. He still used the old shop for dirty projects. He liked the smallness of it; he could reach all his tools without going too far. He remembered where each oil stain came from. Manny stepped onto a lift and worked the controls. The Marauder was on the third level of containers, second to last box on the left. Linda enjoyed riding the lift. One afternoon she took Polaroid pictures of each car to place on the door of its respective container. The Marauder's Polaroid was of the Mercury's grill, nestled between the four simple round headlights.

He had to admit. That thin slash of chrome was dazzling against the black.

Manny still held out hope that Bonn would let him fix up the engine someday. Manny steered the lift into place. He unlocked the container and swung open the door. The containers were only eight feet wide inside, so he had to turn sideways and step past the car's wide body to get to the trunk. He wrapped the document up in an old wool blanket and put it gently on top of the spare. He shut the trunk carefully, just leaning on it until the latch engaged. It was hard to see anything but the silly dice in the dark container. Everything on the car except the chrome was black. Manny turned a light on and wiped a thin layer of dust off of the sinister machine. He locked up the container and rode the lift down.

A proper restoration job made something old even better than new.

It was the first car they'd dipped a frame on. Bonn was more than a good mechanic—he was an artist. Manny wouldn't have chosen the black interior though. A cream interior would look nice—however, with the dice inside it'd look like a big dumb domino.

All the black with the chrome was ominous. If the pale horse gave out on Death while in the Finger Lakes region, he might come for the Marauder.

Manny imagined the Grim Reaper riding the lift and opening the door.

That's one bad machine. I like the dice.

Manny had an idea: he'd tell the history buff he gave the document to someone to check it for authenticity—that sort of thing might take a while.

Maybe the guy would stop asking about it.

~Conus

The trawler's top speed was eight knots. It took several days to reach the fishing grounds. The tongueless boy was tasked with watching Henna. Each morning he brought her bleach coffee with a starch-thick breakfast of rice with breadfruit. She washed it all down with rationed sips from the bottled water she'd bought in Malé. Chlorine was in everything, but by the end of the fourth day it didn't bother her as much. When she explored the boat, the boy followed. The crew shot her odd glances, but left her alone. Many of them were African. She tried some polite greetings in Swahili, but they refused to speak with her. It was as if they'd been told not to.

Time passed despite her discomfort. She read a bit. She watched for birdlife to indicate nearby islands or atolls. Her lips became chapped from the sun and the bleach. Early one morning the boy knocked lightly on the door of the storage room. The engine had slowed. She felt the big boat turn. Henna pulled the loose end of the hitch holding the door shut and peeked outside. "Are we there?" The boy nodded. He gestured excitedly with his hands. She'd started to understand his rudimentary sign language. He was a good kid. Henna correctly guessed his meaning and he nodded happily.

They'd pull the first net in two hours.

Henna was surprised how many men were actually on the boat. The deck seemed cluttered with bodies. Everyone but her knew what to do. She kept getting in the way.

The ship was a freezer trawler. The primary goal was to get fish in the freezer quickly. When the first haul was pulled aboard, everyone who didn't run a machine was on deck. They scrambled to throw different fish down different hatches. When a giant turtle became entangled in the net and disrupted the mechanism for gathering the net together at the top, Henna dashed forward to inspect the mass of writhing creatures. It was mostly mullet, so the odd turtle or tuna really stuck out. It was difficult to look past the suffering of the animals brought aboard. Henna understood why the woman on the telephone advocated abolishing the practice of trawling.

But she had to admit—it was effective.

Henna forced herself to search the periphery of the net while the crew worked. The boy with no tongue was there at every turn. Henna stumbled over him more than once. Henna cursed herself.

She should have brought more cash.

She only had a couple hundred pounds left. Using the captain's math that would buy her ten specimens. She wondered for a moment if the boy was also tasked with her specimen count. Life at sea was nothing like life on land. An uneducated, barbaric loser on land became a god when he was named the top person on a boat. Henna watched how the captain ruled the crew. He used fear and violence. He carried a sjambok with him to point and direct people.

He was not a kindly man. The meaning was clear: This is my sea scepter. Do my bidding, or I'll remove your skin one lash at a time.

He didn't just carry it either—he used it. Two meals were served to the crew each day. One day during the second meal a cook stumbled in the galley. A large bowl of rice was spilled. The captain was immediately on his feet. He strode forward angrily and lashed the man three times with the weapon. Henna shivered.

No one dared say a word.

They fished around the clock. Henna saw a few cone snails, but they were known species. The trawler's nets opened, the pickers rushed the pile of creatures, the catch was sorted. They fed the nets back out. Each time a live turtle came aboard the fishermen performed a show for Henna by gently returning the creature to the water. Forced smiles and nods indicated they always treated the gentle giants with such reverence, but Henna knew the truth. The captain likely choreographed the act. When a dead turtle was brought aboard, the real excitement started.

"One to eat? One to eat!" A man yelled in Swahili. Henna kept a mental tally—though turtle was one of the main sources of protein on the boat, Henna was sure most of the drowned turtles were in the freezer, awaiting lucrative black-market sales in Zanzibar. She doubted the crew usually ate them; they were worth too much money to be crew-food. Henna forced herself to look past the dead turtles. She even feigned joy when she was served turtle in the galley for the second meal. Everyone watched her closely. She was determined not to bring more attention to herself than necessary.

On the third afternoon a porpoise slid from the net. It was exhausted but alive. A man took a short knife and cut the animal.

"One to eat."

He flashed a smile at Henna. Guiltily, he added, "Already dead."

It wasn't already dead. He likes the taste of porpoise.

Henna jumped when she realized the captain was behind her. He clapped and then put a hand on her lower back. He leaned in to be heard over the machinery, but it was much too intimate a gesture.

"Truly a shame. We won't waste the body of the fish, though. We will give thanks to the fish when we eat him."

Henna swallowed the bile in her throat and managed a nod.

She despised hypocrites.

The captain slithered off to congratulate the man with the short knife.

What a loathsome boat. What malevolent practices. They had no right to kill the porpoise.

The boy was at her side. He shook a plastic bag in her face to get her attention. She took the bag and looked inside.

Cone snails—the ones she needed!

Five of them. They were darker than any she'd seen before—nearly black. Each was near ten inches long and had beautiful light blue patterns, like loosely interconnecting delicate sine waves. The shells had obconic apexes and sharp bases. One snail probed its surroundings with a phosphorescent blue proboscis.

They were alive.

The boy pointed to the porpoise and mimicked sadness. He raked at his cheeks to indicate tears. Henna nodded her head. The captain stepped forward to direct the bleeding of the porpoise. The boy appeared nervous. He'd waited for just the right moment to show her the snails. He held a finger to his lips and pointed to a small cooler next to the door of the galley. Henna understood.

Take these, but don't tell.

The snails were a peace offering.

The boy missed home. He wasn't like them.

Someone shouted. Something was wrong with the net. The captain swung the sjambok wildly. He yelled. It seemed part of the net was caught on a reef. They had to take a smaller boat out to free it. Henna tucked the bag of snails in her satchel and took a few tentative steps toward the cooler. The snails were heavy. Each one must weigh nearly a kilogram. Her heart raced. The captain leered at her and yelled. Henna glanced around for the boy, but he had his back to her. He seemed intent on helping with the net.

"You will come, too. We take the small boat."

You. He meant her.

The captain smiled broadly. "We send two men into the water to free the net. You inspect the net for shells when they do it." Henna's blood ran cold. She held her stomach as if she was ill, but the captain pointed to the skiff with the sjambok. "Real quick. We are quick. My best men. They know what to do."

"Thank you, no. I will stay here." The captain shook his head at Henna. Then nodded to the men who awaited orders from him.

She was in trouble. Getting on that skiff would be the biggest mistake she could make.

The men had her arms. They roughly marched her to the ladder.

"Let go of me NOW—I'm staying here!"

Henna landed hard in the little boat. Whether she fell or was thrown didn't matter. She heard rather than felt the impact and rebounded despite the blow.

She was going back up that ladder.

She reeled and touched her head. Men climbed down and blocked her way. The outboard started on the first pull. They started for the reef. Henna looked for the boy on the trawler. He was there. Watching her. He cried—he didn't use his fingers to indicate crying—tears actually streamed down his cheeks. The ladder, her lifeline, was gone. The captain took over the controls in the skiff. He knelt in front of the outboard motor and spun the throttle full forward. The crew knew to lean forward, but Henna fell backward and hit her head on a fuel tank. Small things whirled in front of her. A buzzing noise inside her head drowned out the sound of the outboard. It felt like several minutes that they raced at top speed, but she wasn't sure. Her head hurt. She felt disoriented. She began to come around as the boat slowed. They were helping her. Many hands were on her arms, helping her up. Someone laughed. They were sorry she was hurt. It was sheepish laughter. She smelled fuel. She must have fallen into some fuel because they took her shirt off.

Please, God, let them be helping her.

~Motivation

Bonn threw some things together. Manny was on the phone, and he felt increasingly anxious to get to Ithaca.

He could use a break from the city anyway.

Lately Manny had been calling him daily. The history buff, Norman Trundle, remained obsessed with the Bill of Rights. More people became involved. "I put it in the trunk of the Mercury like you asked me to, but this is Norman's new hobby, son. He just won't let it go."

"It'll all work out Manny. How is Linda doing?"

Bonn's question seemed to make Manny angry. He didn't answer it.

"He snuck a picture of it, by the way—Norman, I mean. A couple guys in suits showed up with the picture. They demanded to see it. I told them I had a university official come pick it up to see if it was authentic, but they wanted a name. I balked. Finally I picked up a ball peen hammer and re-invited them to leave. One of them tossed a card at me. They said they'd be back with a search warrant. Card reads: Warfield and Rainbolt, Attorneys at Law."

"I'll have Rupert call them. He'll take care of it. Listen, we are overdue for a visit. I'll take the train up tonight. We can catch up in person. I want to break open that CNC machine."

Manny was quiet on the other end of the phone. Something else was going on. Neither of them spoke for a few moments.

"The other thing, son—I've considered skipping this detail— when the lawyers were here Linda came down with some lunch. She does that most days anymore, but, like I said, the lawyers were here. She and Jelly Bean got all tangled up coming down the stairs. They're fine, but Linda took a big spill."

Manny was trying to hold it together, but his voice shook.

"After I helped her up and checked her over, I noticed one of the lawyers leaning on my workbench with a big smile. I don't think Linda heard what he said—she was yelling at the dogs not to eat the sandwiches, but I heard what he said. It's the real reason I picked up the hammer. For a minute I considered beating him to a pulp." Bonn stopped packing. He looked out the window toward the park. "'Clumsy nigger.' That's what he said. Just loud enough to hear, but he said it. I'm sure they'll come back with a warrant and if they're the types who would use that language. I'm not sure what other tricks they're capable of."

Bonn pulled on his coat. He swung a messenger bag over his shoulder and made for the park. His jaw muscles felt tight. His heartbeat felt fast. When he hit the heavy bag, he could get his heart rate above 120, but it felt faster than that now.

"That was ignorant."

And reckless.

"I'll ask Rupert to give them a call. I doubt you'll see those guys again—"

And what I mean by that is I guarantee it.

"—when I get there, let's make those oddball parts for the GT you told me about. I suspect the CNC machine will work like a charm."

At the mention of the GT Manny's voice brightened—it was a Ford GT. The son of a collector took it out on a joyride and rolled it. Bonn bought it at auction. Manny wasn't sure they'd ever get the thing going again. The frame was even better than new, the body was pristine again, but some of the specialty parts under the hood were difficult to replicate, even for Manny. Manny liked iron and steel. Bonn knew that. All of the cars from the farm were sold now, but Bonn kept a steady stream of interesting and collectable cars coming. Manny liked to stay busy, but he was over his head with the GT. When he became overwhelmed with the project, he'd put the Ford away. He took a month to fix up a Superbee to clear his head. Supercars like the GT were intimidating. The tolerances were too tight.

"It'll be great to see you, son. I'll be glad to finish that GT up and be done with it. Heck, I'd rather work on another Marauder. Do me a favor and don't buy any more cars like that Ford. I'm nearly retired. I don't want to discover more things I'm not good at."

Bonn had things to do before he headed north. He needed to test himself before taking on the racist attorneys that harassed Manny and Linda. He felt his pulse. It had returned to normal.

He was ready for the test. This had been coming for years.

146

~True White Devil

Henna looked at the man in front of her. Her vision was clearer now. He had her wrists. He was helping to steady her. She needed to vomit. Henna tried to turn her arms to free her wrists from the man's grip, but he shook his head and smiled. It was the man with the short knife—the man who wanted a porpoise dinner.

My best men. We are quick. They know what to do.

She turned her head to look behind her. The captain had his pants down. Someone had her hips.

Her pants were off. She didn't remember taking them off. A sharp pain.

They weren't helping her. The man who held her wrists squatted down and squeezed her wrists so hard she couldn't feel her fingers.

Oh God. Oh God, please send me help—send me a pack of glass-toothed wolves. Send me Stephan. Pull us into the water. Anything.

The men laughed casually. She wasn't fighting. Someone new was behind her. "Porpoise Lover" squeezed her wrists even tighter and mocked her. She wasn't fighting—yet.

But she could.

The captain was finished. He pulled his pants up. He walked to the front of the boat. Instead of his sjambok, he held a panga. When they'd finished with the rape, he'd kill her with the short machete and throw her overboard. No one on the trawler would ask what happened to her. They wouldn't need to—they'd know.

They knew already.

Enraged, Henna screamed. She bore down and screamed until her grim breakfast shot from her mouth into Porpoise Lover's face. He lost his grip on her. Henna twisted and rolled. Men laughed less casually. They celebrated her willingness to fight.

Something was underneath her—the satchel?

Henna shoved her hand blindly inside.

There—a cone snail.

She gripped the animal around the center of the shell and rolled quickly toward the captain.

Things slowed down.

Stephan spoke to her. She couldn't see him, but she knew Stephan had his wig in his hand. She heard his voice as though he were standing at her elbow. "They don't expect us girls to fight, but we always do." She attacked. She rolled onto a knee and thrust the base of the cone snail into the Captain's groin with all her might.

"Jolly good," said imaginary Stephan, "now the others."

Why wouldn't he help her? Maybe he was—at least he told her what to do.

Down again—she rolled for the satchel. The other idiots were frozen. They looked at the Captain, who gasped for breath in fetal position. The snail had harpooned the man—the toxin appeared to work on vertebrates.

Imaginary Stephan did something that slowed time. When he spoke again, even his voice was slow. "Hey, Henna, those snails are pretty hot—the captain can't breathe. You're onto a fish-eating species."

Henna grasped a cone snail in each hand and stood. Porpoise Lover reached for the panga, in slow motion, while the other two looked on. Each of the men had their pants down. They wouldn't move fast even if imaginary Stephan sped things back up. A surge of anger fueled her. She was ready. She rammed the base of the shell in her right hand into Porpoise Lover's neck. He spun, but remained upright. He felt his neck with his free hand, then raised the machete to strike her. She raised her left hand to ward off the blow. Something stirred inside the shell. In a flash, the snail thrust its harpoon. It pierced the man's upper lip. He dropped so suddenly, it appeared his bones had melted. A man with a tiny penis took a tentative step toward her. She crouched and held the snails in front of her like knives.

"Shake 'em up, old girl," her imaginary friend said in his best *African Queen* voice.

Good idea.

She aimed the business ends of the snails at "Tiny Penis" and shook them hard. One of them answered with a harpoon. A bone-melting dose of injectable death dropped the man. Henna spun to face the last of her attackers. He looked frightened. He'd pulled his pants up. He appeared terrified of the snails in Henna's hands. She rolled her shoulders back and readied herself, aiming the snails at his abdomen.

A calm came over her. She spoke to him in Swahili. "Take me back to the ship."

The man's eyes bulged and rolled in his head, not unlike the eye of a wildebeest cut from the herd in the last few steps of chase, when it knows it has lost. Not wanting to look, but looking back all the same, for the terrible hooks about to pull it down. He nodded vigorously. He worked his mouth like an oxygen-starved mullet, but was unable to conjure a fearful word past the gatekeeper of his mouth.

Henna stepped forward. "If you try anything I'll whistle," Henna promised, "the True White Devil will come. I'll let the snails spear you, but I'll keep you alive for the True White Devil. You know what *he* does." The man's eyes flashed wider still. Tanzanians were superstitious people—they imagined many fates worse than death. He turned to pull the starter on the outboard and Henna picked up the panga. She swung the machete hard. It cleaved his skull easily. The superstitious man fell still. Henna turned in a circle to look for *real* Stephan.

He wasn't there of course.

The motor was pitched askew, tilted to one side. The boat turned in a slow, tight circle.

Four dead men.

How many of them raped her? She didn't know. Porpoise Lover held her wrists—did he rape her first? Henna felt her sinuses burning. Her nose was broken and bled badly.

Blood. She needed blood samples from these men. They could have HIV—they could have anything.

She couldn't breathe through her nose. She felt herself hyperventilating through her open mouth.

What did people do for that?

Stephan didn't answer, but Henna could think for herself now.

They breathe into a bag.

She had a bag. Henna looked for her satchel. It was open. Simply having a plan to do something helped slow her breathing. A cone snail was at her foot. She picked it up carefully and looked around the boat. There were four left—she'd driven the first snail, sharp end first like a railroad spike, deep into the captain's pubic symphysis. Henna decided to let the captain keep it. She placed the remaining snails in her satchel. She still needed blood samples from these men. She looked at the panga.

There was a way.

She pried the big knife from the skull of the superstitious man. Next she tied a tourniquet tightly around the captain's right wrist. She placed his arm across his chest. Holding it steady, she chopped at the arm until it came free. Suddenly she realized she was completely naked. She looked for her shirt. It was in shreds. She took pieces of her shirt, wrapped the hand of the Captain in it, then placed the hand in her bag with the snails. She repeated the process with Tiny Penis and Porpoise Lover. She was winding the last of the cord around the superstitious man's right wrist when she noticed the trawler coming at her.

She'd have to work on the move.

She turned the throttle on the outboard and straightened the till. She pointed the skiff toward what she hoped was Diego Garcia. She couldn't see well; with her nose broken her eyes were full of tears. It felt like looking at the sun through water. The ship corrected to head her off. The outboard on the skiff was small. It was a short, wide boat. The trawler might be able to overtake her.

She'd have to dump the bodies.

She turned the skiff sharply 180 degrees and backed off the throttle. The ship corrected to intercept her. She had to focus on one thing at a time.

First, the arm.

She made short work of the superstitious man's arm. He was thin.

She probably outweighed him.

She squatted and dragged him to the side of the boat, then tipped him headfirst into the ocean. Porpoise Lover was even thinner. He and Tiny Penis were easier to move now that she had a method.

The captain was last.

The trawler closed on the skiff, but she took the time to roll the captain's body back and forth to remove his shirt before she hoisted him overboard. He floated face up. Henna glowered at the corpse with rage. "Porpoises are mammals, jackass." The ship was close now. It slowed and turned sharply. She guessed someone wanted to board the skiff—

But they surely didn't want to help.

She slipped the captain's shirt on and spun the throttle hard. The ship was now only feet away. She turned the skiff to the rear of the trawler. They'd need to swing wide to chase her. That should buy her some time. With just Henna's weight, the skiff was faster. She rubbed her eyes to clear them and steered for the only landmass she could see. Another boat raced toward her from the island. Henna reached into her satchel and pulled out a cone snail. She found the heavy machete and wedged it into the gunwale.

If they wouldn't help her? She'd kill them too.

~Survivor

The boat from Diego Garcia reached her first. From 150 meters they hailed her with a bullhorn. "Power-skiff headed for Diego Garcia: halt your progress and cut your engine. Prepare to be boarded." It was a British voice so Henna spun the throttle to low. When the boat pulled alongside her, men pointed automatic rifles at her. The man with the bullhorn put the device down and gave commands. "Miss, turn off the outboard. Place your hands on top of your head." Henna turned off the outboard, but the captain's shirt was short. She was not going to give the Brits a show. The military boat was longer and much faster than the skiff. It flew a ragged flag. It looked like someone pinned a British flag to a flag from the USA. Several deeply-tanned mildly-drunk men were aboard. One held a volleyball. The man who gave orders spoke into a radio, then barked some orders to the others. The men with rifles held them at low ready. Henna felt dizzy, but held her chin high.

The small whirling things were back.

"I'm a Scottish citizen. I've been raped and beaten. I need immediate medical attention. In my bag I have a fax from British Indian Ocean Territory London office that allows me to collect scientific samples from these waters—" Henna collapsed. Two of the tanned soldiers boarded the skiff.

"Jesus—" said the youngest of the men, tiptoeing around the pools of gore that shifted with the men's steps. "That's a lot of damned blood." One of them removed his shirt and tied it around Henna's waist. The trawler was nearly on top of them. The man at the console spoke into the radio. The men with rifles trained their weapons at the incoming vessel. The man in charge shouted into the bullhorn. "Shut down your vessel. Set anchor. Prepare to be boarded."

When Henna awoke she was in the military boat. She was covered in an assortment of shirts. She followed the eyes of a tan man with a broad back as he grinned toward Diego Garcia. When he spoke, she was relieved. "I thought they were sending out the patrol boat."

"They are," the man with the bullhorn answered tersely.

The man with the broad back shook his head and held a hand to his ear.

"But I hear them firing up the Harrier," the Brit with the bullhorn answered with understatement. "They're sending it all out."

Once ashore, four of the British Royal Marines escorted her to the clinic in the back of an ambulance. One read her fax from BIOT London en-route. They took her to an examination room. A woman entered and the Marines excused themselves. When the door swung open she saw a policeman and some US Navy officers in the corridor.

They had her satchel.

She heard the Marines argue with the policeman, but Henna couldn't tell why. Through the window in the door she saw someone standing guard. "I'm Dr. Becky Phillips. Please call me Becky." Becky covered Henna with a blanket and put the head of the bed up for Henna. "I don't need to examine your nose. It's broken. Before I examine the rest of you, do you feel like you can tell me what happened?" Henna tried to speak, but choked on her own voice. Becky brought her a cup of water. She sat on the foot of the gurney. After a sip of water she coughed and cleared her throat.

"Thank you."

"Seems like something terrible happened?"

"Yes." Henna felt amazed. She drank the remainder of the fluid.

The water tasted like water.

"I boarded a trawler in Malé bound for these fishing grounds. I wanted to collect cone snails—I'm a toxicologist. A boy with no tongue found some for me. The captain of the trawler—" Henna's voice cracked. Becky nodded encouragement and put a hand on Henna's foot. Henna clawed at the captain's shirt. "I need this off—" Becky pulled a pair of trauma shears from a pocket and unceremoniously cut off the shirt. She helped her into an exam gown. The shirt was still on the foot of the bed. Henna drew her feet away from it. "It's the captain's shirt. They ripped my clothes. I took it after I killed him."

Becky put the rapist's shirt in a clear plastic bag and handed it to someone in the hallway. Henna felt a little better with the shirt off. "I killed four men who raped me. I need their blood tested for STDs, hepatitis, and HIV. I brought their—their hands with me. They're in the satchel the men in the hallway are arguing about."

The cone snails.

152

"I need you to get the satchel. There are cone snails inside—with the hands. Extraordinarily venomous animals. They shouldn't be handled." Becky stood. She went to the door. The policeman didn't want to surrender the satchel, but Becky pulled rank. She carried the satchel to a small stainless steel tray to open it.

"Probably overkill on the tourniquets, but I admire your spirit." Becky appeared unflappable. She unwrapped each hand and placed it on the tray. She didn't attempt to handle the cone snails, but did peer into the satchel at them for a moment. "These need a cooler or something, don't they? If you want them to stay viable?" Henna nodded.

Too much. This was all too much.

Henna heard her own voice. She sounded to herself as though she babbled nonsense. "The trawler is out of Zanzibar. Most of the crew is Kenyan. Not the boy. The boy with no tongue—he's Indonesian."

The boy!

"There is a boy from Indonesia on the trawler. He tried to help me. I hope he isn't hurt. Can you make sure they don't hurt the boy with no tongue?" Henna stood. She needed to help him.

Everything was going too fast.

It felt like she now paid for the extra time Stephan gave her on the skiff. "I told the superstitious one I would whistle to conjure up the True White Devil if he didn't take me back to the ship, then I chopped his head open with a machete—"

Becky draped a towel over the gruesome row of hands. "We'll work it all out. Come, sit down. Let me examine you and we can go from there." Henna couldn't sit.

"—one of them held my wrists after I hit my head. At first I thought he was trying to help, but he was holding me down. He held me down so they could take turns." Henna sobbed. She didn't know if Becky could even tell what she was saying. The stress from her week at sea came out in a flood. "He had a knife. He cut a porpoise. He killed it because he wanted to eat it, but he didn't have to." Becky sat on the bed with Henna and put her arm around her shoulders. A nurse came in to ask how she could help.

"We have plenty of time. I'm going to give you something for pain and an anxiolytic," Becky nodded to the nurse and she left the room. "I need to examine you, but do you need to just cry for a bit? I think I would. I'll stay here with you."

Yes. I need to cry.

Henna didn't say it, but Becky seemed to know. Henna sobbed. She clung tightly to the woman. Becky held Henna and glanced at the towel covering the hands on the tray. After a couple of minutes, Henna relaxed and laid back on the bed. Becky handed her a washcloth for her face. The nurse came in to start an IV. She gave her morphine and lorazepam, then drew up more medicine. Becky spoke in a matter-of-fact tone that was soothing. "I'm going to start you azithromycin and a cephalosporin. Let's just treat you empirically for everything. I don't have antivirals here and if I did, they would make you feel terrible. Since you'd have to wait to start them anyway, I'd advise you to wait until the test results are back." Becky cleaned up Henna's nose. She reduced her nasal fracture and taped it up like a boxer. After examining the rest of her body, Becky brought her fresh blankets.

Warm ones.

Henna looked at the tray. The hands were gone. Becky followed her gaze. "I pulled samples from the hands, but the tests are send-outs. The samples will be flown to our mother hospital in Japan." Despite the warm blankets, Henna began to shake. The nurse came back carrying a small cooler and some surgical scrubs. She handed the items to Henna. She opened the cooler so Henna could see inside.

The snails.

The cooler was full of water. The nurse smiled at her. "It's salt water." Becky left to make some phone calls. Henna listened to the men in the hallway argue about her satchel. The police were concerned about evidence, but there were more Marines than police in the hallway. Henna put on the scrubs and pulled the blankets over her head. She didn't feel cold, but she couldn't stop shivering.

Just the aftermath from the adrenaline.

A few minutes passed. Becky was in the hallway. She barked orders and a short argument ensued. It sounded like the Marines escorted the police out. The nurse brought in Henna's satchel and wiped at the beat-up bag until it was clean. Henna wrapped her arms around the small cooler and hugged it hard. When Becky returned, she gave Henna a sweatshirt. It was blue with an embroidered yellow helicopter. She had two Popsicles in a cup. She offered Henna one. She took the other by the wooden stick and bit into it. She chewed as she talked.

"The police want to question you about the hands. Do you have any interest in talking to them?"

"No—but I probably have to don't I?"

Becky smiled. "Not exactly. We aren't really prepared for this type of thing. No one really knows what to do with you." Becky took another bite of the Popsicle, but tucked it into her cheek so she could talk. "As far as I can tell, you're a good woman who got on a bad boat. My question is why make things any more complicated than they have to be?" They were both quiet for a few moments. Becky looked blankly at a wall then nodded her head confidently. "How about this: why don't you leave me your phone number so I can call you with the results from the blood samples. I'll put you on the next plane to the States—I know that's nowhere near Scotland, but it beats staying here until they do figure out what to do with you."

~Timing Screw

Marauder: pillager, raider, bandit, buccaneer, corsair, freebooter, looter, outlaw, pirate, plunderer, ravager, robber, thief.

Bonn bought a ticket for the late train. It left for upstate in three hours. He slipped the ticket in his pocket and hailed a cab. As he rode from Penn Station to 77th, he replaced his running shoes with sparring shoes. He entered the park at 77th west and headed southeast toward the lake. After a group of cyclists pedaled by, Bonn slipped on some light police-style gloves. He slung his bag across his chest as he walked. He prepared himself, sliding a friction lock police baton into a tube he'd sewn between two belt loops on his jeans. He pulled his sweatshirt down over the weapon then took out a can of wasp spray. As a boy he'd watched a hired man prepare to use the stuff. He was a tough guy—a retired bull rider. The man showed great respect for the wasp spray. He'd put on safety goggles before climbing a ladder to douse a hornet's nest. As he climbed he told Bonn something memorable:

Got some of this in my eye once. Just a speck of it really. It hurt so bad I screamed like a mashed cat. I fell off a roof and broke my pelvis—worst pain I ever had—including being stomped on by a bull.

As an afterthought, the man paused on the ladder and looked down at Bonn to clarify.

The eye—not the pelvis.

Bonn held the spray in his left hand—the shortened nozzle oriented away from his face—and carefully tucked the can in his sweatshirt. He slid a black sweatband high on his forehead then stretched a pair of swim goggles over the band. The fabric would keep the lenses on the goggles from fogging up. He pulled the hood of his sweatshirt over the goggles so they were hidden above his hairline and eased his left hand back into the long pocket on his sweatshirt. He held the wasp spray in the pocket as he walked. With his free hand, he pretended to talk on his cellphone. A woman walked by. Bonn threw his head back and laughed into the phone. He strove to blend in, but his left eye didn't lend itself to blending in. He usually wore sunglasses, but he had to simplify things if he needed to use the wasp spray.

People seemed averse to a person who laughed on a cellphone. It was difficult to tell what a person usually looks like when they smile: eyes became colorless wrinkles, a belly laugh allowed a great view up one's nose, but won't allow an observer to identify specific features. There was a social barrier that accompanied cellphones. Even panhandlers avoided Bonn when he pretended to be on the phone.

Bonn knew Central Park well. He knew where people walked their pets, he knew the trails cyclists preferred—he knew where drug dealers and gang members met. Despite the surrounding urban crush, Central Park was relatively safe. Police presence fluctuated with crime levels and vice-versa. Everything came down to timing.

Everything.

Good timing was crucial to all successful endeavors. A person who understood timing could become rich. Good timing even allowed an average man access to beautiful women. Bonn thought of the old Mercury. The Marauder had a timing screw on the carburetor. Manny could make a carburetor purr; he knew the sweet spot between the coughing death rattle and the too rich whine of a humming bird. When he hit the sweet spot, his friend always turned to him and flashed a satisfied smile.

Just right.

It was, of course, the volume of fuel that caused a change like that in an engine, but it was the flow that mattered. Manny was a carburetor artist. He knew what perfect sounded like by ear.

All of it was timing.

A professor, who had accused Bonn of cheating, would have argued that in the energy conversion, there was always more energy into a system than out. Bonn knew this was true, but recognized something his professor didn't: where the laws of physics stopped explaining the success of certain people, the phenomenon he thought of as artistry picked up the conversation. Artists of physical timing weren't physicists. Artists were regular people with great reflexes. They didn't struggle to make quick estimations.

They acted.

Babe Ruth became a phenomenon because he knew where a baseball would be before it got there. By the time it left the pitcher's fingertips it traveled roughly fifty-eight feet to get to the plate. That gave him time. Babe was a legend because he used that time wisely. The ball was a victim of physics during each fifty-eight foot trip. Physics don't change mid-flight. Babe had the bat ready when the ball

157

got there. Babe Ruth was no athlete—he had a famously flabby midsection. He was, however, an artist. In comparison, even an amateur lightweight boxer required exponentially faster timing to avoid the fists of a skilled opponent.

Gifted reflexes, immense core strength. The willingness to keep going when damaged.

A boxer was just an opponent's arm length away from damage. Consequences became dire quickly when they didn't block or dodge. And how did a good boxer differ from a legendary boxer?

Superior timing.

Bonn turned off of Terrace Drive. He headed northeast. The trail ended at the lake. There was usually activity there. Bonn walked fast. His footsteps were nearly silent in the sparring shoes. Three young males were ahead of him on the trail so Bonn slowed. They couldn't hear him approach from behind. They took their time. They waited for an opportunity.

Gang members.

They could be his opportunity.

Time would tell.

Bonn heard hooves and a snort behind him. Two mounted police approached. Bonn stepped off of the path and sat beneath a tree. As the officers passed by he shrugged his shoulder into the phone and pretended to write something important on his hand. The officers ignored him. They continued toward the lake.

Everyone headed toward the dead end.

Bonn glanced at his watch. He had an hour and a half to catch the train. As the officers slowed to pass the thugs, one of the men on foot spoke. "She's not that cute, but the other girl? The one in my calculus class—" Once the officers were out of earshot, the banter stopped. There was no jocularity or laughter from his companions.

They had a method.

A man and a woman approached from the lake. Bonn backed further into the trees to watch as the two groups converged. One of the thugs stopped to tie a shoelace. It gave them all a reason to pause there. Tension grew as the couple neared. The gangsters assessed the situation. The man was big and fit. When they passed the loiterers, the man put his body between the woman and the strangers. He kept his hands free. He moved fluidly. He waited to wrap his arm back around the woman's shoulders until they were past the thugs.

Gallantry was not dead.

158

The thugs exchanged looks. One spoke. The others nodded. They'd agreed on a plan but hesitated. Bonn guessed they speculated on the likelihood of the cops return. If the cops didn't return on the path?

Maybe they'd mug the couple—maybe they'd hassle the woman. Maybe they'd taunt the woman to humiliate the man after battering him.

There were many worse scenarios, but none of them mattered—

He would intercede.

The couple neared Bonn's hiding spot. He remained still and watched, unobserved. From the looks of the man, the thugs might have their hands full with him, but they would certainly have weapons. The sun dipped beneath the trees. In the distance, Bonn saw the mounted police gallop off the path, through a grassy expanse. Either the horses needed to run or they'd received a call. Either way, they wouldn't return on the path. The thugs noticed too. They didn't hesitate. They went after the couple with purpose. Bonn waited to commit until they passed his hiding spot. Maybe he'd misread their intentions.

No. He'd been right.

Two of the men held guns and the third pulled a lead sap from his back pocket. They'd just passed Bonn when the guy with the sap spoke. "Drag her back here to the trees."

No doubts now.

The couple disappeared behind a grassy knoll. Bonn pulled the goggles down over his eyes. He grasped the wasp spray firmly in his left hand. He removed the baton with his right.

Here I go.

Bonn swung wide and ran up behind the men.

Fast, quiet, low.

His mind slowed. He perfected his plan on the move. With each step, his next movement became clear.

The one on the left has the sap. His hood is up—the calculus student. He will be last. The middle one is a step behind the others—he has a gun. He is first. The one on the right also has a gun. He is second.

Bonn approached like he prepared to kick a field goal. Just before he reached the thug in the middle he flicked the baton open. *Click.* It was loud, but it was too late—the thug just began to turn his head when the baton smashed into his right temple. The thin bone caved like an eggshell. Bonn wasted no time. He lunged toward the man to his right and swung the baton backhand.

Babe would be proud.

The effect was devastating. The baton impacted the second man's trachea and he instantly folded in half. He dropped the gun to grasp his throat with both hands, and Bonn kicked the gun a safe distance away. Bonn wheeled left and leveled the spray at the third man. The confused thug held the sap out like a remote control. Bonn circled him until he was upwind.

"This is your final exam. Calculus can be described as the study of how things change. Two elements are important in this study. The first element is numbers—what is the second element?" The gangster was dumbstruck. He glanced at his companions, but they were of no help.

"You're crazy!"

"The answer I would have accepted was 'functions.'" Bonn sprayed the man for several seconds with the wasp spray.

The stuff does work.

The thug wheezed and dropped the sap. He pushed his fingers into his eyes. Bonn strode forward and rained blows down on the would-be rapist.

One collarbone, two—left mastoid insertion site, right. Nasal bone.

Bonn stayed low, but pivoted slightly to check the others. The first man appeared dead—he was motionless. His right eye bulged from his head like a lemon. The man on the far right was frothing blood from his lungs in an odd arched position. His eyes were open but glazed. His pupils were huge.

No oxygen to the brain. He wouldn't last another minute. Neither was a threat.

Bonn turned back to the third man. He had mechanically destroyed the guy's ability to use accessory muscles above his neck. The man's two-decade-old sternocleidomastoid muscles pulled in vain on his broken clavicles. The muscles were no longer tethered to the man's skull either. Since his nose was shattered, he had to breathe through his mouth. He made grunting noises. Bonn timed his inhalation attempts. When the cretin struggled to take his next breath, Bonn emptied the rest of the wasp spray into his mouth.

Timing—it was everything.

While Bonn walked toward where the couple disappeared, he pulled off the swim goggles and sweatband. The goggles went into the bag and a small bottle of isopropyl alcohol came out. Bonn squirted some of the fluid onto the sweatband. He used it to wipe down the baton.

The couple was visible again—two hundred meters off.

Bonn finished cleaning the baton and jogged to a maple tree. He struck the tip of the baton on the tree to collapse it, then slipped off the sparring shoes.

The couple was at the fountain now.

He placed the sweatband inside one of the sparring shoes and pulled his running shoes on. He jogged south. At a fork in the trail there was a refuse bin. Bonn paused there and pulled a pack of cigarettes from the bag. He tapped one out and lit it. He pulled just enough of the noxious smoke into his mouth to make the tip of the cigarette glow hot. He turned in a slow, casual circle. To the west a man and a boy walked toward the lake. They didn't seem alarmed.

No one to the north but dead thugs.

Bonn pushed the sparring shoes into the refuse bin. He doused them with the rest of the solvent and threw in the cigarette. *Whoosh.* The shoes were alight. The rubber soles curled and bubbled in the hot blue flames. Bonn used the cigarette pack to prop open the hinge on the refuse bin and dropped the empty can of pesticide in. He took off the gloves. The fire was really hot now. He threw in the gloves. The shoes no longer looked like shoes. Bonn glanced back toward the lake. The man and the boy skipped rocks, oblivious to the black smoke that came from the bin. Bonn pulled out his phone. He pretended to talk on it and made for the fountain. The couple sat on a bench near the fountain. They moved on when Bonn neared. The woman rubbed the man's back vigorously. Her wedding ring fell off.

She didn't notice.

Bonn followed them. He picked up the ring. It looked old—traditional. An inscription inside the simple gold band read: H & M 5/5/1966. He flanked the couple from a distance. The woman's nose was taped as though she'd been in an accident. She had bruises around her eyes as well. She looked his age. The man appeared a few years older. They stopped to embrace. The man stood too straight. It didn't seem a romantic hug, more like he consoled her. He wore no ring.

They weren't married.

Bonn stuck the ring in his pocket. He put the cellphone to his ear and passed the couple.

The woman's hands looked very slender.

The ring in his pocket wasn't made for a slender finger.

Why did he follow them? Why did he care about the ring at all? He'd helped them already. Was this momentum? He felt obligated to see them safely home.

Bonn paused at East Drive. He checked his watch and looked around like he expected to meet someone there. The couple passed him and left the park on 72nd. The crowded walkway made it easier to follow them inconspicuously. Bonn hunched his shoulders and blended into the throng. At the next light, however, the man seemed to look right at him for a few moments, then the light changed. The river of people flowed on. Two blocks later the couple entered a boutique hotel. Bonn waited long enough for them to get into the elevator, then went in.

"Hey." Bonn used a thick Midwestern accent on the desk clerk, who peered at him over the top of trendy eyeglasses. "I just shared a cab with a super nice couple—I saw them come in. A block down the street I noticed this ring on the seat. One of them must have lost it. I ran back to try and catch them." He held the ring up for the desk clerk. The prissy-looking man raised his eyebrows and forced a purse-lipped smile.

"I'll let them know it's at the desk." Bonn frowned at the ring. He seemed to consider the offer.

"Would you mind just passing along my cell number to them? I would rather return the ring in person." Using a pen tethered to the counter by a thin chain, Bonn wrote his number on a nearby pamphlet advertising city tours. "No offense, I don't know how things work in big cities. I just want to make sure they get the ring back." He pushed the pamphlet across the desk and slapped the pen back on the counter. "Nice hotel." Bonn looked around the lobby and nodded like a hayseed. The clerk forced another smile past his obvious distaste for the task and shrugged consent. "Thanks—if I don't hear from them today I'll stop back in tomorrow." Once on the street, Bonn hailed a cab. "Penn Station."

He'd done well. He had a train to catch. The lawyers should not be much of a challenge.

He wasn't sure why he'd risked the business with the ring. Something about the woman struck him in a way he couldn't place.

A baby cried on the train. People shifted nervously, trying to ignore the sound. The mother held the infant to her neck and whispered something. It reminded him of Jelly Bean. The train accelerated after the last stop in the city. The baby settled down. Bonn pulled the ring from his pocket and rubbed it clean on his shirt.

The woman in the park ... she was grieving.

~Magic Show

Becky saw Henna onto the plane herself. The first stop was Singapore. Since the pilots were at the end of their duty day, they'd remain in Singapore for eighteen hours before continuing on to San Diego. Henna found a couch in a lounge and plugged in her cellphone to charge. As soon as she could, she called Stephan. "It's going to be OK, Henna," Stephan promised. "I'll take care of things. I'm going to send a courier for the snails so you don't have to worry about them. I'll meet you in New York. We will get a hotel room and just relax. When you're ready, we'll fly home." Henna didn't share many details, but Stephan could hear the pain in her voice.

"I'd be dead if you didn't teach me what you did."

"It's going to be OK," Stephan repeated. "I'll meet you in New York. I'll wait for you at the airport. You're going to be OK."

"Do you think so?" Henna started to sob. She didn't know it was going to be OK—all she knew was she was nauseated and sore and she didn't want to think. Stephan was patient and gentle. Long silences filled the conversation.

He'd take care of everything. She could just sleep.

Stephan, it seemed, was a magician. Before she knew it, a polite man stood before her with a bag of lemon-lime sodas, some crackers, and a really nice cooler. "Ms. Maxwell? I am here to transport your animals to Scotland."

Henna was numb when she arrived in New York. Stephan held her hand in the cab. When they got to the hotel, she collapsed onto the bed. He took her shoes off for her. Henna slept for hours. When she got up to shower, Stephan called room service. When she stumbled out of the bathroom in a hotel robe, the sheets on the bed were crisp and fresh. A few tubs of gelato sat on a room-service tray with sliced fruit and coffee. "I'm not eating without you," Stephan said softly.

She pulled him into bed and laid her head on his chest. He stroked her hair. She slept some more. Early the next morning Henna awoke to Humphrey Bogart's voice. Stephan was still in bed with her. *The Maltese Falcon* played on an old movie channel. She got up to use the bathroom and shower again. Stephan was asleep when she came out.

He was such a beautiful man.

She crawled quietly back into bed with him. He rolled toward her and pulled her close.

On the second day Henna managed dry toast. Stephan was in the shower when Becky Phillips called. "All the tests are negative, Henna. I'm reading the results now. There's no reason to start antivirals. I wish you all the best—I'm sorry we met under the circumstances we did."

"Did they determine my fate after you helped me escape?"

"I spoke to my liaison in London. The Marines have scuttled the ship. BIOT London plans to move forward on the fishing ban. Hey, I've got your little buddy here drooling popsicles on my office chair. As far as I can tell, he's from Padang. He's only fourteen, Henna. I'm going to get him home. He remembers his family. It's been many days of painful questions, but I used a translation phone service. He can nod yes and no. He remembers his parents. They snatched the little guy from the beach between four and five years ago. Henna, if you hadn't said anything about him, he might've died out there." Henna wiped at her face. It took her a moment to find her voice.

"Thank you for finding him. Tell him—please tell him—thank you for doing what he could."

"I will," Becky promised.

"So no one is—looking for me?" Henna bit her lip nervously.

Becky laughed. "There is not much drama out here. When London gave the go-ahead to sink the trawler, they all forgot about you. The boys acted like a shipment of man-sized Tonka trucks got dumped on the beach and they raced right out to play with them." Henna hung up and knocked on the bathroom door.

"Stephan, the labs are back. I just found out. They are…" Henna wiped at her face "…they are normal." Stephan opened the door in a towel. He wrapped his arms around her.

"I knew they would be. Now will you eat some gelato with me? Then let's go for a walk—we need to celebrate."

Henna caught a glimpse of herself in the mirror. She'd failed to wash her hair despite all the showers. She looked like hell. The bruises around her eyes were fading, but her nose looked worse than ever. Once Henna felt more presentable, she and Stephan went to find food. They bought sandwiches from a street vendor and took them into Central Park. The sun was low, but there were lights along the paths. It was a nice night. Although it wasn't cold, Henna stopped and shook several times. When they passed some loitering teenagers in hooded sweatshirts she shook badly. She was far from OK, but knowing the boy with no tongue might see his family again helped. Stephan was protective and affectionate. She was so lucky to have him—some people had no one.

Would she have called Alvar if she didn't have Stephan in her life?

Alvar would have taken this very hard. She might have tried to weather the storm alone. She admired Stephan as he opened the bag of sandwiches. He had dropped everything for her, and here they were in New York City. They sat on a park bench near a fountain.

The sandwiches were terrible.

Stephan read advertisements for better food from a newspaper someone left behind. A few of the places were within walking distance. Suddenly Stephan got goose bumps. He stood and looked around then held his hand out for her.

"Let's just go back to the hotel, order a few tubs of gelato—we'll eat it until we're sick." He wrapped his arm around her and pulled her close. "I'll let you pick what to watch on TV, as long as it's in black and white." Henna nodded, unable to smile at her friend's exhausted joke. The walk was adventure enough. She wanted some walls and a door that locked. She wanted to curl up with Stephan again and sleep.

~Homecoming

Sean Warfield and Casey Rainbolt jogged together every day after their morning meeting. It got the blood moving. Since they were more productive the rest of the day after exercising, the partners encouraged everyone in the firm to jog like the young attorneys did. They pulled on their running shoes even before the first cup of coffee. They ran forty-five minutes every day, rain or shine. Lately, they'd taken to the trails around Cayuga Lake. It added a few minutes to their day, but the partners didn't mind. They were longtime friends. Fraternity brothers. They worked well together. Their wives were beautiful, they were rich—in theory—they were unstoppable. They worked together like wild dogs.

Until they were accosted by a man in a black hooded sweatshirt.

Bonn wasn't cruel. He killed them quickly. He slit each man open, from pelvis to jaw, and sunk their bodies in Cayuga Lake.

Both Manny and Linda were thrilled to have Bonn home. Linda roasted a turkey for the occasion. Bonn programed the CNC machine to cut an intake manifold for the Ford GT. "There." He took a huge bite of his turkey sandwich and started the machine. Linda watched her husband become transfixed—immobile. The machine chirred and hissed—an immobile swarm of precision locusts. Metal was removed in the most beautiful and efficient sequence. When she spoke to Manny, he couldn't listen. The CNC machine had his full attention.

Linda shook her head and pinched the cheek of her high school sweetheart playfully. "Congratulations. You've been replaced by a robot—now you're my sous-chef and my dishwasher."

Manny ignored her. He kept his eyes on the gleaming manifold as it took shape. "It's beautiful—I had no idea how it could work. Just—beautiful."

Bonn gave the rest of his sandwich to Jelly Bean. The dog picked the turkey out of the sandwich and guiltily eyed Linda. "Hey now— that mayonnaise will give her the trots! Do you want me to wake you at two in the morning to supervise you while you clean up that dog's mess?" Bonn laid his ears back in mock fear. He hung his head shamefully but snuck a hand toward her plate. Jelly Bean wagged and urged him on, licking at her whiskers conspiratorially.

Linda playfully slapped Bonn's hand away.

It was good to have him home.

The dogs cut the loneliness a bit, but everything seemed better when Bonn came to visit. Linda felt brighter with him around. He was still an unnatural character, but he was good to them and she liked to mother him.

It was a bit like having an alien baby come to visit.

By Tuesday the GT was finished. Manny couldn't believe how quickly things had gone with the boy's help.

What a machine.

Manny raced the ridiculous car around on some back roads, then he and Bonn washed and polished it. As they finished up, a thin man in tweed skulked into the doorway of the shop. Bonn wiped his hands on a rag and scrutinized the skinny character without saying a word. Finally, Manny sighed and waved the history professor in. "Bonn Maddox, meet Norman Trundle." Bonn didn't offer a handshake. He continued to look Norman over. "The history professor I told you about," Manny offered. Bonn frowned as if trying to recall mention of such a man then sprang forward with a jolt.

"Oh." Bonn nodded. To Manny, the boy seemed suddenly manic. "Manny did mention you."

Stepping much closer than necessary, Bonn offered his hand to the slight man. Norman put his own hand out, and Bonn grasped it tightly. He turned Norman's palm up, which made the professor visibly more uncomfortable, then stepped even closer. The invasion of Norman's personal space caused the man obvious distress.

"The 'Bill of Rights' guy—Mr. Tott mentioned your interest in it. It was my father's. Professor Nagel at Tufts came up to take a look. He was excited also at first—he even took it to compare with one of the originals." Bonn released Norman's cold thin hand and the man stepped back, relieved. He removed his spectacles. He nervously polished the round lenses. "You got my hopes up. If it were an original, I would have sold it. That would have been a nice windfall, but as it stands, Mr. Tott took a financial hit to fly Nagel up here. Nagel said he didn't expect it, but Mr. Tott reimbursed him for his

168

time anyway." Norman pulled his glasses off to clean them some more. Manny smirked.

Mr. Tott?

"I didn't intend to cause problems," sputtered the history professor. "I'm only here to check on the—" Bonn cut him off.

"The reproduction is a good one. Nagel said it was from a batch printed in the 1960s. A place in Boston still sells them, but they are worth more than the cheaper reproductions." Bonn moved raggedly. Manny shook his head.

He's even making me nervous.

Norman backpedaled with a jolt. He found a handkerchief and pressed it to his mouth.

"The Indian," Norman managed, "I just came to check on the Indian."

"Too bad," Bonn said, ignoring Norman. "I would've been famous. You say you didn't intend to cause problems, but Norman, you have. Tell me about the lawyers you sent to badger Mr. Tott." Norman looked at the floor, as if he hoped a crevice would form large enough to hide in. "You sent over some lawyers, didn't you, Norman?"

"He sure did," Manny offered helpfully. The boy's ears seemed to lie back across his skull, like a mad dog.

"Well, Norman, you seem to be a man of few words. Maybe that's because you're an exceedingly good listener. Here's your chance to shine. We do good business here—we mind our business." The boy hooked a thumb toward the GT. "We just finished a project for our own lawyer friend in Manhattan—surprising, huh? A couple of greasy mechanics like us have friends like that? Word of mouth, Norman. It is the best advertisement. So here is the deal: The guy who bought this car has a bunch of pals at his firm. He passed around pictures of his new toy, bragged a little. Now each of the partners wants one. You know how it is. Competition. They all want to outdo each other." Manny watched Norman closely. The man turned pale and a bit—

What is that—angry? It's nice to have the boy do the talking. Hell—this is fun! Norman's a bit of a dichotomy, isn't he?

One of Norman's feet pointed toward the door, but he tapped the toes on his other foot impatiently. "Where's the document now?" He blurted, then looked behind him, like a dog surprised by his own flatulence. Manny laughed.

What fun.

"I burned it. We can stop talking about the damned thing forever, Norman. We burned it." Bonn nodded and gave him a slight wink.

"We've got a big project. The owner of the firm wants us to work on his dream car now. Mr. Tott will not have the time or space to work on your motorbike, so it is time to settle up." Manny raised his eyebrows.

Big project?

"That Bugatti, Mr. Tott, is going to take much more time than you think." Manny stifled a laugh.

"I suspect you're right."

Where'd he come up with this stuff?

Bonn returned to the GT and ran a clean shop rag along the crease of the Ford's hood. "We haven't worked on magnesium before. There will, I suspect, be a big learning curve. We don't have time for motorbikes. Our dance card, as they say, Norman, is full. Mr. Tott, do you have Norman's motorbike running?"

"No," he replied—Manny actually did have the Indian running.

But he could assure it wouldn't.

"But I cleaned it up some. How about I push it outside the shop doors there. You come get it in the morning, Norman." The skinny fellow nodded. Manny knew the man didn't believe a word of their ruse, but would he call their bluff?

That's right, Norm. We didn't burn the Bill of Rights. There is no Professor Nagel and there is certainly no big time lawyer from Manhattan bringing a rare Bugatti to Ithaca.

Norman glared at him. Manny had to chew on his lip to hide his glee. He fished around in his pocket, found a toothpick, and popped it in.

He's going to say something. He's going to demand to know the truth about the document. Don't do it, Norman. The boy is on a roll.

"I understand." Norman looked behind him again to see who'd said it. Manny chomped the sliver of wood to occupy himself and counted to ten under his breath to let the tension rise. Then he gazed up at the ceiling, as if doing a difficult calculation. He tapped his thumb against each finger, doing math on his fingertips. "Let's see, $1,500.00 should cover the bike—figure in another $2,000.00—that should cover the consultation with Nagel..." Manny nodded with finality "...$4,000.00 even."

"Thirty-five hu—" Norman started to protest but reconsidered.

170

What if the bluff failed? As soon as he had his bike back, he'd probably call the lawyers. They would get the warrant.

"Yep—sounds fair." Manny gave the boy a bewildered look as Norman wrote a check. Silently, he mouthed a word at Bonn.

Bugatti?

Norman fumed as he drove away.

The nerve of these hicks!

At this point the bike didn't matter. He placed a call to Casey Rainbolt, but it went to a recording. He hung up, disgusted.

He'd dropped a $10,000 retainer to hire the guys—the least they could do is answer the phone.

In the morning Norman turned a rental van down the alleyway to retrieve his motorcycle. He nearly ran into a car-hauler. The behemoth backed up the alley the wrong way. Several people milled around the entrance to Manny's shop. A stern-looking man wearing a suede vest and a driving cap glared in his direction and barked orders at everyone. Norman cracked the window to hear what he said. "Left. More left!" Norman backed up and waited at the entrance to the alley. A man opened the doors of the trailer and stepped inside. Moments later a 1935 Bugatti Aerolith coupe rolled out. Norman was dumbfounded. He craned his neck to see the treasure, yet failed to notice the approach of an enormous man in a suit until he tapped on the window with a class ring the size of an egg. "Roll this down all the way." Norman did. "Back up, point the nose of this vehicle in any other direction, and find another place to be," the bodyguard hissed.

"I just—"

He could see his Scout.

Norman pointed at the motorcycle for the huge man, like a toddler who knows what they want but can't verbalize it yet. The bodyguard was impatient. "Mr. Turnbull will be done in twenty minutes. Do you understand me? It would be wise to look at me and indicate your understanding." Norman nodded. "Then back up and go. If I need to, I'll get in and do it for you. Do I need to do that?"

There were two bodyguards now. The second guy made the first look like a dwarf. He approached the van like a carnivorous rhino wearing a suit the size of Norman's refrigerator. His head was lowered. He swayed side to side, each step a notable event. He flared

171

his nostrils and looked at the grill of the van as though he'd either eat or molest it. His jaw looked borrowed from an Asian beast of burden—

Norman put the van in reverse and did as he was told.

~A Good Man

Her mother's ring was gone. Henna never did have the ring re-sized. She hadn't needed to. She usually wore it around her neck. Ever since the Viesträ Alvar gave her the ring, she'd always known exactly where it was. She'd put the ring on her finger when Stephan held her in bed. She didn't know why—it was too big for her, but she slid it on and spun it around her finger while she listened to Stephan breathe. She fell asleep with it on. When she felt it on her finger in the morning, she decided to leave it there for a while.

Stephan made her feel safe.

He was kind and funny. Gentle, intelligent. When anything exciting happened he was the one she called.

She couldn't imagine life without him. Would it hurt to imagine being married to him?

She was too busy to be married—and too young. She had too much to do, but if she ever did get married, she'd want to be married to a man like Stephan. It didn't matter anyway. She was certain she wasn't his type.

She was wrong. It did hurt. The ring was gone. Leaving it on her finger was so foolish.

Henna searched her pockets. Then, in desperation, made Stephen search his. She cried with her eyes open so she could keep searching. She felt frantic and didn't bother to wipe at her tears.

There wasn't time.

The sadness swelled through the sinuses in her fractured nose, and she was forced to breathe through her mouth. She tasted tears and sat down. It was really gone. She'd lost so much lately, but the ring— it was too much.

It was the only part of her mother she had left.

Stephan called the front desk. A cheerful woman answered and looked in the lost and found drawer. "Sir, I don't see any rings here, but I'll check with the dayshift clerk in the morning." Henna eavesdropped on the call and felt increasingly unbalanced.

Even through the fight on the boat, she'd kept the ring. It had been so stupid to wear it.

It was the size of her mother's finger.

She should have kept it around her neck.

Henna looked at her hand again. She closed her eyes and willed it to be there, but when she opened her eyes, it wasn't. She wished for Viesträ.

If she broke gingerbread into three pieces, she'd have a wish. Childish. Her desperation was making her childish.

It wasn't just that the ring was her mother's. It was the reverence her grandfather showed the ring that magnified the loss. When Henna wanted to hear a story about her mother, she'd let Alvar hold it until the story was finished. It was a part of her history.

Winters were for remembering. That's when the ring was passed back and forth between them.

Henna had nothing of her father's. As a girl she had made up stories about him. She imagined him tall, with kind blue eyes and straight white teeth. Her father had loved to tickle her—she did remember that. If there'd been no fire, he would've taught her to dance—to swim. He'd wear a thin blue sweater when he got home from work. He would have distinguished touches of grey in his hair. He'd smell like cedar. He'd wear glasses that made him look as smart as he was. Her parents were married in graduate school. Alvar said they were madly in love. They'd traveled the world together. Her father would've touched the ring, too—when they were married—whenever her parents held hands. She felt her neck for the string. It wasn't there of course.

She was losing herself. Could she remember the stories without the ring? Were the stories inside of it somehow?

Stephan checked them out of the hotel two mornings later. It was time to return to the living. Henna stood in front of the hotel while Stephan checked them out. She couldn't help but look along the edge of the sidewalk for the ring.

It was ridiculous. Several hundred thousand pairs of eyes would have seen it already.

It was in someone's pocket now. Or in a pawnshop. It was melted down into something else. The stories burned out of it.

Gone forever. Vaporized. Stuck to the windows of the tall buildings around her, where her stories didn't belong.

Stephan joined her. He had a smirk on his face. A note was stapled to the hotel receipt. He read it to Henna. "I found a ring that may be yours. Please call me at the following number." Henna couldn't believe it. She shook as she pulled her phone out of her satchel and had to sit down on the steps.

174

Please. Please. Please be true.

She got an answering machine. Her heart dropped. Henna left a message—along with her cellphone number. She considered giving a brief synopsis of what the ring meant to her, but what to say? The machine would cut her off before she could, so she left a simple message: "Thank you for doing the right thing." Stephan gave her an optimistic look, but Henna felt worse. "Do you think they still have it? I lost it days ago. Will they pay roaming charges to talk to me if we fly back today? Will they believe me when I promise to pay them for the postage it'll take to ship it to me?"

Stephan shrugged. "It's more than we had—I think you'll get it back."

They had to go—Henna knew that.

Airplanes don't wait for rings.

Stephan hailed a cab. On the way to the airport, Stephan held her hand. "The type of person who'd leave a note will also return your call. Try not to worry." Henna wondered if they had to stop holding hands when they got back to Edinburgh. She hoped not.

She checked her phone on the layover in Birmingham.

Nothing.

It seemed worse knowing that someone tried to return it. Maybe they sold it or turned it into the police by now. She sat and stared at her phone while she waited at the gate. She willed it to ring. Stephan brought her food and a magazine to take her mind off things. Too soon it was time to board the last leg home. Upon landing in Edinburgh, Henna checked the phone again.

A text?

> *Of course I would be*
> *glad to send your ring*
> *along. Text me your*
> *address?*
> *Warm regards,*
> *Bonn*

Henna dialed the number again. She needed to thank them. Him? Bonn must be a man? No one answered. Henna texted back.

175

I insist on a reward. How
did you find my ring? It
means so much to me.
Thank you~
Henna

She texted her address next. Her heartbeat quickened. She stared at the screen of her phone, waiting for him to respond. When he didn't, she texted again.

I want to thank you for
being honest. I called
you, but your mailbox is
full. It wouldn't allow me
to leave a message.

Stephan pulled at her elbow. It was time to get off the plane. He steered her through the airport by her elbow while she stared at her phone. Finally, in baggage claim she got another message.

My phone acts up. I
can't access voicemail
anymore. Time to
upgrade I guess.
I'll head to the post office
after work. Glad to help.
Let me know when you
receive the package?
Cheers

Henna relaxed. She would get the ring back.
Bonn.
Henna mouthed the name. "Bonum" meant "good" in Latin and the French translation for the word "good" was even closer: "Bon." Henna smiled.
There were still good people out there.

~Marionettist

Bonn waited in a tree. The night was calm. The object in his hands was a rifle, though most people wouldn't recognize it as such. He'd made it. He'd loaded the cartridges for it—he'd even turned the bullets for it on a lathe. The riflescope, however, was recognizable. Bonn looked through the glass on the Schmidt and Bender scope as a group of teenagers began to gather near a park bench on the path near Sheep Meadow. Bonn finally felt useful—the trouble with the history professor that led to the lawyers was a catalyst. A violent one, but one he'd been destined for.

This was his calling.

He didn't share his secret with anyone. He didn't really know anyone to share secrets with anyway.

Maybe the Germans—certainly not Rupert, Manny, or Linda.

If the Germans found out they'd be ambivalent. They were like machines and reminded him of Hedwig. He imagined Hedwig out in the rain. The rain turned her body into a worm. He imagined that he picked the Hedwig-worm up off the wet sidewalk and pulled her in half. Each worm-half became one of the German men. Her body, her age, all equally divisible. The German worm-babies would heal and morph on the rainy nighttime sidewalk. By morning they'd sprout legs, arms.

And razor tipped shoes.

The Germans weren't normal. He knew that. They were interesting characters. A bit mysterious.

They weren't bad, though. They were like him, only less human.

If he needed to confide in them, he could, but he didn't need to. If he asked them to go do these things, they would. They'd do them perfectly—but this was his calling. This gave him purpose. Maybe when he had a larger project in mind, he'd ask them for help. Manny and Linda would be crushed if they knew about the lawyers, but there was no reason for them to find out. Since the trouble with Norman Trundle, Bonn checked in with Manny most mornings. Manny sounded relieved each time.

Still no word from the lawyers, son—and I haven't seen Norman since the Bugatti charade.

The trick with the Bugatti worked flawlessly. The Aerolithe now occupied the container next to the Marauder. It was pristine. The car cost him a fortune, but it served its purpose perfectly. Norman didn't need to die—he just needed a show of power. The actors were compensated well. Bonn hoped Norman didn't attend too many plays in New York—or if he did that his seats didn't provide good views of the actor's faces.

Bonn adjusted the scope. More teens joined the group. They loitered—high fives were exchanged. This wasn't a sophisticated group. They moved to a park bench where Bonn had mounted a microphone. He turned on his headset and listened in. Snippets of conversation came through the static:

"Dude. The car was like—"

"That stupid job. When I get a real job I'm gonna—"

Banal stuff. Nothing much. Nothing damning. Just dumb kids. The scope was amazing, though. Bonn checked his calculations and adjusted for windage. He let his thoughts drift on the light breeze that had kicked up.

Henna Maxwell.

With a name, an address, and a couple of razor-shod worm-Germans, you can find any information you could possibly need. Henna was born in a youth hostel in Chile. Her parents were also deceased. A grandfather had raised her. Henna was a toxicologist—a child prodigy who'd kept her momentum. Unlike most child prodigies, Henna didn't fade into obscurity in her late teens.

She'd turned into a smart and productive lady.

The man with her in the park was a friend from the university—a martial arts instructor turned scientist. He had some strange hobbies: he liked to dress like a woman and sing show tunes in public.

But who was he to judge? He was in a tree with a homemade rifle pointed at somebody's head.

Bonn thought about the wasp spray.

Henna could concoct something so much better.

Two more joined the group by the bench. Older guys. Tension in the group increased. Bonn counted heads. Seven. All male. It was almost dark, which in the city wasn't very dark at all. Regardless, the timer on an automatic lamp hummed to life near the bench. It disrupted his view of the group through the scope. Bonn pulled an ultraviolet laser from a pocket and peered through a night vision monocular. He could see the beam clearly through the device, but it

178

would be invisible to the group of teenagers. He focused the beam on the light sensor on top of the lamp. In a few seconds the bulb winked out. It was set to an eight minute delay. Bonn looked through the scope again.

Better.

There were nine teenagers now. A new arrival lit a cigarette. Several other boys hurried to light their own cigarettes to mimic him.

He's the alpha.

Alpha jumped onto the park bench with a flourish and sat on the backrest. He was right over the microphone so Bonn could hear every word. Alpha explained a point system to the group. Different actions were assigned points.

They were going wilding.

'Wilding' was a new term for an antediluvian activity; bands of kids got together and howled at the moon. Raised hell. It was usually random. They broke windows, bullied strangers. Recently, however, a woman was raped in the park and "wilding" was all over the news.

"Knock someone out? Five points," Alpha explained.

Bonn adjusted his headset.

"Take a wallet? Ten points."

The guy smoked his cigarette like a movie villain, blowing smoke out of his nostrils for effect. Bonn increased the magnification on the scope until he could make out Alpha's facial expressions. Bonn had spent a lot of time in the tree. He'd ranged the distance to several landmarks. The bench was 271 meters away. Bonn adjusted the scope a touch—fine tuning the elevation—then pulled a long sound suppressor from his bag and screwed it onto the muzzle of the rifle. The baffle stack inside the suppressor was unlike any other. He had fitted flexible silicone O-rings between each baffle. Bonn could fire twenty shots in rapid succession before the silicone began to break down. It functioned more like a wet suppressor than a dry one and increased the accuracy of the rifle. Since each huge bullet traveled at sub-sonic speeds, the system was extraordinarily quiet.

"Rape a woman? Twenty points—but you have to bring me proof."

In fourteen syllables, Alpha turned them all into targets.

Bonn spoke under his breath. "OK, guys. If you don't believe in rape, leave now."

Why didn't police bug park benches? Where were they when things heated up in the park? Feeding the horses?

179

Perhaps it was all talk. The First Amendment allowed even potential rapists to blather on about doing evil things, as long as they met peaceably while they did so, but if Bonn let it slide, one or more of these guys might deprive people of their inalienable rights somewhere he couldn't intervene. He shouldn't be so hard on the police. It would be a tough job if you had to follow rules. He didn't want to live in a police state. Bonn put the crosshairs on Alpha's nose. The young man's minions milled about as he exhaled. "None of you are leaving, are you?"

Alpha dragged it out.

Would he stop assigning points at rape or up the ante even more? His minions would wait. He was in charge. If he didn't die today, he would die in prison. After making many people's lives complicated and miserable. This is better. Here he can die outside.

One excited wilder broke away from the group. Bonn tracked him in the scope. He kept the crosshairs in the middle of his head. The guy walked a few meters and unzipped his pants. His urine began to flow. The sniper pursed his lips, thought of the curled letters on the Bill of Rights, then shrugged and pulled the trigger. This was not a peaceable assembly.

Click. The 402-grain bullet entered the base of the teen's skull at 1050 feet per second. He dropped like a marionette—strings cut. Bonn worked the bolt mindlessly and tucked the spent cartridge into the fleece-lined bag on his belt. He trained the crosshairs back on Alpha, but adjusted the field of view to see the whole group. Their behavior hadn't changed. No one noticed the dead guy. Alpha lit a new cigarette. Two guys shoved each other. Perhaps eager to prove himself, one threw a punch at the other. Things escalated. Soon they flailed their arms at each other. Neither had much technique, so the fight lasted last long enough to be a good distraction. A straggler loafed near the rear of the circle.

Click. Pink mist. The puppet master dropped another one. Bonn worked the bolt and adjusted the scope. Alpha joined the fight. He knocked one of the brawlers to his knees. The guy held his nose and spat on the ground. Alpha cocked his fist to punch the other fighter. Bonn's bullet zipped through his eye socket just before Alpha threw his punch.

Click. Alpha grinned proudly and held his arms aloft. "That's how to do it." The celebration didn't last. Alpha looked past the guy with the broken nose and pointed. The others looked too. "I didn't hit him—why's he on the ground?"

Click. A bullet severed Alpha's spinal cord. Bonn shook his head, disgusted.

Dead's dead, but that one was sloppy—too low.

The four remaining targets circled like dogs preparing to lie down. Voices rose in pitch. They chattered like birds. "He cut him—he cut Aldo!" In the chaos, one assumed the fighter bleeding from his nose stabbed Alpha. They kicked the offender brutally. One broke off. He shook and sat on the park bench.

He had a cellphone.

"Things got out of hand—yeah. Aldo got cut." He stood and paced a few meters from the bench. "Looks like his neck. He looks dead. The—"

Click. Bonn shot the delinquent in the liver. He dropped the phone and slumped. The shot had the effect Bonn intended. The others turned toward him, confused. Two boys' skulls lined up in the crosshairs.

Click. The last target standing tilted his head and cautiously approached the guy with the nosebleed. He was unconscious. He inspected his hands for a gun but found none. Then he did a peculiar thing: he turned to face Bonn. Through the scope, he appeared to see him.

Click. The bullet was perfectly placed, just below the guy's eye. The one with the nosebleed moved an arm. His neck was at an unnatural angle. Bonn adjusted the scope and prepared to pull the trigger.

"Oh God!"

Bonn spun the knob to increase his field of view. A bicyclist stood by the park bench. He had a light mounted on his helmet and shined it at the bodies in the grass.

"Oh Lord." The man dialed his cellphone while Bonn rappelled out of the tree. Once on the ground, Bonn pulled one side of the rope. It dropped at his feet. He bundled it and placed it in his bag. The cyclist leaned on the bench and yelled into his phone. Bonn broke the rifle down while he listened.

"Yeah—one guy's breathing."

"I don't know, it's dark! Maybe ten bodies? Twelve? Why does that matter?"

"Central Park. Sheep's Meadow—I told you that already."

"You've got to be kidding me—are you sending anyone or not? Oh for God sakes—Sheep's Meadow, Sheep Meadow, who cares if I've mispronounced the name of the damned lawn—send out some cops!"

Bonn walked. His long strides landed softly, carrying him away from Sheep Meadow. Static filled the earpiece—he turned it down. He knelt for a moment and turned on his headlamp. He had fired seven shots and needed to account for seven casings. Bonn opened the fleece pouch and counted the spent casings twice.

Seven. They were all there.

Bonn put the pouch in the bag next to the suppressor. He could still hear the cyclist. He switched off the earpiece and put it in the bag.

Now he looked less like a sniper and more pedestrian.

Bonn walked west quickly and gritted his teeth.

The neck shot was low.

He pulled on disposable gloves. When he reached West Drive, he pulled the surgical booties off his feet then zipped them into his coat pocket. He pulled out a small bottle of fox urine. This place would be swarming with police in twenty minutes. This time they'd bring dogs. Bonn sprayed the whole bottle of urine on the road, palmed the empty bottle, then pulled the glove off over it. He held that glove in his other palm and repeated the trick. Trappers used the stuff to hide human scent from animals; foxes mark their scent on everything. In theory, police dogs would also focus on the scent. They might stay away from his tree, at least until the ballistics experts showed up. He had hoped to retrieve the microphone, but no one could trace it. He hadn't touched it without gloves. Nevertheless, the dogs would find it. Police dogs probably found weird stuff all over the city when they were set loose. It didn't matter if they tied the microphone to the bodies. A sloppy private detective attempting to prove an infidelity could just as easily have left the device there.

Bonn mounted the old bicycle he'd left behind an earth-toned utility shed. He slung the bag across his back and rode north, exiting the park at West 72nd. He pedaled hard then paused and pulled the bike onto the sidewalk on Broadway. He leaned against a post and checked his watch. Twelve minutes had elapsed since he left the tree. Bonn watched for a gap in traffic and darted back into the street. He pedaled east and waited at a bus stop near the park until he heard sirens. An old Italian woman in her shirtsleeves, wearing a mustard-colored scarf on her head, looked at him for a moment too long. He

182

pulled out his phone and pretended to dial it. He squinted as he talked as if he couldn't hear well.

He disliked it when people stared.

The bus arrived. People got off. People got on, including the woman in the scarf. The first police vehicles entered the 72nd street entrance at the twenty-eight minute mark. Park police would already be on scene. Bonn noted the time, watched for a gap in traffic, and pedaled toward his apartment. Once inside, the apartment seemed very small. Bonn emptied the bag, spread the contents out on a table and began to clean everything. Bonn didn't have much in the apartment, but it still seemed cluttered.

It was time to move. He'd call the Germans in the morning.

~Homicide

Terrance Grimaldi clung to his soda cooler nervously as the big car swerved. He'd been a cop for eighteen years and was promoted to homicide after only two. His marriage lasted only nine years. The late hours took a toll.

It didn't matter that he didn't run around. He was married to the job.

Terrence paid his child support. He paid the rent at the apartment his ex-wife lived in. He paid the electricity and refuse bills and was otherwise agreeable to all the terms of the divorce. His ex-wife took their ten-year-old son to Connecticut anyway.

That wasn't the deal. He never saw him anymore.

The boy wouldn't talk to him on the phone. He wrote his son letters but never got any in return. Terrence applied optimism to his bleak existence as a coping mechanism.

Now he was left without distractions. Now he could do more of what he did best. Drink Fresca. Catch murderers.

Terrence was a phenomenon: he didn't have cold cases. He didn't fret over a file with gruesome pictures that would haunt him in his retirement. He never missed a thing … operating as everyone should—in the black.

Until recently.

Once Terrence got ahold of a case, he found the perpetrator, male or female. Two of the nine serial killers he'd brought down were of the fairer sex.

Fair. Sure. Like taking my kid to Connecticut—

All in all, Terrence was not terribly angry about the loss of his family. He was more—disillusioned. He wanted to be a good father. He'd never had a good father.

Matter of fact, his father was an abusive drunk pederast—may he rot in peace.

Terrance's mother remained in the old country when he and his sister boarded the boat for the United States with dear old dad, and he never wondered why. His father bought a bar, chewed cigars, and brutalized the remaining members of his family until they were old enough to flee.

In the sixteen years he'd worked homicide, Terrence hadn't been eluded. The insomnia helped. Since the divorce he'd only slept between cases. He didn't smoke or drink—not because he was a health nut, he wasn't religious either—he just worked better unaltered. Co-workers knew better than to ask Terrence out for a beer. No one who knew him even offered him a cup of coffee.

He wouldn't drink it.

His cooler kept him company when he was on the clock, which was always. He kept it stocked with Fresca and string cheese. He could get both at the Corner-Mart when he filled up the car. Once a week he bought a small bottle of conditioning shampoo and a tiny tube of toothpaste from the section where two-packs of condoms and three-dollar emery boards were sold. If he died on the job, it would be easy for someone to clean out his apartment.

There was nothing in it.

His sister sent him packets of gourmet nuts in royal blue Mylar wrappers from California. He kept them in the glove box of the unmarked sedan. The unlikely diet proved superior brain food for the middle-aged Italian. He was indefatigable. Until recently, Grimaldi had a lazy Irish partner. The heavy drinking Mick teased him for his clean living until he saw Terrence in action. He'd boxed Golden Gloves and still had the moves.

Thirty-eight and two.

He helped out at the gym a few times a week. He liked to spar with the hopefuls. It was the closest he could get to feeling like a real dad. At the precinct they called him "Bubbles" for all the Fresca he drank, but at the gym? At the gym he was known as "Hammer." Hammer Grimaldi: the Sober Wop. The portly Irishman retired to a desk job in Pennsylvania a few weeks back. "I wanna be closer to my new grandson," he'd said.

As though he'd go help around the house. Change a diaper? Please—the man couldn't be bothered to zip his fly.

This left Terrence at odds. He didn't want a new partner. He'd become used to doing it all himself.

They'd only get in his way.

He was assigned one anyway. A Puerto Rican woman named Estelle. Estelle was young and Estelle was late. Not late for work. She was in trouble. Knocked up. A couple weeks in, they'd started to click, but their first case together remained open. It'd been open for

185

five weeks now. That made Terrence nervous. It was not a good sign. Estelle seemed unaffected by the work—she had other things going on in her life. To Estelle, it was just a job. She made frequent declarations. Some were more sentimental than others. Terrence worried about the declarations also. The longer they worked together, the more liberties she took.

Oh, Bubbles—you are quirky, but trustworthy. I'm glad I have you.

After she warmed to him, things got worse.

Good Lord, could the woman talk.

They were on their way to a murder scene. Another one in the park. Terrence needed silence. To breathe, to prepare—to focus.

Drink a Fresca maybe.

Estelle, however, seemed obligated to catch him up on every boy she ever liked, every sandwich she ever ate—and what the sandwich looked like when she passed it later. The Latina suddenly slammed on the brakes and swerved around a group of pedestrians. Terrence clung tighter to the cooler.

"And Terry? I'll tell you—the chipotle chicken? That bird changed in my guts—it may've even changed my guts. Maybe forever. The baby? I think he took a few bites of the chicken as it passed him by. Couldn't help himself. It tasted good, Terry—good, spicy chicken, Terry. First thing in the morning? That bird woke me up with a burning, desperate sensation—I almost didn't make it. And, Terry? I'm not kidding even a little bit—in the toilet that bird rearranged itself to look like Australia. The shape of Australia. I'm not kidding you. And the bite the baby took? Tasmania. A tiny little Tasmania shaped chipotle chicken baby poop. Floating right next to mine. Oh, Terry—it was so cute." Estelle paused to take a drink of her banana-oat smoothie. She steered and honked with the other hand. "Is Australia a continent or an island, Terry? Because I almost couldn't hold it." Terrence hoped Estelle would stop talking, but he knew better. Talking was how she relaxed.

She needed to talk like he needed Fresca.

"Terry. I was almost incontinent of an entire continent." He tried not to react, but suspected that Estelle had seen the corner of his mouth jump a little. One day he had introduced Estelle to an old boxing colleague who'd happened by. The guy bragged about him in the old days. Estelle was all over his nickname.

Hammer? Oh! I like the sound of that. Well—not Hammer exactly, but we can shorten it up a little—Ham? Yeah. Ham sounds good.

Estelle called him "Terry" approximately a hundred times at the beginning of each day, but the rest of the day she called him "Ham." Grimaldi found that he didn't actually hate the nickname. In fact, he shortened Estelle to "Stella."

"C'mon, Ham. That's some funny sh—hey—watch out!" Stella steered around a jaywalker and honked the horn. When the sedan came out of the fishtail, Terrence pulled a piece of cheese from the cooler. Stella dropped the empty smoothie cup between them on the seat. "See, Ham? I drive better when I'm distracted with other tasks." She banged at the steering wheel with her elbows and adjusted the clasp on her necklace. A seasick St. Michael bobbed from the chain. Terrence forced himself to look away.

"Were you wearing that St. Michael when you got yourself in the family way?"

Stella smiled at him as though he were an older, ugly, sweaty brother. Terrence's attempts to keep her jabber to a minimum didn't work. Today he was trying dry humor—cutting remarks—just a little too true to be kind.

If he found a technique to hush her, he would stick with it, but so far he had struck out.

"And for God sakes, slow down. They'll still be dead when we get there."

Stella's smile spread. "Dead? Yeah, Ham. You're right, as always. That reminds me—two days ago? When we stopped at that stand for pulled pork? An hour later? Bam. I think the baby didn't like the way it looked to him. The shredded chunks floating by in globs of fat. I think he held on to a bend in my guts and flutter kicked it out of me fast, because it didn't slow down on the way out at all. I felt like a hippo-mommy marking her territory—Ham? Have you seen a hippo poop its guts out? What a sight—hippos, Ham. They wag that tail like they forgot to pay their union dues and got caught. Like a salad shooter, flinging little bits every which way. Ham. I did that. Imagine if a pregnant hippo ate pulled pork from that place. No one could touch her."

Terrence shook his head. He tried to look at the horizon—a trick that he heard kept people from feeling seasick—but they were in the thick of the city and the horizon was just the inconsistent line where tall buildings met concrete.

Homicide is a weird job.

187

Lately Stella had been sharing bits of her work philosophy. Sophomoric observations.

It wasn't really much of a challenge.

Real life was very much unlike TV. He didn't have to play either good cop or bad cop. Most people were predictable—most of them wanted to talk. Once he had a suspect in custody, there were stages people went through. The guilty folks? They had a set of stages. Innocents had stages too. If he were asked to write a book describing his inner sense about the phenomenon, he couldn't. It was just in him. It might be different in other cities, but in New York, people seemed obligated to fill silence with information. Eventually, if they were guilty, that information led to a conviction. Sure there were quiet ones, but they still gave him information—whether they knew it or not.

Sometimes silence WAS information.

Years ago the FBI sent a team of profilers to shadow him, one of them a blond woman—not a bad looking woman. He worked a serial killer case and caught the guy while the FBI got mired in the minutiae of graphs and the like. On wrap-up, the blonde asked him to write down the steps he'd taken in a decision tree. He sat and looked at a pad of paper, but he couldn't write anything—it just came to him.

Who knows—they might send him a psychic next.

This guy they were after now? He talked to him, even though they didn't have him in custody, he communicated.

But in a language he didn't understand yet.

Their open case involved three victims in Central Park. Two died from devastating blunt trauma. Something was swung with unbelievable force, caving in one guy's skull, another's trachea. The last guy was picked apart with the same type of instrument, but not with brute force.

It was surgical.

Both clavicles demolished and also the victim's insertion sites for a muscle called a "sternocleidomastoid." The medical examiner had nearly scratched a hole in his scalp.

Indicates the attacker has knowledge of human anatomy, as structures supporting respiratory accessory muscles were of focus.

Terrence thought best out loud. It drove Stella nuts when he did it, but he did it anyway. "That lands you on the angry end of the spectrum." Stella shot him a sideways glance—concern-laced disdain. She picked at her teeth with a fingernail and studied what she found.

188

"It makes me nervous when you do that."

"What?"

"Talk to yourself. Unless you were talking to me, in which case, I'll advise you to back off. You haven't seen me angry, Ham." Terrence shook his head dismissively.

So you've got a smart guy—he knows anatomy. Powerful too. Wastes the first guy with one blow. Second guy? One blow. Last guy …

Terrence asked himself questions under his breath, but found that he had to vocalize out loud to think.

"Do you know the last guy? Did he insult you? What makes you tick? Did he fight back so you took him down slow, or was he the only one without a gun, so you had the luxury of time to do him in?"

Gibberish. The actual cause of death was the bug spray—sprayed down the victim's throat.

"Why take so much time on him? Were you playing? Experimenting? Learning?"

The scene of the crime was huge.

There was a trash can fire. The perpetrator burned some things but didn't do a bang-up job of it. The bug spray had some manufacturing marks. Some bits of shoes were recovered. The grommets on the shoes were traced to a company in Japan. It was a martial artist's shoe—a sparring shoe. There were no witnesses.

The precinct tried a new thing: a morning "think-tank." Tuesdays and Fridays, unsolved cases were presented to a group. He was required to go. He didn't need the jokes. It didn't give him leads. It just provided some of his less productive peers the opportunity to be hucksters. Last Friday he'd presented the Central Park case to the group. They had a merry time with him. Some fool posited a theory that involved a band of ninjas. They read meeting highlights from surrounding precincts also. The information was too dilute. It was a waste of time, however being forced to explain the case aloud had made him realize a few things.

"You're a tough character alright, but you do some very stupid stuff. Why the fire? Did you think you'd be caught with the stuff you burned? Was it a distraction? The fire was a bad idea—likely nobody would've checked the trash can if you hadn't set it aflame." Without witnesses there were no tangible leads. The killer made boutique weapon choices—no Japanese medical students or black belt respiratory therapists were implicated in interviews with known

189

associates. A police baton might be able to create the devastating trauma, but the medical examiner nixed the idea.

Detective, a man couldn't generate those forces with something as light as a baton. It'd take a silverback gorilla.

And now, here they were. Eight youths shot by an unseen sniper. Ninth kid beat nearly to death.

The only survivor.

That kid was still in the ICU—not expected to make it.

Minimal brain wave activity, the doctor had said. He'll never prove useful as a witness. Even if he woke up and recounted the whole scene, it wouldn't be reliable information.

He wasn't beat by the shooter either; to Terrence it looked like the shooter took advantage of the fight. The gunman had capped all the other kids as they milled around. It felt good to be out of the car. Stella spoke with a crime scene investigator then joined him to stare at a patch of grass. She caught him talking aloud again.

"That no one ran when the shooting started speaks to a suppressed rifle." Stella shrugged, unimpressed. She pointed to a body.

"He was shot while he took a leak." Terrence frowned. He expected that level of hardware from a mob contractor, but mob contractors don't typically off high school kids. They watched a spatter-monkey scrape brain matter from the grass while Stella told him where the technicians were at with the scene. Tissue patterns indicated the shooter was platformed in an old oak tree about 300 yards off. It always upset the crime scene investigators when he wanted to see a fresh scene.

He generally disliked the technicians, but appreciated their work.

Lab-geeks swarmed the tree but found no DNA. The tree was recently pruned, however. The technicians worked to match the saw marks to a known tool—no luck yet. The lead arborist for the park was no help. Terrence held up his pen—he looked down the body of the implement at the oak tree as one of the scientists approached. Terrence disliked small talk and didn't greet the man like he expected.

"How fresh are the pruning marks?"

"Within the past two weeks, sir."

He'd guessed as much. This was opportunistic. The sniper was on an elongated stakeout.

"And no DNA in, on, around the tree—not a hair?"

"No, sir. Not yet. Some rope marks. Nothing useful. Rope fibers were collected. They'll look at them in the lab."

Terrence shooed the forensics expert away and continued his thoughts out loud. "The kids were probably raising hell, and at some point, the guy—who'd been camped out waiting for someone to pop—decides: 'Yeah, you know what? They're bad enough. I'll shoot the lot of 'em.'"

Stella chimed in. "If he just wanted to pop someone and get away with it, Ham, he'd have popped a jogger."

"Yeah—not entirely random, but a little bit random—maybe two clicks from random. We've got ourselves an opportunist." Stella sat on his cooler, squinting. She had found his cheese sticks.

"Most of these teenagers had knives," Stella said as she chewed. "They're small-time thugs, Ham. Basically bored kids and they just happened to organize their night near a sniper camped out for weeks in an oak tree? See, Ham, when you say things like, 'two clicks from random' it makes me wonder several things, like what comprises a click? Ham, you're no sniper and you were never in the military, so when you use the word 'click' it makes me wonder about you. I might be touchy because I'm hungry and thirsty and I've gotta pee, but I wish you wouldn't say things that don't mean anything to anyone." Terrence stretched and rolled his shoulders. She wouldn't appreciate his specific thoughts just then.

He'd wait to share.

"Don't let the baby have any of that cheese. It's stolen. It'll shoot right through him." Stella rolled her eyes and took another stick. A technician approached. He had recovered a bullet, which he dangled in front of him in a small bag.

It wasn't a regular bullet, so that could be something.

"It is approximately .300 caliber diameter, but not exactly .300 . . ." He showed Terrence and Stella the evidence bag and filled them in. ".3034 caliber diameter at the unexpanded base—400 grain recovered weight. Beautiful expansion. I don't know how they accomplished that in a subsonic. Some sort of alloy. If it were a .303, we'd have two archaic rifle calibers to choose from, but not this. This was probably shot out of a home-made rifle."

No casings. Fastidious shooter. Rope fibers. Bonsai Sniper strikes again.

Terrence didn't like it when the lab-geeks were impressed.

Stella swallowed the last of the cheese sticks and tossed the empty wrapper in his dwindling cooler. She opened one of his sodas and

191

took a big drink. A different tech brought her a stack of papers from the van. "Ham, these were high school kids. Not angels, but not card-carrying gang members either. Three of these guys though? Recently acquitted. Rape charges. Two others were on juvenile probation. One for assault, one for shoplifting. Somebody's taking out the trash. Boys don't gather in groups like this to help senior citizens get their grocery shopping done." Terrence sat on a nearby park bench.

"So how do you judge character from three hundred yards away?" He spoke softly to himself. The Mick had been hard of hearing and didn't try to be helpful.

He missed him.

"Did you read lips through the scope or was the fight enough? You don't break up a fight with a rifle. Was the fight enough to justify killing everyone except the kid getting kicked to death? Were you trying to help that kid?" Stella looked thoughtful for a moment. A crime scene investigator brought her a telephone bagged up. Stella pushed buttons on the phone through the bag and looked at the screen.

"Ham—there's an outgoing call that would've been placed around when this all happened." Stella dialed the phone number from her own phone. A man answered in a shaky voice.

"Hello?"

"Detective Estelle Castillo calling, sir. Would you identify yourself please?"

"Is Bobby in trouble? I'm sorry—this is Bobby's dad. He called a bit ago, but we got cut off. He didn't answer when I called back. He said somebody got cut? Is everything OK?"

"Sir, I'll need your address. My partner and I will come speak with you." Stella wrote down the address and hung up the phone. Terrence knew she hated that part—telling people their loved ones were dead. She shivered. He didn't mind it. It helped to be matter-of-fact with people. "Ham, it sounds like the kid called dad to tell him about a knife fight that got out of control. We should head over there. He sounded like he knew about his boy already, but I don't want to make him wait."

"Give me a minute." Terrence slid down on the park bench and put his hands behind his head. "None of the boys were cut or stabbed. None of the knives had blood on them. There was a big fracas—things were out of control—no one knew what was happening, they just saw their buddies all over the ground. There was a suppressor on a weird rifle fired accurately from a faraway tree. It was quiet enough not to raise suspicion—since none of them heard the rifle and most of them had knives on them, the kid deduced it was a knife wound—he panicked, which was appropriate. He called Dad just before he got popped—" Stella was visibly upset. Perhaps not about the phone call, or him talking to himself, but something was certainly brewing. Terrence finished his thought. "So we've got an opportunistic sniper in a tree, out of earshot. What's missing?"

Stella ignored his question. "You don't know anything about women, Ham. I'm using that cheese as a binder. Otherwise, we're going to have oatmeal smoothie soft-serve to deal with and it's gonna be really distracting. Ham? I'm so serious—you know what I'd give to have a normal bowel movement right now? I'm eating bananas and cheese to slow my guts down. My midwife says it'll help—and Ham? If you paid attention to women at all, you'd know that you only see us desperately eating cheese when our bodies have been sabotaged by either spicy food that's turning us into an airbrush nozzle, or by a little baby who thinks your colon is his hammock—either way? Don't mention any stolen cheese to me, Ham. In answer to the question I asked you? What would I give to make a normal-looking slow-moving light brown turd with a gentle taper on each end? I would give you up. Yes, Ham. I'd give up my relationship with you as my partner." Terrence had stopped listening. He was down on a knee looking under the park bench. Stella squinted her eyes, as if something besides her bowels just occurred to her. "And for perspective, Ham? I respect you. I respect you and I'm starting to like you a little—that, Ham—that's how bad I want my body back. Hey, why do I think this is our guy? The one from before? The open case—"

Terrence waved down an investigator and he came running. "The bench is wired. Shooter could hear everything down here. There's a little microphone taped under the bench. He might be listening to us right now."

193

~The Myth Of Closure

Ruka always smelled the same. Henna felt thankful for that. She kept the window down despite the light rain and the flecks of mud that found their way into the car from the bumpy old road. She needed to smell the sweet wet smells of the local foliage. She needed the mountains.

She needed Alvar.

She wouldn't tell him what happened. Just being home would be enough. The farm seemed smaller than she remembered, but more orderly. A stack of beekeeping materials lined the garden fence. There were more goats and their faces were different. A woman came out of the little stone cottage. She wiped her hands on a towel she had tucked into her apron as she approached the car.

"You must be Henna?" The beaming woman looked in her mid-seventies. Her big smile showcased straight long teeth that bore the honest stains of a life in the country—a diet consisting of starchy root vegetables and dark juicy berries—dental care only when there was a problem.

"Hello, there—"

Maybe she was the bee lady?

Alvar stood sheepishly in the doorway. The lady bustled back to Alvar. She handed him the towel then patted his hand.

"You two catch up. I'll see you in a bit." She leaned forward and tackled Henna in a running hug. Henna was enclosed in the woman's soft arms before she knew it. Henna hugged her back, polite, but unsure and the woman became even softer. She sighed contentedly then chirped like a warbler and grabbed Henna by her face with her plump, warm hands. "Maybe you could all come to dinner? Not tonight, of course, but soon?" She lunged into another embrace, but thought better of it at the last moment and offered her hand. "I've forgotten my manners. Perhaps Alvar hasn't mentioned me—I'm Akka." Alvar fidgeted on the porch. His face turned red but he remained silent.

"Very nice to meet you, Akka—" The soft-armed woman walked to an old bicycle propped against the chicken coop. She whistled happily as she mounted the bike then bared her long teeth in a smile. She pedaled out of sight. Henna hugged her grandfather.

"I didn't know how to tell you—I have a girlfriend."

Henna jabbed a playful finger into her grandfather's ribs. "I see that. She seems nice." Alvar opened his mouth to speak, then grumbled and closed it again. Henna smiled at Alvar and admired his face.

He looked younger somehow.

"Should we go for dinner then, or are you shopping around?"

Alvar blushed some more. "She's the bee lady. Sometimes she brings me food."

"Sometimes? Well, I approve, in case you need my approval. She gives warm hugs. I could get used to them."

Alvar fidgeted some more. "I was going to tell you this week. I wanted to tell you in person."

"Sounds serious." She hoped her hug felt as warm as Akka's did. Alvar put his hands on her face. Henna smirked and he gave her a dismissive pinch on the cheek.

"She wants to impress you. She left us a peach pie."

It was good to be home.

"Well, let's go have a piece. I'll want to make sure she can bake before I commit to dinner." Henna brought her things inside. The pie was still steaming. There was brandy in the filling.

Akka, indeed, could bake.

Alvar stoked the fire like he always did. They sat where they'd always sat. Henna fed a bit of piecrust to the curly-faced dog. He wagged his tail and dozed by the heat of the hearth. Henna thought of Mortimer and glanced up at the mantle-wolf. Alvar seemed to read her mind.

"That dusty old beast doesn't have much use without Mortimer around—maybe in the morning we should go bury him somewhere. If we get up early enough, we can have a basket of berries ready when Akka comes over."

Henna couldn't shake the feeling of dark, deep melancholy. She was happy for her grandfather—it wasn't him—she was different now. She was no longer the girl who really knew this place. Henna put her hand on the stone fireplace and thought of all the lessons she'd learned there—lessons she used every day. The dusty wolf skin was a lesson. Alvar probably never wanted it there. It was hung there for her: to remind her of monsters.

Enjoy the pie, but there are monsters—
I love you. Watch out for monsters—

Monsters exist, Henna—be ready.

Henna looked away from the wolf pelt. She knew monsters too well now. "Berry pie, Grandpa? Are you using poor Akka for her pie-baking skills?" Alvar played along, but he could feel Henna's tension. This wasn't a simple visit.

"I think she wants me for my money."

Their smiles died down. Henna watched Alvar wring his hands. For decades he'd sat by the hearth and loaded his pipe. Now that he'd quit smoking he didn't seem to know what to do with his hands.

She looked at the mantle-wolf. "Let's burn him."

~Truth

The building on 79th came along nicely—bureaucrats were bribed. *With enough money, most problems could be solved.*

Permits were granted quickly. The biggest expenditure was time. The concrete had to cure between pours. Although the polished stone and green mirrored glass building appeared light from the outside, it contained more concrete than the Empire State Building— and it went up in less time. Most of the windows were a façade: if a tank fired upon the first five floors, a concrete wall would be visible behind broken glass. The base of the hardened structure lay four stories below street level. The walls were fourteen feet thick and hardened with fly ash. The walls thinned at each level. On the top level the walls were a mere four feet thick and there were real floor-to-ceiling windows. No structure was literally impenetrable, but it would take some time for even the military to breech this building. Underground parking, blast doors, biometrics—the structure had it all. A tunnel led to an adjoining building, which Bonn also owned. Three sets of blast doors separated the two.

Bonn was pleased. The Germans had understood his vision.

There was a situation room with solid-state computers. There were secure phone lines. Flat screen monitors showed the exterior of the building. Images were recorded on immense redundant hard drives kept in separate Faraday cages. His cellphone rang. It was Henna Maxwell.

"Ms. Maxwell?"

"Yes. I got the parcel. I've tried to call a few times. My texts don't seem to go through, so I'm thrilled I reached you! The ring arrived just fine. I'm going to send you an appropriate thank you, but there was no return address on the package. How did it even get through customs like that?"

Bonn wasn't prepared to answer that question, so he indicated with his silence, that he considered the question rhetorical. Soon enough, the attractive toxicologist continued.

"Anyway, I want to reimburse you the postage and send along a box."

Bonn shook his head. "You're very kind—that is unnecessary. I'm pleased the package reached you."

"Flowers then."

"Thank you. No. Good karma should suffice." Bonn smiled into the telephone, as he'd been told to do as a child.

It was evident in some way to those on the other end of the line.

"You believe in karma? Very nice." Henna laughed, "A kilt then? A kilt will bring you some seriously good karma."

Bonn didn't know what to say. He was no good at banter. "You think it would?"

Henna smiled. "Sincerely now—you've no idea what the ring means to me."

She was insistent.

"How did you find it anyway?" Bonn had prepared for this particular question. He had prepared to tell her an elaborate lie about a blind man. A blind man at a crosswalk who had waited next to him for the light to change. A blind man who had thought Bonn dropped the ring. A blind man would hear the ring drop. He would ask Bonn if he dropped something. He had prepared to tell Henna he had looked up, saw her crossing the street, but missed the light and saw her enter the hotel. He had planned to tell her he made it there too late and left the note.

But he didn't.

"I was following you."

Henna was silent. Bonn prepared to hang up. He could remove the SIM card from the phone and crush it.

She couldn't find him.

She only knew his first name. It was an odd first name, but she didn't know his last name. The phone was secure. The number led to nothing. Even crushing the SIM would be overkill. Why had he told the brilliant scientist the truth?

It was reckless, but it felt right. He decided to trust her—what did he have to lose?

"Why would you follow me?"

The moment of truth. He could pull the SIM card now. He'd be a puff of smoke—invisible in seconds.

"I wanted to make sure you and your friend made it to your destination safely. Some bad men planned to hassle you in the park." He had already said too much—he might as well tell her. "I killed them." A long pause. The lady breathed, but didn't speak. "Your ring fell off near the fountain. I couldn't think of a good way to return it to you without incriminating myself. I'm not good with people."

198

She was still there.

"Which I am doing now, I suppose. Incriminating myself."

Henna was still there. He could still hear her breathing.

Everything else became silent. Bonn stood on the top level of his fortress. He looked out of the thick glass window. A mote of dust floated up into view. It just hung there.

One shiny speck. It was beautiful, defying gravity like that. It had no reason to.

Henna swallowed hard. Bonn guessed at her thoughts.

The truth was easier.

He had given her no reason to fear him. He didn't want anything. He was kind and polite, but he had said it himself—

He was not good with other people.

"Why were you watching me to begin with, Bonn?" The speck pirouetted into a bright beam of sunlight.

Henna's voice sounded measured. She didn't sound afraid.

Sparks of blue and pink reflected from the unlikely particle. Bonn was reluctant to speak; the air it took to answer Henna could create a draft and blow the shiny speck away. "I wasn't. I watched the men. They were going to harm someone. They picked you and your friend. I decided to stop them."

"What's your last name, Bonn?"

The shiny mote of dust twirled and rose in an updraft. It spun toward the sun in little circles, switchbacks that led to thick ballistic glass.

That led to nowhere.

"Maddox." Bonn told her despite the possible consequences. "My name is Bonn Maddox." The speck was gone. A falling star lost— winked out. Several seconds passed. Bonn listened for the dial tone.

Now he'd be caught. He'd have to run.

"Thank you for what you did, Bonn Maddox."

Not gone?

The speck multiplied. Hundreds—thousands of shiny specks now danced in the sunlight. Pairs of dots drafted each other, a messy cartwheeling cotillion whirled from an invisible spot on the sun-warmed concrete floor.

Brownian motion without the fluid.

Bonn didn't know what to say, so he didn't say anything. He simply stood in the sunlight. He looked out the window, watched the

199

world come to life around him, and listened to Henna Maxwell breathe on the other side of the Atlantic Ocean.

~Incarnation

Henna waited nervously at the airport. A thin man in a tailored suit held a sign that read "Maddox." The man held a soft-sided canvas bag with what appeared to be a box inside.

To thank Bonn for the return of her mother's ring, she had sent him a copy of her latest book: *An Illustrated Field Guide to Toxic Fauna of Australia.* She'd sent along a note as well. The note was difficult to write. There wasn't an established protocol exacting how to thank someone who may have saved your life from hardened street thugs.

What if Stephan had been hurt? She couldn't bear to imagine it.

When they spoke on the telephone, her savior had seemed painfully honest. Of course, there were vigilantes in the world—their crimes propped them uncomfortably atop a moral fence, teetering left and right as prosecutors and defense attorneys assigned different weights to facts ultimately damning or redeeming the person in the balance—but all of that happened if they were caught.

A man on a subway who'd had enough. A father or mother who become proactive when some creep showed too much interest in their child.

Those events made the news all the time. Bonn was different. He went looking for trouble and something told her he'd never get caught.

The man in the suit held the bag at arm's length, as if something alive moved inside. He grasped the handles delicately with just his fingertips. Henna stole glances at the man's face. Beads of sweat formed at his hairline. He glowered suspiciously at the bag until a herd of people approached. Stragglers broke from the migration to seek restrooms and coffee, electrical outlets and French fries. The thin man held the sign high, his arm a desperate metronome. The movement advertised his urgency to rid himself of the bag.

Bonn knew what Henna looked like from the dust cover of her book. It was a big advantage. Henna had no idea what he looked like. She searched the faces of travelers and watched for one to recognize his name on the thin man's sign. A dark-haired man came toward them—six feet tall, grey wool pants.

Nice shoes.

He approached the thin man with the sign in confident strides. He was muscular, but not bulky.

He looked—flexible.

His movements reminded Henna of a bipedal cat—dense muscles rolled beneath tailored wool skin. Stephan was fit, but this guy—

This guy was unreal.

His shoulders moved easily, as if they had ball bearing joints the size of shot puts. He tipped the thin man in the suit and took the canvas bag. He turned toward Henna fluidly. "Hi, Henna."

In the letter, Henna encouraged Bonn to visit her in Edinburgh. He called her soon afterward to tell her he'd like that: next week, in fact.

I read your book. I'm fascinated by toxicology, but don't know much about the field. I've been busy with school and a recent move. Your letter came at a good time for me. I could use a break from the city.

Have you been to Scotland before?

No—I'm embarrassed to admit I've never been out of the States. I'd like to remedy that.

And here he was. Strong square jaw. Great skin. One green iris corralled by a thick dark limbal ring—and one white iris, the lost looking pupil floating conspicuously in a milky pool. A faint scar ran from Bonn's cheek and terminated in a disfigured ear. He was an incredibly intense-looking man, and he seemed aware that the eye was off-putting.

"Welcome to Edinburgh, Bonn. Did you get your first ever passport stamp?"

The cat-like gentleman smiled and patted his pocket. "I did. It feels good. I'm a man of the world now."

A small shock of white hair grew from the scarred area near Bonn's ear. He looked so smooth, so symmetrical everywhere else, the irregularity drew Henna's attention. Bonn ran a finger along the scar. He'd noticed that she'd seen it.

"Childhood was rough on me."

She was quick to smile. "I keep mine on the inside. Now that my nose looks like a nose again, I mean. Last time you saw me I was pretty banged up." Henna touched her own face to mirror Bonn's scar. "What happened there?"

With his squared off features he reminded her of a taller, more handsome version of her gargoyle.

"My mother shot me on my ninth birthday."

Henna's eyebrows shot skyward. "Wow—you're serious aren't you?"

"I'm not very funny—serious is all I've got."

Henna nodded. "Let's go get your bags." She felt a slow smile adorn her face and didn't try to fight off the welcome feelings that accompanied her expression.

"No need. I've had some things delivered to a hotel." The well-dressed American offered her his arm and held up the canvas bag. "I brought you a gift. They may be a bit cramped, so do you mind if we stop by your lab on our way to conquer the city?"

"They?"

Had he brought her something—alive?

Bonn returned her smile, but his face seemed unaccustomed to the movement. "Cramped may not be the correct word. You'll see. It's a surprise."

They took a cab to the university. Bonn slid down in the seat of the cab so he could more easily see out the window. One after another historical buildings drifted past—some older than the United States itself. Henna pointed out some of her favorite landmarks.

Henna passed cab fare up to the driver. "You can let us out here." They were a few blocks away from the school, but Henna wanted to show the visitor one of her favorite spots on foot. It was raining, but the New Yorker didn't seem to care. They walked down ancient stone steps into an even older cemetery. The verdant expanse was overgrown with moss-covered headstones and crosses. Some were so old the inscriptions were gone.

Bonn drank in his surroundings. "Everything seems so—"

"Old?" Henna squatted to read an inscription.

"I was going to say green. Green and gray. It reminds me of upstate New York. They used a lot of stone in the buildings there too. I snuck out of our house a lot to explore when I was little. Stonework always interested me." The rain let up. Bonn looked inside the bag, then felt the box. "It probably isn't accurate to say I snuck out. No one would have come for me even if they knew I was missing, but I practiced my stealth, nonetheless." He seemed satisfied that the contents of the bag were dry.

They continued along the winding path through the graveyard. Bonn seemed awkward—he was so careful to choose the correct words that he seemed wooden. He spoke slowly, as if he wasn't used to talking to anyone at all. "In fact my German nanny might have locked all the doors if my absence wouldn't have rendered her nonessential."

"A nanny? Where were your parents?"

"My father was either working or philandering. My mother was similarly occupied, minus the work."

They left the graveyard. Bonn walked on the sidewalk closest to traffic until they entered campus. When they approached a bald panhandler with a spider web tattooed on his head and one pink contact, Henna noted that he positioned himself between them. He seemed naturally protective—like Mortimer. Henna told Bonn about Mortimer and the wolf. She couldn't actually tell if he listened until the story was finished.

"That's amazing. I've never seen a dog do anything like that." When he looked at her, his eyes were so intense. Piercing.

Unsettling.

He seemed aware of it. He obviously tried not to look at her, as if he knew it would be painful and rude to do so. Henna attempted to break the tension with yet another story—about the day she picked wolfsbane. This time she could tell he listened. He was odd but apt.

He seemed a bit robotic.

He didn't nod knowingly, interrupt, or even smile as she talked, but he definitely listened. He seemed to see and notice everything. It didn't look comfortable to be inside his brain. There was an awful lot going on up there. But by the time they reached the University, she'd adjusted to his lack of emotion and expression and their conversations fell into a rhythm. When Henna opened the door to her lab, Bonn's eyes widened slightly to take it all in. "Oh. Fantastic."

It was the least enthusiastic utterance of the word Henna had ever heard, but the odd man said it with genuine intent.

Henna walked him through the lab. She pointed out animals. She used their common names and gave Bonn interesting facts like Alvar used to do for her. When Henna came to an enclosure housing a coastal taipan, she told him about her search for the inland taipan in Queensland—the snake that had eluded her. "I liked that part of your book the best. You mentioned road hunting in the foreword—the excitement of searching for one thing and finding another—I thought about that philosophy a lot, in fact, Henna. Without the motivation to find the inland taipan, you might not have encountered that perentie, but you recognized the opportunity. You took it. We are alike in that way."

"You really did read my book. It was such an amazing trip. I remain optimistic about the taipan. Sooner or later I'll have a pair of them in my collection." Bonn handed her the canvas bag.

"I've found that optimism pays extraordinarily well."

~Hard Objects

Bonn felt at home in the new building.

The living space was on the top floor. The architect was a fan of Fibonacci's golden ratio. She'd made each space, each room, each window feel right. A great room divided six apartments. Each apartment was similarly furnished with simple modern decor. Two of the corner units didn't have windows. Depending on an occupant's perspective, they were either luxury safe rooms or elegant dungeons. A floor-to-ceiling window on one end of the great room delivered an illusion: it appeared one could float out into the cityscape. The glass was treated for privacy, yet still gave a dose of natural light to the room that made it feel alive. An immense mosaic occupied the other end of the great room. Constructed on a monolithic stand-alone wall, the artwork served to camouflage the unsightly elevator shaft. The artists used reflective bits of glass to create a nautiloid swirl: black, copper, cobalt, June-bug green—great plates of weathered copper covered the walls surrounding the mosaic.

The effect was bewitching.

The team of artists that created the piece was busy two floors below, on an even more impressive project. Each apartment was comfortable for two people. They were intuitive spaces. Each surface, each seat, the placement of each light made sense. They were ready for visitors, though Bonn didn't yet know who those visitors might be. The finest materials were used in construction, yet nothing was overdone. A basket of toiletries sat crisply on each bathroom counter. Even the toothbrushes were luxurious. Soft, white, organic bristles sprung from wooden handles ready for grateful hands to make use of them. Bonn swung open the heavy door to one of the windowless apartments and carried in the Bill of Rights. He considered each wall in the main room and chose one. He propped the frame gently against the wall. It would be safe here. More secure than any museum. He'd be sure to invite only the most appropriate visitors to see it.

The floor below the living space would be Henna's lab. His visit to Scotland had been fruitful. Henna agreed to help him outfit his own toxic menagerie, but the lab would be as much hers as it would be his. Bonn would staff it with a hand-picked team that could care for the animals and produce useful substances. The Germans worked out a floor plan for the space that optimized work areas, while tastefully showcasing the animals. One level below the lab was Bonn's church. The gym was large and simple. Divider walls separated gear from the main area. The architect used a Japanese aesthetic to create a space where Bonn could practice Kendo and meditate. Shoji doors led to spaces where Bonn could climb ropes, use kettle bells, and practice powerlifting. One room housed only a fist-polished teak Mook Yan Jong, a wooden training dummy nearly two centuries old.

If you strike soft objects, you stay soft—to become hard, you must strike hard objects.

Bonn rode the elevator down two floors. He wanted to check on the progress of the larger mosaic. The artists were all women—two sisters and a cousin. They were born in Japan, but were very much New Yorkers. They worked together quietly and with great affinity. They'd measured Bonn before they started the project—both barefoot and with shoes. They'd rolled an elaborate jig up to him. He peered through tubes to determine the exact height of his pupils when standing and at rest. They'd measured his gait, his stride. Precision was imperative. They measured the room the piece would occupy, sketched and diagramed, talked in hushed tones and sourced materials for a week before they ever laid the first glass piece. Bonn gave them a blank check and a theme. They were determined to create a masterpiece.

This project, sir, is the challenge of a lifetime. We will assure that you are pleased.

The glass pieces were placed painstakingly. Each was now in place, but individual portions of each piece of glass were polished. As one woman adjusted and moved a large light on a boom, another woman polished the pieces. The third woman wore what appeared to be black suede blinders and stood on a small stool that brought her to Bonn's full height. To further limit her vision, she peered through small black tubes at each piece as it was faceted. Bonn was unsure how she communicated with the woman polishing the glass. She twitched her hands like a spider checked its web. Bonn moved closer to her. He heard tiny tonal utterances. She seemed more conductor than director. She ignored Bonn for several minutes, so he sat to appreciate the process of creation. The woman on the stool made a curious gesture after a few minutes and swept off her blinders. She lithely dismounted the stool and took Bonn by the hand. She led him around the room so he could view the mosaic from several angles.

It was breathtaking.

The scene showed Musashi Miyamoto. He knelt in a rowboat. The water shimmered, clean and deep. Musashi wore tattered peasant clothing and carved a long bokken out of an oar. His most famous opponent, Sasaki Kojiro, angrily awaited him on the bank of a small island as Musashi put the finishing touch on the edge of the bokken with a small carving knife. The woman squeezed his hand. "Observe, please—the hamon." Kojiro's sword. The polished edge of the long weapon shone as Bonn moved through the room. He nodded in appreciation. "Amazing."

"No," the woman said softly, her eyes dancing from his face to the mural. The glass polisher pointed to Musashi's bokken—where Musashi ran the carving knife along the cutting edge of the improvised wooden sword and a dazzling shimmer reflected back. Bonn walked around the room again to watch the effect—the oar seemed alive. The shiny edge of the wooden weapon illuminated the self-assured expression on Miyamoto's face. "Only for you—the hamon on the oar. It can only be seen at your height—the pieces were set just so."

Bonn considered how difficult it must have been to cut, set, angle, and polish the thousands of tiny bits of glass the way they had done. The woman grasped Bonn's hand again, to hold him in place. She nodded to her sister, who adjusted the lights. The mosaic changed. The sun came from behind clouds. Musashi, Kojiro, even the boat cast shadows now—all three women watched him. The room was thick with anticipation. This was the moment that would make or break the mosaic.

There—he saw it.

Musashi's shadow lay coiled in the water.

It was his true nature—

The woman closest to the mosaic, the one who'd set the pieces, spoke reverently. "Watatsumi." Bonn felt a shiver of excitement. He sucked in his breath and sighed in genuine appreciation. He knew the legend.

Watatsumi—the dragon-deity of the sea.

208

~Forty

Henna shook as she entered the ICU. The physician on the phone said it was a subarachnoid bleed from blunt force trauma.

He looks better today, but he's not out of the woods yet. I apologize that you have not been contacted sooner. We didn't know who he was for a while. You are Stephen's power of attorney. Are you related in some way?

A lapse of time had occurred. She couldn't recall anything between that phone call and this moment. Peering in the small window to his room, she wasn't even certain how she got to the hospital.

It couldn't be him.

His whole head seemed purple and swollen. A tracheostomy tube embedded rudely in his neck.

Oh, my poor Stephan.

A nurse came in to check vital signs. She asked him some questions. He nodded and coughed a bubbling wet cough. The nurse suctioned out the hole in his neck and plugged it with a small valve so he could talk then went to retrieve pain medicine. Henna was horrified.

At least she knew where he was now.

It had taken the police three days to sort out what actually happened at the cabaret—two of Stephan's friends were killed in the senseless attack. Stephan reached for her hand. Orthopedic pins stuck out of both hands and he winced with the effort. He tried to smile. Henna couldn't smile back. She touched the tips of the broken man's fingers and he seemed to relax, but then his breathing seemed too fast, as if he were preparing to dive underwater. Henna stood to get the nurse, but Stephan shook his head stiffly. He tried to say something. She bent down. Stephan's eyes moved as though he watched a moving train beneath his swollen lids.

"Can you see me?"

Stephan strained to answer. "Um ..." Stephan coughed more.

Everything about his airway looked uncomfortable.

He tapped her hand with his fingers, but it seemed involuntary. The nurse was back. She gave Stephan some pain medicine through a huge intravenous line that ran underneath a clavicle then helped him roll onto his side. He relaxed a little. His eye movements persisted, but the train slowed. "Forty of them, at least."

"Forty? Stephan, it's me, Henna. Forty what?"

Stephan coughed again. The nurse assured him his cough was stronger then stooped to check on some drainage devices strapped to each side of the bed. "Call me if you need anything, OK? I'll check on you in a few minutes. Here's your call bell—" The pain medicine made Stephan drowsy.

"Forty what?" Henna repeated.

Stephan strained to open his eyes. He seemed angry. The train was back and was up to full speed. Stephan's eyes jittered back and forth.

"Didn't I already tell you this?"

Henna recoiled. "No—I just got here." She could see how easy it would be to become disoriented in this environment. "Do you know who I am, Stephan?" Her friend closed his eyes, but the train sped along. His face drew tight and he looked like he might cry. Then he did. He cried. And tapped his fingers frantically. When he opened his mouth, Henna could smell blood. Most of his teeth were broken or missing.

"Forty of them, Mama." Henna stooped awkwardly, trying to hold him. She hovered, looking for a place to touch him that might not hurt. There weren't any.

"It's going to be OK, honey." Henna didn't believe her promise, but she had to say something. She wiped her own tears with a sleeve and found some tissues nearby for Stephan.

"Forty," Stephan said again, then drifted off. "Too many to fight."

A man stood at the door. He appeared surprised to see Henna. He didn't appear to be a medical person, and for a moment it appeared that he would walk past. Henna felt her jaw clench and squared herself to the door.

"You know him?" the intruder offered. Henna stepped toward the man and in front of Stephan to block the interloper's view.

She answered rabidly. "Who are you and why are you here?" The man quickly found his manners.

"Chief Superintendent Forsythe. I want to help."

He wants to help. Too late for that.

"I'm Henna Maxwell. Stephan's power of attorney." Forsythe nodded. He stuck his hands in his pockets.

"How is he today?" Henna looked at Stephan—he either slept or ignored them.

210

"How is he? Not good. I'm his close friend and colleague, but he thinks I'm his mother." Forsythe nodded.

"The doctor has kept us from talking with him much. He said we had to 'minimize stimuli.'" Henna crossed her arms and paced at the foot of Stephan's bed.

"His brain was bleeding. They couldn't allow anyone in, I guess. I only found out he was here this morning." Forsythe nodded again. The man obviously had questions to ask, but pursed his lips and was silent.

Chief Superintendent—impressive title.

Henna broke the silence. "Who did this?"

"A hate group. White supremacists." Forsythe stepped closer to Stephen and tilted his head. "Your friend here took a few of them out. He fought like hell. We have video footage from the bar." Henna shook. Forsythe kindly pretended not to notice.

"Do you know Stephan through the Synagogue?"

"No. Through the university." Henna did a double take. "Synagogue?" She forced a laugh to make her point. "Stephan isn't Jewish. You're thinking of someone else." Forsythe raised his eyebrows. He rummaged through his pocket for something, then handed Henna a copy of Stephan's passport. Stephan looked so young in the photograph: on his head, he wore a Kippah.

It was unmistakable for anything else.

"He may have worn that for the photo as a joke. He's got an odd sense of humor." Forsythe shook his head confidently.

"He's young for a rabbi, but he's a bona fide rabbi. He was ordained eighteen months ago. That's a big deal. He must've grown up orthodox, because the knowledge it requires to become a rabbi is intensive. He likely studied hard from the time he was a young boy." Forsythe watched the information sink in. Henna felt dumbfounded.

How didn't she know? She knew he was a drag queen. Hell, she knew his shirt size. How could she not know Stephan was a rabbi?

Forsythe held his hand out for the copy. "Let's get some coffee."

Forsythe filled her in. Forty-four aggressors, most with shaved heads and neo-Nazi tattoos, descended on the cabaret en masse. Security cameras caught the event. Each carried a framing hammer. None wore masks. The attack was long and deliberate. Forsythe watched Henna wince at the mention of the hammers.

211

He had to read her correctly to know if this would succeed.

Henna set her jaw. Steam rolled off her untouched coffee. "How many have you arrested?"

"It doesn't work that way, Ms. Maxwell. We're in the information gathering phase of the—" She didn't let the detective finish.

"Forty-four criminals entered a building with weapons, battered eight, but killed two men in a premeditated act and it's on videotape?" Henna knew she was shouting, but she didn't care. "On *video*, Mr. Forsythe—and not one arrest has been made? All of those men—have they vanished into thin air?" Forsythe looked into his cup. Although he'd already sweetened his coffee, he tore open a sugar packet and slowly stirred it into the cup. Henna leaned in to assure Forsythe saw her glare.

At sixty-one, his career was nearly over. Forsythe had worked hard to keep peace in the city. He'd been young once. Unjaded.

He got promoted because he was a good officer.

A good man.

He looked at Henna apologetically. "I'll be honest, Ms. Maxwell—by that, I mean if you repeat what I tell you, I'll be fired. That'd be OK—I'd go learn to fish. I'd seek peaceful spots. I'd sit and take time to listen to the birds. I wouldn't hold it against you, but I think I still have some good to offer the community, so I hope you don't repeat this." He felt sad and defeated. "Some of the skinheads are connected."

The girl waited. Forsythe felt embarrassed to have said what he did.

Connected—the mobster cliché.

"Connected to what?"

He stirred his coffee some more.

He had already said too much. The stunt would get him canned.

"Connected to someone important?"

Forsythe sipped at his coffee. The woman across from him was so young—so full of energy. Ready to change the world. He envied her. He remembered those feelings. Unyielding certainty and vigor are only friends of the young, but he was thankful the traits still existed. The decades of disappointment had changed him. Even good people lost their certainty in jobs like his.

212

He couldn't feel it anymore. No sure things existed. Disappointment and injustice taught him that.

He'd lost himself—his hunger for change and justice. At the end of the day, cops that last are the cops who know when to stop asking questions. He shook his head, disgusted with himself. With the injustice of the system.

She even looked a little like his wife—before she passed.

She was gone even before he lost faith in the system. Before he realized he was powerless to make grand changes. He was only one cog in a machine. No matter how well he did his job, no matter how precisely he matched the teeth of his gears with the rest of the machine, the machine often failed. It failed by design. It was bigger than any individual. It was more powerful. The machine that men built to ensure justice didn't run justly. It didn't thrive on goodness and light. It was simply a massive delivery vehicle. Someone operated the machine for a while and it delivered money from one account to another until the balance of power shifted. Then it delivered money to the next god. The cogs of the machine, like himself, never even felt the transitions. It was easy to convict a homeless miscreant who does wrong, but it was routine for criminals who had friends in power, friends with money, or friends with influence, to go free. It was a hard lesson to learn, yet for some reason he still clung to the machine like a tidewater limpet. The naive part of him still hoped it might someday work, though he'd run out of motivation to fix it.

"I'm not ready to learn to fish, young lady." Henna glowered at him, so he focused on stirring the sweetener into his coffee.

"Not just yet."

~Great White Hope

Brownsville was Bonn's new proving ground. Bonn walked the streets just after dark. He wore a black hooded sweatshirt, loose jeans, and sneakers. He kept his hood up and his head down. It was much harder to blend in—in Brownsville—the population of whites hovered between two and three percent, so if anyone saw his face, they'd consider him an oddity. He'd spent time getting to know the streets. The first few times he'd ventured into Brownsville were uneventful. Tonight he planned to walk down Pitkin Avenue. There were more businesses and fewer apartments on Pitkin, so he was sure to encounter more people.

Just another guy looking for drugs.

Bonn kept his hands in the long front pocket of the sweatshirt. He'd cut holes in the pocket to allow quick access to the baton, oleoresin capsicum spray, and karambit strapped to his belt. He'd painted upas, tincture of arrow poison wood, on the blade of the hook-shaped knife. Bonn was certain the tincture hadn't been easy to come by. He didn't entirely understand the poison and treated the blade with great respect.

To most people the gruesome gifts he and Henna exchanged would seem macabre. They were certainly not romantic gifts.

The odds of being shot in Brownsville were good, even if you didn't go looking for trouble. Accordingly, Bonn wore a ballistic vest under the sweatshirt. He also carried an unregistered .357 in case things went truly sideways. He took the gun from a guy on the subway one day. As the thug watched his heavy-hitter friends beat someone over a perceived infraction, he'd noticed the outline of the revolver in the man's back pocket. Bonn sunk an ice pick just left of the man's spine, hoping to hit his descending aorta. He made a quick circling motion and pulled the pick out. His estimation worked. The man bled out in a couple of minutes—well before his thug buddies finished with the beating. Bonn wore skin-toned rubber gloves in public. Since he had never handled the revolver without gloves, it was an ideal backup weapon. He set it up for a weak side draw, in the event his dominant arm became injured.

As Bonn walked, he noticed differences in the clothing worn by gang members. Even from block to block the colors were different.

Basically an enormous public housing project, gang activity was common. Gang members advertised their turf with their clothing. Prostitution was rampant. Drugs could be found every hour of the day—sadness of every flavor. For sale, cheap. A young man approached on a BMX bicycle, a Yankees cap sat high on his forehead. He wore a flannel shirt tied low around baggy chinos but was bare-chested. He looked lanky and awkward on the small bike.

"Smack downs, boy?" he asked.

Was he even sixteen? Certainly no older. He would call the kid BMX.

BMX seemed shocked when he saw Bonn's face. "Aw no—You want girly girl instead."

Bonn had worked to develop an understanding of local street language. It was a challenging task. "Boy" definitely referred to heroin. Cocaine was more a white man's drug and was commonly referred to as "girl." Since Bonn didn't look like a heroin junky, BMX likely offered to sell him either cocaine or a session with a prostitute. "I'm good. Thanks anyway."

"You a narc?" Bonn held his left eye mostly closed, like he'd been punched or possibly had a palsy. He'd brought props along, so he pulled out a pack of cigarettes and lit one.

"Sure, kid. I'm a narc." They faced each other for a moment. BMX smiled and shook his head in disbelief.

"Why you walk Pitkin this late?"

Bonn worked hard to smoke the cigarette naturally. "I should ask you that. What are you, about fourteen? You should be at home where it's safe. You'll only get yourself in trouble out here. Why did you ask if I was a cop—you have drugs on you?"

"At home where it's safe?" The kid gave Bonn a look of incredulity. "You don't know where I live." They neared a row of three-story apartments. The boy gave a shrill whistle and pedaled away quickly.

Housing projects in various stages of decay surrounded him. Cooking noises rattled from open windows. Cigarette butts lay in thick piles. A man in a blue windbreaker sat and smoked on a stoop. He stood as Bonn came near. He tilted his head and squinted past the brim of his cap to get a better look at Bonn.

"Playa, why you in the pro-jects?"

Another man stood quietly inside a nearby doorway, listening. Bonn knew both were armed.

The guy on the porch must sell what the guy in the doorway hands him. If the cops came by, the hood on the street would hand his pistol inside so he didn't have anything incriminating and the man in the doorway would disappear. If rivals came to shake them down, the man inside would have a long gun—it was a good strategy. The police wouldn't do anything without a warrant.

"You can't help me."

"This my hood, bumpkin—I be yo' ONLY help."

BMX watched from the corner. He held a cellphone to his ear.

Time for improvisation.

"I need ten keys of raw." It was an unreasonable amount. Men who sat on porches couldn't access that volume.

Bring out the boss.

The man laughed. "You travel pretty light. What, you gonna write a check?"

He had a point.

Bonn took a drag from the cigarette. "You think I'm alone? You have your boss, I have mine." The man on the porch shared a look with his backup then stepped onto the sidewalk. He looked up and down the street to exaggerate his disbelief.

"OK, great white hope—conjure up the man. Let's see who shows up." Both BMX and Backup spoke into their phones. Bonn may have sold them short. They were patient and organized.

Did they have a call tree? How many guns would point his direction in a couple of minutes?

Bonn panned the myriad windows that faced the street.

They could be anywhere.

Bonn shook his head dismissively and started down the sidewalk. "You have had enough playtime. You must not have the resources. I'll go find the varsity crew." The screen door creaked open. Backup stepped off of the porch with a pump shotgun. He held it along his side as he approached and surveyed the block. BMX was on the move too. He pedaled toward him on the bike.

Bad odds. Take the fight on the move.

Bonn pulled his hands from his sweatshirt pockets and held them to his sides, but he didn't stop. He kept walking.

"Hey," Backup yelled from the porch, "We ain't done!" The slide of a pistol racked home a round. He stepped sideways. Glancing back, he saw that BMX had a semi-automatic leveled at his chest. An old car approached. "Hold a minute," Backup ordered. "This your boss rollin' up on us?"

216

Bonn nodded to buy time. BMX held the pistol down to his side and watched the car. Bonn slid out the baton and held it collapsed in his fist like a kubaton. "I always wanted to meet Gerry Cooney. That who gonna roll down the window and show me the briefcase full-a-money?" The car slowed, then stopped at the curb.

An old Toronado.

"Problem is—that there? That there's my boss." Bonn felt an impact on his back. He spun as he swung the weapon, crushing the dealer's temple with the steel base of the baton, then flicked the weapon fully open.

He got cut when he turned.

The knife didn't penetrate deeply into the vest, but the back of his arm stung and felt wet. A shot rang out.

BMX. Point blank.

The boy looked confused as Bonn swung the baton. He took the blow to his jaw, and peered up at him from the ground. Bonn kicked away the pistol and swung the baton again, destroying the sentry's trachea. A shotgun blast made Bonn's ears ring.

That was a much greater impact than the pistol round. Guess the vest works.

Backup pumped a fresh round into the chamber. Bonn dropped and rolled toward him. He held his breath and squeezed his eyes shut as he emptied the can of OC into Backup's face, rolled, and pulled the karambit. As the doors of the Oldsmobile swung open, he registered shouting despite the ringing in his ears. Bonn unzipped Backup's abdomen with the knife. Reflexively, the man brought his hands from his stinging eyes to protect his core. Bonn spun the knife by the ring on the end of the handle and sunk it into Backup's ear.

He had tunnel vision. That couldn't happen right now.

Tunnel vision would get him killed for certain. Someone just got out of that car.

Run.

Bonn ran. He heard gunfire but didn't feel any impacts. He heard footsteps of people as they took chase. Though disoriented, he sped up.

How many gunshots had there been?

He squeezed his right fist, then felt his groin and hips for blood as he sprinted. His right arm was drenched in blood. It was hard to tell where else he might be hurt. Risking a glance back, he saw that two people chased him—two men, but they weren't gaining on him.

They didn't appear to be athletes. Time to take stock.

The OC spray was behind him in the street. No prints would be found on it. He still had the karambit. In fact, he had been running with the poisoned blade. He slowed, re-sheathed the knife, and felt for the revolver, then ran even faster to increase the distance while he planned his next move.

He still had the gun, but the baton was gone. That wouldn't do.

That level of ineptitude would get him caught. It was bad practice. He ran past a group of guys with red shirts and white shorts. They laughed at Bonn until they saw who chased him—then they ducked into a doorway.

Next hood over—as good a place as any.

Bonn stopped in the street and turned. The men closed on him slowly.

Flagging after only a few hundred meters? Weak effort.

Bonn pulled the .357. He stood broadside to the men as they approached and concentrated on his breathing.

He'd be ready when they got there—all he had to do was aim true.

He cocked the hammer on the revolver and relaxed his right arm along his side. With a deep breath, he crouched. The men cartwheeled in on worn-out legs and burning lungs. The faster of the two brought up his pistol as he slowed.

They didn't expect the revolver.

Bonn shot him in the brain through his frontal sinus cavity. The second man was a few yards behind. He understood too late that Bonn was armed. Fatigued, unable to control his forward momentum, he slid as though he'd stolen third base. As his sneakers caught on the pavement, he began to tumble. He dropped his weapon. The gun skittered past Bonn as he fired two quick shots into the man's torso.

Breathe.

He picked up the thug's ball cap and put another bullet in his head. Bonn pulled the hat onto his own head in a fluid motion, tossed the .357 on the ground next to the owner of the hat, and picked up the dead man's submachine gun to check the chamber, then the magazine. He flicked the selector from "full-auto" to "three-shot burst" and engaged the safety.

It was sloppy, but it was done. Now he'd go back for the baton.

As Bonn walked, he listened for sirens. Hearing none, he approached the scene confidently.

Just another curious thug.

He pulled the Yankees hat low. A large woman knelt over Backup's body. She didn't seem to notice him.

The baton should be close.

People hung out of windows. Some held cell-phones. Others brought their dinner plates with them.

They must not have cable.

The large woman began to wail.

There. The baton.

Bonn retrieved the stick from the gutter and walked to the Toronado.

The car was still running.

After a quick sweep of the interior with the submachine gun, Bonn got in the Oldsmobile and pulled the stick to "D." At a light he felt dizzy and short of breath. He fastened his seatbelt and dialed Ryker's cellphone.

"Can you meet me in the garage? I've lost some blood. Yes. If it is something we can fix ourselves, I would prefer that."

~Modus Operandi

Terrence threw Stella a glance.

She'd heard it too.

It was the first "morning think tank" of any worth. The Brownsville case was well presented. A ton of witnesses, but none of the accounts matched. The detectives on the case gave a synopsis over the speakerphone.

"One woman swore she saw a policeman shooting up the neighborhood. When asked why she thought he was a policeman, she had said, 'Cause he was white.' No one came forward who could identify the man."

Drug deal gone bad? Doubtful.

"One witness swore there were many white guys rampaging through the block just east of Pitkin. Some wore baseball caps, some wore sweatshirts. They all ran like hell. The way the guy worked the neighborhood over is confusing ..." The detective took a demoralized breath. "One victim took a blow to the temple. Another was doused with OC spray, disemboweled, then stabbed in the brain. He had a cardiac glycoside in his system. Lethal dose of it. Don't ask me which one. One kid had a broken jaw and a fractured trachea— he'd apparently been riding a bicycle while attacked, or while on the attack—his prints were found on a pistol at the scene. Piece had been fired. He did manage to get a shot off—"

Stella returned Terrence's look. She leaned in to whisper, "I want that coroner's report. We should compare it to the Central Park case."

"—the bullet from the bike-hoodlum's gun hasn't been found, but there was blood on the street that didn't match the victims. Some of it on a knife. No local hospitals reported gunshot wounds or stabbing victims not otherwise accounted for."

Again. Stella leaned in. "Vest?"

Terrence nodded. "Maybe."

Not our case, but maybe our guy.

The detective cleared his throat and continued to report his findings in an increasingly dismal tone. "—and up the street two more men were shot. One a head shot from approximately thirty feet. Second one, double tap to the chest, one to the head. Looked to the

CSI like the guy was down already when he was shot. Prints found on one gun on scene matched Martin Stone Slattern, aged twenty-eight. Long rap sheet. Martin was wanted for grand larceny and several counts of assault in Pennsylvania and New Jersey, but that lead didn't pay off. I used 'was' because Martin was killed with something like an icepick on the subway a few weeks ago. His prints weren't pristine, so someone likely took the gun from him on the subway—"

Someone with gloves on.

The trachea injury definitely reminded Terrence of the Central Park victims, but much of this was nonsense.

Why would you poison someone by disemboweling them? If you can disembowel someone, then stick a knife in his ear, why would you need poison? Why the overkill?

"—a can of OC spray was recovered. Surprise—no prints."

Sure a thug can get some gloves on, but in a drug deal gone bad, is a guy going to pull OC spray? No. He's going to pull a gun. Is it likely that an armed kid chased someone down on a bicycle, shot but missed, then is taken out with a lead pipe to the trachea?

Stella leaned in. She had found some gum and cracked it in his ear. "It's a populated city, Ham—but the trachea thing? That's a pattern."

Terrence hurried to his desk to make some calls. Stella rolled her chair close. She took a soda out of his cooler and droned on about kids' names. Terrence was getting to know her.

Sure, she filled the air with noise—mostly junk—but the woman came up with good leads while she did it.

"Daniel?" Terrence looked at her quizzically. "For a boy, Ham. Daniel. I think it's sweet. Traditional. Simple. Danny for short—what do you think?" Terrence nudged his cooler under the desk with a toe and pointed at the phone he held to his ear.

"Ringing—Stella, how is 'Danny' any shorter than 'Daniel?' They both have two syllables." Estelle frowned. She tapped her finger at the air, ostensibly to count syllables. Suddenly she jabbed at the telephone, disconnecting the call.

"If this is our guy and Brownsville's guy, he's a very busy guy. Let's assume it is him—what's the body count including Slattern?"

"Including Slattern? Sixteen."

"That's what I got too. After you talk to the guys at seventy-third, let's get something to eat, Ham. Something mild. I'm tired of you always asking about my bowel habits. It's getting creepy."

~High Art

Exercise helped Bonn think. He needed the burn. The ache—the stretch. It cleared his mind. He jumped rope, worked with the Mook Yan Jong, and swung kettle bells. He felt strong but remained troubled. The shot in the park was low. Though it had been a week, Bonn still needed to know why. Yes, it killed Alpha, but the neck shot was not his point of aim.

What was perfection?

Musashi knew better than he did. He looked to the mosaic. He willed the legend in the boat to talk to him.

What would he say? One has to find limits to surpass them? Perhaps, learning from failure negates the failure itself?

He doubted the master would go that easy on him. Bonn had lost sleep over the neck shot. He should be reviewing the events in Brownsville—only dumb luck got him through that night—but to Bonn, events were linear. He couldn't move forward until he understood the low shot in Sheep Meadow. He put down the kettle bell and padded to the machine shop. He sat before a CNC machine and turned it on. He'd already pored over the rifle. It was pristine. He'd studied the brass. Earlier, he'd pulled and studied the primers from each empty cartridge, but he still couldn't explain the low shot. With the tap of a few buttons, the expensive device began to carve a perfect looking bullet out of the alloy bar stock.

Since human error was out of the equation, was the alloy to blame?

The bullet was done. Bonn placed it on a small digital scale.

406.22 grains. That was it—the bar stock.

Bonn felt relieved. He reset the machine and cut another one.

405.75 grains. No wonder. At subsonic speeds, the weight differences mattered. Even at short ranges.

He had calculated bullet drop based on 402 grains. Bonn clenched the two projectiles in his hand and made his way back to the gym. Musashi remained in the boat—forever carving an imperfect wooden sword from an imperfect oar. The carving knife he used was—imperfect.

Maybe guns weren't the way to go.

Musashi always made do with what was at hand. He had used his mind to win battles before they were fought. His lack of convention was what made him a legend. Bonn thought about the rifle. It was close to perfect. He'd succeeded in building an (unconventional) conventional weapon. Bonn ran his fingertips over the wound on his arm and allowed his thoughts to fall into their natural places.

Surprise was more important than perfection. Precision was good, but artistry was better.

Bonn reviewed his many mistakes in Brownsville. It seemed a laundry-list.

Under-armored and under-gunned ... he let people get behind him. He had to set the terms. Do something more meaningful ... would the world be a better place because he killed five dealers? No. They were already replaced.

Bonn decided to go back to Brownsville. He'd bring surprises. He'd pick his fights better.

He'd hone his art.

~Everything That Comes After

Henna waited in the green hallway to see Forsythe's boss. His avoidant and long-suffering act was lost on her. She wanted to see some action. She'd gone through the trouble of making an appointment, but the time of that appointment was now long past. Henna felt her ears become hot as she became angrier. Finally the door opened. A slight-shouldered elderly man with a shock of unruly white hair shuffled out and turned to close and lock the office behind him.

"Deputy Chief Constable Abernathy?" The man peered at Henna over the tops of his bifocals, then looked down at his big gold watch.

"Yes, lass. Late for an appointment—Maxwell is it?"

"Late, indeed. For my appointment." Henna glared at her own watch. "Over an *hour* late—you can stuff the attempt to dismiss me and refer to me as 'Doctor Maxwell.' Give me five minutes. We're both busy people."

Actually, Henna skipped a rung in the chain of command. Forsythe's direct supervisor was on vacation. He wouldn't finish his African Elephant photo safari for another week. Henna couldn't wait another week. She needed to see the men that hurt Stephen and murdered his friends behind bars. Abernathy's head turned as red as his nose. He smelled of alcohol. Since he couldn't quickly find a way to escape her, he turned back to the door he'd just locked. His jaundiced fingers fiddled with the keys until he had the door open again. Henna found the man repulsive. His liver appeared to be the only organ in his considerable abdomen. Henna followed Abernathy into his office. It was as she expected: big desk, crystal decanter. Expensive wood.

At his pay grade it should be nice.

There weren't windows in the room, however.

Abernathy's boss would certainly have windows. And probably a decanter, since Abernathy got away with having one.

She immediately disliked the man. Deputy Chief Constable Abernathy gripped the edge of his large wooden desk to ease himself into his comfortable chair. Once planted, however, his mild countenance changed. "I heard some talk about you meddling with an ongoing investigation, and I want to hear your thoughts, Doctor

225

Maxwell. Why would that seem prudent, or even practical, for such a busy scholar?"

Asshole.

"I'd be happy to expound, but I'm not inclined to use my time that way. Tell me about the barriers to appropriate arrests when there are known and identified murderers free in the city. Don't underestimate my resources or resolve, Mr. Abernathy. You may see a girl, but I know some people that may impress you and my temper is short. Consider this a motivational courtesy call." Abernathy was unprepared for the challenge. He'd not been challenged by anyone in years. Henna gave him a moment to process things, but his eyes didn't seem focused, so she pressed on. "This is when you tell me why no arrests have been made and we talk about action. Chief Superintendent Forsythe was forthcoming about these murderers. They're connected to someone important. Who? Your boss is out photographing elephants. He's been out of the country since the attack on the cabaret. I doubt he took a moment between epic dust bath and watering hole shots to jaunt over and tell Forsythe to drag his feet, so you must have … Why?" Abernathy looked vacant. Henna seethed. "Forsythe was a gentleman, but he wasn't at the hospital to interview victims. He was there to canvas for friends and family who might cause trouble, because someone—perhaps you— told him to."

Abernathy glanced longingly at the decanter with the lovely burning elixir inside. He hadn't had a drink in a half hour now. The comfortable film protecting him from demands and decisions had become too thin. He operated better at a drink every fifteen minutes.

Of course he'd ordered Forsythe to gather information and halt all arrests, but he didn't know why. It came from up high.

His job was to be a stern and punctual middleman. He was told what to say, what to order.

He was, in fact, ordered what to order.

"Ah, well—" Abernathy poured himself a drink. He skipped the part where he offered Henna one. That would make him an obvious target. "Ms.—" Abernathy winced and started over. "Doctor Maxwell …" He poured the fluid down his throat. The comfortable film returned. His tongue relaxed. It knew what to say without the brain.

226

Add scotch, tongue helps brain. Repeat. It'd worked for years.

"I'm certain you're very important indeed, although I myself have never heard of you. I've no doubt but that you are acquainted with important intellects of all kinds who are ready to storm the castle in their petition for justice. In due time, that very justice will be had— certain investigations take more time than others—to determine how to proceed with measures such as arrests. I'd humbly ask that you give our system the time it needs to—"

He was stuck on a word. To what? To cover up the decimation of a group of drag queens? To allow criminals to escape? To hide? To literally strike again? The blood on those hammers was dry a week ago. Perhaps a sip would help? Ah, there.

"To digest this tragedy and pick the correct course in assuring that the correct people are brought to the fore to answer for it." The pesky girl's ears shone red, so mad she appeared nearly on fire.

The anger was lovely on her. Show us your tits, lass.

"Digest?" The scholar pinched her earlobes and twitched. "How long does it typically take a 'system' to correctly digest, cleanse, gather the fortitude to take the appropriate action, Mr. Abernathy?"

The film was back—just then. What a relief.

He allowed his eyes to rest solidly on the girl's bosom. He saw her mouth moving. He knew she was angry, but his tongue would take care of it.

He could relax.

His tongue spoke: "What are you a doctor of, lass?" A momentary trouble rested in his mind's periphery, but the tongue was quick. It would get rid of the pest. He watched his hands pour another drink into the glass from the decanter. The hands served him well, and he smiled at them in thanks.

Old friends—each little part of him. All was fine when he bathed his brain in enough scotch.

"If you're seeking a way to minimize my title, you won't find one, you pompous drunk." Doctor Maxwell stood. She plucked a card from his gleaming desk and was gone.

He could rely on his tongue. It always helped him. It always knew just what to say.

O̲nce outside, Henna began to shake. She had to walk. She needed Stephan, but not the new Stephan—she needed the old Stephan.

The whole Stephan. Stop—that was wrong—Stephan needed her. For the first time, he needed her. She wouldn't let him down.

It was time to stop asking herself what Stephan would do— *Stephan DID.*

Henna convinced the owner of the cabaret to show her the tape. It was horrible—the men with hammers rolled in like a tide and started swinging. Stephan managed to take about six of the forty-four out before they had him on the ground. They swung the hammers at his face—they held down his arms and crushed those capable, loving hands. Stephan fought like no one she'd ever seen, but they still got him. Henna walked. She ruminated. Soon she stood in the graveyard she'd shown Bonn. She held the phone to her ear. Even as she did, she couldn't remember who she had dialed. She could hear her heartbeat and paced.

"Hi, honey—are you calling to check on my weight? I'm trying to limit myself to one pie a day."

Alvar.

Henna breathed into the phone. She didn't know what she needed—she didn't know what to do. "Are you there, Henna? Can you hear me? I hear you breathing, I think. Are you OK?" Henna found her voice.

"No, Grandpa—I'm not."

"What's going on? Do you need to come home?" Henna sat on an old stone bench and tried to calm herself. The bench faced a large headstone over two hundred years old.

A girl. Twelve years old—the perspective was just what she needed.

"I need some advice, Grandpa."

Perhaps Alvar sensed the distress in her voice?

"I've managed to get quite old. I might have something useful to say."

What had Abernathy said? Oh yes. I heard some talk about you meddling with an ongoing investigation. They could have her phone tapped. She wouldn't be able to flesh out any details for Alvar, but she probably didn't need to.

"I've never asked you about the war, Grandpa. I've been afraid to ask. I'm certain you witnessed horrible things. I can't imagine the injustices you endured." Alvar was quiet. She pictured him leaning forward, like he did, intent to glean a salient meaning from her jumbled words.

228

"Injustices are a part of everyday life on different scales, dear, but yes—wartime brings out the worst in people—not all people, though. It brings out good qualities buried deep inside others."

"How did you make it? Out, I mean, and with your decency? Oh, Grandpa—I don't even know what I'm asking you."

Should she just tell him what was going on?

She was suddenly reminded of Mortimer—the day he broke the window to kill wolves.

"How did I make it?" Alvar became deathly quiet. Henna pictured him back in a trench, a burning rag tied around a wine bottle filled with petrol and soap—perhaps the first of many he'd throw at tanks, but this was the very first anyone threw—since he designed it, he threw it. Was he fighting injustice? Nothing about war was just. At a certain point justice is no longer expected. Even the idea of it feels like a trap, somehow built to trick you into the ideal, but what mattered? What could Alvar distill to tell her about resolve? Was she asking for advice?

Or permission ...

"When you're at war, it's important to fight. If you're committed, you aren't fighting for yourself, you're fighting for everything that comes after you—" Henna focused on the young girl's headstone. She nodded into the receiver. "—and once you start to fight, or fight back—once you've made the decision, you tear a hole in Hell, make what escapes work for you. Don't stop until it's done. And Henna? If what you've done isn't enough, tear a bigger damned hole. Invite every last devil. Point the beasts in the right direction and light their tails on fire." Henna breathed a sigh of relief. She'd received his blessing. Of course leveraging a corrupt legal system wouldn't work—

She would kill them all herself.

~The Act

Bonn showered and dressed.

Tonight, he would be—an artist.

A scene from a movie had struck a chord with him. The main character had a prosthetic third arm. In the scene he rested the arm on the bar and had a philosophical conversation with the bartender. He paid the man for information. Despite having superior skill, he took no chances. Out of sight, the man's real hand held a pistol leveled at the barkeep. The scene was comical, yet there was some utility there. Bonn took the idea to an extreme. He brushed his teeth with his left hand before reviewing his gear. Though right handed, he'd used his left hand for everything for several days. He'd adapted quickly. His dexterity improved. He could pass for a left-handed man now. Bonn looked at himself in the mirror. A prosthetic right arm held a large artist's portfolio bag. It was a believable arm. It appeared to articulate naturally out of his shoulder, which was the biggest trick. A loose fitting car coat allowed the illusion. He could pass for an architect or a graphic designer. His real arm rested inside the portfolio. It held a suppressed bullpup rifle with a fifty-round magazine. It was ideal for the bag: the brass dropped from the bottom of the stock as each round was fired, and it never jammed. The cartridge contained a fast moving round. It wasn't as quiet as he'd like, but the bag itself muffled much of the operating noise. Only a half-inch of the suppressor was visible outside the long flat black portfolio case, but since the suppressor was also black, it wasn't noticeable.

Bonn used a bore-sighting laser while he practiced.

The bullets would go where the laser shone.

He'd practiced for hours each day, checking his aim by dry firing the trigger on the laser device in the chamber. Practice truly did make perfect—though essentially shooting from the hip, he now felt confident to engage targets out to twenty meters. Bonn removed the costume. He field stripped the rifle down to the firing pin, lubricated all metal parts that touched other metal parts, and then re-assembled the rifle with a new firing pin. He cycled a dummy round into the chamber and squeezed the trigger to check the primer strike. Next, he slipped on a ballistic vest and a light sweater then put on the coat.

He arranged the prosthetic arm—a lightweight glove was stretched over the faux hand. Even the finger joints on the hand moved. Bonn walked back to the mirror and adjusted the hand to hold the strap of the bag. Bonn finished the outfit with a porkpie hat, which he sat at a jaunty angle. The hat was black with a small red and yellow feather. He sought to appear a likely victim. The feather reminded the vigilante of a lure. He entered the park tentatively and walked without confidence. Without purpose. He made his way meekly through the park and avoided eye contact. A skateboarder passed him from behind and he jumped, startled. Bonn ambled for twenty minutes. He shrank from joggers. He held a large paper coffee cup in his left hand and pretended it was full. His body language declared he couldn't bear to spill even a drop of precious coffee. Bonn trained the bullpup at each passerby. It felt natural. He startled frequently. It was an important part of the role, but he wondered how believable the act was.

The fish weren't biting.

Was the hat too much? Generally people steered clear of crazy. Had he overdone the outfit? Maybe he'd jumped meek and nailed schizophrenic? Bonn challenged himself to stay in character even when no one observed him.

Discipline. Patience.

Two uniformed policemen on mountain bikes nodded in passing. Bonn stood aside. He appeared to toast the officers with his coffee.

Movement on the left.

Something rustled in the bushes. Pivoting slightly, he leveled the cup at the figure as it broke cover—a coyote—after a feral cat. Many coyotes lived in the city. The canid dodged at right angles, but the cat made it to a tree in the nick of time and clawed up to a fork. It rested for a few heartbeats, then hissed loudly at the predator. Two women approached. A third figure, a man, sat on a bench near a pond thirty meters off. One of the women held a phone to her ear. The man on the bench sat angled to watch.

"Sweet hat," offered one of the women. Bonn tipped the cup in silent thanks.

She was about eighteen—and dressed like a runaway.

The girl seemed committed to engage him. She was thin and pale. She stunk. She had sores around her mouth and was missing teeth. "Where you from?"

231

Bonn kept the cup pointed at her face, but looked at his shoes. He shook his head and backed up a few steps.

"I do not want to seem rude, but I am married. I am not looking for company."

The girl on the phone laughed. "Don't got any spare change for a runaway?"

They were digging in.

The man on the bench stood. He glanced around, then strutted toward them. "Oh hey—I wish I could help. Listen, my church lets people crash in the basement—are you girls all right? Are you really runaways?"

The girls are the distraction—the man plans to mug me.

"Oh—that's so sweet, Captain Save-A-Ho. Thanks, though—we got a place to sleep. How about twenty bucks—can you kick in a little if we do?" One of the girls tried to slide to Bonn's left, but Bonn stepped back to keep everyone in sight.

The guy was within range.

Bonn aimed the bullpup at the man's nose, but kept the small can of cholinergic agent inside the coffee cup aimed toward the girls. The hand holding the cup was also a prosthetic—his actual hand was balled inside the cup, aiming the nozzle attached to the can of aerosolized poison. "What about it, honey? You got some change? Or a smoke?"

There.

The approaching man pulled a revolver from his jacket pocket and brought it up.

TCHISSS. TCHISSS.

Bonn put two bullets in the man's brain. He spun toward the girls. The girl to his far left held a cheap .380 and gaped at the fallen man. Bonn didn't hesitate. The jet of cholinergic hit the girl in the face. She dropped the gun, but her hands reacted too slowly to block the aerosol. She fell. She foamed and convulsed, as though seizing.

"What did you do?" Bonn asked the remaining runaway—he hoped his voice sounded frightened.

She may be a victim here.

The girl seemed frozen. She held her arms stiffly to her sides and let the phone drop from her fingers.

Was she new to the ruse?

232

She might be a runaway—it would be easy to fall into the wrong crowd when you're trying to live on the streets. "No, retard—what did YOU do?"

He wasn't very good at reading people.

Bonn sprayed a metered blast at her chest—she looked down for a moment, glared back at Bonn and then started to leak.

Everywhere.

She coughed foam. Her eyes ran like faucets. She lost function of her bowels and bladder. Although the spray hadn't hit her mucosa directly, it killed her in seconds. Her eyes ran even as her pupils bloomed open to indicate brain death. Bonn reached for the stopwatch inside the portfolio and started the clock. He stood in the midst of the melee for a moment. He panned for possible witnesses. He wouldn't kill witnesses, but they'd affect what he did next. Seeing none, Bonn turned on his heels and walked back the way he'd come. He worked his hand free from the paper cup and placed it in a zip lock bag inside the portfolio. Ninety seconds passed before he came across the first pedestrians. A young couple—dizzy in love. They stopped to kiss often. It would take them awhile to reach the bodies. Bonn sped up. At thirteen minutes he reached the garage entrance to his building. Once inside, Bonn stripped off the portfolio bag, the coat, and prosthetics. He tossed the porkpie hat and replaced it with a bicycle helmet with a rearview mirror coming off of the brim. He kicked off his Chelsea boots and ratcheted on some expensive road bike shoes. He tucked a pant leg into his sock, slung a trendy messenger bag over his shoulder, and scanned the door open.

Presto—I'm a bike messenger.

The bike was a "fixie." No brakes, one speed—only serious cyclists rode them. If he were searched for any reason, police would find an NYU ID. "Steve Thompson" carried two energy drinks, a thin book on economics, a cheap blue plastic calculator, and some highlighted class notes in his bag. Bonn stopped at a light and glanced at the stopwatch.

Twenty-eight minutes.

Sirens could be heard in the distance, but that was normal. Park police would be on scene now. The homicide detectives would be there soon.

They were who interested him. That's why he'd gone hunting tonight.

He pedaled into the park. He took paths that swung wide of the crime scene. He reached forward to activate a light on his handlebars, then another button to make the red light pulse under the seat.

Safety first.

Thirty-seven minutes. They should be there now. Bonn headed for the crime scene. Around a bend an officer spoke with someone in a sedan then moved aside a temporary traffic barrier.

There they are. Homicide.

An officer waved a flashlight at Bonn to stop him. Bonn pushed a small button on the back of the helmet mirror, which turned on the fish-eye camera hidden in the helmet's sun visor. He kept the visor pointed at the sedan. "Go back the way you came and take another path. This one's closed." Bonn rotated a heel to disengage a shoe from a pedal. He put a foot down for balance. "What's going on?"

"Investigation. I'll need you to exit the park as soon as possible."

"I know CPR." The officer gave him a pained smile that didn't appear sincere.

"We're past that. I need you to move along now." The detectives got out of the sedan. The man held a can of soda and eyeballed him hard. Bonn kept the camera on the detectives, but glanced down to check his watch. "If you have someone walk me through, can I go this way? I'm going to miss Frasier—my girlfriend will be really mad and I've just recently been invited out of the doghouse." The officer gave a more genuine smile, but pointed Bonn back the way he'd come with the flashlight.

"Could be worse. Trust me." Bonn shrugged and clipped back into the pedal.

He had what he came for.

He'd get to know the detectives in the sedan. He realized how risky it was to come back, but if things worked out, the video would pay him back in droves.

Terrence watched the red blinking light fade as the cyclist rode off. For a moment he considered sending a unit to detain and question the guy then thought better of it. No reason to waste time on him. Revisiting a crime scene just as the homicide cops rolled in was simply ridiculous.

The lack of sleep was getting to him. That was all.

Stella chatted up a storm. They drove another fifty yards and she swung her swollen ankles out of the sedan. "I miss coffee, Ham. And beer. Oh, little St. Michael, thank you for keeping the bad mommy away from her beer."

The crime scene investigators recognized the sedan. The one in charge loped quickly toward them. It was Tuesday. During the morning think tank, Terrence read a transcript from upstate—a couple of bodies washed up in the Finger Lakes. One in Cayuga, one in Seneca.

Just bodies—no heads. No hands or feet

What may have been a tattoo on the upper chest of one of the bodies had been skinned off. The abdomens of both men were opened, presumably to sink the bodies, but whoever dumped them forgot to perforate the intestines. Bacteria continue to thrive in a corpse's gut—that creates gas. Dead people don't fart, so intestines grow and grow. If they're in water, you've got a nasty gut buoy. Some kids out canoeing came across the flotsam. They towed it aboard to inspect it, then saw a corpse hanging below the surface like a fishing weight. The kids freaked out, capsized the canoe, and swam for shore. Authorities dragged Seneca Lake and found the body. Next day? One shows up in Cayuga Lake. The bodies may have been dumped together. The Finger Lakes were connected through underwater caves. Both had male bone structure, but the fish ate the genitals. Water does a job on a body quick. Terrence had seen a few floaters. They turned soft and black fast. Fish don't care what they eat.

Including corpse dick. It threatened to turn him off fish altogether.

Five weeks before the bodies were found, two lawyers went missing in Ithaca. Hair samples matched. The report spoke to solid police work. He didn't envy the guys working that case.

No leads, no known enemies. That's a cold one.

"I can't let you in yet ..." The crime scene investigator in charge was blocking their way. "But I'll give you the rundown so far. Why do you keep showing up so fast? Are you two driving on sidewalks or what? Don't answer that. I like surprises. First girl there..." the investigator pointed with his pen "...no ID. Several credit cards in her pocket. Different name on each. Cellphone in the grass. Last call in the log placed to the phone of that male corpse..." the man pointed with the pen at a body a few yards away "...who has two in the head. The girl looks like hell. She has pink froth all over her face, pee pants—lost her bowel function, too." The CSI took a breath and

235

looked to make sure the detectives were following him. They nodded. Terrence gestured to keep the information coming. "Second girl." The pen pointed at another figure in the grass. "Same thing. Pink froth. Soiled. They may have been sprayed with something."

"Bug killer?" Terrance asked.

"No. Nothing that benign." Stella looked back and forth between the girls. She had an odd look on her face. The technician who collected evidence from the second girl approached them.

"This one had a baggie of rock methamphetamine in a pocket, but no pipe to smoke it with. No paraphernalia on her. No spoon, no tourniquet."

"So not a double OD? Bad batch?"

"Unlikely."

The investigator in charge of the scene had something else. "Two guns on scene: neither one has been fired. She has one, he has one. The shooter isn't here. OK, you know the rules. I know you are itching to go roll in something important. Don't. Go gawk at the dead people. Don't touch."

Nothing seemed easy anymore.

Terrence hadn't slept in weeks. He was breaking down. He'd have to force himself to sleep. Maybe he would go home. Take a Benadryl. Force the rest. He was no closer to solving the other two Central Park cases and now they had a mystery poison? Delivered by whom? Someone who also, conveniently, had a gun. He couldn't imagine how this one went down. Terrence pinched the flattened bridge of his nose and closed his eyes.

Stella seemed manic. "We're up to eighteen that we know about. It's our guy." She snapped her fingers, then pointed this way and that, like she saw things. "Yeah. You know, Ham? Yeah." She made for the sedan. She took two cold sodas out of the cooler. She sat on the seat and waved her arm out of the window for Terrence to join her. Terrence ambled begrudgingly to the car. "It's all a little different, huh, Ham? Different guns, bug spray, poison. Blunt objects, but he's a slasher too. Does he want us to think he's different people? No. He doesn't care what we think. He's not in this for glory, Ham. He's practicing." Stella held her index finger up to keep him silent while she gulped at the bubbly drink. "He's a little fledgling who's spreading his wings, getting ready to fly. He's trying on a few pairs of wings to see what he likes to fly with—and when his real wings sprout, Ham? We're gonna have the Angel of Death on our hands.

Eighteen's a lot, Ham. You think he's counting? I don't. I think he's just coming up to speed. I think our guy's using Central Park as a playground. As an incubator. I think he tried out Brownsville when he felt ready and got schooled there. Sure he killed everyone who came after him, but he took some licks too, because he came back to his incubator. This is his safe place." Terrence put his soda back in the cooler.

It wouldn't help.

"So what? What's your point? Let's say it's our guy and you're right—he's ramping up to fry the big fish next. He's in his research and development phase, but soon he'll jump out of his comfy little Central Park nest for good. That he's already stuck his toe in Brownsville's pond to test the water. It didn't go so well because he took a bullet and he limped back here to 'incubate' some more. So what? Where does that leave us?" Stella was making chewing movements. She'd discovered the shiny, blue bags of nuts in the glove box.

God, he missed the lazy old Mick.

Stella could chomp and talk at the same time. "I'm no profiler, but we need one. I know you don't like profilers, but that's where we're at. We got a real interesting guy here, Ham. He's going to have books written about him—maybe even a TV special. I'm saying I don't want to be the cop who skips the profiler and lets the guy spread his wings to float out over the city like Saint Michael here, Ham. I'll tell you what—I'll call one in. You don't even have to listen. You keep on not catching him the way you've done, but I need some help and you aren't it. Know what you need? Sleep. You're so far gone you don't know you need it, but you do."

Bonn reviewed the footage. He paused a frame and expanded the view. He'd captured what he needed to on the helmet-cam. He took still shots of each of the detective's faces, then zoomed in to read the woman's ID badge. "Estelle Castillo." He ran a public record search. In a few keystrokes he had her phone number and home address. The man hadn't worn a badge.

It didn't matter.

Bonn dialed the non-emergency number for Castillo's precinct from a secure line. "Twenty second dispatch, how can I direct your call, please?"

The woman who answered sounded weathered.

"Yeah, hey—I got a money clip down here—must have eighty or so bucks in it. You got a pregnant gal in the twenty-second? Comes for a meatball sub every couple days? Gal can eat. Chatty one. Anyhow, the old guy, her partner—he left a money clip down here at Vince's. What's his name? Drinks sodas, but brings his own— cheapskate, you know? Won't buy a thing."

"Ah …" The dispatcher perked up. "Bubbles?"

This was likely the most fun she'd had all night.

"Terry Grimaldi. Terry won't even eat a sub down there?" By her tone, Bonn realized the dispatcher planned to tease Grimaldi a bit when he rolled in.

"You kiddin'? Can't make a dime on 'em."

Terry Grimaldi? Could be Terrence.

Bonn tapped at the keyboard.

There you are.

Divorced. Old-school boxer. Bonn leaned back in his chair and studied the man's flattened nose and scarred forehead. "He's damn lucky I'm Catholic. Guilt wouldn't let me sleep if I took his money. Have him swing by?"

~Conviction

Henna did her own police work. All she needed was one and here he was—he'd lead her to the others. One man stood out in the footage from the cabaret. He'd laughed when he crushed Stephan's hands with the hammer. When he was done—when the men who'd held Stephan down left to bludgeon other victims, he stayed. He sat beside Stephan. He leaned in and appeared to talk to him—almost as if he knew Stephan. She took still shots of the man's face and printed them on her computer at the university. Stephan was slowly getting better. He called her by her own name now. That morning he'd gone in for his third surgery—hand specialists needed to move two pins in his hands that migrated, and since he'd be under anesthesia anyway, other surgeons would work to reconstruct his sinuses and jaws. Teeth would come later. Still—Stephan would never be the same— although his brain was healing, a lot of anesthesia accumulated from the many surgeries. It was hard to tell what he'd be like in a year, or even two.

His door was open. Stephan was awake. Henna sat on the bed and stroked her friend's hair. After a while he noticed the pictures in her other hand. He reached for them. He couldn't focus. The neurologist was hopeful the traumatic lesions causing nystagmus would shrink when more swelling went down and his trochlear nerves healed. Stephan moved the picture on top of the stack back and forth for a long while.

"I know him—I'm remembering more now." It took Stephan some time, but he accurately described the man in the picture. "I know him from school. He took a class from me. I thought he liked me." The parts of Stephan's face that still moved looked sorrowful. "I'm sorry I didn't tell you I was a rabbi—I grew up Hassidic. Like all fundamentalist upbringings. It created shame and resentment. There weren't options or choices of any sort in our house. It was hateful— my father starved me when I couldn't recite teachings verbatim. I didn't want you to know me like that. An instant victim? No. I learned long ago that you can feel sorry for yourself and limp through life, or you can choose to be what you want others to see. I want you to know me as strong, capable, independent, fearless. It's who I want to be for myself too. That's why I dressed up for drag shows. I—I

239

suspect you might think I'm gay, but Henna, I'm not—I spent time at the cabaret because I was surrounded by friends who were facing their fears head-on. It wasn't what they were doing that was important. What they chose to do despite their fears mattered. It was a festive atmosphere—lighthearted and ridiculous, but exhilarating. No judgments were made. Nothing was too serious. That acceptance allowed people of all sorts to be kind, patient, understanding with each other. It was the farthest I could venture from the pain of my upbringing. It's a wonder I still want to be Jewish." Henna smoothed at a bit of hair that hadn't been shaved from Stephan's head.

"What else don't I know about you?"

Stephan teared up. Secretly, Stephan had loved her for years. He had almost told her thousands of times, but it was better she didn't know. He loved her unconditionally. There was no one on Earth like her. He'd always felt lucky just to be near her and if she knew, if things became uncomfortable between them, he'd cheat himself out of the only relationship he'd ever cherished. If there had ever been an appropriate time to confess his feelings, it had passed long ago. It was especially true now—with him in little pieces.

"You're a great friend, Henna." Henna teared up but had to stay on task.

"I actually knew that—OK, not-gay rabbi. Tell me about him—let me go get him."

"He seemed to have romantic intentions, but I'm celibate—let's add that on for fun. I'm a *celibate* not-gay cross-dressing rabbi." Stephan was trying to joke.

That was a good sign.

Henna forced a smile. "Don't forget ninja."

"Yeah—I was a ninja too."

"You still are—"

She couldn't lose it right now. She had to stay on track, or she'd just crawl in with Stephan and never leave. The men who hurt him would get away with it.

"—so he was mad you didn't want to date him?"

"Maybe—I think he looks for boyfriends, but it's a secret he compensates for with the hate group. He seemed mad when I told him I was busy. He knew I sang at the cabaret because he went there. He must have assumed I was gay. When he saw me at school he recognized me—maybe he was angry and embarrassed? Marcus? Marcus. That's his name."

The earth stopped rotating under Henna. She focused on the tick and hum of Stephan's IV pump, on the smell of astringent, on her friend buried beneath the macramé of cords and wires. Her heart pounded her anger awake with whale coughs and Tibetan mountain horns. Each *whunk* of electrified meat sent hornets to the tips of her fingers, to her scalp, to the arteries below her tongue.

Marcus—she had a toehold.

The planet groaned for relief under her. It waited permission to spin. Somewhere mountains buckled, stones splintered into the air like popcorn boulders from the pressure.

Marcus.

Henna took a breath and allowed the globe's skin to judder forth. Each relief valve in its skin, each volcanic boil, each geyser and crack that spewed heat and magma seemed to line up beneath her feet like the tumblers on a lock. She was the epicenter—white-hot vexation escaped her in sulfur-scalded bursts. "What semester was that?"

"Last fall—the three o'clock in 216. Wait..." Stephan tried to sit up "...what do you mean by 'go get him?'"

This was the crossroads. Stephan was unaware no arrests had been made.

Even the media had moved on to other stories. Henna chewed her lip and brushed at the bit of hair left on Stephan's misshapen head.

He must feel her hunger for destruction.

"Remember something for me, Stephan: I know things are hard right now, but they will get better." Henna found his cellphone in a plastic bag in a thin closet. She plugged it in to charge and sat it on his bedside table. "In about a week I'll call you from New York. It won't be from a number you recognize, but please answer. I won't leave a message if you don't answer, but I'll try again. If you see a call from area code 917, it's me." Stephan looked confused, but nodded. "What's the area code I'll call you from in a week Rabbi Ninja?"

"Nine-one-seven. So you're leaving me?"

"No." Henna cupped Stephan's face in her hands. "I'm paving the road for us."

Henna made a call from the lobby. The university's registrar found Marcus in moments.

She had an address.

She went to an internet cafe and dug. Marcus Blackshaw lived with his parents. His father was a powerful lobbyist, cozy with the

241

Scottish parliament. He was a rainmaker. A damned tycoon. Now Henna understood: Marcus believed himself untouchable.

Well, prepare to be touched, you evil bastard.

~Metal Crowd

Henna rented a car to stake out the Blackshaw estate. She ignored a large Bentley that rolled from the tall iron gates, but when a small sports car pulled out shortly after, she followed it.

Marcus.

She spent the whole afternoon watching her quarry. He ate at an Indian restaurant near the Royal Mile then went to a bar that catered to the metal crowd. She followed him in. Although it was risky, she sat just a table away. Finally she got a good look at him. Bleached hair. Healing black eye. Expensive wool jacket. A large man with a shaved head joined the evil asshole for a couple of minutes. They spoke in hushed tones. Shortly, the skinhead nodded. He walked behind the bar and made several phone calls. The skinhead looked dirty. Marcus, however, looked fastidious—as though he bathed twice a day.

Henna stayed at the bar when Blackshaw left. She flirted aggressively with the dirty skinhead. When she invited him to the toilet for some fun, he jumped at the chance. Henna followed the monster down a filthy hallway. She slipped a thin aluminum tube from her pocket and unscrewed a cap from one end. A black rubber cone sat beneath the cap. It housed a thick spring-loaded needle.

They were alone.

She drove the device deep into the giant's elbow. She watched him drop then locked the door.

It was as if lightning struck him.

He curled involuntarily around his arm and groaned in anguish through clenched teeth.

"Stonefish venom," Henna said calmly, though she didn't feel calm. Henna held the aluminum tube up. She screwed the cap back on so the writhing dirt bag could see the device. "I ask the questions. If you answer believably, I'll give you a shot of antivenin. You don't know what that is, do you? I'll tell you—the first shot hurts like nothing I can comprehend. The pain will kill you if I don't intercede. The next one helps. You need the next shot ... you want the next shot. It'll make you feel better."

243

Henna rotated the tube as if she revealed an exclusive magic trick. She raised her eyebrows and squatted near the grimy beast. She tapped the second cap then unscrewed it as he watched. A second black rubber cone lay underneath. The criminal nodded eagerly at the tube.

"Of course, you want it—I've told you as much. Questions first. Who is Marcus Blackshaw to you?"

The man hissed a stale-breathed answer past clenched teeth. "He leads the Runes."

God, that stuff must hurt.

"Good. Are you a Rune?"

"Yeah. I'm a Rune. Now give me the shot!"

His breaths had become labored. She had to hurry.

"I know you need it. Look whose hand it's in, dumbass. I'm the only one who can save you. Focus. When do they meet next? The Runes, that is, and where?"

The miscreant wasn't thriving. He'd fouled his pants and exhibited both nuchal and diaphragmatic dyskinesia. He tried to breathe past the vomit the involuntary movements had caused, but he'd already aspirated. Beer, rye, and smoked meats mixed with the smell of blood and smoke, feculence and scum. Henna recalled the morning she and Alvar came across a hunter squatting over a moose on a crisp fall morning. When the hunter had opened the massive animals body with the tip of his knife, the intestines steamed. They roiled, still alive, while the man sliced the connecting tissues from the animal's huge liver. It was an earthy smell—a deep metallic, clean smell.

Humans smelled so much worse, even live humans who were mostly intact.

This man smelled of rot, of disease—his eyes rolled wildly inside their sockets like loose old clams. The putrescence of hate clung to every surface of the small room.

From the looks of him, she might not get her answer.

"You'll be dead in thirty seconds if I don't give you this shot—no time for nonsense."

"Tonight—the Hall. Ingliston. Gray one-story. North of the track."

"Will Marcus be there?"

"Yeah—" The animal had become more helpful as his hypoxia worsened. "We all will." Henna screwed the cap back on the aluminum tube. She'd planned to give the second injection of stonefish venom as a painful sendoff, but he only had seconds left. She might need it later.

"I will," Henna promised. "You won't."

~Ingliston

Henna raced to Ingliston. A building that matched the skinhead's description was where he'd said. Henna approached warily.

One-story. Flat roof. North of the racing track.

Otherwise nondescript, it reminded her of the blue cinderblock building in Malé. There were two doors: the back door swung in, the front door swung out.

Reinforced metal.

They'd put a heavy stone planter a few feet from the front door. The planter contained sand and cigarette butts. She imagined they'd put it there to block a vehicle from ramming the door, or maybe for cover if the building were attacked. Henna removed her belt and measured the distance from the planter to the door. The wind kicked up and a thin metal sign buzzed against the block walls.

The Hall.

Bars covered a small window to one side. They were welded to a steel frame set into the heavy block wall. Sun-yellowed paper was pasted to the inside of the window, but someone had scratched a small hole in the paper to see out. Inside, Henna made out some plank benches, a podium, some folding tables and chairs. She imagined the room full of racist skinheads, each giving off a different chemical stink.

This is where they met to plan the attack on Stephan and the others.

One of them yelled "hammers" and the rest had cheered. These were no Vikings. These were not even men. These were demons— loathsome rummagers who consecrated atrocities while clinging to the underbelly of the world. The room seemed light inside, as if there was a skylight. On her second trip around the building she found a stepladder behind some scraps of plywood. She unfolded the ladder and looked up at the roof. Henna had a moment of doubt as she climbed. Her legs felt weak and her mouth dry. In a moment, her anger returned. She willed her legs to move. The tar roof was covered in gravel. There was a skylight at one end, near a metal pipe shaped like a candy cane, but the glass was too grimy to make anything out. The cane shaped pipe must be an air intake. It was eight inches or so in diameter. She guessed the shape kept rain out. Henna reached into the pipe and pulled out a rusty mesh screen—a gob of papery filth

246

dropped out with the screen, put there by either insects or birds. She tossed some gravel around the bend in the pipe. She heard it land inside the building. Henna stood. She brushed the filth from her hands and surveyed her surroundings. Activity at the track was light and it was quite far off. There was no reason for track patrons to look toward this nondescript building. Other industrial buildings were scattered around, but it was Friday. Unless someone worked late and came out for a cigarette, odds were no one would see her.

Well done, Runes. You've picked a very discreet spot to die.

Henna glanced at her watch. She had her work cut out for her. She'd have to hurry.

~Sympathetic Tone

On her way to Ingliston for the second time that day, a surge of adrenaline hit Henna. Her heart raced. A sheen of cold sweat coated her forehead. The top of her head felt hot, but the rest of her was freezing. She glanced in the rearview mirror. The cardboard box she'd carried out of the lab sat in the middle of the back seat. Her blood pressure surged until she heard buzzing in her ears.

What if she couldn't do it?

Henna slowed the car. She had to think.

She had a good life here. She adored her flat. She'd miss her gargoyle. There'd be no coming back. She was on Abernathy's radar. She'd all but threatened the drunk's personal safety.

"Second most important cop in Edinburgh," Henna murmured. "Well done, Maxwell."

They'd know who did it. She had the motive and the means.

Henna squeezed the steering wheel until her hands ached. She tried to focus on her breathing, but other thoughts swarmed her.

She'd paid for her ticket to New York with a credit card in her own name.

Her bowels went cold.

No doubt they'd catch her, but she wouldn't make it easy.

Henna narrowed her eyes. She curled her lip into a sneer and nodded. She bit down on her lip until she tasted blood. It wasn't her blood.

It was Marcus's. Abernathy's. It was the putrid clam-eyed giant's blood.

The earth shivered beneath the car. She drank molten rock from the deep well of resolve.

I'm doing it.

Henna pulled over to make a phone call. The phone rang twice and she hung up. Then, as he'd promised, her own phone rang. "Hi—how are you doing?"

Bonn sounded so calm. So smooth.

"Good," she lied. "The device you gave me worked like a charm. I wouldn't change a thing."

"Oh. Good. I'm glad it came in useful."

"It did." Henna sucked at her lip. "Are you settled in enough at your new place to take on a visitor?" Bonn seemed to sense the urgency in Henna's voice. He didn't answer immediately. "Sort of an—indefinite visit?" Henna added. A familiar car sped by.

Marcus.

The brimstone settled in Henna's ears. She eased back onto the road and forced herself to keep her distance. "Of course—" Bonn answered. "Bring as much or as little as you'd like. There is some passable shopping nearby. Should I expect you soon?"

"Tomorrow night. Can I call you from the airport?"

"I'll wait for you there," Bonn promised. "Call me sooner if you need a hand? I'm happy to help."

"Thank you." Henna glanced at the cardboard box. "I've got everything I need."

Henna pulled past the low block-clad building. Marcus's car wasn't there. Either she was early or the big skinhead lied. He hadn't seemed smart enough to lie—especially under that much physiologic stress. She drove past and pulled into the parking lot of a transmission repair shop. It looked closed for the weekend. Henna pulled in next to a beat-up Fiat.

She doubted a new transmission would fix it.

She sat in the car and counted to a hundred.

Nothing stirred in the shop. She had to hurry.

Henna grabbed her satchel and slid into the backseat. She dumped the contents of the bag onto the floor and opened the flaps on the box. She pulled out a spool of thick cordage and two squat glass jars of oily fluid, then considered the pile of stuff on the floor.

What do I need?

The cold sweat was back. Henna preferred fury to terror. She felt limp and damp. Her joints and bowels felt loose. Henna rolled a scarf around a jar and placed it in her satchel. A pair of wool leggings padded the second jar. She placed it carefully next to the first, then pulled it out again. Her tongue felt big and Henna swallowed hard against it. She was so nervous she could feel her heartbeat in her throat.

I'm going to do this—for Stephan.

Henna sat the second jar on the seat beside her and bent down to paw through the toiletries she always carried.

Dental floss.

She held the roll at an angle and read the label in the diminishing light; it was a travel-sized roll.

Fifty yards, but she'd used it daily for months.

Henna tried to remember when she'd bought the floss but couldn't.

The success of this plan hinged on a few meters of dental floss?

Henna laughed nervously and shook her head. She retrieved a pair of nail clippers and used the file to pry off the top of the floss container. She squinted at the small spool.

It seemed like enough.

She tied the end of the spool beneath the lid of the second jar and padded it with the leggings then slid the nail file in her pocket. She lifted the roll of cordage. Alvar spent many winter evenings practicing knots with her by the fire.

Hopefully, she remembered them.

She tied a lineman's loop on one end and left the rest on the tube. Henna breathed through her mouth. Her tongue felt dry and rubbery.

How long can I function under this level of sympathetic tone? Did Bonn get nervous? Did he get angry? She doubted it. He looked built for this. He seemed immune to this.

Henna tugged at the knot with slow, heavy fingers. It held. She willed her saliva glands to make something to swallow.

She hoped the cord would hold. Nothing she could do about it now, though. It was time to go.

Henna slung the satchel over her head and rounded the transmission shop.

Still no cars in front of the block building.

She felt emboldened. She found she could now breathe through her nose. The movement seemed to help.

She'd do the hardest part first. The roof.

Henna ran to the rear of the block building and listened. A car slowed in front. Henna froze. Her heart drummed a frantic tattoo inside her chest. She dropped to the ground and concentrated on breathing. She crawled to the corner.

The car was gone. Just someone headed to the track. Get up. There's no time to waste.

As Henna climbed the ladder, the jars clinked together. She winced but kept moving.

Please God, don't let them break—not yet.

She was on the roof. The gravel crunched under her feet.

250

At the pipe. Open the satchel. Unwrap the leggings.

Henna pulled some floss from the spool and carefully fed the jar up the cane-shaped pipe. She was mouth breathing again. Small extra hisses of breath escaped with each heartbeat. She nudged the jar past the bend in the pipe and paid out more floss until she felt the weight of the jar. She felt her eyeballs jolt in their sockets with each heartbeat. She was short of breath. She pursed her lips with each exhalation as though she'd just been sprinting. She paid out more floss and estimated the jar's position in the pipe.

Just above the ceiling now.

Henna backed toward the edge of the roof. The spool dwindled quickly, but she was almost to the edge.

Another car.

Henna dropped to prone. She clenched the spool tightly and wrapped a length of floss around her fingers, pulling the rest of the floss off the small plastic spool.

It wasn't enough.

Henna sucked at her lip, her mouth felt chalky. To be able to swallow anything would be a luxury. Her lip was as barren as her tongue. She couldn't even taste the blood from earlier. Henna panted to catch her breath. Sounds were amplified—a dog barked somewhere close. She held her head steady and opened her mouth. She needed to concentrate on the front of the building.

The flick of a lighter. The smell of cigarette smoke. Someone jerked the handle on the front door. Must be locked—someone early for the meeting.

Henna looked at her watch.

The rest would be here shortly. She craved water. This plan lacked water. It was essential. All future attacks on murderous demons would take place near large bodies of clear, cold water.

Henna focused on the taut line of dental floss tied to the jar of mustard gas suspended in the pipe. She'd hoped the floss would stretch to the ground. She could've wedged it in a crack in the wood that had hid the ladder from view.

A voice—the early bird was on his phone. Do it. What? Anything. Move. Remember what Alvar said—when you're at war, it's important to fight. Commit.

Henna tied a loop in the floss and held it in her teeth. She rolled a little and retrieved the nail file from her pocket then brushed at the gravel until she reached the layer of tar that sealed the roof. She held the loop flat on the tar and pushed the nail file through it. It held. Henna shivered. The buzz of doubt and fear was back in her ears.

How did Bonn function under this amount of stress? Maybe he didn't feel stress like this. He probably brought water.

Another car pulled up. Doors opened and closed. Henna rolled some more and removed her sweater. When she did something, the buzzing stopped.

If the floss were long enough, she'd be down there now. It was better up here. Please don't let anyone see the ladder.

Henna held the loop and pulled the nail file back out of the tar. She held it in her chattering teeth and pushed the file through the sweater near the wrist then stuck the file back through the loop into the roof. With the scratch and jangle of keys, she heard the front door scrape open. Voices came up the pipe. Someone dragged a metal chair. "Put that out. Marcus will freak if he smells it in here." The scuff of a boot extinguished a cigarette. "The big one in yellow. He's the one that got Alec."

"How's Sorcha?"

"How do you think she is? Alec's dead." Henna got to her knees. The argument was loud. She hoped it'd mask the gravel sounds. She held the nail file steady in the tar and bunched up the remainder of the sweater. She tossed it over the side of the building. It dangled below the top of the ladder. The top of her head was hot again. Her teeth stopped clacking. Henna felt her head with her hand. She expected it to come away wet with blood, but it didn't.

Focus. Stop thinking about how you feel and finish it. This wasn't about her—this was about Stephan. A nail file, a sweater, some dental floss? It was a terrible plan, but it'd have to do.

A car at the track revved its engine. Henna took advantage of the noise. She swung her legs over the edge of the roof and felt for the top of the ladder. She crept down quickly. It felt good to move. She folded the ladder and rested it beside the scrap pile. The sweater was a different shade of gray than the building. It stood out like a sore thumb.

Hopefully, none of these idiots scout the perimeter.

Henna tiptoed to the rear of the building and ran the end of the cord around the base of a flowering dogwood, then passed the spool through the loop. The back door was, at most, three meters away. Henna held on to the cord and backed toward it. She needed another loop in the cord about a meter from the door. Her hands shook. She

252

had a hard time focusing her eyes on the task. She felt tired and cold—and stiff. She shook her head and willed her frozen hands to move. She managed to get the second loop in the cord just as someone turned the latch inside the door.

Run.

Henna dropped the spool and sprinted for the transmission shop. She slid around the corner of the building and dropped.

They must hear my breath.

Henna took choppy, open-mouthed breaths. She swallowed hard against her dry tongue. She listened for footsteps but didn't hear any. After a couple of minutes she peeked around the corner. Cigarette smoke wafted from the open door. Someone either stood inside the door waiting for others to arrive or they'd propped a chair. Either way, the spool of cord in the grass hadn't sent up an alarm. She heard more cars and glanced at her watch. The high-pitched sounds of the car at the track drowned out the sounds from the road. Henna felt disoriented. Now she was too far away.

What if there were so many cars they'd park at the transmission shop too?

She was too exposed.

What would they do if they caught her? Movement—

A skinhead with a cigarette dangling from his mouth stood by the dogwood and urinated on the cord. The car at the track made another wheel-shrieking lap. It was pushing the corners. The skinhead seemed distracted enough by the car not to take notice of the spool of cord on the ground tied to his pee-tree. The man heard something inside and hurriedly zipped his pants. He flicked the cigarette at the dogwood and went inside. Something metal scraped on concrete and the door closed with a *whunk.*

Marcus must be inside. Make sure.

Henna forced herself to stand. Her knees didn't feel like they'd support her. She wasn't just stiff—it felt like her bones were fused. She braced her hands on her knees and slowly crept alongside the building to the road. At least two dozen cars were outside.

Marcus's car, too.

She craned her neck past the corner of the transmission shop. The front door of the block building was closed. A surge of fresh adrenaline cured her legs. She ran along the side of the building and behind the dogwood. It was dark, but enough light from the track let her see the cord. She checked the loop and pulled the cord to feel the tension on the bush—she grimaced as she picked up the spool.

253

Not long now.

Henna ignored the urine and ran the spool through the door's heavy handle, then doubled it back to the second loop, fashioning a trucker's hitch. She used the loop like a pulley and cinched it tight before she tied it off. When they tried to pull the door open, they'd have to uproot the bush to get out, or the cord would break and they would catch her. Henna ran for the stepladder. She unfolded it on the run. She rested the ladder on one side, legs braced against the rock planter. The top of the ladder was still centimeters from the front door.

It wouldn't work. They'd get out.

She ran for the scrap pile and grabbed all she could carry. A short piece of plywood was wet and warped. She was able to fold it. She wedged it into the space between the ladder and the door, but the voices inside became quiet—

They'd heard her.

Someone inside pushed on the door until the ladder and the spongy plywood stopped it. Breathless, Henna shoved wood scraps between the ladder and the door. They kicked the door from inside, so she jammed her makeshift shims in between kicks. Although she saw her hands doing what they needed to, she felt like she fumbled with the materials. She couldn't feel her hands.

Were they still hers? No time to contemplate it. They'd be struggling against the cord now too.

Henna rammed a last piece of wood in the gap and ran for the sweater. She jumped to grab the dangling arm, but couldn't reach it. In desperation, she took a few steps back and ran at the wall. She pushed the ball of her foot against the blocks and leaped to jerk the arm of the sweater.

Got it.

The sweater came free, so the nail file must have pulled free too. Henna grabbed a piece of scrap wood from the stack and ran for the back door. The cord danced violently as at least one skinhead hauled on the inside handle. Then all at once the line went slack—Henna saw fingers wrap around the edge of the door. "One—two— THREE!" The door bounced open several centimeters. The remaining tension in the cord stopped its progress. It sounded like someone tried to wedge a chair into the temporary gap, but it wasn't wide enough. "Again. One—"

The gas should be working. The skinheads should be screaming—they should be dying! Didn't the jar break?

Henna heard screaming. It was her. Overcome with rage, she smashed at the sets of fingers with the wood. A small, curious part of her brain took over. It spoke to her in a pragmatic voice. It was a man's voice. It sounded like a British naturalist dryly narrating why her silly plan was doomed from the start.

Unfortunately for Henna, the jar didn't break. What Henna didn't know as she struggled to contain the villains was this—the skinheads didn't even know about the mustard gas. Why should they? The pea gravel she'd tossed down the pipe into the room went through another grate, one just above the false ceiling— the deadly agent she'd worked feverishly to concoct would rest safely nestled above the second grate—for years.

"—two—" The bloodied fingers were gone. They pulled on the handle again, where their fingers were safe.

"No!" Henna roared. New fingers popped through the door crack. So many fingers. Her throat raw, Henna raged as she swung the wood again and again. For each set of fingers she crushed, more shot into the crack.

Too many—they were going to get out.

She unwound the scarf from the second jar and held it aloft—

When they jerked on the door, she'd throw it in.

Henna heard a new voice inside. One with more authority. "Again! On three. One—" The gap pulsed open as the men inside revved like bobsledders. "—two—" Henna tossed the jar through the gap. She heard breaking glass. She backed from the door and gripped the lineman's hitch with both hands. Henna pushed the cord to the ground and stood on it.

Finally. The screaming.

The fingers trapped in the door danced like spittle on iron. Thirty seconds passed. The screams stopped. The fingers trapped in the doorjamb were still. The car at the track whined by. Henna eased one, then the other foot off of the cord and cautiously let it droop. Sets of dead fingers fell from the doorjamb to join the dead arms inside. The naturalist was back. With an even bigger lilt in his voice. He'd fooled the audience. Of course he'd known the outcome already—but he'd narrated well—he was a showman after all.

With that, Henna bludgeoned the skinheads' dirty fingers and surprised them with a second jar of mustard gas. The oily fluid would us-u-ally take hours, or days to cause victims to expire, but the wily tox-i-cologist had added some garnish to the recipe to make it faster acting. She flung the jar into their midst and secured the rope while they died. Victorious, Henna stumbled toward the transmission shop in need of water and sleep. She was on the run now—and life as usual had become, well, quite un-usual indeed.

~Mala Mujer

Henna slept a dreamless sleep on the plane. Bonn met her, as promised. Her whole body ached. She felt like she had a crust—a rind—a scaly caul over her. She worried that she smelled bad.

Did evil cling to you when you wallowed nearby? If she did stink, Bonn was too kind to say so.

"I'm excited for you to see the lab." She was glad for the reason not to talk about her spur-of-the-moment arrival. She bought a large bottle of water. Bonn led her to an old black car. The water was clean. It was cold, yet warmed her. She felt her cells suck at it before it even hit her stomach. When the soil of her brain got what it needed, she felt more like herself again. A stronger version of herself.

A galvanized version.

A thought warmed her from within—

Now, Stephan is safe.

The lab was amazing. She walked the wide aisles. At the end of one, an odd dark man on a ladder painted something on the wall. It looked like Vitruvian man. Unlike da Vinci's original, however, the man held bouquets in each fist. Each cluster of flowers reached the edge of the circle he stood within, so although his hands weren't open, the idea of proportion remained. As she got closer, she recognized each bouquet.

"Mala mujer!" Henna exclaimed.

The dark man was gifted.

His work channeled—hearkened the shouts of ancient Dutch masters, with an even older, darker religious flavor—Vermeer-like with an inkling of dread in the style of Hieronymus Bosch. The shine and shadows of life and decay, a snake in a bride's bouquet, a spider perched on a perfect ripe plum. The painter tilted his head at a birdlike angle to peer down at her. He had remarkably thin lips. He flicked his head, unceremoniously—like a woodpecker who has paused to look about, then remembered his goal, and returned to his work. His fingers moved delicately as he painted hair-like thorns on each stalk. The figure also held a shock of bright red castor flowers.

The mother of Ricin. Did the figure have breasts?

Henna stepped back to take in the whole painting. The third and fourth hands held western water hemlock and wolfsbane. Henna felt a chill. She stepped closer.

It was her face.

It was unmistakable. The odd man had given the figure her face. It was more beautiful than she was—eyes wise and calm—they saw through the rubbish of time and temperament, past the walls of the lab into space. Not only did various snakes adorn her crown of death, her Medusa-like hair also hid several blue-ringed octopus tentacles and half a dozen dripping scorpion tails. The chemical makeup of each beautiful, poisonous horror faded in smoky calligraphy in the background. Unlike Henna, the painted figure had no weakness. Here was a sister of Freyja—a cousin of Enyo, of Agasaya. She was in the company of Kali, but instead of blades to do her work, she might summon the Valkyries to carry a corpse to Valhalla, or just as easily, Bastet—to heal with her ointment jar. "An ode." The man looked at her—intense. Hawk-like.

Had he spoken? She wasn't sure—

"An ode—in paint." The man's thin lips moved again. The inside of his mouth seemed black and tongue-less. His lips were stiff, like a sea turtle. His hawk-like eyes blinked with un-hawk like slowness that somehow seemed respectful.

His lids were wrong. She must be seeing things.

Henna swore she saw a nictitating membrane. One human set of eyelids, but also a second set.

Like a crocodile. She needed sleep. That's what it was. No doubt the man was a master of paint, but he was just a man. Her brain played tricks.

Bonn didn't bother to introduce the painter. He continued the tour as though they were alone. Down another aisle, a similar thin-lipped man lurked inside an enclosure. She looked closely at him. There were only subtle differences between him and the man on the ladder. This man squatted among a knot of cane toads. The amphibians appeared lined up for communion—in an orderly fashion. The guy tossed a baby mouse into each grateful mouth then popped one in his own maw. He swallowed the hairless, pink rodent whole and appeared satisfied. Henna rubbed her eyes and felt her own mouth open involuntarily. She bunched her eyebrows together and looked from the man to Bonn and back with disbelief. "Did he just eat a—a—"

"Rickard," Bonn offered. "A mouse, yes—they eat all manner of things. I'm not certain why. The one on the ladder was Ryker. They'll grow on you. They can do anything and are helpful." Rickard peered at her through the glass. She felt uncertain. Then, swiveling his head like an owl, he focused on something distant. She followed his gaze—a television appeared to be his new source of fascination. Bonn walked quickly to the screen and increased the volume. When Ryker materialized at her elbow, she jumped. She'd not heard him approach. The television played a commercial for a mobility chair. Her intense host nodded. He held his hands out to mimic the infirm but ecstatic grandfather who toggled the freedom-delivering joystick. "Yes. That's it," Said Bonn. The raptor-men, now side by side, nodded in unison. "Let's get started."

~Spectacle

Bonn usually talked to Manny twice each week. The machinist no longer needed to work. He worked when he chose to. Many times they only discussed cars.

You know what I'm doing, son? I'm fitting an SRT 10 Viper power plant into an old Challenger—I've even got it rigged with paddle shifters.

Not stock huh? What a shame, Manny. You are ruining it.

Manny got the joke on their last visit, but he'd really laugh if he saw Bonn's current project.

The power chair wasn't a classic. It was ugly as sin, yet functional. Just the tool he needed to enter the lion's den.

Bonn tightened a bolt. He ran a compression check. It worked. He was done. Rotational weight minimized, chassis lowered—the chair's new top speed was 35mph. The frame was pressurized. It could deliver short and mid-range bursts of Henna's special recipe as slurry or a juggernaut of corn-plastic shells full of death-powder at a cyclic rate. The barrel was shrouded but not terribly quiet. It didn't need to be. If he squeezed that trigger, everyone around him would die. Bonn checked the time. He'd been in the shop for hours. It was time to stretch his legs. In the lab, Ryker worked inside a pharmaceutical hood. Henna supervised as he cleaned up the last of the powder inside the hood with a solution which rendered it inert. The German pulled an arm from a gasket-sleeved gauntlet to pop a mealworm into his mouth. The lovely scientist shook her head and closed her eyes. Rickard worked over a small still containing green tobacco leaves. The temperature was set to facilitate nicotine distillation. The plants were so heavy with nicotine in their natural state, Henna encouraged the German to wear gloves throughout the process. Checking the yield from the still's last batch, their resident toxin guru tapped some numbers into a calculator.

"Unless we make a second still, the eleven hundred milliliters the chair needs won't be ready for another—two days."

"I'll take what I can get." Bonn looked from one German to the other. The men seemed to adore Henna. They acted funny around her—as if they wanted to please her above all other things. They'd always seemed like robotic lizards to him. He couldn't recall ever shaking hands with either man, but imagined if he did, their skin would feel cool.

They consumed their own weight in lab-animal food.

He hadn't noticed it until Henna came to stay.

She was so—normal?

No—she wasn't normal. The Germans who repulsed her likely revered the lady because she shared their stratospheric level of brilliance. He wondered what the world was like for Henna—what the world seemed like to her. What would it feel like to be shocked? It wasn't lost on Bonn that he kept odd company—even Rupert was off. Manny and Linda were the only normal people he knew. "I'm going to see my grandfather tomorrow," Henna told him. "I think you should have what you need for the chair." Henna looked around with her eyebrows raised, perhaps to see if the Germans had heard her. The reptilian duo became immobile. They gawked at Henna like infatuated iguanas. Henna flipped through a stack of menus from local restaurants. "Does anyone want human food? Thai? Indian?"

"Indian," Bonn offered. The Germans looked at each other and shared a long, quiet moment. Finally, Ryker held up a squat Styrofoam cup and shook his head. Their meaning was clear:

We have crickets. Who could want more?

When Henna returned with the takeout, she gawked around the room as though a freakish spectacle had taken place. Bonn looked around for the Germans. The men had set up a camera to monitor the still, but watched the gauges on a monitor they had installed in the shrikethrush enclosure. Sporting speedos, they basked under the full spectrum light as if they required it—their foreheads pointed toward the light though their eyes stayed on the monitor. Bonn imagined vestigial third eyes on their foreheads as they made small neck corrections, as though their heads were satellite dishes listening for that elusive alien *ping*. The shrikethrush hopped happily to Ryker and nestled into the arch of his foot. Bonn saw that the scene had intrigued Henna, somehow, and wondered himself, for a moment, at the Germans behind the glass.

The men were so pale an hour ago. Now they looked like mottled, brown parchment.

Without her, he no longer registered the Germans' odd behaviors. Early on, the men had been a distracting source of entertainment and speculation, though somehow their usefulness had kept his questions at bay—before he'd grown accustomed to them. Certainly, people

261

who kept exotic, scaly pets were similarly riveted at first. As a boy, Bonn had fantasized that his father had made a deal with the Devil: that these were his capable henchmen. Later, he imagined they were the product of a mad scientist. Finally, he decided that Europeans in general were unpredictable. He hadn't met too many Germans. Certainly Henna had met more … what were Henna's thoughts about the pair? There was nothing to gain by asking. Perhaps when she returned from Ruka, he would notice that they had grown claws—or even tails, but those nuances might escape him in her absence. Bonn maneuvered the wheelchair to the boxes on the counter and poked around to find his order. He paused to take a bite of tandoori, shrugged at Henna, then raced away again.

~Bespoke

Henna married Alvar and Akka in the garden. Since she wasn't a minister, it wasn't a legal wedding—but no one required one. Akka clutched a simple bouquet of daffodils and Alvar bragged about his suit.

"A bespoke suit!" he declared, tugging at the sleeve. "The stitching is solid. It should last me another twenty, maybe even thirty years."

Akka's daughters came, as well as her two granddaughters, and nine great-granddaughters. Pies were everywhere. Sugared-up children chased each other and squealed. A tiny girl squatted next to a basket of puppies.

Why had she worried that Alvar would be lonely?

She loved seeing him so happy. Akka doted on him. She watched as the gleeful bride cut Alvar several thin wedges of pie. Akka sat on Alvar's lap near the hearth and spooned bits of the treats into his mouth. Each time she offered a new bite, she whispered into Alvar's ear, presumably the next flavor.

It was lovely.

A girl of seven stared awkwardly at her. She had wild curls and deep blue eyes with a speck of brown in one. Henna stood and offered her hand to the girl. "Can I show you a game I learned when I was your age?" Happily, the child took her hand. They walked through the old gate, past the garden. Henna closed her eyes and held her arms wide.

It could be a new world. She could help change it.

"I smell something delicious—"

~Hunting the Devil

Bonn rolled into Brownsville on the weaponized wheelchair just before dark. He wore a helmet on his head, which he allowed to loll about loosely on his feeble neck. He left his mouth agape. He forced his head back to hide his strong jaw and drooled a bit. He'd worked to replicate the adenoidal sonorous breathing someone with a bad traumatic brain injury might exhibit and it was believable. He didn't remember it, but he'd sounded similar after Raquel shot him. A cheap fleece blanket covered his invalid lap. A garish tiger's head decorated the blanket—the type people bought at state fairs after too many pitchers of beer. The black barrels of the weapon systems on board were camouflaged by the stripes of the cat, just inside each armrest. Bonn wore a huge grey sweatshirt. Heavy armor plates that would stop most bullets were hidden underneath the sweatshirt. They covered his chest, back, and sides. They could withstand multiple strikes from rifle-caliber rounds. Two ballistic Kevlar blankets lay beneath the head of the massive tiger. Even the soft collar Bonn wore to keep his head from bobbing about was made from ballistic cloth.

He'd never before been so armored.

The plan was simple: enter Brownsville, do the right thing, make the time count. Bonn rolled up the street at a lazy pace. He paused for a stray cat to cross his path and pivoted the chair in jagged movements to watch it, as though his neck didn't articulate.

"Kitty?" Bonn grinned like an idiot. He forced his tongue out in a grotesque smile. Some school-aged girls pointed and giggled. The woman with them hurried them along. An old Buick with bare brake pads announced danger with a metallic hiss. A shirtless man hung his arms out of the window. He wore a purple baseball cap with a marijuana leaf emblem on the front. Bonn stopped the chair and toggled the joystick to face the car.

There was a second man in the passenger's seat—taller. Also shirtless—no cap.

Bonn couldn't see through the darkly tinted rear windows. "What up, retardo?" Bonn flicked his middle finger of his right hand quickly. A jet of nicotine-laced silica slurry blasted the driver squarely in the eyes. The man recoiled, his mouth open with surprise. Bonn delivered a second blast. Laughter came from the rear of the car.

There were people in the back. They thought the driver mimicked him—the handicap.

Bonn spun the chair a quarter turn and rounded the rear of the car. He stopped even with the passenger's window.

He'd give everyone a reasonable chance to do the right thing.

"Quit playin'." The passenger yelled at the driver. He had realized something was wrong. Turning from the dead man, he saw Bonn looming outside his open window. Bonn blinked slowly.

"Hi." He let his head bobble like a newborn baby for a moment. The man pointed a pistol at Bonn. With the slightest shift of tiger stripes, Bonn sprayed him.

The chair turned on a dime.

Now at the left rear door, as if on cue, a fat man with a purple hat stepped out.

Shotgun.

Bonn tapped the switch. The man buckled, retching. The sound of a round being chambered in a carbine came from inside. Bonn drenched the back seat. A fourth man stumbled into the street opposite Bonn. He made gasping sounds and fell.

The concentrated nicotine was bad stuff.

Even indirect blasts did the job—of course the slurry splattered a lot—some of it must have hit their mucous membranes.

Henna said it had to.

Bonn motored back to the sidewalk and sped around a corner. A block away a group had formed. It looked like a fight. Bonn sped toward the group. A tight circle of teenage boys stood around something.

Something screaming.

He was just behind the circle now. The teens ignored him—in the center of the circle a boy had a girl's pants down. She cried out. She struggled to free herself. Bonn coughed loudly and the nearest delinquent startled. He looked Bonn over with a mixture of confusion and disgust. Bonn forced his face into an idiot grin.

He couldn't hit the girl.

"Ar-r-r-re you helping her?"

More confused faces looked up. None of the teens appeared willing to help her. Bonn rammed the nearest boy with the chair and pivoted it in a circle. He'd welded a spike to the footrest and the metal ripped the thug's calf muscle away. He spun in an arc, got the chair up to speed, and rammed the circle again. A few of the miscreants broke away, but none ran. Bonn tapped the slurry switch several times. They dropped like flies. The boy with the ripped calf screamed, and the circle scattered. The remaining boys acted like hyenas. They ran few yards and shifted back and forth. They looked for weakness. One pulled something from a pocket. Bonn twisted a knob and toggled the switch. The slurry flew in a fine jet and dropped him.

Bonn maneuvered the chair to the girl. "Can you move?"

She struggled with her pants. Bonn peeled back the tiger and covered her with a ballistic blanket from his lap as he nodded at a parked car. "When you can, get yourself under that car until I'm gone, OK?"

The boy with the torn calf was up. He hopped toward the sidewalk. With each movement, the loose muscle bobbed angrily behind him like a kangaroo tail. Bonn toggled the switch and dropped him. Only one was left. Some of them had escaped. The rapist raced down the street at a sprint. Bonn pushed the joystick forward and ran him down. The pants tripped him.

Should've kept them fastened.

Bonn eased off the joystick. He aimed the spike at the fallen rapist's liver. With the spike sunk to the hilt, he turned the chair sharply. Blood filled the street in a great red swoosh.

The girl.

Bonn slalomed the chair around the bodies. She was still there. She sat up, crying. Holding the ballistic drape against her, she peered over the edge of it as Bonn approached.

"El Diablo!"

She looked to be about eleven. She'd called him the Devil.

Bonn shook his head. "No," he replied in Spanish, "I am hunting the Devil."

A screen door crashed.

A matronly Hispanic woman rushed from a nearby building. She picked up the girl and whisked her inside. Curious onlookers began to flock to the scene and Bonn raced away. He zigzagged several blocks and turned onto Pitkin. He paused at a bus stop and backed the chair up against a hedge. A young woman with a baby glanced at him then turned back to the street.

Just waiting for the bus.

266

A tragedy-weathered young woman pulled dentures from her mouth, added some paste to one side, and replaced the ill-fitting teeth with a wince. A man wearing sunglasses and a blue jacket sat on a nearby stoop. A police car pulled into the bus stop. A pudgy cop emerged. He approached the man in sunglasses. They spoke for a moment. The man handed him a fat white envelope and the portly cop left.

A payoff—no efforts at discretion were made.

Bonn read the license plate on the cruiser as it pulled away. This was the real problem in Brownsville: the cops paid to protect and serve were either too frightened to patrol or were on the take.

That was food for thought.

The bus rolled up. People got on. The man in sunglasses stalked Bonn. He walked in front of him and lit a cigarette. He gave the fake invalid a casual once-over. Bonn crossed his eyes a little. He pushed his tongue out like a newborn baby who's had enough squash. "You look like you'd smell bad—but you don't." Bonn raised his eyebrows and smiled an idiot smile, as if he'd passed gas.

"Thanks." The man nodded. He inhaled his cigarette. Bonn smiled even bigger, as if he'd just made a friend.

Something was off. Did he see the spike?

Sure enough, the man took off his sunglasses. He bent to inspect the bloody spike jutting from Bonn's footrest.

He's paying the cops off for something. That's enough to go on.

Bonn backed the chair up and toggled the switch. The man fell forward. Bonn swiveled the chair to avoid him.

Sirens.

Bonn still had a few minutes. With the messes he left behind, legitimate patrols would wait in the periphery until SWAT responded.

He had time.

Bonn crossed Pitkin and took the next left.

This was near where he'd been shot.

A man in a blue cap rested his elbows on the window frame of a second story window.

Drug dealers were like shark's teeth: one got yanked, another fell into his place. Hundreds of thugs awaited their turns on the porch. He had to make something happen.

Bonn swerved the chair back and forth. He sang at the top of his voice. "Street drugs, neat drugs! Street drugs, neat drugs!" To Bonn's left, a man stepped from an alcove, laughing. Bonn sped toward him and brought the machine to a stop. "Hi. Do you sell drugs? I wanna buy some." The man laughed so hard he couldn't stand straight.

"Neat drugs, huh? Can you pay?" The man collected himself. He pulled a small baggie from his pocket. He dangled it in front of Bonn shamelessly. Bonn toggled the jet and the man dropped. A woman, naked from the waist down, ran from a doorway with an AK-47. She stood over the dealer, panting. Yells came from another building. He backed the chair up a few yards.

He'd let this evolve for a moment.

More people collected around the downed man. Bonn reached beneath the fleece blanket and found the old gas mask. He removed the helmet and pulled the leather and glass mask tight across his face to assure a good seal.

He was a motorized steampunk. A carnival nightmare.

The woman gestured with the rifle. A man with a shotgun stood on the porch. He barked orders into the building.

A call to arms? Every man on deck.

Bonn flipped a switch to activate the chair's other weapon. He backed up further. The woman pointed at Bonn. The man raised his shotgun. Bonn held down a button. Balls of powdered death breathed from the shrouded barrel, torquing the chair to the left. Bonn compensated with the joystick. He kept his finger on the button until a fog of powder billowed before him. When he released the button, whistling sounds filled the street.

The last stridulous breaths of the dying.

The woman, the man with the shotgun, all the others who had spilled into the street to attack him were down. Bonn turned the chair and rolled away quickly.

If he could avoid it, he wouldn't use that one again.

Bonn's ears rang. The breeze had dissipated the powder, so he pulled off the gas mask and performed Toynbee's maneuver to relieve the pressure in his ears.

Time to go home.

Bonn weaved through the projects for a few blocks then paused behind a dumpster to replace the helmet and regroup.

Back in character.

He used the joystick to move the chair along the sidewalk at a believable speed. He checked his watch. It had been only twenty-seven minutes since he rolled the chair out of the rented van. The sidewalk ended at a construction site. The curb was sharp and Bonn got off of the chair to ease the machine into the street. Police lights pounded at the dark. A cruiser squealed around a corner, but didn't slow down when they saw him. He re-mounted the chair quickly and pulled the tiger blanket back over his lap. Bonn brought the power chair up to speed and approached his turn. "Hey!" Several figures hopped the construction fence.

They might have seen him get out of the chair.

"Hey." Bonn returned. One kid bent over and pinched his nose. He pulled a leg to his chest, as though stretching to prepare for a race, then laughed.

"Let's tip him over." There were several kids. Some looked frightened, some looked amused, but all of them were children—some not yet ten. Bonn straightened his head.

"All of you go home." The young ringleader pulled a pistol from his pocket. Reflexively, Bonn threw back the blankets and rushed him. A shot rang out. It was a wild shot. Bonn took the pistol away from the boy and slammed him to the ground. He estimated how much pressure he could apply to his throat without killing the boy.

He needed for the boy to listen.

"All of you, listen—things are different now. After tonight the streets will be filled with people like me. You won't know we are there until we spank your bare bottoms in front of your friends for nonsense just like this. Bonn yanked down the shooter's pants and spanked him. The boy began to cry. "That's if you're lucky—guns and knives won't run us off. Go home. Drink less soda and more milk. Don't smoke. Read books. Work on your grades, whether your parents care about you or not. Make something of yourselves. The guys selling drugs on your block will be dead in a year. You can all do better than that." Bonn yanked the boy's pants back up and hoisted him to his feet, then spun him, their faces less than an inch apart. He opened his eyes wide so the boy could see his scars.

"Even you."

Bonn got in the chair and sped for the step-van. He rolled the chair up the ramp, slid the ramp into its pocket, then swung the doors closed from inside. He'd rigged up a shower in case he had to use the powder. Bonn stripped and washed his body twice, then toweled off quickly and donned a sweatshirt, paint spattered jeans, running shoes.

Helicopters.

Bonn started the van. He pulled slowly from the parking space. He avoided Pitkin.

It probably looked like the New Year's Day Parade.

Bonn pulled over as a string of Lenco Bearcats thrummed by. The turrets were manned. Each vehicle bristled with uniformed men wearing SWAT vests.

That went better.

~Tiger Man

The wheels of the van shrieked as Bonn sped into the garage. He made for the lab. Since the Germans spent most of their time there, the lab had become the unspoken meeting place. Bonn suspected they slept in the lab, although he'd given each of them a beautiful living space. The news was on—the Germans watched with interest.

Brownsville was rioting.

Ryker and Rickard shared a tube of aquarium food as the scene unfolded. Bonn pulled up a chair. Ryker offered him the container of tubifex worms, but Bonn declined. A news team reported from the road closure on Pitkin. Gunfire could be heard. When the reporter ran out of salient things to say, she cut to the crew filming from an overhead helicopter. Some of the gunfire sounded automatic. The earth-bound newswoman was back. She cast nervous glances toward Pitkin and repeated herself often. She pushed a device hard into her ear and grimaced as she struggled to repeat the information she was fed.

"Gang violence is at an all-time high tonight in Brownsville, emergency crews struggle to access unsafe areas. People in need are suffering for help they might not get. No body counts are available as yet. It's easy for some to dismiss these neighborhoods—violent crime is much too common for the impoverished, however tonight we see how organized lawbreakers can be. These are no simple turf skirmishes playing out behind me. It appears the gangs of Brownsville are at full-blown war. Droves of ambulances are staged in safe zones established by SWAT personnel—here on Pitkin Avenue, even as I look at a river of emergency lights, I hear active gunfire and until that gunfire stops, the emergency crews will not be allowed in. As I said before, this is, I think, a war zone."

Video footage from the helicopter showed people swarming the streets with guns. People who didn't hold guns bashed each other with various other items. Businesses were looted. Riot police were on scene. Crowds gathered to hurl anything not bolted down at the police.

Police.

Bonn sat at a computer. He quickly found the officer that the man with sunglasses handed the envelope to. Ryker glanced over his

271

shoulder and sat at his own computer. He tapped at the keyboard and spun the monitor toward Bonn then turned back to the TV.

Ryker used a much better database.

No surprise: the man was a dirty cop. Not just a "protection" racket either—he was connected to the sex trade. If he wasn't a pedophile, he enabled them.

The Latino girl was on TV.

The cameraman tried to keep her off camera, but she wouldn't be denied. She jumped. She yelled. A skinny guy wearing a headset attempted to usher the girl out of the frame, but a blocky woman with a mustache bowled him over and charged the camera. The newswoman seemed to try to make the best of it. She knelt and held the microphone for the girl. She wasn't one to thwart a human-interest moment. The girl babbled in Spanish, but the microphone didn't pick it up. The reporter didn't speak Spanish and tried to cut the girl off. Exasperated, the blocky woman wrenched the microphone from the woman's hand and handed it to the girl.

"Thank God for you, Tiger Man!" the girl shouted in Spanish. The Germans looked at each other. Ryker turned to a monitor to look up the translation, but Bonn understood. "Good hunting!" the girl added.

The blocky woman passed the microphone back to the reporter and blew kisses at the camera. A Hispanic man hugged the girl, crossed his heart, and kissed a rosary. The reporter stood, adjusted her skirt, and brushed at her hair.

"Back to you, Dean—anything new from our eye in the sky?" Dean didn't have much—they played a loop. The same rioters threw the same projectiles.

It was still a riot.

Rickard found more information on the dirty cop. He was known to associate with many convicted felons who'd served time for crimes against children, but not for legitimate reasons. He was no parole officer. The Germans took a moment to read the Spanish translations on Ryker's monitor. Ryker pantomimed a cat scratching at the air. Rickard nodded. They each regarded Bonn with a respectful reptilian gaze.

Tiger Man.

~Rabbis' Anonymous

Henna dialed Stephan's number from her new phone.

No answer.

She straightened herself in the vinyl chair and stretched her legs. People flowed by in the concourse. She wondered which one of them would recognize her.

It would only take one.

The passport Rickard forged was amazing. It didn't look like her exactly, but with her hair dyed red, she didn't look like herself either. Henna turned back to the newspaper. Her new phone vibrated in her pocket. She pulled it out to look at the screen—

Stephan!

She pushed a button to pick up the call. His voice sounded strong. "Rabbis' Anonymous—we're taking pledges. Is this area code 917?"

"How are you?"

"Blind in one eye, but walking. I always wanted an eye patch. It should cut my makeup costs roughly in half." Henna clenched her teeth.

Stay positive.

"That's the optimism I expected."

"Detective Forsythe visited me. He asked about someone I used to know, but my memory's not very good. I guess there was a big to-do in Ingliston. Did you hear? A bunch of skinheads bit it in an alleged chemical attack. You should look it up."

"I think I heard about that." The loudspeaker announced Henna's flight. "I'm off to see the wizard, Rabbi. I hear he's got a fish I need for my collection. Will you be ready to travel in two weeks? I know a place you'd like—there is world-class healthcare and the best gelato this side of Bergamo."

"I'll keep my phone on. I'm glad you're OK—so much of this seems imagined. It feels good to do something normal, like dial a phone."

"Don't get used to normal, Rabbi..." Henna scanned the crowd nervously "...normal doesn't exist anymore."

~Free Wi-Fi

The Germans observed the watchers as Bonn looked on. They'd set up a car detailing service. It was a huge operation—forty-one shops in the greater metro area. Bonn mailed stacks of coupons to each of the seventy-six police precincts as a promotion. Black and white police cars detailed free for a full year, unmarked vehicles free with accompanying official ID. The city's Chief Financial Officer called to assure it wasn't a scam. Ryker answered the phone on the first ring. He laid his ears back along his skull and, oddly, a booming Southern accent with softened edges cast forth.

"So good to hear we may be embraced by the city's finest, ma'am. Let me tell you more about our service—we're an international company. Our cash crop is coffee and coffee roasting. We use ancillary businesses such as Trojan Wash to market our brand. We grow our brand not only by providing superior product, we aim to build a reputation for excellent service. We've other promotions, but I'm certain you're most interested in the money we can save the city—"

The silver-tongued German made it happen.

A union contract was cancelled. Over the course of mere weeks, Trojan Wash, LLC, washed, polished, and detailed thousands of official and unmarked police cars while the city's finest drank good coffee, dropped off their dry-cleaning, and enjoyed free Wi-Fi from rows of luxury massage chairs. Unbeknownst to the pampered cops, extras were provided, too—GPS tracking devices, fish-eye cameras, microphones, and more. All installed in their rearview mirrors. The Germans grew their database. There were some straight shooters out there, but many of those who appeared to walk the straight and narrow were just good at hiding their secrets.

Just not good enough.

~Behest

A nurse wheeled Stephan to the hospital entrance. He could walk but didn't feel like arguing hospital policy with the nurses to be allowed to do so.

How strange—

He couldn't remember what his apartment looked like—he remembered the address—but couldn't remember his furniture.

Did he have furniture?

He sat on a bench outside to wait for the cab. A white Audi wagon pulled into the patient-loading zone. Two pale, thin men emerged from the car. They walked to his bench and sat down. One of them pointed to the plastic bag that contained his few things. He spoke in a monotone German accent. "Is there anything remaining at your apartment that would enrich your life if we were to retrieve it?" Stephan shook his head.

"I don't understand. You must think I'm someone else."

"Perhaps." An awkward silence followed. The men didn't look for someone else. They seemed to orient their faces to the sun to recharge their ability to speak.

Odd thin men with facial solar-powered batteries?

Then the other man spoke—to Stephan their voices sounded identical. "Is there anything at Ms. Maxwell's apartment you suspect may enrich her life if we were to retrieve it?" Stephan strained to focus his good eye on the man, but his remaining eye was his bad eye before the attack. Without stereovision, the man looked like a creepy paper doll. His features were too thin—his ears looked translucent. They seemed to pivot like a bat's ears. The condition didn't help. Since his brain injury, Stephan couldn't see things directly in front of him unless he looked back and forth quickly. The doctors said he'd learn to tolerate the disability.

It hadn't happened yet.

"Is Henna here?" He knew better, but what do you say when mysterious Teutons materialize unexpectedly and engage you as though you're a Cold War operative ready for relocation? It felt much like the set of a noir-film. He considered the men closely. He jittered his eye back and forth. He could imagine them in black and white, chain smoking—adjusting the brims of their felt hats to broadcast a certain mood.

"No. We came at her behest."

"Oh. OK—"

He could just go with them. What did he really have to lose?

His other friends were gone. Edinburgh seemed sour. Maybe it was time for a new city. And Henna sent them—he loved her. Henna wouldn't send anyone to hurt him, but the invitation was abrupt. "She does have a gargoyle she's quite fond of and obviously some particular animals from her lab." Stephan remembered Henna's apartment better than his own. "It probably weighs two hundred kilos—the gargoyle that is. It's a part of a building the police likely have under surveillance." The nearest man shrugged. The odd men stood. They made for the wagon. "So I'm not being abducted?"

"We don't have orders to abduct you."

"You're going back without me then?"

"No. We will stay until you are ready to go."

"What will you do if I decide not to go?"

"We will drug you in your sleep and take you with us."

"That sounds like abduction—"

"It does."

"But you don't have orders to abduct me?"

"No." Stephan jittered his eye back and forth and weighed his options.

It didn't matter that he was broken. He needed to be with Henna.

"Are we stopping for the gargoyle?"

~Out of Business

Word of mouth was the best advertisement. Officers flocked to Trojan Wash. Bonn installed big screen televisions near the massage chairs in each station. Within a week they had ninety percent of Metro area police vehicles processed. Ryker hired bike messengers to dirty-up outstanding units. Before long, all of the city's functioning police vehicles were under surveillance and Trojan Wash went out of business. The GPS modules only broadcast when in motion. Units were just green dots on a map when unoccupied. Voice-operated microphones recorded only when there were sounds above seventy-four decibels, but the cameras ate up battery life—they ran full time. Each battery pack had to retain enough energy to activate one of two switches. One switch released a puff of powder. The other activated foam that would encapsulate the powder stored in the mirror and render it inert.

They couldn't wait too long.

Shortly there wouldn't be enough power in the units to accomplish either task. Two days at the most. Bonn looked from the Germans to the monitors. One wrote source code while the other edited, then they switched to check each other's work.

He couldn't imagine what could stump them—their output appeared infinitely adjustable. Their efficiency was astounding.

As he watched, Ryker trialed an algorithm in a test environment. There were too many active units to monitor concurrently, so he'd written a program to do it. Rickard nodded his approval. It worked. In a few keystrokes, they applied the program to the live environment. The Germans leaned back to watch as processors analyzed patterns of speech, movement, and interconnectivity and measured them against conditions that ran opposite freedoms outlined in the Bill of Rights. Infractions were graded and organized by severity. Images subdivided the screens.

Bonn couldn't quite follow what had been accomplished. "This is real-time?" Rickard popped something crunchy in his mouth and nodded. "Amazing."

Ryker reached for the cup of crickets and Rickard handed them over. Ryker dumped the remains inside the cup into his mouth as though the insects were ice chips. He spoke with his mouth full of musky wings and legs.

"Introducing the top ten offenders." He expanded screen number one and they got an audio and video feed from inside a police car. "Let's listen in for a while—make sure it isn't just the president on the radio." Rickard nodded gravely. Bonn wasn't entirely sure it was a joke.

~Rohypnol

Terrence finally slept. He had the nicest dream. They were at a Yankees game—he and his boy. The stadium was full of people who hadn't died.

They were alive because he was a good cop.

Passers-by went for hotdogs and beer, but each stopped to pat his shoulder or to shake hands to thank him. Some were people he'd seen dead, but today everyone was vibrant. There was no cause for decay in the ballpark. Everyone was young. They were happy and fresh. His boy caught a ball—a home run. The batter jumped the fence to sign it. He asked for a bite of Terrence's hotdog. He'd run the bases later. Stella was there too—happy and strangely quiet, sitting beside them. The Central Park vigilante spoke to him through a device deep in his ear. Now he was in front of a room of cops. He was the vigilante's puppet. He explained the microphone under the park bench to a room full of his biggest lab-geek fans. Stella asked to listen in, but there was only one ear bud. He couldn't afford to miss any leads.

"You ROOFIED me?" Terrence's eyes flew open. This wasn't his dream. "Your place is nicer than I imagined." Stella sat up in bed next to him. She wore white pajamas. She rubbed the bed linens like you might pet a dog. Her eyebrows rode high on her forehead, as though she were confused, but pleased. "The sheets are really soft." She looked as bewildered as he felt. Terrence sat up. He, too, wore white pajamas.

This wasn't his apartment.

"Wait a minute—you ROOFIED ME?"

"This is not my place," Terrence managed. "And you're not my type." His head ached mildly.

They were drugged.

Stella looked under the covers. "You've got pants on. I've got pants on. That's a good start." She looked around the room. "Well, it isn't Heaven, 'cause I gotta pee." Stella swung off the covers and went to find the bathroom. Terrence got up slowly and walked to a massive door.

Locked.

A camera lens sat above a keypad shielded by thick glass. He tapped on the solid-looking steel door with his fingernails—it was very heavy—maybe even filled with concrete. There were no windows. The walls were concrete too, but were stained in warm earth tones. "There are little soaps in here," Stella called from the bathroom. "Oh—they smell nice—like root beer and some kind of tropical flowers." Terrence stood straight. He looked at his feet. He tapped a foot on the solid floor, then pushed hard on his eyeballs with his fingertips.

This was no elaborate extension of his dream—this was real.

Stella padded out of the bathroom and rummaged through the refrigerator in the small kitchen. "You do love Fresca, don't you, Ham?"

She still didn't get it.

Stella sorted through a massive wooden bowl full of pomegranates, avocados, and mangos on the counter. Terrence opened the refrigerator to see for himself. Several cases of Fresca sat perfectly aligned on two of many shelves. Stella found a knife and cut up some fruit. "This isn't my place."

"Yeah. You said that. So where are we then, Ham?"

"We're captives."

"Uh huh. We're captive. Spa-captives—with ten thousand thread count cotton sheets and little soaps made from beach flowers. I'm gonna go look in the bathtub—if we've got those little fish that nibble the nasty bits off your feet I'll be a while, so do you need to pee first?" Stella paused to bite into a slice of mango, then raised her eyebrows in a serious look. "Only. One. Bathroom."

She was right. He didn't understand women at all.

Whirring sounds filled the apartment. A massive impressionist painting slid sideways. Beneath it, a huge television screen flickered to life. A well-coifed newscaster tapped papers he wouldn't glance at and turned to face Terrence with his two-foot wide face. "Brownsville's riots are losing momentum this morning. The National Guard continued to patrol the streets last night in an attempt to enforce the 8:00 PM curfew—some locals seem thrilled to have the uniforms on the ground."

Riots in Brownsville? How long had they been here?

A well-dressed Latina wearing a ridiculous orange hat popped onto the screen. "A grassroots uprising is born from the tragedies that plague our streets. We've needed a catalyst to bring the citizens of Brownsville to our senses. We're awake now—we are Brownsville! We're not going to hide anymore. We'll swarm! We'll identify and flush out the enemy."

"Thank you, ma'am—back to you, Mark." Mark explained an uprising of law-abiding citizens calling themselves "The Tigers" now patrolled the streets. They'd already run off known drug dealers and criminals and planned to tackle gang violence next. "An unlikely hero began this movement when he aided a twelve-year-old girl in need—he put himself in harm's way when he didn't have to." A new camera angle framed the newest edition to the studio team—the attractive street reporter wore a smart new suit and sported freshly bleached teeth.

"I like her blouse." Stella sat in a comfortable leather chair with her bowl of fruit and kicked her feet up.

"Welcome to the crew, Mary."

"Thanks, Mark. It's an honor to report the unknown hero who started this movement appears wheelchair bound. He saved a girl from a fate of shame and degradation, a story all too common in Brownsville—the mystery man inspired those who've felt powerless to enter the streets and take action. It may be just what Brownsville needed and for his efforts, if he's watching tonight, Brownsville and the News Center Team thank him for the brave things he did—and the ongoing bravery he's inspired." Mark reported the recovery of a policeman's body from the East river. "The officer, whose name cannot yet be released had laminated photographs of himself with multiple children in various vulnerable states—suicide has not been ruled out at this time." Mary shook her head for a couple seconds in an awkward attempt to illustrate both disapproval and remorse. With all her culturally appropriate bases covered, Mary raised her eyebrows and in the next breath, wrapped up the morning news.

"Two other police officers remain missing—veteran homicide detective Terrence Grimaldi and his partner Estelle Castillo went missing Monday morning—no evidence of a struggle was found at either detective's residence when officers performed safety checks. However, in each of the detective's homes, an ominous note was found—allegedly written *IOUs* were left for each officer." A picture of Stella filled the screen.

"They chose that one? I have helmet hair in that one!"

Mark and Mary in the Morning gave a phone number for viewers with information helpful to authorities. Stella stood and stormed around, looking for a phone. "I'm gonna call and tell them where to find a better picture. Nobody's gonna look for me looking like that— I look like el Coco." Stella didn't find a phone, so she went back to the kitchen. Ham heard the freezer open.

How long had they been here—three days? More?

"We got Ben and *Jerry's*. One, two—"

The last thing he could remember was going home to shower.

"—like fifteen little tubs of it." Terrence made his way to the bathroom. Some routines couldn't be put on hold. He picked a small soap out of a large bowl of toiletries and smelled it.

She was right—it smelled nice.

He heard Stella outside the door. "Leave the little white soaps for me, Ham. The ones that smell like root beer. You can use the flowery ones, but we're gonna have to conserve a bit to make them last. You should know—I'm due in fifty-two days. And Ham? It's our guy. He got us, Ham. I'd bet there's gonna be a test on something, so we've got to figure out what it's on. We've got to get out of here. I don't want you to deliver Daniel, Ham. You've gotta figure a way out of here before we're out of ice cream."

~Fresca

Had it been a week? It was hard to tell. Terrence tried sleeping in one of the chairs, but each time he awoke, he was in bed with Stella. Whoever kept them stocked in fresh fruits and toiletries also tucked him in at night—after the gas put them to sleep. They developed a routine. The news came on in what he guessed were twenty-four hour intervals.

It could be taped news—he wasn't sure.

Everything felt out of balance.

Well, one thing was reliable.

Terrence looked up at the document. The copy of the Bill of Rights was set into a heavy glass shadowbox flush with the wall. It remained dimly lit until the news came on—during the news, however the light changed.

It pulsed.

The oscillating amber tones were difficult to ignore.

Stella was right. There was going to be a test.

Terrence studied the document for at least an hour a day. He'd known each of the amendments loosely before his incarceration, but now he knew them by heart. He'd sold Stella short. She'd merely glanced at the ancient looking document and she had it. She quizzed him when the lights went out. While they waited for the gas. She didn't just paraphrase each item either—she could recite each amendment verbatim. As Terrence took on the role of pupil, he lost track of how he fit into the world. He'd stopped struggling with modesty and physical barriers. Since he began each day extracting himself from Stella's aggressive spooning techniques, he'd surrendered. Stella moved him about like a stage prop. Terrence got into bed first. Stella lay down with him. She put her head on his shoulder.

"You should really know these by heart, Ham. The amendments, I mean. You know why? You weren't born here. Like me. My great grandmother used to quiz us. She was so old she remembered what it was like before the Spanish American War. Aren't you a first generation immigrant? You should know them, Ham. Even if most folks born here can't tell you which amendment is the freedom of

283

speech, we should know. It's why I'm a cop, Ham. Why are you a cop?"

He'd never asked himself that question.

The faint smell of butterscotch and propane filled the air.

The sleep gas.

They had just a few seconds. Since neither of them would remember the conversation in the morning, he answered truthfully. "My dad."

"He was a cop?" Stella blinked, fading.

"No. He beat us. And molested my sister."

"But not you?" Terrence couldn't open his eyes.

"No—well—yeah … me too. We needed a cop, so I became one." The butterscotch swam into his sinuses and Terrence felt his mind expand into a broad field of nothing.

Stella was up first. With nothing pressing Terrence to hurry into the day, he lay still and listened to the pregnant woman sort through the kitchenette. "We got four more tubs of ice cream." Stella called out. Terrence wondered what the end game was. It'd been weeks. Stella acted differently—she hoarded things like a squirrel prepared for winter. He pretended not to notice the pyramid of toilet paper rolls she'd amassed under her bedside table. He wondered if she'd weave a multi-ply quilted nest when the time came to push the baby out. He willed his neck to move and shook his head to clear the image from his brain.

He had no inclination to find out.

"And a new book." Stella wore Terrence's sweatshirt, which their benefactor left one night. Stella got one too, but she said his fit better. Terrence dared not argue, so he wore his pajama top around the clock. He got up and poured himself a cup of coffee. The deliveries of Fresca had ceased and the bitter brown fluid did help the morning headaches that came after the gas. Stella looked like a woodchuck. She wore reading glasses. With her legs tucked under her, swimming in his big sweatshirt, she looked like an intellectual rodent reading John Locke in a custom stitched Scandinavian lounge chair. Terrence sat in his chair and sipped the coffee. The Bill of Rights glowed brighter than usual. "I would've ripped the wig off of one of these stodgy fools and made him chase me for it." Stella declared. Terrence stood and walked to the document. He was certain they were watched on camera.

If he appeared trained, could he go home? Home—did he have one? He had an apartment—did he pursue happiness? He had the right to, but did he do it? What was happiness?

"All he'd see is my big ol' bustle, Ham—peeling out like I hit the nitrous switch."

Stella seemed happy. Despite recent events.

Terrence felt envious. The painting slid aside and the television came on. "Tell me what happens—I'll be right back." Stella ran for the bathroom. She returned in moments. She handed him a Fresca, then popped the tab on her own can of the warm but coveted beverage. Terrence realized that hoarding his sodas somewhere in the bathroom was Stella's attempt to do something nice. A treat—something to look forward to.

Missing people quickly become boring when they don't turn up dead—some trees were stolen from an elementary school courtyard, a woman was on the lam after she submitted a counterfeit lottery ticket—then their story.

Third in line.

A choppy video of Terrence in the boxing ring filled the screen. With a devastating right cross, young Terrence 'the Hammer' Grimaldi knocked out his opponent and looked to the referee to call the fight. Stella cleared her throat, as if prepared to say something, but didn't. "Forty-two and three." *Mark in the morning* misreported Terrence's boxing record and filled the next few seconds with tidbits of information about him that Terrence suspected summarized him as a man.

Is that all he was? It didn't seem like much.

Stella couldn't contain herself. "We know. Ham's still missing. Now me. Do me." *Mark in the morning* looked to his left as *Mary in the morning* pantomimed the guy who'd been knocked out. "Oh, that hurts."

Mary had no idea what a punch felt like.

Stella was on the edge of her chair. She bounced in anticipation. "YES!" A glamor shot of Stella filled the screen. She appeared to have an entire container of lip-gloss on her lower lip and hoop earrings so big they rested on her shoulders. Stella did a victory dance. It looked two parts running man and one part sprinkler. Gas prices were down. More trouble in the Middle East. The painting slid back into its parking space. The Bill of Rights glowed and pulsed. Stella tucked back into John Locke with a smile on her face. Terrence patted his belly. There'd been a time he could crack a walnut on his abs. He was still pretty firm, just saggier. He went to the side of the bed where Stella couldn't see him and sat on the floor in his strange pajamas. He did sit-ups as quietly as possible. It didn't take many before he felt the old familiar burn. If Stella heard him she didn't poke fun. Pushups were next. He didn't know what life had in store for him. Pushups probably wouldn't prepare him for it—but they wouldn't hurt either.

Thirty-eight and TWO, Mark in the morning. Thirty-eight and TWO.

~Catch and Release

Stephan left the door to his apartment ajar and walked to the center of the great room. He wasn't sure how many people lived in the building. The Germans hadn't provided him with anything as useful as an orientation packet. One door looked different. Thick metal. He approached the door cautiously.

Did he hear voices?

When he dipped his head and opened his mouth to really listen, he only heard normal city noises. Bonn was an aloof, albeit polite host. He seemed to have no expectations of him. When the Germans delivered him to the building, Bonn gave him a blue plastic card with a clip to wave in front of the sensors as he moved about, but the thick metal door that stood out didn't have a sensor. Stephan had spent the morning poking around. He didn't feel ready to explore the city yet, although the envelope of cash on his kitchen counter would allow him to do so in style. Stephan shrugged. He went back to his own apartment to brush his new teeth. A full set of zirconium—a bit too white to be believable. They'd installed them on the very last surgery, just before they took his eye. The oral surgeon joked with him in the recovery room. He'd said:

You can chew ball bearings now if you choose to.

Stephan washed his face and put the eye patch on. He jittered his eye back and forth to see himself in the mirror. Would the idea of chewing steel balls have been funny before? Before hammer blows pounded all perspective out of him? He stopped moving his eye back and forth and lost himself in the mirror. He could see the access badge on the counter. His peripheral vision seemed to be getting clearer, but it was frustrating. No. Not frustrating.

The word was infuriating.

Most mornings Stephan felt he had eggs for brains. Whipped into custard. He couldn't talk the way he wanted. He even had to watch his feet in order to walk. He felt self-conscious about everything. It felt good to be out of sweatpants, however. That was all he'd worn at the hospital. Stephan pulled on some jeans and clipped the access badge to his belt. He left the apartment and took the elevator down a floor. The Germans seemed to be working on a computer program. They didn't appear to notice him as he walked in. Their bat-like ears were translucent when viewed toward the light of the screen. He either saw or imagined that each man twitched an ear to track his approach. The ears searched him for importance, found none that was notable, then swiveled back to join the heads of the men pointed at the monitors.

Bonn reached up to turn off his own computer monitor. He stood to greet him. "Are you getting your sea legs, Stephan?" Stephan shook his head.

"I'll be honest, I'm still trying to find my own legs. I'm not certain I'll ever be shipshape."

Bonn nodded. "You will. It takes a while—I've been there myself. You don't know you're getting better until you are. I understand we share an appreciation of animals. Have you had the grand tour yet?"

Stephan shook his head. Bonn walked quietly and slowly down the aisles with Stephan. Stephan felt himself come alive. He missed his work, and the lab was world-class. Stephan couldn't imagine how much the place had cost to build. He couldn't have even fed this many animals on his old salary.

"Fantastic."

Stephan paused at an enclosure. A pair of eastern brown snakes. If he looked through the glass at an angle, he could see the snakes without looking back and forth. The female had the opaque eye caps and grumpy demeanor that promised an impending shed. "Do you mind if I meddle a bit? I'd love to have something to do." Bonn shook his head and reached into a recess on the side of the enclosure. He offered Stephan a snake-handling hook.

"I need an expert." Bonn spoke candidly. "I'm a novice myself. With Henna in Finland, we're doing the best we can." Stephan looked into the recess and gathered a few other items. He opened the snake's cage, gently placed the female inside a plastic box, and slid the lid home with a *click*. He carried the box to a stainless steel counter with a freshwater tap and ran the water until it was the right temperature.

He hadn't looked at his feet.

When the water was the right temperature, Stephan ran a couple of inches into a second plastic bin and deftly maneuvered the lids and the snake. "I'll just let her soak a bit. It'll loosen up her eye-caps enough that she'll want to rub her old skin off. It'll help her with the shed and she can calm down a bit. They get jumpy when they can't

288

see well and I feel bad for them. The less stress they're under, the happier they'll be."

Bonn nodded appreciatively. "Thank you. I didn't know that. If you have any other pointers, I'd love to hear them. Do you want to poke around for a bit? I need to finish something, but then maybe we could go get some lunch."

Stephan started at the first cage. He moved slowly and talked to each animal in a soft voice. After a while he felt his stomach rumble. He couldn't recall feeling hungry—ever actually. It felt good. This time when he approached the computer monitors, Bonn pulled a chair up for him. Stephan joined him and looked at the screen: it appeared to be his apartment, but different people were inside. A very pregnant woman sat reading a book while a man did pushups. Bonn seemed to wait for Stephan to comment on the scene. When he didn't, Bonn offered an odd explanation.

"Not all the enclosures are on this floor." Stephan's host seemed to be counting the man's pushups. "This pair is almost ready to set free."

~The Oath

Terrence opened his eyes—in the kitchen, the coffeemaker sputtered—Stella must be making him coffee. She didn't drink it. His arms felt heavy. It seemed much too early to start the day. The painting slid aside next.

Too early for the news.

Terrence willed his neck to move, but it refused. Light came from the television screen. It sounded like a sitcom was on. Recorded laughter came from the screen at reliable intervals. Stella turned the volume up. Kelsey Grammer's voice echoed through the luxury prison. A woman's voice came from just beside him. "Hold still. Someone's here."

Stella was still in bed?

Now that she'd spoken he could feel her head on his shoulder— her eyelashes ticking against his cheek with each blink. He felt her heart beating fast against his arm. A surge of adrenaline hit him. Feeling returned quickly to his hands and legs. If he had to jump up and fight he might stand a chance—but Terrence guessed he wouldn't face fair odds. The *Frasier* rerun malfunctioned. Kelsey Grammer repeated, "Consider this," a few times. "I'm not going to pee this bed." Stella tossed back the covers and ran for the bathroom. Terrence sat up slowly and wiped his eyes. Fighting seemed ridiculous now. Their captor would've planned for that.

Time to find out what they want.

There was more furniture than usual. A third recliner faced the television screen with a man sitting in it. Terrence couldn't see his face. He moved cautiously. It seemed the man was alone. No visible torture equipment lay about. Terrence remembered a scene from an old movie—a villain had the protagonist strapped down. The antagonist did horrible things to his captor's mouth, then asked him "is it safe?" several times.

Well, is it? I guess we'll see.

Stella came out of the bathroom. They approached the man together. He stood and turned to face them. He was ridiculously fit and dressed casually in jeans and a tee shirt. He had bare feet, like his captives. He seemed to toast them with a large smoothie. Hot food steamed from trays in front of each chair. The young man swept his palm toward the offering. "Please. Join me for breakfast. We have a big day ahead."

"The guy on the bike." Terrence remembered him. "Central Park—Frasier date with the girlfriend. The doghouse."

"Good memory. I recorded you on my helmet cam. I admire your work. I had to catch you before you found me and here we are."

Stella didn't wait to eat. She was halfway through her eggs Benedict before he sat down. When they joined her, she shot the newcomer a suspicious look and peeled her blood orange. Terrence poked at a piece of bacon and watched the mysterious figure put on a wireless headset. He handed game controllers to each of them. Stella finished her orange. Her impatience showed. "We're going to play video games?"

The stranger pushed some buttons and *Frasier* was gone—when the screen blinked back to life, it was a map of the city. "Not exactly—you'll see."

Hundreds of blinking dots lit up the map—maybe more. Some of them moved.

The man spoke into the microphone and tossed his own game controller on the table, then kicked his feet up and relaxed back into his chair as if they were all old friends. A cursor moved on the screen. Someone somewhere minimized the map and opened other windows. Terrence had an epiphany. "Government hits? You're a spook. What are you—CIA?"

It was clear to him now—they were in protective custody. It had to be. It explained the safe house.

"Sure would've been easier to brief us and leave us home—did we stumble across some weird top secret thing?"

"Interesting theory, detective—that I work for the government. It raises some philosophical questions. In that employees get paid, I do not. Do I labor for the people? Also unclear—I think so. I will reassure you—I do represent the people's best interests. In fact, I am like you and Detective Castillo. I yearn to protect and serve, albeit in an enthusiastic fashion. The fundamental difference between us is one of a bygone era—you and Detective Castillo are encumbered by an absurdly top heavy government, whereas I have chosen to operate light and fast."

Not a spook.

Terrence locked eyes with the guy.

"I know you both well—we share many ideals. I do like the CIA's oath—I've never taken it, but I would." The screen changed—video feeds from inside police cars popped up. "I will paraphrase my favorite part of the oath: 'I do solemnly affirm to uphold the Constitution of the United States against all enemies, foreign and—'"

Stella sucked in her breath and Terrance saw that the color had left her face. She pointed at the screen and finished the sentence for their captor.

"Domestic." All views collapsed but one. The interior view of the police car was clear. The cursor scrolled over a toolbar and activated the microphone. A battered teenage girl screamed something in Russian to the officer in the front seat. She threw herself against the partition. She was badly bruised and bled from her mouth and nose. The plainclothes officer wiped his hands with a towel and stopped at a traffic light. The officer's name, rank, badge number, even his precinct rolled across the bottom of the screen, followed by the English translation of her plea.

"You CAN'T! You CAN'T take me back to him. HE WILL KILL ME!"

Stella understood before he did. She stood to pace in front of the screen. "Sex trade? Vice cop on the take. No partner with him in the car. She escaped—" Terrence nodded and bit his lip.

"He's taking her back." The man with bulging muscles picked up his controller—the screen divided. Now the map shared the screen. Their view zoomed in on one blinking dot.

"That's them." Stella spat. The girl sobbed hysterically.

"I will do anything. Please. Don't you have sisters? He will kill me. I will be dead in an hour. Or worse! I will do anything you want." Stella ran to the bathroom. Terrence clenched his teeth.

"Is this live?" The fit stranger nodded, put down the controller, and leaned back to drink his smoothie. Stella was back, but couldn't hold still. She paced behind their chairs and wrung her hands.

"Call it in."

Shaking his head, the man with the answers took a bite of bacon. "Too slow. The girl is correct. She really will be dead before legitimate police get there." The officer pulled over and rolled down his window. He dialed a cellphone. On the screen, a dialogue box opened below the map. Both sides of the call were typed into the screen—

>Hey. I've got her down here.

>In front?

>Yeah. Right outside.

>Where was she?

>She'd made it. She was almost to Cape May—I grabbed her on the ferry. Listen, you got what I asked for or should I let her go? It's been a long night.

>I've got him.

The call ended. A couple of tense minutes passed. The dirty cop smiled at someone outside the window. The Russian girl sobbed with renewed terror and hid her face with her arms. "NO. NO, NO, NO, NO, NO!" The officer got out. The girl was dragged from the backseat. A young boy was flung inside in her place. Stella roared. She grabbed her controller and toggled the joystick.

"How does it work? Why? Why are we watching?" To the left of the screen, someone typed in a list of Officer Clark's offenses—

>**Facilitator of illegal sex trade, human trafficking.**
   ~**Human rights violations:**
         *****Article 3: Right to Life, Liberty, Personal Security**
         *****Article 4: Freedom from Slavery**
         *****Article 5: Freedom from Torture and Degrading treatment**
   >**Pedophilia.**
      ~**Human rights violations:**
         *****Articles 3, 4, 5.**

The car pulled away. The little boy looked malnourished. He held his haunted face to the partition and peered at Officer Clark with hope. He, too, spoke in Russian and they read the translation: "You are an officer. This is a police car. That is good? I am safe now?" Officer Clark adjusted the rearview mirror and smiled at the boy. Stella lost it.

"Stop this. Get me a telephone. Let me intervene. ENOUGH!" Their jailer nodded calmly.

293

"OK. I will stop it." He picked up the controller and the cursor hovered over the blinking light on the map. The cruiser turned down a street in the warehouse district. Choices populated the screen—

>Disconnect?

The intense young man hovered the cursor over the word. More choices opened.

>Yes.

Officer Clark looked baffled as the engine cut out. He studied the dashboard as arms reached into the backseat and pulled the boy out. The provider of Fresca, of eggs Benedict, of sweatshirts, clicked more ominous words—

>Terminate? >Yes.

With a small popping noise, fog filled the screen. When the camera cleared, Officer Clark lay slumped over the steering wheel. "Save my place?" Their accomplice asked politely. "Green tea is a strong diuretic."

Stella sat on the edge of her chair and pressed her hands to her mouth—speechless. Back from the bathroom, the strong-looking cop killer sat. He pushed some buttons on his controller.

"What about the girl?" Stella asked. Terrence had to do something. He went to the refrigerator for lack of other options.

Would there be sodas?

He pulled out a six-pack of Fresca and handed one to Stella. She wouldn't take it. "WHAT ABOUT THE GIRL?" The man in the tee shirt held his hand out for a soda. Terrence gave him one. He opened the can, took a drink, and pointed to the screen. The cursor moved— a dialogue box answered Stella.

>Intervention in progress, Deputy Castillo.

"What the hell does that mean? Does that mean you're sending in the feds to take down the operation?"

294

"No. Too slow. It would take hours to brief them. They would waste time with warrants, struggle for jurisdiction with Vice and the girl would die. The system, as you know it, can't save her."

"So what's the intervention?"

"An odd little man with twice my IQ and a belt-fed rifle." Stella seemed speechless, but their captor waited politely for a moment to make sure. "Let's do another one. We will have to pick up the pace a bit if we want to make a big difference, though. That's my goal—to make a big difference."

Terrence whistled quietly.

How'd he put this thing in motion?

"Let's try an easy one. A confidence booster."

Terrence watched the man's thick hands as he worked the controller. They were thickly scarred, but his nails were clean. Well manicured.

Those conditions didn't frequently accompany each other.

A new sedan interior was on screen. A female officer sipped coffee as she drove. Her partner scanned the road in front of them. Information on each officer populated the screen, then it split—to the left, pictures emerged.

A slideshow.

A baby. The officer riding shotgun proudly holding a trout aloft. Their barefoot company chose:

>Stop Feed? >Yes.

The microphone crackled. The driver glanced into the camera for a moment, then shrugged. She asked about someone's birthday party. "They're good, so they live. I get it—" Stella picked up her controller and hovered over a light on the map. "Doesn't pay child support?" She glared at Darryl "Nix" Ford. The nine-year veteran worked the Bronx. Ham watched and picked up his own controller. Officer Bob Graahl rode shotgun—aside from the child support, both officers were clean. Stella chose their fate.

>Stop Feed? >Yes.

They all looked up at the map.
There were too many lights.

295

"How'd you know the first guy did that?" Terrence asked.

"We applied a program that grades malfeasance. We watched him all night—that is how we had people positioned."

"Do you have all the information on file? Do you save it?"

"Yes."

"Then let's stop—let's do it the right way." The man in charge pursed his lips and worked the controller. He opened a file.

>Top Ten

Their own precinct chief, Bill Turret's car blinked on the map—he was in New Lots. Stella barked angrily. "Why is Bill in New Lots?" The jaw muscles on their benefactor peeled his face into a genuine smile. He nodded at Stella with enthusiasm.

"Now we are getting to it. Thank you, Estelle. We may share ideals detectives, but I'm more of a realist—do you remember the cop found in the East River? The one with kiddie porn on him? I killed him. I killed him in person, ten hours after I discovered he'd hurt kids. Why didn't I kill him sooner?" Stella glared. Terrence shook his head. "I had to know who else he was connected to."

"Bill?" Stella pulled her legs inside her oversized sweatshirt and rocked back and forth. The rippling killer nodded.

"And eight other cops. If I don't get them all, they will spread." Stella rocked harder. Her voice sounded cold. And small.

"Like cockroaches—"

The man's strong jaw muscles pushed hard teeth into another bite of bacon. "No. Cockroaches serve the food chain—more like cancer." He locked eyes with Terrence for a moment. On screen, their precinct chief consorted in illegal ways with a minor a block from a junior high school. "The system won't stop it. It's too big, too slow, too inefficient—too many offenders inside pumping the brakes for their buddies." The cursor confirmed what they saw.

>Commercial exploitation of children.
*S 230.05: Patronizing a prostitute in the third degree.

He was right. The system was broken.

When the act came to a close, Bill refused to pay the child for what she'd done. He pushed her from the car and rewound a small camcorder. The police chief looked tired but serene. He reviewed the tape for a few moments, put himself in order, and started the car. Stella tapped furiously at her controller. "He taped it, Ham—he even taped it." She hovered over a word.

>Terminate?

"Where is the yes? Why doesn't it give me a choice?" Terrence tried his own controller. He hovered over the ominous word to no effect.

"Is it broken?"

"No," said the man quietly. "That's where I come in. I didn't keep you here to act—I brought you here to understand." His scarred hands did his bidding. The cursor hovered and clicked.

Terminate? >Yes.

Bill Turret, family man, officer of the year, cousin of the mayor, pedophile, took one last breath.

Terrence put down his controller. His shaking hand reached out for his soda, but knocked the can over. It landed on the floor and spilled. Stella seemed frozen. The stranger, the man with the power and the will, spoke. "I'll do the rest. Hundreds will die, but they need to. It doesn't affect me like it affects either of you—I'm not wired the usual way." Stella's cheeks were tear-streaked. She seemed to manage only quick, jabbing breaths. Terrence absently considered how trivial the pool of soda that spread on the floor really was.

Yesterday it would've been an event.

Tall, graceful, their visitor walked to the door. He waived a card in front of the scanner. With a hum, the door rolled open. "I doubt you will be on the news for a few days—considering. Take care of yourselves. Tomorrow, when you wake up in your own beds, think about how you fit into the system. Do what you can to make it better. I'll do what I can from here." The heavy door closed behind him. The television screen flickered to a national news station. A tropical storm was upgraded on Florida's panhandle. There was discontent in the Middle East. Fuel prices were up.

~Epilogue

The Belcher's sea snakes multiplied. As Henna and Stephan tenderly sorted, sexed, and inspected each tiny marvel before freeing them in a coral rich habitat brimming with tiny bright orange fish, Henna excitedly told Stephan about her newest discovery just upstream of Perth on the Swan River.

"The bull sharks come upstream, so not many people dive there. It's quite urban until it isn't—anyway, I worked my way upstream. Some aboriginal kids floated toward me in a raft of plastic buckets. One of them had a Ziploc bag. He held it up to the sun and pointed inside. I went over to see what he had—"

Stephan watched Ryker. He had paused to listen to the story. He'd been brushing at the Gargoyle's remaining horn inside the shrikethrush enclosure. Although the unassuming bird had hundreds of live-branch perches to choose from, she seemed to like the weathered horn of the gothic statue best. The naked German seemed a part of the exhibit. The little bird hopped around cheerfully and tilted her head. She caught a colorful beetle and flicked her wings to land on the specter's shoulder. Ryker opened his mouth and the bird fed him the beetle—It was toxic enough to kill eighty normal people, but that didn't concern Stephan.

The Germans ate them all the time.

"—the kids all laughed until I unzipped the bag—then they freaked out. 'Sick-fish! Sick-fish, lady!'" Rickard continued his work, quietly at a computer. He had announced that he was automating what could be automated—the program showed promise, although the blue-rings seemed to escape more often to hunt for their neighbors when people weren't around. Stephan guessed the invertebrates removed the filter from the aerator when they went marauding—they were smart enough to figure it out. If that was the case, they put the filter back when they were done—he tried to film them doing it, but they refused to misbehave on camera. Stephan hadn't seen Bonn for a long while. After culling seventeen percent of the city's police force, he got quiet. He wiped down his old muscle car frequently and appeared deep in thought. Stephan saw Bonn reading an article on Route 66 the night they'd celebrated Henna's return. He might be out there now—driving between windblown gas stations, eating cherry pie under buzzing old neon signs. Sleeping in bad motels.

"—they don't know where the fish go when they aren't schooling together, Stephan, I couldn't convince the kids to give me the bag. I even offered to trade boats with them. I think they thought I'd eat the fish. So what do you say, Rabbi? Next spring? You and me on the upper Swan in Perth? I know a guy who can make you a passport— what should we do with your hair?" Stephan looked at his reflection in the glass. The prosthetic eye looked perfect behind his new glasses. He didn't need to jitter his good eye anymore.

"I think I'll grow it out—let it get long. Go for the 'Robinson Crusoe' look."

"That sounds a bit Hassidic. Are you getting serious about religion on me?"

"Always have been, Doc."

Always have been.

Estelle awoke to a telephone. She hiked herself up on an elbow. She was surrounded by familiar things. "I thought I'd call and make sure you got home, too—"

Ham.

"—there is a note here, with a phone number: call if you need help on the job. Thing isn't signed, but we know who it's from." Estelle rubbed at her eyes. She looked around her bedroom.

Nothing interesting here.

"It's only Christmas morning for you, Ham—that or he knows I don't need any help to get things done." Estelle took a shower in her own shower.

She would miss the tiny root beer soaps. After breakfast she'd call to announce her return—several days of questions would follow. A physical at the least. It'd be like an astronaut's re-entry protocol. They had to make sure she wasn't brainwashed or in love with her recent captor.

Hair still wet, Estelle decided to splurge on a cup of coffee.

Ham won't know. One won't hurt, will it?

The Bill of Rights hung in a simple frame above her kitchen table. With goose bumps everywhere they would fit, Estelle read the short message written on the table in permanent marker:

~Trust your instincts

Lochlann Blackshaw handed an envelope to the craggy man. Inside were eight-by-tens of an attractive redhead. Abernathy pulled out the stops to make things right—he'd delivered the photographs to Lochlann himself. The woman's face was captured from several angles as she made her way through customs at LaGuardia. The man flipped through the photographs, slid them back inside the envelope, and passed the packet back.

"Don't you need to take them with you?"

The craggy man shook his head disdainfully and tapped his temple. The lobbyist wondered what was next. He was used to being the heavy. When he made a promise, it affected the economies of nations. If he didn't pull through on those promises, someone like the man before him would visit. He'd remove him—a stubborn nail from a weathered fence. Lochlann knew about these people, but he'd never before looked one in the eye—the life he led was a gamble and so far he'd won. "What should I call you?"

"You shouldn't."

"How will I pay you?"

"Now."

Lochlann nodded—angry, but nervous. Marcus usually dealt with the bottom-dwellers.

Now he'd do it himself.

Marcus was dead, but this man would make it right. Lochlann reached across the table and handed the man his fee.

Bottom-dweller wasn't an insult—they were just very hard to get to.

Lochlann solicited help from wealthy friends, who recommended someone—who notified the apparition before him. Although he couldn't recognize the man's nationality, he did recognize the need for such men. It took money to make them surface and this particular man hailed from the deepest depths. If Lochlann was the head of a hammer, building wealth and industry for those who kept the world in balance, this man was the claw on the opposite end of the same tool. Lochlann knew the man's name. Not many did. Osgar didn't bother with promises.

He probably wasn't even in the business for the money.

The killer moved gracefully to the door of the coffee shop. Lochlann heard the door open, but when he looked out the window—the man was gone.

~About

I'm a full-time independent author living in Alaska with my family. *Inhumanum* is my first novel.

Though some are bad asses, and others jerks, all characters appearing in this work are fictitious—so please don't become flattered, ashamed, angry, or the like if you believe that you resemble one of the jerks.

Instead, seek therapy … or take up yoga. Perhaps you could adopt a pet who doesn't know your past.

I'd love to hear from (most of) you. Join me on Facebook, Goodreads, and see my next projects at http://bradleyernst.com/

Bradley

61456521R00192

Made in the USA
Charleston, SC
21 September 2016